The Supreme Progress
and Other French Scientific Romances

also by Brian Stableford:

The Empire of the Necromancers (1: The Shadow of Frankenstein; 2: Frankenstein and the Vampire Countess; 3: Frankenstein in London); The New Faust at the Tragicomique; Sherlock Holmes and the Vampires of Eternity; The Stones of Camelot; The Wayward Muse.

also translated and introduced by Brian Stableford:

Anonymous: Sâr Dubnotal vs. Jack the Ripper; *Anthologies*: News from the Moon; The Germans on Venus; *Richard Bessière*: The Gardens of the Apocalypse; *Félix Bodin*: The Novel of the Future; *André Caroff*: The Terror of Madame Atomos; *Charles Derennes*: The People of the Pole; *Henri Duvernois*: The Man Who Found Himself; *Henri Falk*: The Age of Lead; *Paul Féval*: Anne of the Isles; The Black Coats (1: 'Salem Street; 2: The Invisible Weapon; 3: The Parisian Jungle; 4: The Companions of the Treasure; 5: Heart of Steel; 6: The Cadet Gang); John Devil; Knightshade; Revenants; Vampire City; The Vampire Countess; The Wandering Jew's Daughter; *Paul Féval, fils*: Felifax, the Tiger-Man; *Octave Joncquel & Théo Varlet*: The Martian Epic; *Jean de La Hire*: The Nyctalope vs. Lucifer; The Nyctalope on Mars; Enter the Nyctalope; *Georges Le Faure & Henri de Graffigny*: The Extraordinary Adventures of a Russian Scientist Across the Solar System (2 vols.); *Gustave Le Rouge*: The Vampires of Mars; *Jules Lermina*: Panic in Paris; Mysteryville; *Marie Nizet*: Captain Vampire; *Henri de Parville*: An Inhabitant of the Planet Mars; *Gaston de Pawlowski*: Journey to the Land of the 4th Dimension; *P.-A. Ponson du Terrail*: The Vampire and the Devil's Son; *Maurice Renard*: The Blue Peril; Doctor Lerne; The Doctored Man; A Man Among the Microbes; The Master of Light; *Albert Robida*: The Clock of the Centuries; The Adventures of Saturnin Farandoul; *J.-H. Rosny Aîné*: The Givreuse Enigma; The Mysterious Force; The Navigators of Space; Vamireh; The World of the Variants; The Young Vampire; *Han Ryner*: The Superhumans; *Jacques Spitz:* The Eye of Purgatory; *Kurt Steiner*: Ortog; *Villiers de l'Isle-Adam*: The Scaffold; The Vampire Soul; *Philippe Ward & S. Miller*: The Song of Montségur.

The Supreme Progress
and Other French Scientific Romances

translated, annotated and introduced by
Brian Stableford

A Black Coat Press Book

Visit our website at www.blackcoatpress.com

ISBN 978-1-935558-82-8. First Printing. February 2011. Published by Black Coat Press, an imprint of Hollywood Comics.com, LLC, P.O. Box 17270, Encino, CA 91416. All rights reserved. Except for review purposes, no part of this book may be reproduced or transmitted in any form or by any means, electronic or mechanical, including photocopying, recording, or by any information storage and retrieval system, without permission in writing from the publisher. The stories and characters depicted in this novel are entirely fictional. Printed in the United States of America.

TABLE OF CONTENTS

Introduction

This is the third in a series of anthologies of French scientific romance that I am compiling for Black Coat Press, following *News from the Moon* (ISBN 9781932983890, 2007) and *The Germans on Venus* (ISBN 9781935543566, 2009). Three of the authors showcased here—X. B. Saintine, Eugène Mouton and Louis Mullem—were previously represented in one or both of those earlier volumes, and the stories reproduced here complete the work they did that is of most relevance to the development of French scientific romance. The four stories by Charles Cros reproduced herein also represent all of his relevant work, while Paul Adam and Victorien Sardou are represented by their most relevant works. "Charles Epheyre" (the pseudonym of Charles Robert Richet) did write considerably more within and on the fringes of the genre, but the two stories included here are arguably his most important contributions to it.

Although the contributions by Louis Mullem were all published posthumously after the turn of the century, it seems probable that they were written at much earlier dates, probably in the early 1890s; if that is so, all the stories reprinted here predate the first translation into French of work by H. G. Wells, which imported the narrative method that became typical of British scientific romance into the French literary arena. They are therefore representative of a distinct tradition whose cardinal influences included the popularizer of astronomy Camille Flammarion and the Comte de Villiers de l'Isle-Adam,[1] the great pioneer of satirical *contes cruels* with a philosophical edge—both of whom were personally acquainted

---

[1] Two collection of Villiers' genre stories, *The Scaffold* (ISBN 9781932983012) and *The Vampire Soul* (ISBN 9781932983029) are available from Black Coat Press.

with several of the authors represented her. Three of the stories—the one by Sardou and the two by Epheyre—were reprinted in the popular science periodical *La Science Illustrée* (1887-1905), which explicitly labeled all of the fiction it serialized as "*romans scientifiques*"—a phrase flexible enough to be translated as "scientific romance" or "science fiction," as one pleases. The term was already in common use, first having been popularized in connection with the relevant work of Jules Verne, but its employment in *La Science Illustrée* and the range of reprinted and original material chosen to appear there under that rubric, provides clear evidence that its users were conscious of the existence of a genre and had some notion of its scope some time before the importation of the parallel British genre.

La Science Illustrée was not the only popular science magazine to feature an episode of a feuilleton serial in every issue; one of the writers who contributed a brief *roman scientifique* to the magazine, Emile Gautier, established his own rival periodical, *La Science Française* (1890-1900) which adopted a similar policy, although he gave much greater priority to stories of future warfare than the less belligerent Louis Figuier, the former periodical's proprietor. The popular geographical periodical *Le Journal des Voyages et des Aventures de Terre et de Mer* (1877-1929) also included many items of speculative fiction among its regular feuilletons, whose scope gradually broadened out from their more rigidly Vernian origins to fill a spectrum not dissimilar to that of the serials in the popular science magazines, albeit with more emphasis on the adventurous aspect and less on the scientific content of the stories.

By the early 1890s, such periodicals as these provided regular dedicated outlets of a sort to which the likes of X. B. Saintine, Eugène Mouton and Charles Cros had not had much access, and whose more general existence might have provided them—and many others, including Villiers de l'Isle-Adam—with a greater incentive to produce *romans scientifiques*, although the continued difficulty of publishing more

8

offbeat examples of such work is readily illustrated by the failure of Louis Mullem to place any of his more ambitious speculative fictions with any publisher at all. Although its existence was manifest some years before the shining examples provided by Wells, French scientific romance was always a fugitive and marginal genre—and it remained so long into the 20th century. It did, however, have a relatively elaborate history somewhat in advance of its British counterpart, and the contents of this anthology, like those of its predecessors, will hopefully help to illustrate the span and strength of that tradition as it evolved from the early 1860s to the mid-1890s.

The first of the authors represented here, the prolific dramatist Victorien Sardou (1831-1908), became one of the leading figures of French drama in the 1860s, although he had endured considerable hardship and a string of misfortunes since the first of his plays to be produced, *La Taverne des étudiants* (1854) had met with a hostile reception because an absurd rumor somehow got around that he had been paid by the government to blacken the reputation of the students of Paris (a reputation that was surely black enough already). By 1857, he was literally starving in his garret, as writers are often said to do, but—as happens far more often in fiction about writers starving in their garrets than in reality—he was saved from both desolation and destitution by the assiduous attentions of a young woman, Mademoiselle de Brécourt, who had theatrical connections. He married her, and by the time she died prematurely, eight years later, he had become a great success.

Sardou eventually combined his relentless playwriting with enthusiastic participation in Allan Kardec's investigations of "Spiritism"—the French rival to American Spiritualism. Sardou met Camille Flammarion through Kardec, and became a regular attendee at Flammarion's weekly salon, which routinely brought scientists and spiritualists into contact with literary men. Sardou gladly offered his services for experiments with "automatic writing" and "automatic drawing" during the early 1860s, and soon began to "receive" messages

9

from Jupiter, apparently dictated to him by the spirits of the composers Wolfgang Amadeus Mozart and Bernard Palissy, who were now supposedly resident there in the city of Julnius. His drawings depicting life on Jupiter were made into etchings and published.

Before involving himself intently in spiritism, however, Sardou had published a short story entitled "Le Médallion" [The Locket] (1861), which adopts a much more hard-headed view of scientific investigation, and also qualifies as a significant early contribution to detective fiction, featuring a police officer who attempts to use "physiology," in collaboration with careful logical deductions made from physical evidence, as a means of identifying criminals. Inevitably, Sardou converted the story into a three-act comedy, *La Perle noire* (1862), and whenever the story was subsequently reprinted— as in *La Science Illustrée*—it bore that title, a translation of which I have retained for the version reproduced here (which was taken from the periodical's pages) as "The Black Pearl." Although it is of somewhat marginal interest as a scientific romance, it is fascinating as a study of the interpretation of evidence, and the relevance of science to criminal investigation; it is—in an admittedly weak but nevertheless significant sense—the first authentic romance of forensic science, and the ultimate ancestor of the currently-fashionable wave of such dramas in fiction and on TV.

X. B. Saintine was the by-line used by a prolific dramatist and novelist who was born Joseph Xavier Boniface (1798-1865). Although he is largely forgotten today, two of his novels, both fictionalizations of actual occurrences, remain fairly well-known: *Picciola* (1836) is about a political prisoner who conserves his sanity by his investment in the fate of a flower growing in a crack between the stones of his prison, while *Seul!* [Alone!] (1857) purports to tell the true story of the castaway on whose experiences Daniel Defoe based the story of Robinson Crusoe.

The fascination with strategies of psychological survival exhibited by these two novels resonates in many of Saintine's other works, including a curious book of visionary fantasies, ostensibly (and presumably genuinely) drawn from a notebook in which the author had long compiled a record of his dreams, *La Seconde vie* [The Second Life] (1864). A translation of the two-part episode forming chapters IV and V of that book was included, as "Astronomical Journeys," in *The Germans on Venus*; the two stories reproduced here are the others that take an obvious and straightforward inspiration from the advancement of natural philosophy.

"The Paradise of Flowers" is interesting, not merely as an extravagant botanical fantasy reflecting a contemporary Parisian passion for the importation and display of exotic blooms from around the world, but also as a sly commentary on current disputes regarding the authenticity of the phenomena of "animal magnetism" and the broadening of those disputes into a general debate regarding the controversial authority of purely materialistic explanations of natural phenomena. The same debate provides the philosophical inspiration of "The Great Discovery of Animules," which attempt to apply neo-atomic theory to the phenomena previously associated with the soul. As in "Astronomical Journeys," the author's deftly unorthodox wit provides both stories with an abundant narrative energy that attempt to compensate for the intrinsic weightiness of their subject-matter and the occasional density of their terminology.

Eugène Mouton (1823-1905) was the son of a military officer who spent his childhood in Guadaloupe. He embarked upon a career as a lawyer, which culminated in an appointment as a prosecutor in Rodez. He began writing humorous short stories on the side, using the pseudonym Mérinos [Merino sheep or wool], making his debut in *Le Figaro* in 1857, and gave up his legal career ten years later to become a full-time writer. He remained best known for his humorous short fiction, much of which was fantastic in a vein somewhat akin to

11

the "nonsense literature" produced in England by Edward Lear, Lewis Carroll and W. S. Gilbert, but he also wrote various non-fiction books, including one on French penal law and of the first ever guide-books for would-be authors. Partly inspired by the example of Mouton's professionalism, his nephew by marriage, Paul Duval, went on to become one of the leading lights of the *fin-de-siècle* Decadent Movement as Jean Lorrain.

Mouton produced a number of items directly inspired by reading contemporary popularizations of science, of which "La Fin du Monde" (here translated as "The End of the World") was the first. Two others are translated in the earlier anthologies in this series: "L'Historioscope" (as "The Historioscope") in *News from the Moon*) and "L'Origine de la Vie" (as "The Origin of Life") in *The Germans on Venus*. The latter stories were both first published in book form in the collection *Fantaisies* (1883), although they had appeared in periodicals at earlier dates. "La Fin du Monde" was initially published in book form in *Nouvelles et fantasies humoristiques* (1872, by-lined Mérinos), but it too had probably been published previously in a periodical.

Like Mouton's other exploits in this vein, "The End of the World" exemplifies the perennial problem that early writers of scientific romance had in finding appropriate narrative forms for their speculative excursions, being as much an essay as a story. It also provides a graphic illustration of the license that the adoption a humorous tone gave to a laconically casual imaginative extravagance that might have seemed inappropriate in more earnest work. It is, of course, an exercise in absurdity, but it demonstrates very clearly that in 1870 or thereabouts, it was only by reaching into the utmost extremes of absurdity that a writer could have any chance of imagining the prospects that would be visible on the horizons of possibility established in the 21st century. Mouton thus became the first writer to imagine an ecocatastrophe precipitated by global warming generated by human industrial activity, and the first to imagine some potential effects of applying a sophisticated biotechnology to agricultural production. Although Mouton's jesting exercises in scientific romance helped to lay ground-work for the more elaborate and sophisticated speculative ad-ventures of Alphonse Allais, Alfred Jarry and Gaston de Paw-lowski, only the last-named came remotely close to duplicat-ing the imaginative reach of "The End of the World," and even he could not match its uncanny targeting.

Despite the thinness of his output, Charles Cros is one of the most interesting pioneers of French scientific romance, by virtue of having attempted to follow a scientific career as well as a literary one; as the four stories reproduced here represent the whole of his contribution to the genre, he—like Louis Mullem—warrants more detailed consideration in this intro-duction than his fellows. He was born in 1842. His father, Henri Cros (1803-1876) had shown excellent prospects as a scholar and had obtained a doctorate in law, but had scorned the bar in order to devote his attention to literature and philos-ophy, settling in the south of France, where he made a modest living running a small boarding-school. Charles was the youngest of four children; his siblings were Antoine (1835-1903), Henriette (1838-1924) and Henry (1840-1907). By the time Charles was born, his father had published two editions of his ostensible philosophical masterpiece, *Théorie de l'Homme intellectuel et moral*, in 1836 and 1838, but its lack of appreciation had extended so far as his being condemned as an unfit educator by virtue of his ardent republicanism and outspoken agnosticism, and he had been forced to abandon his boarding-school in 1839. The family was in dire straits by the time Henri Cros moved it to Paris in 1844 and tried unsuccess-fully to obtain academic post.

At the age of 18, Charles obtained a job at the Institution des Sourd-Muets; Henry joined him there in 1861, but was expelled in 1863 for dueling with one of his colleagues and Charles was suspended soon thereafter for chronic absentee-ism. He began medical studies, following in Antoine's foot-steps—the latter had established a medical practice in 1857—

but did not finish them, although he acted as his brother's auxiliary during the cholera epidemic of 1865. By that time, Henry was ardently pursuing a career as sculptor, having exhibited work in the famous *Salon des Refusés* in 1863. Charles lived an unsettled Bohemian existence, but thought that he might make a career as an inventor, and began work on an "autographic" telegraph system—a primitive fax machine—for which he applied for a patent in 1866.

Antoine hosted a literary *salon* in addition to his booming medical practice, and frequented several others, along with his younger brothers, including the one hosted by Camille Flammarion, who was then in the process of writing his *Récits de l'infini*, the most important of which was *Lumen* (1866-69). The other regular attendees included Paul Verlaine as well as Victorien Sardou. Charles had become interested in the problem of color photography—he sent a paper on the topic to the Académie des Sciences in 1867—and Flammarion took him under his wing. The friends he made at Flammarion's salon introduced him to another, hosted by Nina de Villard, which was a very different kettle of fish.

Nina's lavish salon was ostentatiously *avant-garde*, and she delighted in hosting performances of various kinds; the star of her private shows was the Comte de Villiers de l'Isle-Adam, with whom Cros became fast friends. Other writers Cros encountered there who were later to make important contributions to speculative fiction included Louis Boussenard and Anatole France, but he quarreled violently with the latter over Nina's affections and tried to strangle him in the climax of a violent quarrel. Nina's *salon* was not to everyone's taste—the Goncourt brothers described it as "l'atelier de détraquage cérébral" (the mental breakdown factory)—but that only added to its fame, and Cros was glad to become a central figure therein when he and Nina became lovers.

Camille Flammarion, who put on a staid lecture series at his own *salon*, invited Cros to talk about another of his hobbyhorses, the possibility of interplanetary communication using light signals, in May 1869. Cros submitted the text to the

Académie des Science in July, and it was published in Victor Meunier's *Cosmos* in August before being reissued as pamphlet. He began publishing poetry in the same year; he and Nina were both admitted to second showcase anthology of the *Parnasse contemporain*, although it did not appear until 1871, the delay in its publication being caused by the Franco-Prussian War and the Paris Commune.

In December 1870, the house in which Charles was still living with his parents was hit by a shell and destroyed. Henri took the rest of the family south, to stay with his wife's family, while Charles was taken in by Madame Mauté, Paul Verlaine's mother-in-law. Cros and Verlaine were good friends by then, but the invitation owed more to the fact that Antoine Cros had nursed both Mathilde Verlaine and Madame Mauté through bouts of smallpox. Charles busied himself with experiments in "modern alchemy," attempting to synthesize gemstones, but acted again as his brother's medical auxiliary during the chaos precipitated by the Commune. Once the Commune had fallen, Antoine and Charles were both denounced as Communards, but the charge failed to stick, because Antoine was held in great esteem by his prosperous clients in the Faubourg Saint-Germain. Nina, however, had entertained many of the leading Communards in her *salon* and thought it politic to flee to Geneva.

In 1871, Verlaine showed Cros the poems he had received from Arthur Rimbaud and Cros went with him to meet Rimbaud at the railway station when Verlaine invited him to Paris (although they missed him). Charles was now becoming interested in theoretical science, and submitted the outline of treatise on *Mécanique cérébrale* [Cerebral Mechanics] to the Académie des Sciences in May—effectively a prospectus for neuropsychology, which was handed for consideration and evaluation to Claude Bernard, the great pioneer of experimental physiology. At the same time, however, he associated himself with an *avant-garde* literary group centered on Rimbaud, known as the *Vilains Bonhommes*. He began to publish poems in *La Renaissance littéraire et artistique*, where he also published his first scientific romance, "Un drame interastral," here translated as "An Interastral Drama," in the July 6 and August 24, 1872 issues.

In July 1872, Verlaine and Rimbaud ran away together, causing a great scandal; Cros, unsurprisingly, sided with Mathilde in the ensuing long-distance quarrel, but left Paris shortly afterwards to meet up with Nina, who eventually thought it safe to return in the following April, shortly after the publication of Charles's first poetry collection, *Le Coffret de Santal* [The Sandalwood Box]. He also struck up a correspondence at this time with the Comte de Chousy, who was subsequently to publish the satirical scientific romance *Ignis* (1883)[2]; it might have been Cros who introduced Chousy to Villiers de l'Isle-Adam, who sent him a complimentary copy of his own satirical scientific romance *L'Ève future* (1887).

In March 1874, Cros launched a periodical of his own, the *Revue du Monde Nouveau*, in collaboration with Henri Mercier; its second issue featured Cros's second scientific romance, "La Science de l'Amour" (here translated as "The Science of Love"). Unfortunately, its third issue was its last. Cros wrote a comedy drama in the vein of Beaumarchais, "La Machine à changer le charactère des femmes" [The Machine for Changing the Character of Women], but it only saw had two performances, both enacted privately at Nina's salon; Villiers served as his co-star. He also wrote another play in collaboration with Nina, "Le Moine bleu" [The Blue Monk], which suffered the same fate. In 1876, Cros and Nina were both blackballed from the third *Parnasse contemporain* showcase by Anatole France—never a man to forgive and forget—but that setback was countered by the success of a series of monologues that Cros wrote for the actor Ernest Coquelin, more familiarly known as Coquelin *cadet* [the younger]. The first and most famous was "L'Hareng saur" [The Salted Herring], in honor of which Nina decorated her salon with salted her-

[2] Available in a Black Coat Press edition (ISBN 9781935543887).

rings hung from the ceiling. There were, however, more disappointments to come.

In March 1877, Cros found a financial backer for his work on color photography in the Duc de Chaulnes, and also began work on a device he called the paléophone; he sent a sealed description of the latter device to the Académie in April, and built a prototype, but the Duc would not provide funds to develop it. Eight months later, Thomas Edison applied for a French patent on a near-identical device called the phonograph, and it was granted.

Cros's monologues continued to be successfully performed, but Coquelin *cadet* pocketed the money they earned him, only paying Cros a small flat fee for each one. In 1878, Cros married Mary Hjardermaal; their son Guy-Charles was born the following year, during which he published a second, much-expanded edition of *Le Coffret de Santal*. He was now attempting to develop an acid-free battery without metal electrodes, and published the early chapters of his *Principes de Mécanique cérébrale* in *Synthèse Médicale*, a journal edited by his brother Antoine, but the journal folded with the text incomplete, and it is doubtful that he ever wrote any more.

While continuing his increasingly desperate quest to make a living as an inventor, Cros joined Emile Goudeau's literary club, the Hydropathes, through which he met and became friends with Alphonse Allais. The club became too popular for its own good and its meetings became unmanageable; it was suspended in 1880, when its journal, *L'Hydropathe*, was revamped as *Tout-Paris*; the latter only lasted five issues, but one of them included Charles's third scientific romance, "Le Journal de l'Avenir" (a later version of which is here translated as "A Newspaper of the Future").

Cros continued his work on color photography in collaboration with an engineer named Jules Carpentier, but could not devise a marketable method. At the end of 1881, however, Rodolphe Salis founded a café called *Le Chat Noir*, with the ambition of making it Paris's leading literary café and Cros became one of its earliest regulars, along with other Hydropathes—Salis had requested Goudeau to revive the club with *Le Chat Noir* as its base. It was there that Cros's friendship with Allais matured, Villiers having fallen on hard times, and Nina de Villard's salon being defunct. Cros missed the "double act" that he and Villiers had put on *chez* Nina, and started a new one with Allais; Gabriel Astruc's *Le Pavillon des fantômes* (1929) recalls Cros and Allais exchanging "des passes d'armes contradictoires où la fantaisie se mêlait au document. Tous deux fabriquaient du Jules Verne ou du Robida avec une profusion et un cachet d'authenticité stupéfiants" [argumentative duels in which fantasy mingled with the documentary. Both fabricated work in the manner of Jules Verne of Robida with an amazing profusion and stamp of authenticity].

It is possible that Cros's finest work in the field of scientific romance was done, and essentially frittered away, in these performance pieces—but it seems probable that some of the humorous scientific and pseudoscientific speculations that Allais subsequently put into the squibs he wrote for various humorous papers originated from these flights of fancy. Unfortunately, the pieces in question were randomly scattered through Allais' various collections, obscuring the extent of his contribution to the rich tradition of French satirical scientific romance. Several of the other writers who hung out at the *Chat Noir* also went on to write scientific romance, including Edmond Haraucourt, Henri Rivière and Charles Laumann (who signed himself E. M. Laumann).

Cros, however, made little or no further attempt to publish any literary work connected to his scientific endeavors. His principal literary effort in the context of *Le Chat Noir* was the founding of a group he called the Zutistes (a calculated echo of Rimbaud) in 1883. It went nowhere, but the eventual publication of the contents of a manuscript intended to be its showcase, *L'Album Zutique*, gave it a certain belated notoriety. He did do some published work in collaboration with Allais, including a series of "*contes sens dessus dessous*" (upside-down tales) issued under the pseudonym Carlemyll, for the periodical *Gil Blas*, but it only included two works of marginal speculative relevance before being cut short.

Cros was not initially involved in the editorship of the café's journal, *Le Chat Noir*, founded in 1882, but he did take a hand in it after April 1883. He subsequently involved himself with *Le Scapin* and *La Décadence*, both founded in 1885, but he was in poor health by then—presumably due to the heavy drinking he had begun in Nina de Villard's salon and continued in *Le Chat Noir*—and both aspects of his languishing career suffered from his increasing incapacity. In 1884, Joris-Karl Huysmans published his "Decadent handbook" *À rebours*, in which he included a remarkably harsh criticism of Cros, with specific reference to "La Science de l'Amour"—a view not shared by all the champions of the Decadent Movement, given that Rémy de Gourmont described the same story as a "masterpiece" in 1891. There was, however, no mention at all of Cros in the second foundation-stone of the Decadent Movement, Verlaine's non-fictional account of *Poètes maudits*. Perhaps the omission was coincidental, given that the book was a hastily-compiled collection of essays, but Verlaine probably had not forgotten that Cros had sided with his wife when his marriage had disintegrated.

It might have been the sting of Huysmans' dismissal that led Cros to reprint "La Science de l'Amour" in *Le Chat Noir* in October-November 1885, but it is significant that he followed it up with a revised version of "Le Journal de l'Avenir" in March 1886—in which, as can be seen in the translation included here, the journal in question becomes a 1986 issue of *Le Chat Noir* rather than a 1980 issue of *Tout-Paris*—and a new (albeit very brief) scientific romance of sorts, "Le Caillou mort d'amour" (here translated as "The Pebble that Died of Love") in the very next issue. He added a reprint of "Un drame interastral" to the series in August. *Le Chat Noir* thus featured all of Cros's scientific romances within the space of a year—a sequence that might have formed a basis to the continuation of a series and the birth of a genre if Cros had not been so prematurely weary and seriously ill by then. He accomplished little more before dying, a broken man, on August 9, 1888, leaving his family nothing but debts.

"An Interastral Drama" is, inevitably, primitive by modern standards, but its interest is not confined to its anticipation of developments in media, or its blithe assumption that space travel will never become practicable. Its greatest fascination lies in what it refuses to say, most conspicuously about the particular charms of Venusian women (which obviously exceed those of Earthly women, in the eyes of Earthly men) and other "Mysteries of the Cupola," but also about the other speculative elements contained in the story, all of which are deliberately consigned to a vagueness aptly symbolized by the moving images of the hero's inamorata, lovingly reproduced in swirling smoke.

"The Science of Love" is far more modest in its speculative content than "An Interastral Drama," but equally interesting by virtue of its cruel satirical account of a scientific mind at work. "A Newspaper of the Future" is of little literary interest, its parodic verses having lost any impact they once had as their targets have become less familiar, but its lurid account of the technology supporting the "reporters" of the future and distributing their wares is a fine phantasmagoria of phonographic extrapolations. "The Pebble that Died of Love" is a euphemistic allegory, which only employs a lunar setting and anthropological jargon in the cause of scurrilous parallelism, but it deserves attention nevertheless as a work *sui generis*.

The calculated vagueness and ostentatious understatement deployed in Cros's scientific romances is also reproduced, more flamboyantly, in the "upside-down tales" he wrote in collaboration with Alphonse Allais, and echoes of it can be seen in Allais' own relevant work, one sample of which is reproduced in *The Germans on Venus*, and more of which will hopefully be showcased in a future anthology in the series. Allais, however, tended to be a much more down-to-earth writer, and the speculative fiction of Allais' most loyal disciples (insofar as their humorous writing was concerned), Gabriel de Lautrec and Paul Vibert, also fails to reproduce the strange surrealism of Cros'. There are, however, hints of the same scrupulous peculiarity in the work of two more famous writers who readily admitted Allais' influence, Alfred Jarry and Gaston de Pawlowski.[3]

Cros was not without influence on subsequent French writers of scientific romance in other regards than the stylistic. His proposals for interplanetary communication were not only echoed by Flammarion in subsequent works but were put to far more robust use by Flammarion's most fervent disciple, Henry de Graffigny, in the *Aventures Extraordinarire d'un savant russe* (1888-96),[4] which he wrote with Georges le Faure, and by Gustave Le Rouge—who was part of Paul Verlaine's entourage before taking up a career as a *feuilletonist*— in *Le Prisonnier de la planète Mars* (1908) and *La Guerre des vampires* (1909).[5]

"Charles Epheyre" was the pseudonym used on most of his literary work by Charles Robert Richet (1850-1935), a physiologist who won a Nobel Prize in 1913 for his work on anaphylaxis. He was the son of the Professor of Clinical Surgery at the University of Paris, and set out to follow in his father's footsteps, although he also pursued his literary interests while he was a student in Paris, and continued to do so thereafter. His career was interrupted at its inception by the Franco-Prussian War, when he did military service at Les Invalides and also as an ambulance-driver—like his father, he was a pacifist. When he resumed his medical studies, he developed a strong interest in abnormal psychology while he did

---

[3] Pawlowski's *Journey to the Land of the Fourth Dimension* is available in a Black Coat Press edition (ISBN 9781935543375).

[4] Available in a Black Coat Press edition as *The Extraordinary Adventures of a Russian Scientist Across the Solar System* in two volumes (ISBN 9781935543818 and 9781935543825).

[5] Both available in a Black Coat Press edition as *The Vampires of Mars* (ISBN 9781934543306).

a stint as an intern in a ward of "hysterical" patients who were being experimentally treated by hypnosis. That same interest also extended to a keen fascination with what would now be called "parapsychology," his initial skepticism being eroded by witnessing the performances of various spiritualist mediums, including Eusapia Palladino. Like Camille Flammarion, at whose salon Palladino performed, Richet was able to combine his career as a scientist with that of a "psychic researcher," and was eventually elected President of the British Society for Psychical Research in 1905.

Richet's earliest literary endeavors were conducted in collaboration with a college friend, Paul Fournier, and the pseudonym they adopted was a combination of the initial letters of their surnames, although Richet continued to use it for solo work long afterwards. The only book that can really be reckoned a collaboration is *Poésies* (1873), although Fournier might have had a hand in some of the short stories subsequently published under the pseudonym. Charles Epheyre's principal outlet during the 1880s was the *Revue Politique et Littéraire*, which subsequently became the *Revue Bleue*; it was there that both "Le Mirosaurus" (here translated as "The Mirosaurus") and "Le Microbe du Professeur Bakermann" (here translated as "Professor Bakermann's Microbe") first appeared, in 1885 and 1890 respectively, before being reprinted in *La Science Illustrée* as *romans scientifiques*. Epheyre's other contributions to the periodical were various as well as numerous, including the satirical psychiatric case-study "Le pensionnaire de M. Lolo" [Monsieur Lolo's Patient"] and "Bonne et mauvaise étoile" [A Lucky and Unlucky Star], a fantasy in the style of the Arabian Nights (both 1883). Richet's pseudonymous production was not immediately inhibited by his appointment as Professor of Physiology at the Collège de France in 1887, but did begin to dwindle away gradually thereafter.

Epheyre's first book was *À la recherché du Bonheur* [In Search of Happiness] (1879). His most interesting novel, in the context of imaginative fiction, was *Possession* (1887), subtitled a *roman occultiste*. His most famous and successful work, "Soeur Marthe" [Sister Marthe], a classic early study of multiple personality, appeared in the *Revue des Deux Mondes* in 1889, before being reprinted in a book of the same title the following year and adapted for the stage—in collaboration with Octave Houdaille, with music by Frédéric Le Rey—in 1898. Several other books appeared under the Epheyre name, including *À la recherché de la gloire* [In Search of Glory] (1892) and *Le Douleur des autres* [The Pain of Others] (1896), and at least two further plays written in collaboration with Houdaille were produced for the stage. Richet also published numerous books under his own name from the 1880s onwards, and that signature virtually monopolized his work after 1898, when he was elected to the Académie de Médecine. Almost all the books he signed with his own name were non-fiction, the principal exception being a volume of *Fables* (1891), but they do include an ambitious work of futurology, *Dans cent ans* [In A Hundred Years] (1892), whose appendices include a brief critical survey of previous literary works about the future.

Although "The Mirosaurus" is on the periphery of the genre of *romans scientifiques*, its speculative element being largely incidental, it an interesting story by virtue of being one of the earliest to pay satirical attention to the culture of science as a profession, an obsession and a social phenomenon. It is a surprisingly bitter cautionary tale, considering that its author had belonged since his early childhood to the Parisian scientific *monde* that comes in for such scathing tongue-in-cheek criticism in the story. "Professor Bakermann's Microbe" is equally acerbic and original, the much closer resemblance of its plot to conventional speculative fiction being deftly offset by its deftly callous characterization of the psychology of scientific research.

Paul Adam (1862-1920) was a prolific writer, whose first novel was *Chair molle* [Soft Flesh] (1885), which had the signal honor of being prosecuted for indecency, landing him in jail for a fortnight. He began his career as a committed Naturalist, but soon moved on to embrace Symbolism; he often

23

collaborated with Jean Moréas, one of that Movement's loudest propagandists, and served as one of Jean Lorrain's seconds when the latter was called out by Marcel Proust.

Adam never wrote a full-blown scientific romance, but he did have a habit of inserting lyrical futuristic sections into his Symbolist novels, often featuring technological innovations and always appealing for social reform. In his *Encyclopédie de l'Utopie et de la Science-Fiction* (1972), Pierre Versins lists and describes these brief inserts in such stories and novels as *Coeur utile* [Useful Heat] (1892), "Grandeur future de l'avare" [The Future Grandeur of Avarice] (in *Critique de moeurs*, 1893), *Les coeurs nouveaux* [New Hearts] (1896), *Lettres de Malaisie* [Letters from Malaya] (1898) and *Clarisse et l'homme heureux* [Clarisse and the Happy Man] (1907).

The story translated here as "A Tale of the Future," *Le Conte futur* (1893), appeared as a book despite its brief length, and thus remains the most prominent of the author's work in this vein. It is not the sort of work that might have been reprinted in *Le Science Illustrée*, but it does echo a Utopian element that can be found in many of the authors who did appear there, and some of those who appear in these pages; it deserves inclusion as an example of a significant vein of French futuristic fiction of the period, although it contrasts strongly with the jingoistic vein of French future war fiction in general, especially as represented by "Captain Danrit,"[6] a pillar of Gautier's *La Science Française*.

The author most abundantly represented in this anthology, Louis Mullem (1836-1908), was by far the least famous of them all; although he was a regular attendee of Edmond de Goncourt's literary salon in the 1880s he was known there and elsewhere as a political journalist rather than a writer of fiction. He met the writer who then signed himself J. H. Rosny at

---

[6] Captain Danrit's *Undersea Odyssey* is available in a Black Coat Press edition (ISBN 9781935558811).

the Grenier, but Rosny's brief memoir of him, penned in the 1920s, reveals no awareness of the fact that he was ever a fellow writer of scientific romances. Rosny obviously never read the collection of stories assembled after Mullem's death in 1908 by the man who introduced Mullem to the Grenier, Gustave Geffroy, despite the fact that Geffroy, as a fellow-member of the Académie Goncourt, must have been in touch with Rosny at the time of its compilation and publication. Rosny was not alone in that omission; *Contes ondoyants et divers* [Meandering and Various Tales] (1909), seems to have slipped into oblivion; there is no mention of the scientific romances it contains in any reference book on speculative fiction.

Geffroy, as a hardened Naturalist, made no attempt to call attention to Mullem's imaginative fiction in introducing the volume in question, and did not mention Rosny in the list of Mullem's friends (although he did take the trouble to mention Villiers de l'Isle-Adam as an old acquaintance of Mullem's and a key influence on his sardonic literary style). Nor did any of Mullem's imaginative stories in the posthumous collection ever find a publisher while the author was alive, although some of the less adventurous items therein had been previously published. Indeed, had Geffroy not wanted to pay homage to his dead friend, no one would ever have known that these stories existed. From the viewpoint of historians of speculative fiction, however, at least one of the works in question—"Le Progrès supreme," here translated as "The Supreme Progress"—is of considerable interest, in terms of its unprecedented scope and its anticipation of certain ideas that were to be subsequently popularized; its imaginative reach even surpasses Rosny's in one respect, and it warrants consideration as a minor masterpiece of sorts.

Mullem only developed literary interests late in life, having followed a career in law for many years. He had been born into a Jewish family with strong interests in music, and was a fine piano player; his older siblings, Julia and Félix, were both first-rate musicians, Julia in a professional capacity. Louis' interest in literature might have been sparked, or at least encouraged, when Julia married the novelist Léon Cladel, a former acolyte of Charles Baudelaire. It might have been through Cladel that he first met Villiers de l'Isle-Adam. Mullem first began publishing short stories in the early 1880s, the most fantastic of his early productions being "Feue Harriet, fantaisie américaine" [Harriet the Widow; An American Fantasy] in *La Vie populaire* in 1882. There is no way to know exactly when Mullem actually wrote the various philosophical fantasies included in *Contes ondoyants et divers*, although one of them contains internal evidence suggesting that it was written within a year or two of 1893, and there seems to be a developmental pattern in the stories that facilitates their being arranged in a logical, if not a chronological, order.

The story that can be dated with reasonable confidence, "L'Éternité chimique" (here translated as "Chemical Eternity"), surely predates "Le Progrès supreme," but probably not by much. Both were probably preceded by Mullem's third outright scientific romance, "Un Rival d'Edison" (translated as "A Rival of Edison" in *The Germans on Venus*) and by the other philosophical romances that seem to lead up to them thematically, which I have included here as interesting prefaces, along with translations of one wry item of speculative nonfiction and a brief allegory. "L'Invisibilité de M. Gridaine" (here translated as "The Invisibility of M. Gridaine"), "Causeries de cercle" (here translated as "Club Conversation") and "L'Ombre et son homme" (here translated as "The Shadow and His Man"), might or might not have been written after the relatively unambitious "Un Rival d'Edison," but they surely predate "L'Éternité chimique," and were probably produced in that order. It seems probable that all of these stories were composed in the 1880s and early 1890s, as Mullem seems to have allowed his literary endeavors to lapse during the final decade of his life, initially displaced by increasing political activity and then by the burdens of ill health.

"The Invisibility of M. Gridaine" and "Club Conversation" have provincial settings very similar to that of "A Rival of Edison;" all three make similarly sardonic comments about the dogged anti-intellectualism of such towns, and its deadening effects on imaginative ambition and endeavor—presumably reflecting, retrospectively the experience of the early phase of Mullem's legal career, before he relocated to Paris. The former story is akin to the fictional "case studies" assembled by the pioneer of English psychiatry, William Gilbert, in *Shirley Hall Asylum* (1863) and *Doctor Austin's Guests* (1866). The story's central idea—that of achieving a peculiar kind of non-existence—is taken further in "Club Conversation," whose central characters discover a happy medium between the traditional extremes of materialism and "spiritualism." As in "The Invisibility of M. Gridaine," the fantastic element of "Club Conversation" can be regarded purely as a study in eccentric monomania—as the notional audience in the club assume it to be—and the same is true of the Paris-set "The Shadow and His Man," which can be regarded as an expansion of an image contained in the denouement of "Club Conversation," in which "the Bonsor brothers" seem literally doubled by virtue of the shadow cast by the body representing them.

Like "Club Conversation" and "The Shadow and His Man," "Chemical Eternity" is a conversation-piece in which extravagant assertions are made whose reliability is carefully rendered dubious, but in this instance the scope of the conversation becomes very great indeed, replete with highly imaginative speculations. "The Supreme Progress" is also provided with an apologetic frame that permits readers (if they are so inclined) to dismiss the whole thing as a product of absurd insanity, but whether readers take advantage of that option or not, the speculations set out there are truly remarkable. Although they follow on to some extent from the cosmological fantasies of Edgar Poe and Camille Flammarion, they have more in common with the much later and more spectacular visions of Olaf Stapledon, J. D. Bernal and Teilhard du Chardin, not only proposing the notion of the eventual post-technological emergence of disembodied "collective minds" but explicitly raising the questions of what it might feel like to exist as such an entity, and how such beings might spend their time pleasurably, purposively and profitably. For its time—especially if its time was 1894 or 1895 rather than the early 1900s, as seems likely, "The Supreme Progress" is an imaginative tour de force, and its fugitive publication invites us to wonder how many more such masterpieces might have languished unread, for lack of a hospitable outlet.

Brian Stableford

Victorien Sardou: *The Black Pearl*
(1862)

I

When it rains in Amsterdam, it rains hard, and when thunder is mingled with it, the thunder is loud. That was the reflection made one summer evening, after dark, by my friend Balthazar Van der Lys, as he went along the Amstel, trying to get back home before the storm broke. Unfortunately, the wind from the Zuyder Zee was running faster than he was. A frightful squall suddenly descended upon the quay, shaking shutters, breaking signs and twirling weather-vanes—and a number of flower-pots, tiles, net-curtains and pieces of cloth, detached from roofs or windows, were blowing pell-mell into the canal, followed by Balthazar's hat. It was all that he could do not to follow it—after which, the thunder exploded; after which the clouds burst; after which Balthazar was soaked to the skin and started running as fast as he could.

When he reached the Orphanage, however, he remembered that it is dangerous to start running in stormy weather. The lightning-flashes were following one another unrelentingly; the thunder was roaring in rapid succession; accidents can happen suddenly. This observation frightened him so much that he threw himself blindly into a shop doorway, where someone—a gentlemen calmly sitting in a chair—received him in his arms and nearly fell over with him. The gentleman in question was none other than our mutual friend Cornelius Pump, whom I may introduce to you as the foremost scientist in the city.

"Wow! Cornelius! What the devil are you doing here on a chair?" said Balthazar, shaking himself.

29

"Now, now!" Cornelius replied, anxiously. "Don't move about so much—you'll break the string of my kite!"

Balthazar turned round, thinking that his friend was making fun of him, but—not without amazement—he saw him gravely occupied in reeling in, by means of a silken thread, the most beautiful kite that Amsterdam had ever seen floating in its atmosphere. This majestic plaything was swaying over the canal at a prodigious height, and only seemed to be coming down to earth reluctantly. Cornelius was pulling, the kite was pulling, and the wind, complicating the difficulty, was greatly amused by the little contest. But what was truly calculated to provoke admiration was the kite's tail, twice as long as an ordinary one, and entirely fitted with little pieces of paper, innumerable in quantity.

"What the Devil possessed you," Balthazar finally exclaimed, "to play with a kite in such weather?"

"I'm not playing with a kite, idiot," Cornelius replied, smiling in pity, "I'm establishing the presence of nitric acid in electrically-charged clouds." The scientist seized the thoroughly-vanquished kite at last, cast an eye over the little pieces of paper with which it was decorated, and added: "Look— as you can see, my litmus paper has turned red…"

"Oh good," said Balthazar, with the slightly mocking smile of an ignorant person who has no understanding of the puerilities of science. "It's research! A nice time for it!"

"I should say so," Cornelius replied, naively. "And what an observatory! Look at it! No houses nearby. A fine horizon! Ten lightning-conductors in view, and all lit up! I've been on the lookout for it a long time, this rascal of a storm, and I made myself a firm promise that I'd come here to look it in the face."

A violent clap of thunder exploded at these words.

"Go on," Cornelius continued, "roar as much as you want—I've got you, and I'll tell you what's what!"

"And what have you seen here that's so interesting?" asked Balthazar, whose feet were beginning to get wet in the water overflowing from the gutter, and who was not in a good mood.

"Poor fellow," Cornelius replied, with a pitying smile. "Tell me, what's that?"

"Lightning, of course," said the dazzled Balthazar.

"Yes, but what kind?"

"The lightning kind."

"You don't understand," said Cornelius. "There's lightning and lightning. To begin with, we have lightning flashes of the first class, in the form of a luminous furrow, compact, very determined in its contours, affecting a zigzag form, colored white, purpurin[7] or violet. Then there's lightning of the second class, an extended sheet of light, generally red, which can embrace the entire horizon. Finally, there's lightning of the third class, rolling rebounding, elastic, and most often spherical in form—but is it really globular, or might that be an optical illusion? That's precisely the problem that has been teasing me for such a long time. You'll tell me, it's true, that globes of fire have been conclusively observed by Howard, Schübler, Kamtz…"[8]

"Oh, I don't say anything at all." Balthazar replied. "The water's rising, and I'd rather get away from here."

"Wait for me," said Cornelius. "When I've seen my spherical lightning…"

"My word, no—I'm only 300 paces from my house; I'll risk it. And if you want a good fire, a good supper, and a good bed if you need it—and, by way of a globe, that of my lamp—I offer you all of it. Are we agreed?"

"Wait a minute—my lightning won't be long…"

Making no reply, Balthazar was about to launch himself into the street when, all of a sudden, a sinister coppery bolt of lightning cleaved the darkness, and, at the same instant,

---

[7] Purpurin is an orange-red dye obtained from madder root.

[8] The names cited are those of three significant pioneers of meteorology: Luke Howard (1772-1864), Gustav Schübler (1787-1834) and Ludwig Friedrich Kamtz (1801-1867).

thunder burst forth with a frightful din, a few hundred paces away. The shock was so violent that Balthazar's knees bent, and he nearly fell over.

"There was definitely a globe," said Cornelius. "This time, I saw it clearly. Let's go eat!"

Blinded and stunned, Balthazar collected himself. "That thunderbolt fell right on top of my house!"

"No," Cornelius replied, "it was in the Jewish quarter."

Paying him no heed, Balthazar started running, in spite of the danger. Cornelius, gathering up his pieces of paper and putting his chair over his head, decided to follow him, in spite of the rain, which was coming down even harder.

At the corner of Zwanenburgerstrasse, where his house was, my friend Balthazar was completely reassured. No flames were lighting up the street, and his house was still intact. He went up the front steps in one bound and knocked two or three times, imperiously. Even so, no one was in a hurry to open the door, so Cornelius had time to catch him up.

Balthazar hammered on the door.

"Can you believe that Christiane isn't opening up?"

Finally, Christiane decided to do so. She was pale with fear, her hands trembling, and she could scarcely speak.

"Oh, Monsieur," she said. "Did you hear that clap of thunder?"

"Did it render you deaf, then?" Balthazar relied, hurling himself into the house. "Quickly, my girl! Dry clothes, a big fire, and the table set!"

He went upstairs four or five stairs at a time and, shoving open the door of the large drawing room, he fell into his armchair with a sigh of relief. Cornelius followed, with his chair.

II

An hour later, the two friends were finishing their supper, elbows on the table, laughing at the wind and the rain that were raging outside.

"This," said Cornelius, "is the best time of the day. A nice bottle of white curaçao, a good fire, good tobacco and a good friend to chat with you; there's nothing better, is there, Christiane?"

Christiane moved back and forth, putting a heavy stoneware jug on the table, along with the antique glasses with slender stems. Pronounced by Cornelius, her name caused her to blush, but she made no reply, shivering as she still was with fear.

Christiane, it is time to tell you, was a young woman brought up by virtue of charity in our friend Balthazar's house, and I ask your permission to tell you her story, so quickly that you will not have time to become impatient.

Some time after the death of her husband, Madame Van der Lys, Balthazar's mother, was at mass one day when she felt a slight tug on her dress. Thinking that someone was after her purse, she acted so promptly that she immediately seized the hand of the thief. It was the hand of a little girl, very dainty, very pink, very innocent and very charming.

The worthy lady had tears in her eyes on seeing those angelic little fingers so soon employed in bad deeds. Her first impulse was to release the child for pity's sake; the second was to hold on to her for charity's—and that was what she decided to do, the good soul! She took little Christiane home with her; the girl was weeping, for fear of being beaten by her "aunt." Madame Van der Lys consoled her, got her to talk, and learned enough to understand that the child's mother and father were gypsies of the sort that travel with fairgrounds; that the little girl had been trained from a young age in acrobatic exercises; that her father had been killed attempting a difficult feat; that her mother had died of poverty; and, finally, that the pretended aunt was a shrew who beat the little girl and taught her to steal, while waiting for better opportunities.

I don't know if you knew Madame Van der Lys, but she was as good a woman as her son is a man. She kept the child—whom the "aunt" did not come to reclaim, as you can imagine. She brought her up, and taught her to read and count—and Christiane was soon a little model of sweetness, decency and good manners. And what a housekeeper! When the poor lady died, at least she had the consolation of leaving to her son—along with her cook, old Gudule, who was deaf and becoming unsteady on her feet—a young woman of 15, alert and lively, who never let Balthazar's fire go out or his dinner get cold, and who knew where to find the good linen and silver for feast days—and was polite, comely, gentle and pretty to boot. That, at least, was the opinion of Cornelius, who had discovered in those eyes lightning flashes much more interesting than those of the third class. But, hush! I shall stop there so as not to seem scandalous.

I can add, however, that Christiane gave a good welcome to Cornelius, who lent her good books; the young man, in his capacity as a scientist, held a housekeeper like Christiane in higher esteem than the most beautiful dolls in the city, who were often good for nothing.

This evening, however, it seemed that the storm had paralyzed the young woman's tongue. She had refused to sit down at the table, where her place was set, as usual, and, under the pretext of serving the two friends, came and went, hardly listening, replying vaguely, and making the sign of the cross at every flash of lightning…until the moment when Balthazar, turning round, could no longer see her, and thought that she had retired to her room.

A few minutes later, he went to put his ear to the door of her room, which opened into the drawing-room, parallel to the study door. As he could not hear anything, he became convinced that the young woman was already asleep, and came back to sit with Cornelius, stuffing his pipe.

"What's the matter with her this evening?" said Cornelius, gesturing toward the young woman's room.

"It's the storm," Balthazar replied. "Women get so frightened!"

"If they didn't, friend Balthazar," Cornelius replied, "We wouldn't have the immense pleasure of protecting them like children…especially that one, who's so dainty and frail. Honestly, I can't look at her, without tears coming to my eyes, she's so gentle, so good…so tender! Oh, the charming child!"

"Why, Master Cornelius," Balthazar replied, "you're almost as enthusiastic about Mademoiselle Christiane as you are about thunder!"

Cornelius blushed slightly, and murmured: "It's not the same thing."

"Naturally," Balthazar replied, bursting into laughter and taking Cornelius' hands amicably. With a broad smile, which came from the heart—the kind that ensured that one could not help liking the fellow—he said: "Come on, do you think I can't see what's going on? You don't just play the kite-flyer on the Anstel, overgrown child that you are. You also play tennis with Christiane…and it's your two little hearts that serve as rackets…"

"What, do you think so?" stammered the disconcerted scientist.

"But it's been going on for three months, friend Cornelius, and I don't think I'm the only one who's noticed—three months that you've been coming here twice a day: at noon, on your way to the zoological gardens, and at 4 p.m., on your way back."

"It's the shortest route," Cornelius hazarded, timidly.

"Yes, to make yourself loved…"

"But…"

"Come on," said Balthazar, paying no heed, "let's reason it out: Christiane isn't a young woman like any other; she has a young heart and a very intelligent young head—I can answer for that: intelligent enough to admire a scientist like you. You squeeze her hands, you worry about her health; you lend her books, which she devours. You give her a lecture on chemistry if she has a stain on her dress, or natural history on the subject of a flower-pot, or anatomy when the cat provides an opportunity! She listens with all ears, eyes wide open—and you don't expect love to come into the picture, between a professor of 25 and a schoolgirl of 18?"

"All right, I love her, damn it!" Cornelius replied, resolutely. "What are you going to do about it?"

"What are you?"

"Well, I want to marry her."

"Well then, tell her!"

"Well, I will."

"Well then, shake my hand!" cried Balthazar. "And hurrah for joy—for I'm getting married too."

"Oh!" said Cornelius, startled.

"And I'm marrying," Balthazar continued, with the enthusiasm of a lover who can only see and hear himself, "Mademoiselle Suzanne Van Miellis, the banker's daughter."

Cornelius made a gesture that might have been translated as "Damn!"—punctuated with admiration.

"Take note, Cornelius," Balthazar continued, "that I was passionately in love with her six years ago—but Mademoiselle Suzanne, who is today the acknowledged daughter of a rich banker, was then only his natural daughter. Her mother was so poor that they both came to do needlework for us. Do you remember? And if I had chanced, in those days, to say: 'Here's my wife!' there would have been an outcry in the family. So I whispered to myself: 'Later…later…!' And *later* has come. One morning, Suzanne and her mother were put into a carriage, and the coachman plied his whip! That gross egoist Van Miellis, who had never seen his daughter, had met her by chance; he was moved…he was remorseful, so they say; personally, I think he quite simply had a whim to care for someone; but whatever it was, you know the rest as well as I do. He died last winter, leaving his daughter one of the largest fortunes in the city."

"The largest…"

"Well, that's what bothered me, Cornelius, and prevented me from seeing my Suzanne—she was too rich. I dared not go to call at her house; I would have seemed to be after her money. You have no idea how many men want to marry her now! The first time I met her, after her change of fortune, was in the zoological gardens. There were half a dozen gallant

36

gentlemen, of all ages, around her, pressing upon her. I would never have had the audacity to approach her. To be exact, it was her who called to me: 'Well, Monsieur Balthazar, you no longer greet your old friends?' Me, I floundered in politeness: 'Mademoiselle! Madame!' They laughed quietly, the others— but when she'd taken my arm, and her mother had invited me to dinner, they weren't laughing any longer, those who weren't invited.... And I spent the evening there, that day...my God, what a fine evening!"

"And then?" said Cornelius.

"And in the end, I no longer left her house. I loved her like a lost soul, but I would never have said anything. It was her mother who pushed me to speak...a worthy woman, you know, who liked me a lot because I was polite to her when she was poor. She said to me one day, while showing me out: 'Say something, then, Monsieur Balthazar, you're worth more than all of that lot, and I'd be happy to call you my son...'

"My word, that decided me; I took my courage in both hands, and that evening, when I found myself alone with Suzanne, I poured my heart out. She seemed to be half-expecting it, but that didn't stop her being as emotional as me... She blushed, but nevertheless, she looked at me...oh, she looked into the depths of my soul, and made everything dance around me.

"Eventually, she replied: 'Monsieur Balthazar, you mustn't take what I'm about to tell you the wrong way, but, since I've become rich, I can assure you that I've been very unhappy. I can no longer distinguish those who love me from those who don't. I see so many people who adore me that I'm suspicious of everyone, and I'd rather throw my fortune into the Amstel than marry a man I thought to be a calculating villain!'

" 'Oh, Mademoiselle,' I protested, 'is that what you think of me?'

" 'Oh,' she went on, 'I know very well that you aren't one of those, Monsieur Balthazar...that would be so sad! But it's not enough. I'll tell you my dream. I only want to choose

37

as a husband someone who would have loved me when I was poor. Oh, I'd be very sure of the love of that man, and I would return it in full!'

" 'But that man is me!' I cried. 'I'm the man who loved you six years ago, and although I never dared tell you so, you must have perceived it!'

"Very softly, she replied: 'Perhaps, yes…' And she continued looking at me in a manner so strange…I could see that she wanted nothing more than to believe me, but that she didn't dare…

" 'Look,' she said, 'do you want to convince me of what you're saying? Do you remember the summer when I was working in your house with my mother? New flowers were brought for the garden…'

" 'Oh, I remember it well, Mademoiselle—they were orchids.'

" 'Yes, and I was allowed to go see the flowers with you. There were all sorts of shapes, and so singular…one resembled a butterfly, another a wasp, another…one might have thought it was a little face—but there was one above all that outshone the rest, and of six flowers on one stem, not one that resembled another; there was one like a little heart, all pink, with two blue wings on either side! And one of such a pretty pink, and one of such a pretty blue! I'd never seen anything like it. And then…'

" 'And then—let me tell what happened next—as we both leaned forward to look more closely at the flower, I don't know how it came about that your hair brushed against mine, and in the abrupt movement that you made to draw back, your hand, which was holding the flower in order to see it more clearly, detached it from its stem. I can still hear your cry. I can still see you, ready to weep over the accident and beg my forgiveness…when your mother appeared at the window and called you, and I…'

" 'And you?'

" 'And I picked up the fallen flower.'

" 'You picked it up?'

38

" 'And I kept it as a memory of that little moment of joy, so short and so sweet.'

" 'You've kept it?'

" 'Preciously, Mademoiselle—and I'll show it to you whenever you wish.'

"If you had been able to see Suzanne at that moment, my friend...it was no longer her, Cornelius—no, it was a new creature, a hundred times as beautiful, if that's possible. Her eyes were shining; her face was radiant. She held out her hands to me in a gesture so delightful that an angel could not have done better.

" 'Ah,' she said to me. 'That's all I wanted to know, my friend, and I'm very happy! If you picked up the flower in memory of me, it was because you loved me already; and if you've kept it until now, it's because you love me still. Bring it tomorrow, our little flower with blue wings...it's the nicest gift that you could put into our wedding-basket...'

"Oh, my friend, when I heard those words: *basket* and *wedding!* I almost fainted on the spot. I got up, and I was certainly about to do something crazy when her mother came in. I threw my arms around the good lady's neck, and I kissed her daughter a dozen times on the cheeks. That calmed me down.

"I picked up my hat and escaped by running away, with the hope of bringing the little flower to Suzanne this very evening...but this monster of a storm has spoiled everything, and I've postponed my happiness until tomorrow...and that's the whole story!"

"Oh, saints in Heaven!" cried Cornelius, throwing himself into his arms. "Two marriages at once!" At this point, the worthy fellow, imitating the scamps at the church door, threw his cap into the air, shouting: "Hurrah for the wedding! Hurrah for the bride and groom! Long live Madame Balthazar! Long live Madame Cornelius! Long live the little Balthazars! Long live the little Corneliuses!"

"Would you like to shut up," said Balthazar, laughing and closing the other's mouth for him. "You'll wake Christiane."

"Oh," said Cornelius, lowering his voice, "we mustn't wake Christiane. Now show me your flower with blue wings, so that I can admire it…"

"It's in a little steel box at the back of my writing desk," said Balthazar, "with all my poor mother's jewels. I've encased it in a glass locket framed with gold and black pearls. I looked at it again this morning. It's charming. You shall see!"

So saying, he picked up the lamp, took a bunch of keys from his pocket and opened the door of his study.

He had only just gone in when Cornelius heard him utter a cry, and rose to his feet. Balthazar reappeared, very pale, on the threshold of the room.

"Cornelius…oh, my God!"

"What is it?" exclaimed the scientist, in alarm. "What's wrong?"

"Oh, my God! Come and see! Look!"

III

Balthazar, staggering as if struck by stupor, raised up the lamp to illuminate the interior of the office. What Cornelius saw fully justified Balthazar's exclamation.

The floor was completely strewn with papers of every sort, and that confusion of pieces of paper was explained by the sight of two green files extracted from their wooden cabinet and emptied out on to the carpet. Add to that a large morocco portfolio in which Balthazar kept his correspondence, gaping wide open despite its steel lock…and it was completely empty, several hundred letters having been scattered…

But that was only the least part of the catastrophe, Confronted by that mess, of which he was no longer trying to take account, Balthazar's first movement was to run to the writing-desk. It had been forced open!

The steel lock had, however, put up more resistance than that of the portfolio, and the bolt had remained bravely in its socket; thus, giving the impossibility of getting it out, it had been necessary to break the lid of the desk. The entire section

40

of wood adjacent to the lock had been literally cut away, broken up and reduced to shreds, and the lock itself, totally detached, was hanging down miserably with its nails twisted and broken.

As for the rounded and movable cover, typical of Tronchin writing-desks,[9] it had been three-quarters raised—enough to permit a hand to search all the drawers and cubby-holes of the item of furniture.

Strangely enough, the majority of the drawers that were unprotected against violence, and contained stocks and shares, had been left alone by the thief; it seemed as if he had not even taken the trouble to open them. All his attention had been focused on the one that contained gold and silver coins—about 1500 ducats and 20 florins—and the little steel box that Balthazar had mentioned, filled with jewels. That drawer, torn from its socket, was absolutely empty, as if it had been turned upside-down. Everything had vanished without trace, gold, silver, and jewels alike—and what, for Balthazar, was the most cruel blow of all was that, when he picked up the steel box from the floor, he found that it was empty too, and that the locket had been stolen along with everything else!

This cruel loss, which affected him more than that of all his money, caused his initial stupor to be succeeded by a veritable fit of madness. Abruptly, he opened the window that overlooked the street and started shouting at the top of his voice: "Stop, thief!"

The entire town, following its custom, would have replied: "To the fire" if the first cry had not attracted a police patrol sent out to observe and repair damage caused by the

---

[9] Standing desks with adjustable legs known as "tables à la tronchin" were first developed in the early 1800s; it is not entirely clear whether the Tronchin for whom the desks were named was the encyclopedist of that name who was acquainted, albeit somewhat turbulently, with Voltaire and Diderot.

storm. Then ran to the window, where Balthazar, shouting and gesticulating, was unable to get to the end of his explanation.

Even so, Monsieur Tricamp, their leader, soon realized that it was a matter of stolen objects. After inviting Balthazar to make less noise, in the interests of his cause, he posted two policemen in the street to watch the coming and goings, and asked the gentlemen to let him into the house without waking anyone up—which Cornelius did forthwith.

IV

The door having been opened quietly, Monsieur Tricamp came in on tiptoe, followed by his third subordinate, whom he left in the hallway with orders not to let anyone in or out.

It must have been nearly midnight; the whole city was asleep, and it seemed certain, given the tranquility that reigned within the house, the Gudule—who was a trifle deaf—and Christiane, worn out by the excitements of the storm, had not heard any of the racket, and were sleeping peacefully.

"Now," said Monsieur Tricamp, lowering his voice, "what's the matter?"

Balthazar drew him into the study and, without finding the strength to say a single word, showed him the scene.

Monsieur Tricamp was a short man, slightly plump but nevertheless very brisk and lively. He also had a smiling face, an attitude of great self-satisfaction—justified by his much-renowned ability—and pretentions to elegance, eloquence and knowledge. He was, however, a clever and cunning man, who had no other defect, in professional terms, than an excessive myopia: a troublesome ailment, which obliged him to look at things at very close range—which is not always the best means of seeing them clearly.

He was obviously surprised, but it is the rule, in every profession, not to appear astonished in front of *clients*. He contented himself with murmuring: "Very well! Very well!" while smiling and darting the expert glances of a master in all directions.

"You see, Monsieur!" Balthazar said to him, in a strangled voice. "You see!"

"Very well," Monsieur Tricamp replied. "The portfolio forced, the writing-desk forced! Very well…perfect!"

"Perfect how?" said Balthazar.

"Money has been taken, hasn't it?" Monsieur Tricamp continued.

"All the money, Monsieur."

"Good."

"And the jewelry…and my locket!"

"Bravo! Theft with breaking and entering, in an inhabited house! Excellent! And you don't suspect anyone?"

"No one, Monsieur."

"So much the better. We shall have the pleasure of the discovery."

Balthazar and Cornelius looked at one another in surprise."

Tranquilly, and without astonishment, Monsieur Tricamp continued: "Let's take a look at the door!"

Balthazar showed him the only door to the study, equipped with a fine old-fashioned lock, a masterpiece such as is no longer found in the Low Countries. Tricamp tested the lock—*crick, crack!* It was sharp, sonorous and easy. He took out the key and assured himself with a single glance of the impossibility of opening the lock by means of ordinary picking-devices. The key had the form of a double trefoil and was complicated by a secret that, exceptionally, was not generally known.

"And the window?" said Monsieur Tricamp, handing the key back to Balthazar.

"The window was closed," said Cornelius, "until we opened it to call you. Besides, Monsieur, take note that it is equipped with a strong grille, whose bars are very close together."

Monsieur Tricamp assured himself that the bars could not, in fact, have given passage to a two-year-old child, and

43

closed the window again himself—after which, he naturally turned his attention to the fireplace.

Balthazar followed all his movements without saying a word, with the confidence of an invalid watching a doctor write his prescription.

Monsieur Tricamp bent down and considered the interior of the fireplace attentively.—but there again he was bewildered. Recent masonry had blocked off three quarters of the chimney, only leaving the opening necessary for the passage of a stove-pipe. That stove, dismantled every year in spring in order to be cleaned, and only set up again when the weather turned cold, was presently in the loft, and the fireplace was quite empty.

Monsieur Tricamp only wondered momentarily whether the stove-pipe conduit might give passage to anyone, and straightened up again, more embarrassed than he wanted to appear. "Very good!" he said. "Damn it!" And he looked at the ceiling, after having replaced his pince-nez with a pair of spectacles. "There again, nothing suspicious, or even dubious."

He took the lamp from Balthazar's hands, set it down on the writing-desk, and took off the shade. Suddenly, that action revealed a detail that had escaped them thus far...

V

Three feet above the writing-desk, almost equidistant between the floor and the ceiling, some sort of knife was embedded in the partition wall. Verification was made that the knife belonged to Balthazar. It was a foreign weapon, a gift from a friend, which was usually kept in the writing-desk—but what was surprising was the strange use that had been made of it.

"Why is that knife stuck into the wall?"

At the same moment, Tricamp noticed that the iron wire of a bell, which ran along the cornice above the writing-desk, was broken and twisted, and that the two severed fragments were hanging down in the direction of the knife. He leapt nimbly on to a chair, then on to the top of the writing-desk, and started examining the object at closer range. He had scarcely stood on the improvised ladder, however, when he uttered a cry of triumph. He had, in fact, only to reach out his arm between the knife and the cornice of the ceiling to lift up a fragment of wallpaper, unstuck on three sides, to discover a large circular opening underneath, pierced in the partition wall, which the paper had closed off until then like the flap of a valve.

This discovery was so unexpected that the two young men looked at it open-mouthed. Their astonishment did not last long, however; Balthazar remembered very quickly, and explained that the opening, closed off and forgotten for a long time, had once served as a primitive bull's-eye window to illuminate the next room, which had then only been a dressing-room. Later, a partial reconstruction of the house had permitted Monsieur Van der Lys to transform the dressing-room into a bedroom, lighting it by means of a window overlooking the street, and to get rid of the henceforth-unnecessary bull's-eye by covering it with on both sides by canvas and wallpaper similar to that of the two rooms on either side.

Monsieur Tricamp pointed out that the square piece of paper previously stuck on that side had been detached with extreme care, which implied that the person responsible intended to stick it back later. By raising himself up slightly, he succeeded in sliding his hand through the opening and assuring himself that the same work had been carried out on the other side, on the paper in the neighboring room, with the same precaution and the same skill, evidently with the same aim.

There was no more doubt, now, that it was necessary to assume that this was the thief's means of introduction, the bull's-eye being large enough to let someone through. Getting down from his pedestal, Monsieur Tricamp set about explaining everything that the malefactor had done from his arrival to his departure, with extreme confidence.

"The knife," he said, "placed at an equal distance from the writing desk and the bull's-eye, is evidently a step that he prepared for the return ascent, more difficult than the descent. The iron bell-wire, broken from the start, since it was within range of his hand, enabled the dangling end to serve him as a means of support, not on the side where it would have rung the bell, but on the other, where it could only shake the pull—and it is, in fact, the fragment of wire attached to the pull that seems to be the only one twisted by that usage.

"As for the files fallen on to the floor, whose pillage is unjustified, it's easy to understand that our thief, while climbing up to get out, made a false step and lost his balance—at which he reached out for the first object within range. The filing-cabinet being higher up than the writing-desk, answered this need precisely. While the right foot reached for the knife, the left foot, swinging in empty space, found momentary support on the filing-cabinet, which swayed, and two files slipped on to the floor—the two uppermost files, as you can see: the ones that would naturally fall first. After which, rebalanced by that slight support, he was able to reach the bull's-eye without difficulty—and the filing-cabinet, freed from the impulse, naturally regained its equilibrium!

"I attribute to the disturbance caused by the fall the thief's negligence in sticking back the pieces of wallpaper that he had detached so carefully, as if he had not planned to return them to their original state. Does all that not seem to you to be reasonable and evident, as clear as day?"

Balthazar and Cornelius were not listening to this ingenious speech without a certain admiration, but the former was not a man to remain spellbound for long. He was no longer thinking about anything but his locket. Certain now of the fashion by which the malefactor had got in, the only thing he wanted to know henceforth was how he had got out...

"Patience," Monsieur Tricamp replied, savoring his victory with all the pride of triumph. "Now we know what the thief did, let us think about his temperament."

"His temperament!" cried Balthazar. "We don't have time…"

"Pardon me," Tricamp riposted, "but there's nothing better we can do—and Monsieur, who is a scientist, will understand that immediately. The application of physiological knowledge to inquests, enquiries and judiciary hearings is now an accomplished fact, Monsieur, which has transformed the empiricism of the old routine from top to bottom."

"But while you're talking," said Balthazar, "my thief is getting away!"

"Let him," replied Monsieur Tricamp. "We shall catch up with him. As I was saying, you cannot get back to the source of a crime if you willingly forsake the study of the characteristics by which the criminal identifies, and, in a sense, denounces himself.

"And what characteristic, what badge, what more infallible trademark is there than that of temperament, which is entirely revealed in the *nuances of the operation*? Nothing bears less resemblance to one theft than another theft, or to one murder than another. In the fashion in which the crime has been committed, in the varying degrees of cleverness, talent, brutality and propriety that preside over his accomplishment, be sure that the author signs his name in full. It only remains to decipher the signature.

"Thus, yesterday morning, of two servants equally suspected of having stolen a shawl from their mistress, I was able to distinguish the guilty one at first glance. The thief had a choice between two cashmeres, one blue and the other yellow, and had taken the blue. One of the servants was blonde and the other brunette; I was sure of not being mistaken in arresting the blonde—the brunette would obviously have chosen the yellow shawl!"

"That's admirable," said Cornelius.

"Well," Balthazar added, "tell me the name of my thief—and quickly, for I have a fever…"

"I can't tell you the name immediately," Monsieur Tricamp went on, "but what I can affirm right away is that the guilty party is a beginner. The skill with which the paper was detached from the wall was able to deceive our faculties momentarily, but paper that has dried in place for five or six years comes unstuck of its own accord so easily that there's no great talent there. The opening was ready-made, so the merit lay in its discovery; and again, the sight of the paper offered a more-than-sufficient clue. I've nothing to say about that portfolio so carelessly emptied, nor the desk forced in a brutal and savage fashion. All that makes one shrug one's shoulders; it's graceless and tasteless work. Look at that lock hanging down—it's lamentable! He hasn't even disengaged the bolt from its socket. He must have the tools of a cobbler, and that's unforgivable, now that English industry manufactures such light, delicate and convenient instruments for us! Oh, Messieurs, I can introduce you, of you wish, to artists who could force your writing-desks in such a way as to invite your admiration!"

"He's a novice, then?" said Cornelius.

"Evidently...and a clodhopper too. A thief with a little self-respect doesn't leave an apartment in this state of disorder; he puts more delicacy into it. Saunderson, whom we executed the other day, would have preferred to come back, in order to put everything back in place. There was an artist! I will add that the person can neither be very tall nor very robust. I need no more proof of that than the employment of that knife and the bell-wire, when a vigorous man of reasonable height would easily have been able to hoist himself up by the strength of his wrists alone. Moreover, a robust hand would have embedded the dagger with a single blow, whereas our thief had to strike several times to penetrate the partition wall—look at the very recent scratching at the end of the hilt."

"That's true," said Balthazar, dazzled by this visual perspicacity.

"But what about the writing-desk, whose wood has been splintered?" Cornelius objected.

"Why, Monsieur, that's exactly where his weakness reveals itself!" exclaimed Tricamp. "True force is serene and calm, for it is sure of itself. It gives one blow of the fist, and

48

one alone, to a round-topped writing-desk, which is only asking to spring open, and its springs open! Whereas this is the work of an impotent individual losing his head. The object resists; he strikes, lashing out this way and that; he reduces it to matchwood, splinters, a mess. No muscles or sinews! The work of a child, or a woman."

"A woman?" exclaimed Balthazar.

"Since I arrived, Monsieur," Tricamp replied, "I have not doubted it for a moment." And, claiming one last prize, Tricamp added: "And, in sum, it's a young woman, for she can climb, short, since she needs a ladder, brunette, for she's bad-tempered, and familiar with your habits, since she profited from a moment when you were out to act at leisure, and because she went straight to the drawer that contained the money, ignoring the others. In conclusion, if you have a young servant-girl, look no further—it's her!"

"Christiane!" exclaimed the two young men.

"Ah—so there's a Christiane," said Monsieur Tricamp. "Well then, it's Christiane!"

VI

Balthazar and Cornelius looked at one another, both very pale. Christiane! Pretty Christiane! Their Christiane, so good, so sweet…a thief! Get away! And yet, they remembered her origin and the manner in which she had entered the household. She was only a gypsy, after all…

Balthazar fell into a chair like a drunk. As for Cornelius, it seemed to him that his heart had just been burned with a red-hot iron, and that he was about to die…

"Let's see this Christiane, them," said Monsieur Tricamp, abruptly extracting them from their stupor. "Let's go to her room!"

"Her room," Balthazar replied, trying to get up, "But that is her room!" And he pointed to the bull's-eye.

"And you didn't guess the whole thing?" Monsieur Tricamp said, smiling.

49

"But she must have heard us!" said Cornelius, speaking effortfully.

Tricamp seized the lamp, went out rapidly, opened the door of the next room and went into Christiane's bedroom, followed by the two young men.

The room was empty.

All three of them uttered the same cry: "She's run away!"

Monsieur Tricamp assured himself with a single sweep of the hand that the bed was not unmade, and, simultaneously, that nothing was hidden in the mattress or the bolster. "She hasn't even been to bed," he said.

At the same moment, they heard a sound in the hallway. The drawing-room door opened abruptly, and the policeman placed on watch by Tricamp came in, pushing Christiane in front of him. She seemed more surprised than frightened.

"Monsieur Tricamp," said the policeman, "this young woman was about to go out, and I arrested her as she was drawing the bolts."

Christiane looked at them all with an astonishment so natural that anyone would have been taken in by it...except for Monsieur Tricamp.

"But what do you want with me?" she said to the policeman who was closing the door behind her. "Monsieur Balthazar, tell him who I am."

"Where have you come from?" asked Balthazar.

"Upstairs," she replied. "Gudule was scared by the thunder; as it was still rumbling when she went up to bed, she begged me to keep her company, and I went to sleep in an armchair in her room. I woke up, saw that the weather was fine again, and came down to go to bed. I was about to make sure that I hadn't forgotten to close the bolts when this gentleman arrested me—and he gave me a fine scare!"

"You're lying," Monsieur Tricamp replied, abruptly. "You were about to draw the bolts in order to go out, and you didn't go to bed in order not to have the trouble of getting dressed again, and to make it easier to keep a lookout for the moment to escape."

Christiane looked at him with the most naïve expression. "Escape? She said. "What escape?"

"Ah!" said Monsieur Tricamp. "We have aplomb!"

"Come here," said Balthazar, to whom this scene was giving a fever. "Come here, and I'll show you…"

He took Christiane by the arm and drew her into the study.

"Divine Jesus!" cried the young woman, on the threshold. "Who's done this?"

The exclamation seemed so sincere that there was a momentary hesitation, but Monsieur Tricamp's emotions did not last long. He drew Christiane to the writing-desk, showed her the broken lid, and said, brutally: "It was you!"

"Me!" cried Christiane, who did not seem to know what was being said to her at first. She looked at Balthazar with a bewildered expression, then at Cornelius. Then, returning her gaze to the writing-desk, she perceived the empty drawer. Then, as if she suddenly understood, she uttered a heart-rending cry' "Oh! You're saying that I've stolen from you!"

No one had the courage to reply. Christiane took a step toward Balthazar, who lowered his eyes before her gaze. Suddenly, she put her hand to her heart, as if she were choking. She tried to speak, and pronounced two or three incoherent swords, of which none could be distinguished save for: "Stolen…! Me…! Stolen…! Me…!" Then she collapsed like a dead woman.

Cornelius ran to her, seized her in his arms and lifted her up. "No!" he cried. "No…it's not possible! This child isn't guilty."

He ran into the next room and lay the young woman down on the bed. Balthazar followed him. Excitedly. Monsieur Tricamp, still smiling, was about to go in behind them when one of his men held him back, tugging gently at his sleeve.

"With your permission, Monsieur Tricamp," the man said, "we already have some information about the young person."

"What information?" said Tricamp, lowering his voice.

"While my comrade was on watch in the street, the baker who lives opposite him told him that this evening, slightly before the great thunderclap, he saw Mademoiselle Christiane at the window to the street—the drawing-room window. She slipped a package to a man with a cloak and a large hat..."

"A package!" said Tricamp, excitedly. "Good...perfect! Take the name of the witness and keep watch on the vicinity of the house—but before that, go fetch me the housekeeper. Her bedroom's on the first floor."

The policemen drew away, and Monsieur Tricamp went into Christiane's bedroom.

Christiane was lying on her bed, still unconscious, in spite of Cornelius' efforts to revive her. Without pausing to look at her, Monsieur Tricamp examined the room, and immediately perceived the bull's-eye opening into Balthazar's study, as well as a piece of wallpaper, unstuck as cleverly as the one in the other room. He took a chair, set it on the marble top of the chest of drawers, and, measuring the distance, assured himself that the climb was quite easy by means of that improvised ladder. After a few minutes of inspection devoted to the chest itself, he came back to Balthazar, with a smile on his lips...

"After all," the latter said, sadly contemplating the chilly and motionless young woman, "what proof is there that it's her?"

"This!" replied Monsieur Tricamp, depositing in his hand one of the black pearls detached from the locket.

"Where did you find it?" Balthazar asked.

"There," the police officer replied. He pointed at one of the drawers in the chest, filled with effects belonging to Christiane, which had been carelessly left open.

Balthazar ran to the item of furniture, shook the dresses and underwear and tipped everything out of the drawer—and the others—but fruitlessly. The locket was not there.

He looked around; the chest of drawers, the bed and a table without any drawers comprised all if Christiane's furniture. There was no trunk or cupboard—nothing that might serve to conceal the stolen objects…

Meanwhile, the young woman came round. She opened her eyes and saw all the people around her; then, remembering, she turned her head away and dissolved in tears, hiding her face in her pillow.

"Ah!" murmured Monsieur Tricamp. "Tears…we're going to confess." He leaned over her very gently, and said, in his softest voice: "Come on, my child, a virtuous gesture! Admit that you succumbed to an evil impulse. My God, no one's perfect! And we'll treat your folly with the consideration due to a pretty girl. So we're a trifle flirtatious, eh? We wanted to make ourselves beautiful? We wanted to please someone, then?"

"Eh?" said Cornelius. "My God, Monsieur…"

"Hush, young man!" Monsieur Tricamp replied, in a low voice. "Be sure that there's an accomplice." Leaning over Christiane again, he went on: "Isn't it true, my dear, that it was you?"

"Oh!" exclaimed Christiane, suddenly sitting up. "Kill me—but don't repeat that!"

The admonition was so sharp that Monsieur Tricamp leapt backwards.

"Monsieur," Balthazar said to him, "have the generosity to leave us alone with this child. Your presence is irritating her, and we'll get further with her than you."

Monsieur Tricamp bowed. "As you please, Monsieur— but be wary. What a villainess!"

And he went out.

Cornelius closed the door behind him, brusquely. Then the two young men went quietly to Christiane, who was sitting on her bed looking straight ahead, her eyes staring—without tears now—her entire body trembling with fever.

"Come on, Christiane, my child," Balthazar said, trying to take her hand, which was clenched on the bed. "We're alone now, there's no longer anyone here but friends. Would you like to say something?"

"I don't want to stay here!" said Christiane, in a dry, hoarse voice. "I want to go away. Let me go away!"

Cornelius sat her down again, gently. "You can't go out, Christiane. You can't do it without answering us."

"Tell us the truth, I beg you, Christiane," Balthazar continued. "The whole truth, my child. No one will do anything to you, I swear on my honor. I'll forgive you, and no one will know…I swear to you, Christiane…before God! Come on—can't you hear me?"

"Yes!" replied Christiane, who was not listening. "Oh, I can't cry anymore! Oh, if I could only cry! Make me cry!"

Cornelius looked at his friend anxiously. He took the young woman's burning hands and squeezed them gently in his own. "Christiane…my girl," he said, with all possible tenderness, "there is mercy for everyone, and we love you too much to be pitiless. Listen to me, I beg you. Don't you recognize me?"

"Yes," said Christiane, looking at him.

His eyes became moist. "Well, I love you…you know that…I love you with all my heart!"

"Oh!" cried the young woman, softening and dissolving in tears. "You're the one who says that I stole!"

"Well, no," Cornelius replied, swiftly, "I don't believe it! I don't say it, dear child—no! But you can see that you have to help me clear you, to find the guilty party—and for that, it's necessary to be frank with me and tell me everything…everything!"

"Yes, you're good, you," replied Christiane, tearfully. "You have pity on me, and you don't believe what they're saying. Defend me! Can't you see how stupid they are with their theft? What do they think I'd steal here? Isn't this house

54

my entire heart? Is there a single stone in that wall"—she rapped on the wall, and continued with increasing excitement—"that I don't adore? Can one steal one's own life and one's own blood? And to think that my good mother isn't here!" She was applying the name to Madame Van der Lys. "Oh, if she were here! She would send you back underground with your theft! But I'm alone, aren't I? And I've been accused because I'm a gypsy…because I stole when I was little…and they called me *thief! Thief! Thief!* They're calling me *thief!*"

She fell back on the bed, sobbing.

Balthazar could not stand it any longer. He fell to his knees beside the bed and, in his humblest and most suppliant voice, as if he were the guilty party himself, he said: "Christiane! My sister, my girl, my child, look at me! I'm on my knees, as you see. I beg your pardon for all the harm I've done. No one will say anything more; no one will speak again; it's finished. Do you understand? But since you love me…you don't want me to be unhappy, do you?… You won't repay in pain and torment all that you've received in benefits? Well, I implore you, if you know where my little locket is… I'm not asking you where it is, you understand? I don't want to know…it's all the same to me…but if you know, I beg you, in the name of my mother, whom you call your own, help me get it back. Nothing else… My whole life depends upon it, and he person who has taken it has taken all my happiness. Give me my locket…will you do that? Tell me, will you do that?"

"Oh!" said Christiane, in despair. "If it were in the blood in my veins, you'd have it already."

"Christiane!"

"But I don't have it! I don't have it! I don't have it!" She was wringing her hands as she spoke.

Exasperated, Balthazar bounded to his feet. "Wretched woman…!"

Cornelius stopped him—and Christiane put her hands to her forehead.

"Oh!" she said, laughing, "When I've gone mad, it will be over, won't it?" And she collapsed, exhausted, hiding her face, as if determined to make no further reply.

VIII

Cornelius drew Balthazar out of the room; he saw that he was tottering like a man suffering from vertigo. They found Monsieur Tricamp in the drawing-room, who had not been wasting his time. He had had old Gudule brought down. Woken up with a start, half deaf and understanding nothing of what had happened, she replied to his questions weeping and lamenting.

"Come, come, my good woman," Monsieur Tricamp said to her. "Pull yourself together."

"Divine Jesus, my good master!" Gudule cried, on seeing Balthazar. "What's going on? They woke me up so suddenly! Oh my God, what do they want with me?"

"Don't worry, my dear Gudule," Balthazar replied, "this doesn't concern you—but someone has stolen from me, and we're looking for the guilty party."

"Someone had stolen something?"

"Yes."

"Oh my God!" the poor old serving-woman went on, desperately. "But that's never happened before—I've been in the house for 30 years, and not so much as a pin has ever disappeared! Oh, my God, my God! It had to happen before I was dead!"

"Come, come," Monsieur Tricamp resumed. "Answer me without any fuss, my good woman."

"Speak a little louder," said Balthazar. "She's deaf, you know."

"We want to know," said Tricamp, raising his voice, "if you were here when the theft took place."

"But I haven't gone out, Monsieur."

"Not at all?"

"No, Monsieur, because I felt the storm coming, and because of my age, these days, I don't have the legs any longer…"

"Then you were in your room?" said Balthazar.

"No, Monsieur, I stayed in the drawing-room all afternoon, knitting by the fire."

"And you didn't budge, even to go to the kitchen?"

"No, Monsieur."

"Is your sight good, woman?" asked Tricamp.

"Monsieur?" said Gudule, who did not understand the question.

"I asked whether you have good eyes," Tricamp repeated.

"Oh, for that, yes, Monsieur. No ears—that's a little hard—but the eyes are still good, like the memory."

"Ah—a good memory! Well, how many people came during the afternoon?"

"The postman came, Monsieur, and then a neighbor to borrow a roll of pastry…then Petersen, who came to ask Christiane something."

"Ah! Who's Petersen?"

"He's a neighbor, Monsieur—a night-watchman. Monsieur knows him well."

"Yes," Balthazar said to Tricamp. "He's a poor devil who lost his wife a month ago, and his two children are ill—an honest man who has done some odd jobs for us."

"This Petersen came in, then?" Tricamp continued.

"No, Monsieur. He only talked to Christiane, through the window…"

"To say what?"

"I didn't hear, Monsieur."

"And after that…no one else?"

Gudule had the question repeated, and replied: "No one."

"And Christiane," Tricamp went on, "Where was she while you were knitting?"

"Well, Monsieur, the child came and went, as always; she took care of the kitchen for me, since I couldn't. She's so helpful!"

"But she wasn't in the kitchen all the time?"

"No, Monsieur—she went into her bedroom at nightfall."

"Ah! She went into her own room, did she?"

"Yes, Monsieur, to have a wash, because of supper."

"And did she stay in her room for a long time?"

"An hour, Monsieur."

"An hour?"

"Yes, Monsieur, a good hour."

"And you didn't hear anything during that time?"

"What did Monsieur say?"

"I asked whether you heard any noise…hammer-blows on wood, for example?"

"No, Monsieur."

"Yes," said Tricamp, turning to the young men. "She's deaf!" And, leaning toward Gudule and raising his voice, he added: "And the storm was already rumbling, wasn't it?"

"Yes, Monsieur. Oh, I certainly heard thunder!"

"She's confused the two noises," murmured Tricamp. He raised his voice again: "And afterwards?"

"And afterwards, Monsieur, it was completely dark; the storm burst; Monsieur didn't come home. I was very frightened. I got down on my knees and said my prayers…and that was when Christiane came out of her room, all trembling…very pale…and at that moment, the thunder exploded so loudly!"

"Ah!" said Tricamp, excitedly. "You noticed that she was pale and trembling?"

"Of course—like me, Monsieur. That storm broke our arms and legs. I couldn't get up, myself…and it was then that Monsieur started knocking, and Christiane opened the door. And that's all I know, Monsieur…as true as I'm a Christian and an honest woman!"

"You can stop weeping, my dear Gudule," Balthazar repeated, "since I've told you that no one is accusing you."

"Who, then, Monsieur? Who, then?" Struck by a sudden thought, she exclaimed: "Blessed Virgin! Is it Christiane?"

No one replied.

"Oh—you're not answering!" Gudule went on. "Oh, Monsieur—that's not possible."

"My dear Gudule!"

"Christiane, Monsieur!" the old woman continued, not listening. "A child who comes from the good God!"

"Come on," said Tricamp. "Since it isn't you..."

"Oh, I'd prefer that, Monsieur!" replied Gudule, desperately. "I'd rather people accused me...accuse me, you hear! An old woman like me...who's *done for*...what can it do to me? I'll settle my accounts on high, before much longer...but that child! I don't want anything to touch her, Monsieur! Oh, Monsieur Balthazar, don't let anything touch her, she's sacred! Don't listen to this wicked man—he's the one behind all this!"

In response to an impatient gesture from Monsieur Tricamp, the policemen each took hold of one of the old woman's arms in order to take her away.

Gudule took a few steps, then let herself fall to her knees near the fire, sobbing and lamenting that she had not died before *such wickedness*, and Monsieur Tricamp signaled to his agents to leave her there, praying...

IX

"Well," said the policeman, turning to Cornelius, "no one has come who could reasonably be suspected...neither the postman, nor the neighbor, nor Petersen. Therefore, it's either the old woman who's a thief, or the young one—and as I don't believe that the old one is in any condition to perform this feat of gymnastics, I beg Monsieur the scientist to draw the same conclusion..."

"Oh, don't ask me for anything," said Cornelius. "I no longer know what to think. It seems to me that I'm dreaming and that all this is a horrible nightmare!"

"I don't know whether it's a dream," Tricamp replied, "but it seems to me that I'm wide awake, and that I'm reasoning very soundly."

"Yes, yes," said Cornelius, pacing back and forth feverishly. "You're reasoning soundly!"

"And my logic is sufficiently rigorous!"

"Yes, yes—rigorous."

"And everything so far has confirmed my reasoning."

"Yes, everything confirms your reasoning."

"Well then, agree with me that the young woman is guilty."

"Well...no!" Cornelius replied, hotly, stopping short in front of the policeman. "No! That's what I'll never believe, until I hear her accuse herself! And God knows...if she said it at this moment, in front of us...I would still swear to her innocence!"

"But in truth..." The agent objected, amazed. "Her innocence...but what proof is there, damn it?"

"Oh, I have none, I know," Cornelius went on. "And I know all those you've invoked. And my reason is ready to find them evident...terrible...implacable..."

"Well, then?"

"But my conscience immediately rebels against my reason! But my heart is there, which says to me: *No, no, those words, that face...that despair! No, all that is not the behavior of a guilty person, and I swear to you, she is innocent! I can't prove it, myself...but I feel it...but I'm sure of it, and I proclaim it with all my might...with all my anguish...with all my tears. Don't listen to those who accuse her! They lie! Their logic is that of the earth, which is deceptive...mine is that of the heavens, which does not lie. Theirs appeals to Reason; I appeal to Faith...*"

"But at the end of the day..."

"*Don't listen to them*," Cornelius continued, his excitement growing, "*and remember that on those bad days when your scientific pride is ready to deny God Himself...it only requires a quiver of the heart to affirm Him! And how could that heart, which never lies, deceive you about the innocence of a child, when God prompts it?*"

"Well," said Tricamp, "if the police reasoned like that…"

"Oh, I don't expect to convince you," Cornelius went on. "Do your job, and I shall do mine."

"Yours?"

"Yes, yes… Search! Investigate! Examine! Heap up proof upon proof to overwhelm that unfortunate child; I shall be well able, for my part, to amass all those that can defend her."

"In that case, Monsieur" Tricamp replied, "I don't advise you to count among the latter what I've just found in one of the demoiselle's drawers."

"What?" demanded Cornelius.

"This pearl, detached from the locket."

Cornelius seized the pearl. He shivered. "In her drawer?"

"Yes, my friend, yes!" cried Balthazar. "In one of the drawers in her chest…just now…before my eyes!"

Cornelius was pale, motionless, overwhelmed. The proof was so convincing, so terrible! That unfortunate little pearl was burning his hand and crushing him beneath its weight. He looked at it, mechanically, without seeing it…but without being able to take his eyes off it. Balthazar took his hand, but Cornelius could not feel anything. He seemed stunned, and was still looking at the pearl…

"Cornelius!" exclaimed Balthazar, anxiously—but Cornelius pushed him away sharply, and leaned over as if to get a better view of the pearl by making it reflect the daylight.

"What is it?" Balthazar murmured.

"Get out of the way!" Cornelius replied—and, abruptly shoving him aside, he ran to the window and looked at the pearl more closely.

Balthazar and Tricamp exchanged surprised glances—and at the same moment, without saying a word, Cornelius launched himself toward the study.

"He's crazy!" muttered Monsieur Tricamp, following him with his eyes. "Monsieur Balthazar, would you care to pour a small glass of curaçao for my men? It's getting light, and the street must be a little cold."

"Done, Monsieur," said Balthazar.

Tricamp went out. On turning round, Balthazar saw old Gudule kneeling and praying in the corner. Swiftly, he went to join Cornelius in the study.

X

The scientist was studying the hilt of the knife, and the scratch observed by Monsieur Tricamp, with minute attention. The examination lasted several seconds, during which Balthazar, weary and discouraged, watched his friend mechanically, without taking the slightest interest in what he was doing.

Without saying a word, Cornelius climbed on to a chair and inspected the iron bell-wire and the manner in which it had been broken with the same care.

"Where's the bell?" he said, abruptly.

"In the drawing-room," Balthazar replied.

Cornelius pulled the section of wire that ought to have been connected to it, but no sound was heard.

"Ah!" said Balthazar. "She's thought of everything—she's unhooked the clapper."

Without replying, Cornelius looked attentively at the continuation of the steel wire. It was encased in a little tin-plate tube; the wire moved easily within it. There was evidently no obstacle therein.

"Look at the bell," he said to Balthazar. "Does it move when I pull the wire?"

Balthazar went to the threshold of the connecting door and obeyed, uncomprehendingly.

"Does it move?" Cornelius repeated, pulling the wire several times.

"A little," said Balthazar, but it can't rung; it's all stiff and upside-down, with its mouth in the air. One would think that something were maintaining it in that position."

"That's good," said Cornelius. "We'll see about that shortly. Hold the writing-desk while I climb up."

Balthazar came back into the study and did what was asked of him. Cornelius climbed from the chair on to the writing-desk and, assisting himself with the knife, hoisted himself awkwardly up to the bull's-eye, as if he wanted to judge the difficulty of the enterprise for himself.

Balthazar was opening his mouth to interrogate his friend when he heard Gudule call out to him from the next room. He went out immediately and found the old woman very emotional. The policemen were running in response to her voice.

"Monsieur!" she cried. "She's just run away!"

"Christiane?"

"Yes, Monsieur. I got up, and I saw her go through the room and escape through the garden. Oh, my God! Run quickly—she's going to do something silly!"

"Oh, the little serpent!" exclaimed Monsieur Tricamp. "She was playing dead. After her, you lot—through the garden!"

All the policemen launched themselves outside, Monsieur Tricamp at their head, and Balthazar ran to the young woman's room to assure himself that Gudule was telling the truth.

Christiane had, indeed, disappeared—but he found Cornelius in the room, who had got down from the bull's-eye. The scientist was holding the bed-curtains apart, and his attitude testified to the utmost amazement.

"Yes, yes, go on—search it," Balthazar said to him, furious and convinced that the cause of his friend's amazement was Christiane's departure. "Search it! You can clearly see that she's guilty, since's she's run away!"

"I can see," Cornelius replied, turning round, with his eyes on fire and trembling with emotion, "that she's innocent,

63

and that we're the ones who are guilty...and the ones who are stupid!"

"Are you mad?"

"And I have him, your thief!" Cornelius added, with increasing excitement. "I'll tell you everything that he's done, myself—and how he got in, and how he got out! And I'll tell you his name! First of all, it wasn't from this room, nor through that opening, that he got in—it was through the fireplace in your study."

"The fireplace?"

"Yes, the fireplace! And as he was attracted, as usual, to metal, to your gold and silver; he ran first to your portfolio, whose steel lock he forced, then to your writing-desk, whose iron lock he broke—and, making a parcel of your florins, your ducats and your jewelry, he carried them all off, leaving you the dagger in the wall by way of farewell...

"And from there, detaching the wallpaper, he leapt into the bedroom of that unfortunate child, where he dropped a pearl...and if you want to see what has become of your locket, come here!"

He drew the curtains back, and showed Balthazar the young woman's little copper crucifix, entirely gilded from top to bottom, resplendent with that new gleam.

"This is what he did with the golden frame..."

Plunging his hand into the seashell that served as the font of the crucifix, he took therefrom the two glass plates of the locket, fused into a single piece with the flower in between.

"And this is what he did with the rest!"

Balthazar looked at his friend in bewilderment.

"And if you want to know how he got out," Cornelius went on, dragging him to the window without giving him time to draw breath—look!"

He pointed at the uppermost pane, pierced by a little hole the size of a tennis-ball, so neat, so round and so perfect that the most skillful workman could not have done better.

"But who could have done all that?" Balthazar cried, finally, thinking that he must be dreaming.

"Simpleton! Don't you see that it was THE LIGHTNING-BOLT!"

Such a bolt might have struck at Balthazar's feet without him being more astonished—and he was about to demand explanations from Cornelius when the latter imposed silence on him and cocked an ear. A great clamor was going up in the direction of the quayside, and seemed to be coming up the street, getting closer all the while.

They opened the window and saw an agitated crowd, shouting and flowing all the way to the front steps, where it stopped to let through a stretcher borne by policemen, on which Christiane's body was extended. The unfortunate child had thrown herself in the Amstel!

XI

At the sight of that pale face, those eyes that seemed to have closed forever, and those two rigid arms through which the cold of death had run, Balthazar and Cornelius precipitated themselves to the side of the stretcher, took the young woman in their arms, and transported her into the drawing-room, putting her down in front of the fire on a mattress that Monsieur Tricamp took it upon himself to set down. There, they tried to reanimate her, warming her up in their arms, pleading with her and appealing to her as if she were able to hear them—but her hands were icy. Her heart was no longer beating.

No one, on seeing their desperation, could have failed to feel his heart melt in tears. They begged her pardon; they accused themselves. Everyone was weeping, for the crowd had invaded the room and surrounded them.

Finally, in the midst of his agony, Cornelius had a flash of inspiration, and, gluing his lips to Christiane's, he set about breathing in and out forcefully, facilitating the operation of the lungs with his hand.[10] In the meantime, Monsieur Tricamp had earthenware and iron jars heated, and any others that might serve the same purpose, in order that they might be placed under the young woman's arms and feet.

There was a terrible interval of anxiety and silence. The women whispered prayers, the men looked on, craning their necks…

"Bah!" said someone. "That's a lot of trouble to go to for a thief!"

Balthazar leapt to his feet, but there was nothing for him to do—the man had already been thrown out.

"She's breathing!" Cornelius exclaimed, breathlessly.

There was a shout of joy. Everyone believed in the theft, but what is the purpose of misfortune, if not to cause distress to the guilty?

A few minutes later, Christiane sighed, and a little life returned to her cheeks. A doctor who had arrived declared that she was saved, and had her carried into her bedroom. The women remained alone with her, undressing her and putting her to bed. Cornelius and Balthazar ran back and forth, mad with joy, giving advice through the door, asking whether anything was needed, running to fetch it, and, in the midst of all that, congratulating one another and shaking hands. As for the men, they gathered around the fire, discussing the best way of reanimating the drowned.

"Monsieur Balthazar," said Monsieur Tricamp, "I shall retire, with my men, for the young woman is in no state to be arrested today…"

---

[10] This description of "mouth-to-mouth resuscitation" was far ahead of its time. Standard practice at the time in dealing with victims pulled from water who had stopped breathing involved supplementing the warming of the body coupled with various usually-futile manipulations such as body-rolling and tongue-pulling. It was not until the 1950s that the method here recommended by Sardou became popular.

"Arrested!" cried Balthazar. "But hasn't Cornelius told you? We've discovered the thief."

"The thief!" replied Monsieur Tricamp. "Who is it, then?"

"The thunder!" said Balthazar.

Monsieur Tricamp's eyes opened wide. "The thunder?"

"Yes, Monsieur Tricamp," said Cornelius, in a slightly mocking tone. "The thunder—or, rather, the lightning. You apply physiology to the investigation of crimes; I apply physics."

"And you're telling me," cried Monsieur Tricamp, exasperated, "that lightning has done all this?"

"It has done many other things!" replied Cornelius. "What about the nails from an armchair planted in a mirror without breaking it; a key extracted from its lock and hung up on its nail; cigarette papers delicately removed from a melted bronze case; money volatilized through the enamel of a purse that remains intact; a cobbler's tools lifted up to the ceiling, so thoroughly magnetized that the nails run after the hammer like mad things; the wall that it uproots and carries 20 paces away; the pretty hole that it made in Christiane's window and the wallpaper that it unstuck so carefully; and the locket whose two glass plates have been fused without the flower being affected, gallantly leaving our friend the most delightful ornament that one could ever see—and, for his future, a wedding-present that no workman could ever have made—and, finally, the golden frame with which it has completely decorated Christiane's crucifix?"

"Get away!" replied Monsieur Tricamp. "That's impossible.! What about the package—the package that she handed through the window to the man?"

"The man is present!" exclaimed Petersen. "That was me!"

"You?"

"Yes, Monsieur Tricamp—and the package was linen that she had prepared for my children, who are ill."

"Good, good—linen!" said Tricamp, exasperated. "But what about the gold and the silver, the ducats and the florins, and the rest of the jewelry—where are they?"

"Of course!" said Cornelius, striking his forehead. "You've just reminded me…"

He leapt on to the table set against the wall, and overturned the bell, with a violent effort.

"Here they are!"

A large ingot of gold, silver and gemstones fell out of the bell, along with the detached clapper, all melted and fused together, as lightning can. The molten metal, charring the precious stones and pearls, had followed the conductive wire with the facility of movement and whimsical means that only electricity possesses, which has something prodigious and miraculous about it.

Monsieur Tricamp picked up the ingot and studied it in amazement.

He turned to Cornelius. "But what was it that put you on the track?" he said.

Cornelius smiled. "That black pearl, Monsieur Tricamp, which you handed to me yourself, challenging me to see it as a proof of innocence."

"The black pearl!"

"Yes, Monsieur Tricamp—look at that imperceptible little white dot. It's a burn! Providence requires no more to save a human creature."

"My word, Monsieur," said Tricamp, bowing to him, "the scientist is stronger than me; I salute you…and I shall start studying physics and meteorology. But it required no less than this evidence to relieve my mind of a suspicion that had begun to grow and for which I beg your pardon…that you were the demoiselle's accomplice."

"In the final analysis," said Cornelius, laughing, "You can console yourself with that thought that you were not mistaken as to the thief's sex: it was lightning!"[11]

---

[11] In French, *la foudre* [lightning] is a feminine noun.

Monsieur Tricamp removed himself in order not to hear anymore, followed by the crowd, whose members wanted to spread the strange news—and Gudule came to announce that Christiane was better, that she knew everything, and that she was asking to see them.

What can be said about that scene? Balthazar laughed; Cornelius wept; Christiane—who had been forbidden to speak—laughed and wept.

"My dear Christiane," said Balthazar, kneeling beside the bed, "if you don't want to offend me, don't refuse the gift I'm going to make to you." And he deposited the ingot of gold, silver and gems on the bed.

Christiane made a gesture of refusal.

"Oh!" said Balthazar, sharply, closing her mouth. "You need a dowry…"

"If you want me for a husband?" Cornelius added.

Christiane made no reply—but she looked at the virtuous scientist who had returned her honor and her life to her with moist eyes. And I can assure you—speaking as one who was there—that her gaze did not mean *no*.

X.B. Saintine: *The Paradise of Flowers*
(1864)

The Graf von Zoellern, a native of Germany, to which his turn of mind still linked him, was a little, slightly hunchbacked man, something of a joker, very knowledgeable, loquacious and methodical, and full of audacity in his theories. Having devoted himself to botany for only two years, he already claimed to be revolutionizing it from top to bottom—which gave rise to spirited debates between him and my savant doctor.

According to the latter, the Graf von Zoellern's mind, knowledge and imagination—which he did not deny—were, like his personality and the first letter of his name, formed in a zigzag fashion. As for me, the little man's eccentricities and audacious ideas did not displease me, any more than my eyes were offended by seeing his right shoulder positioned more highly than his left.

One evening, when there was to be a table-turning session at my house, and I was counting on the presence of Monsieur Marcillet and his faithful Alexis,[12] the Graf and the doctor were the first to arrive—an alacrity which, I confess, astonished me on the doctor's part; I strongly suspected him of having only come in the capacity of critic, opponent and spoilsport.

Having a few orders to give, I left them alone for a moment. When I came back, Zoellern was already in mid-

---

[12] The famous "somnambule" Alexis Didier (1826-1886), usually known by his first name alone, and his "magnetizer" Jean-Bon Marcillet, were a famous double act between 1842 and 1855, performing at séances all over Europe; they once had a famous confrontation with the great stage magician Robert-Houdin, who attempted to expose them as frauds.

argument, proving, or claiming to prove to his eternal antagonist that plants and animals not only manifested certain points of analogy and parallelism but a complete correspondence of structure and organization. That was, he said, a commonplace that was not even worth discussing. Plato and Empedocles had sufficiently elucidated the question 22 or 23 centuries ago, so he did not know why Geoffroy Saint-Hilaire, in the philosophical system of *L'Unité de l'Être*, had not boldly commenced his zoological series with the most minimal of vegetables, to continue as far as humankind.

"Come on, Doctor, let's reason it out. Taking the animal as the highest degree of the scale, what are its principal functions? It breathes, it absorbs, it digests, it reproduces itself. Doesn't a plant do as much?

"Its leaves, veritable lungs, pump from the atmosphere the oxygen that will modify its sap, transforming it in the cambium, like our venous and arterial blood. But I don't intend to give you a lesson in vegetable physiology. You know as well as I do that the assimilation of absorbed gases produces in plants, as in us, hydrogen, carbon dioxide, alkaline salts, calcium and magnesium phosphates, even nitrogen, which as thought until recently to be reserved to the animal kingdom. Liquids and solids similarly collaborate in developing their strength and furnishing their alimentation. Thus, plants nourish themselves, just like you and me. Look at enormous oaks and tropical trees, so tall, so stout and so sturdy; their cuisine is as good as ours!

"I agree that oaks are more vigorous, and even generally more upright than us," said the doctor, with a certain malicious intent. "I also agree, wholeheartedly, that vegetables and animals have a few points of resemblance between them in their constitutive elements—but animals can move. Do you hear, Monsieur le Comte? They can move!"

"Not all, Doctor, not all! By no means! The polyp in its coral sheath, the oyster and the barnacle, fixed upon their rocks, and many others—are not they animals, although they remain in place?" Zoellern winked in my direction and added:

71

"besides, plants—notably trees—have their own kind of locomotion. Once freed from the bonds than chain them to the soil, they have been seen to come and go, leap and caper, just as well as the most agile of quadrupeds."

The doctor opened his eyes wide. "What trees do that?" he said. "Pray name the trees in question, Monsieur le Comte."

"Only mentioning the most well-known, I cite the elm, the oak, the fir, the walnut—when they are transformed into table, of course…into turning tables."

The dear doctor burst out laughing, got to his feet, articulated "Zigzag! Zigzag!" two or three times between his teeth, and started striding back and forth across the room in the manner of a man refusing to prolong a conversation.

I did not like to see it terminated thus; I picked it up at the point where it had been abandoned. That diabolical little man had the gift of amusing me royally. I smiled at the notion that before my guests were treated to a table-dance that evening, Zoellern's idea might serve up, by way of accompaniment, a new theory on the much-debated subject. Unfortunately, he did not have and fully-formed opinion on that subject, so he came back very quickly to his plant-animals.

Zoellern was planning a new classification, a new nomenclature, in which he would include, pell-mell, fish and certain aquatic plants, which respire like them by means of veritable gills, and rise above the water like them to dive back into it by means of something akin to an air-bladder.

He found surprising analogies between reptiles and creepers or climbing plants; between vegetable and animal parasites. The family of rodents ought, in his view, be augmented by those plants that hollow out stone or wood—and he told me about 1000 other intentions that, if they sometimes lacked reason and logic, at least testified to the ingenuity of his mind and the activity of his imagination.

In the meantime, the doctor continued to stride back and forth across my floor in every direction. Soon, wearying of his stroll, and perhaps even more so of the silence that he had imposed on himself, he abruptly returned to us and, with his eyes flaming and his arms cross over his chest, he interrupted Zoellern in mid-sentence.

"Wretch!" he cried. "Is it chaos that you're pretending to systematize, then? There exists between vegetables and animals one unbridgeable line of demarcation: sensitivity. Vegetables grow, they live, I grant you—but *sed non sentiunt*, as the great Linnaeus said."[13]

"The great Linnaeus would be a donkey today," Zoellern retorted.

On hearing this blasphemy I got up abruptly to protest, but on reflexion, I sat down again. I was curious to know how the little man would justify his enormity.

He did not give an inch. Without respite, arguing against the *non sentiunt*, he maintained tenaciously that all vegetable species bestirred themselves, not automatically, but purely by virtue of a sentiment of self-defense and self-preservation. He cited the means employed by the whole great family of mimosas to protect themselves from an impact or the violence of a storm; those by which the *Dionaea*[14] traps an insect that wishes to live at its expense; the gyratory movements of the sainfoin; the evolutions of stamens toward pistils, and the modest quiverings of pistils at the approach of stamens—clear evidence of will, an aspiration toward a goal, sensation. How many animals of an inferior order seem to be endowed with less activity and rationality!

"Any wisely-calculated action is evidence of thought, and no thought can be conceived other than under a sensitive influence. By what right to you refuse an intellectual life to plants, since they know the emotions of love and the joys of maternity?

"As for their purely physical sensitivity, in spite of the *non sentiunt*, has your great Linnaeus observed that after the fatigues of the day they recuperate their strength by means of

---

[13] Actually, this Latin assertion regarding the insensibility of plants was initially associated with Pope Gregory the Great.
[14] The Venus fly-trap.

73

sleep? Monsieur Buffon himself, one day when he had forgotten to put his cuffs on, was prepared to admit that a plant resembles a dormant animal. The animal has woken up, doctor, it has woken up! After the scientific works by Borelli and Sébastien Vaillant on vegetal sensitivity, Jean de Gorter was the first to credit vital irritability to plants as well as animals.[15] Jean Lups of Moscow and the Comte del Covolo of Florence established the proof of it.[16] You can see that Russians, Germany and Italians are in accord in preaching that doctrine. The illustrious Charles Bonnet, a Swiss this time, and the Englishman Adanson have steered their research in the same direction and added further supporting evidence to the demonstration of this great verity.[17] But that congress of sages lacked a Fren-

---

[15] Giovani Borelli (1608-1679), better known as the "father of biomechanics" (the study of animal movement), was the first microscopist to study the opening and closing of plant stomata. Sébastien Vaillant (1669-1722) worked for many years at the Jardin des Plantes, and published a notable discourse on flowers in 1718. Jean de Gorter (1689-1762), a follower of Herman Boerhaave, actually contended, along with the British anatomist Francis Glisson, that there was a vital force operating in both animals and plants independently of the soul and nervous system, which was responsible for movement.

[16] Jean Lups (1667-1732) was actually a Dutch arms dealer who supplied weapons to Russia, but he was named as "Jean Lups of Moscow" in a history of medicine published in 1815; the reference in question was slavishly copied by several other 19th-century reference books, one of which Saintine must have seen. The "Comte del Covolo", however, seems to have only one significant mention, in Gall and Spurzheim's monumental work on the anatomy of the brain (1810-19), which founded the science of phrenology.

[17] Charles Bonnet (1720-1793) published a book in 1754 which did indeed credit plants with sensibility and powers of discernment. Michel Adanson (1727-1806) was not an Englishman but a Frenchman of Scottish descent who produced a

74

chman; the good Desfontaines has arrived, who has demonstrated in an *ad hoc* memoir that plants enjoy a real life.[18] I therefore have against you, doctor, European science in its entirety. But don't be so impatient! Let me finish...

"Do not plants, like us, need air and light? Do they not have their periods of growth, sometimes so risky; their diseases, so similar to ours; their hemorrhages of sap, like our hemorrhages of blood (pardon the pleonasm); chlorosis and phthisis? Frostbite, sunburn, wounds, asphyxia, even poisoning; everything that threatens our life puts theirs in danger; and, strangely enough—a further point of concordance between plants and animals—the same remedies are employed for their cure: iron sulphate for chlorosis, bleeding for plethoras; and moxas,[19] incisions and amputations!

"All these maladies that they have in common with us, plants feel if they are suffering from them, and they do suffer from them, since they die of them."

Thus spoke the Graf.

Truly, one would no longer dare to pluck a rose or have one's grass mown.

The audacious little man was not about to stop there. Moving from induction to induction, he came to pose this question, which made the doctor and me start on the spot: "Why should plants not have souls?"

I protested; the doctor made no reply, but he drummed his fingers on his snuff-box, murmuring: "Zigzag, zigzag!"

---

system of classification markedly different from that of Linnaeus, which lost out in competition with the latter.

[18] René Desfontaines (1750-1833) worked at the Jardin des Plantes before becoming director of the Musée National d'Histoire Naturelle. He was one of the founders of the Institut, parent of the Académie des Sciences.

[19] Moxa (mugwort) was and is extensively used in connection with acupuncture to warm the skin before insertion of the needles.

"The idea is not mine," Zoellern hastened to add. "It was originated by Thales—one of the seven sages of Greece, gentlemen as one contemporary members of the Académie des Sciences put it—but it has had its partisans a long time after that. Leibniz, who is also the great Leibniz, in his essay on *Theodicy*, was not afraid to propose that the divine seeds destined to become human souls, pre-exist in organic substances, where they are first subjected to a kind of apprenticeship. Malebranche and Bayle seem to be marching along the same road and, nearer to our own day, one even counts a physician among the declared partisans of that opinion—do you hear that, doctor? The physician Dédu—who was only on the faculty of Montpellier, it is true—has written a very curious book on the souls of plants."[20]

"Zigzag! Zigzag!" muttered the doctor.

"That's on the part of Europe," the Graf continued. "As for the Orient, no one there doubts the doctrine, generally professed throughout the Far East." He stroked his chin, and continued: "I recently had the good fortune to discuss the question with the Japanese and Siamese ambassadors, who were both passing thorough Paris. The former spoke at length about a certain god Fottey,[21] whose breath is sufficient to give a soul to the most vulgar of plants; the latter affirmed that, in his

---

[20] *De l'âme des plantes, de leur naissance, de leur nourriture et de leur progrez* [sic] (1682) is signed "N. Dedu [*sic*], docteur en medicine de la Faculté de Montpellier", hence the narrator's slightly dismissive remark. Dedu must have been a botanist of some reputation, however, because he also co-authored a book on plant anatomy with the much more famous Nehemiah Grew and Robert Boyle in 1685. Nicolas Malebranche (1638-1715) and Pierre Bayle (1647-1706) were among the rationalist philosophers who pioneered the Enlightenment.

[21] This name produces no relevant hits on Google and no name bearing any similarity to it appears in any readily-available list of Shinto deities.

country, the theory of souls, applied to vegetables, is so well-recognized that no one there mutilates a tree without expiating the sacrilege by an act of contrition, and no one there pulls up a culinary herb without addressing a mental prayer to the soul thus condemned to displacement." As if in parentheses, Zoellern added: "Take note that these beliefs are not mine."

"I'm glad to hear it," the doctor put in.

"No, in this respect, I still envelop myself in philosophical doubt: do plants have soul, or don't they? A weighty question, gentlemen, a weighty question!"

For my part, what can I say? However bizarre it might be, this animation of all organic substances, no longer forming any but one single complex being, moved by the same laws and marching by a thousand roads toward the same goal, was beginning to impress me. God alone knew whether it was impossible—and who among us can put limits to the great and mysterious theology of nature?

Then, within myself, I returned to my turning tables. Why should not the spirit or demon, which could so implausibly become invisible guest of the table, simply be the soul of the tree that had furnished it? I decided to interrogate that vegetal soul that very evening, demanding that it yield its secret to me. What a discovery, if I could clarify a question so hotly debated, and finally provide, dogmatically, an explanation of the phenomenon!

On the stroke of nine, almost all my guests arrived. I immediately ordered that the table be brought in—a table in which I had particular confidence, the most impressionable, the most alert and the chattiest of all my tables.

As often happens on such occasions, in spite of the chain of fingers obstinately fixed upon it, the table did not budge.

The dear doctor was radiant, and sniffed pinches of tobacco one after another, with the attitude and gestures of an insolent victor. The Graf von Zoellern voiced the idea that the presence of a skeptical unbeliever is sometimes sufficient to abort the operation completely. I had every reason to believe that the little man had hoped to have his habitual contradictor massacred in the midst of a popular uprising.

I ordered that the tea should be served on the same table. The doctor, who was now playing the leading role, criticized my imprudence. "What if it starts to dance a saraband at the moment when it's least expected?" he said. "Watch out for the Chinese porcelain!"

Zoellern called him an atheist.

Fortunately, Monsieur Marcillet and Monsieur Alexis had just made their entrance into the drawing-room. There was no longer any topic of conversation but magnetism.

The doctor rubbed his hands; he was counting on a disappointment in that regard as in the other. To get I ahead of the others, he hastened to propose a card game to Alexis— who, with his eyes blindfolded, named his cards before touching them, taking the trick, then read the contents of pockets, counting up the sums of money to be found therein, in gold, silver or copper, and finished up by telling him that he had dined that day on vegetable soup, fillet steak with olives and sole normande.

"How do you know that?" asked the doctor, somewhat nonplussed.

"By means of your restaurant bill, which is still in your waistcoat pocket."

Zoellern rubbed his hands in his turn. He begged the magnetizer to put him to sleep right away; he had an urgent voyage to make.

After a few conscientiously-administered passes, he did indeed go to sleep, and so obviously that some time went by before he was even able to reply to the questions addressed to him.

Finally, he released a sigh, and his lips moved.

"The moment has arrived," said Monsieur Marcillet— and he resumed the interrogation. "Can you hear me now?"

"They have one!" replied the magnetized man.

"You don't understand. Do you know who is speaking to you at this moment?"

"The god Fottey, honored in Japan and throughout the Indian archipelago."

Monsieur Marcillet recommenced his passes, and interrogated him further. "Where are you?"

"In the *paradise of flowers*."

The magnetizer paused, looked at us with a slightly disconcerted expression, turned to the gallery and said: "Gentlemen, I think I ought to warn you that dreams sometimes interfere unduly with magnetic influences. I don't think the subject is in a perfect state of lucidity. Let's try, without jarring him too much, to put him back on the right path... According to you, then, flowers have a paradise?"

"Why not, since they have one?"

"One what?"

"A soul! Is it not just, then, that like us, they have their places of recompense and punishment?"

At the point, there was a slight murmur in the assembly, in the midst of which I distinctly made out a certain *zigzag!* and the tapping of a finger on a snuff-box.

Monsieur Marcillet continued, with perfect condescension: "Are you quite sure, Monsieur, that you're not mistaken?"

"How could I be mistaken? At this very moment, thanks to the benevolent intervention of the Japanese ambassador, the divine Fottey has opened the abode of floral felicity to my curiosity. In spite of Thales, Leibniz, Malebranche and Monsieur Dédu, I doubted—I repent of it! Now I see, I am forced to believe! Oh, what spectacles! What perfumes!"

"Come on, let's try to divert the course of these ideas..."

"Shut up!" the sleeper shouted at him, in an imperious tone. "Stop disturbing me in my delight!"

The magnetizer made as if to wake him up; I stopped him, and on my request, he consented to put me in fluidic communication with the patient.

Zoellern continued talking almost without interruption; he described what he could see, or what he thought he could see, with such precision that I was unable to suspect the slightest trickery in his narration, utterly strange and utterly supernatural as it seemed; his mind, his knowledge and his imagination alone would not have been sufficient for such an improvisation.

The circle tightened around the visionary; with a gesture to the doctor, I indicated a vacant spot next to me.

"Zigzag!" he replied, drawing away in order to pour himself a cup of tea.

I noticed nevertheless that he had sat down at the end of the table nearest to us, with his ear turned in our direction.

The Paradise of Flowers, created by Fottey, the god of vegetation, in one of the Maldive Islands, had its eastern part divided into a series of little parallel valleys. These valleys, separated from one another by gentle slopes from the top of which fell sheets of water, forming cascades on either side, blossomed in the midst of a warm atmosphere; humid vapors, colored pink, blue and violet by the sunlight, filled them with the radiance of rainbows; the inhabitants of the location lacked nothing, either in the way of gentle sunlight or balsamic dew—but I shall not dwell on that paradisal poetry, with which the sleeper perhaps overindulged himself.

To get back to purely topographical matters, all the squares of this great chessboard were occupied by plants assembled without any classificatory order, having no other link between them than their virtuous qualities and the kinds of services rendered by them to human society.

Pell-mell, in the cheerful part of the garden that had been consecrated to them, the first to display themselves to the visitor's eye were the Nutritious Plants: wheat, maize, rice, and then the numerous family of legumes—green beans, broad beans, peas, lentils—all elegantly sporting their pretty caps on their heads.

Also found in the Paradise of Flowers were the benevolent plants that ease suffering and sometimes even render life to the sick. Zoellern therefore visited the Valley of Medicinal Plants.

He was greatly astonished to find an extremely restricted number there; cassia and senna did not figure there at all; and, as if the magnetic fluid had added a stimulant to his natural malice, he credited to the god Fottey the explanatory opinion that the marvelous virtues of so many plants formerly praised as universal panaceas but rejected today to the ranks of harmful herbs, had never profited anyone but messieurs the physicians, either in Europe or Asia, all of them beings charlatans.

As a faithful reporter of the séance, I am obliged to declare that at that moment, my dear doctor noisily sniffed another pinch of tobacco and poured himself a second cup of tea.

Continuing his narration along with his route, the Graf went through the Valley of Industrial Plants, textile or tinctorial. Cotton, hemp, flax, madder, the indigo plant and a thousand others of similar importance seemed to form up in ranks to either side of his path, in order to be inspected by him.

On mounds reminiscent of altars, silphium,[22] sesame and the lotus, so dear to the ancient priests of Egypt and the Brahmins of India; vervein, the *herba sacra* that served to purify the temples of Jupiter and Apollo; the mistletoe of the druids of Gaul and Germany; persea,[23] the subject of so many pious commentaries; the acacia, the ultimate mystical tree; the rose of Jericho, symbol of death and resurrection, and a whole series of holy herbs no less worthy of veneration, displayed themselves surrounded by the attributes of various ancient and modern cults. God as he was, Fottey bowed down as he passed them by; Zoellern was obliged to do the same, but he reserved his admiration and his surges of enthusiasm for the joyous Valley of Beautiful Plants.

---

[22] *Silphium* was in such great demand in the ancient world that it was driven to extinction, perhaps due to overgrazing by cattle to whose meat it was supposed to impart a special virtue. It is generally thought to have been a kind of giant fennel.

[23] The best-known member of the genus *Persea* is the avocado.

More sensual or less hypocritical than the Occident, the Orient has made plastic beauty a virtue. Beautiful women, be they former fisherwomen, enter authoritatively into the paradises of Mohammed and Brahma, and are elevated by right to the rank of houris or apsaras. It is the same for beautiful plants in the paradise of the god Fottey.

When that magnificent vegetable, the pride of floral creation, MacDonald's cactus,[24] whose corolla, as large as a grape-gatherer's basket, displays its long silver petals implanted in a golden calyx, with its style standing up like an ivory column surmounted by a purple feather, and then the great Aristolochia, the Gustavia, the Victoria Regia, the Nelumbium and the magnolia presented themselves on the shores of his isle,[25] did he say to them: "Where do you come from? What good have you done?" No; he said to them: "Come in."

And after them, when the other royal flowers of every climate and every country, the lily of Japan, the Tigridias of Mexico, the Strelitizia of the Cape,[26] the orchids of Central America, the hollyhocks of Syria, the Agapanthus of Africa, all the way to the peonies of Siberia, offered themselves to him, similarly recognizing the right of their beauty, he opened his door again and breathed on them to give them a soul.

And, thinking about our European gardens—even the winter gardens in Paris, London and the Hague, Zoellern told himself that to compare them with that luxuriant valley would

---

[24] It is not obvious which species of flowering cactus is cited here.

[25] *Aristolochia* is the birthwort genus; *Gustavia superba* is also known as the Heaven lotus; *Victoria regia* (or *regina*) was the name originally given by John Lindley in 1837 to the water lily nowadays known as *Victoria amazonica*; *Nelumbium speciosum* is the "sacred lotus."

[26] *Tigridia pavonia* is the most commonly-cultivated species of "tiger flower;" *Strelizias* are sometimes known as "bird-of-paradise flowers."

be to compare the Societé d'Acclimatation's aquarium to the vast Ocean.

And yet, although dazzled by the spectacle unfolding before his eyes, he thought he noticed, especially among the royal species, certain irregularities of form, certain abnormal accidents that he was astonished to find associated with so many perfections.

He did not hesitate to impart these critical observations to his divine guide. The latter, smiling, immediately refuted them. What Zoellern suspected to be deplorable irregularities were no more than further perfections, additional organs accorded by Brahma to the inhabitants of this blissful abode.

In the paradise of the Maldives, flowers can move and detach themselves from the earth, which scarcely retains them, their roots being formed like birds' feet; they can walk, hopping from one place to another; better still, they have wings, pretty white, blue or variegated wings, depending on the color of their petals or stems, and which, when folded up, become almost undetectable by eye. With a single flight, they can cross the borders of their respective valleys if it pleases them to visit one another.

The god Fottey uttered a cry then; that cry, repeated by a thousand echoes, ran from valley to valley, soon filling the whole island with a clamor.

Zoellern thought he was prey to vertigo. A unanimous, spontaneous movement was manifest in the plain and along the slopes where, until then, ranked by size, all those floral marvels had stood motionless. The plain, the hills and the sky itself seemed to quiver before his eyes. Breathless, gripped by anguish, almost terrified, he witnessed a spectacle that it has not been given to any man down here either to see or to imagine.

Confusing their colors and their perfumes, the flowers of the splendid valley crossed paths in every direction, flying through the air by means of beating wings. Hurrying from adjacent valleys through the damp dust of cascades, appearing over the crests of hills, they mingled together and, all together,

83

whirled about as if at play—but without Fottey's preliminary warning, the Graf would certainly have been able to believe that a furious storm had just descended upon that abode of enchantments.

Now, he saw them slowing down in their flight, breaking up the vortex, gliding, and then descending with fluttering wings to settle on the earth again.

After a few moments' rest, some started walking in groups; those were generally the largest, and the most remarkable in their forms and colors. Zoellern took note of their precious attitude and ladylike gait; during the promenade, with a perfect art of coquetry, they showed off their large petals in such a way as to make their varied hues stand out, while maintaining their leaves in good order and correctly angled.

Other flowers had landed beside little lakes formed at the bottom of hills; they bathed their roots therein, doubtless to refresh their tints or straighten their stems, slightly fatigued by the heat of the day.

On the edges of these same little lakes, aquatic plants had naturally chosen their domiciles. Like their terrestrial sisters, they could detach their roots from the soil, draw away from the bank and, moreover, tour their lagoons by swimming. To the former the benign god of vegetation had given wings; for these he had determined that their lower leaves were prolonged in the form of oars; these oars were adequate to sustain them above water, so that they could move around with their stems straight and their corollas spread out.

Butterflies are admitted to the Paradise of Flowers, for flowers and butterflies can scarcely live without one another; but, attached to the soil or some rocky projection, they are captive, their wings paralyzed, unable to take part in all that celebratory movement, and it is the flowers that, contrary to the established order here, fly to meet them, make their choice, caressing them or neglecting them according to their whim.

The Paradise of Flowers is the butterflies' Inferno.

Zoellern then asked the god Fottey how that attractive sympathy could have arisen between two species of beings that seemed, at least on Earth, to belong to entirely different races.

"By virtue of a great harmonic reason, of which you cannot take account in your backward Europe," Fottey replied, "the transmigration of souls. According to the laws of metempsychosis, the soul of a flower, after its time of proof, passes into the body of a butterfly, or some other insect—a fly or a beetle. That ought to suffice to make you understand the secret attraction than brings these various species together."

The Graf dared to follow up his question. "And what becomes of a butterfly's soul?"

"It passes into the body of a sparrow or an animal of similarly scant importance—but not alone, however, for it requires three butterfly souls to form that of a flycatcher, as it requires three flower souls to form that of a butterfly, and so on; the souls of three flycatchers or wrens form the soul of a wood-pigeon; and always three by three, always progressing in strength and intelligence, they thus climb the scale of beings, step by step, until a myriad of souls of every sort, newly purified by the breath of a god, eventually forms the soul of a human being, the only one created immortal."

Delighted with these cosmogonic confidences, Zoellern collected them carefully, promising himself firmly to propagate them for the instruction of poor Europe, so backward.

While chatting, the god and the voyager advanced toward the most elevated regions of the isle. The latter was astonished to see that the valleys and hills that had been so cool and cheerful a little while ago were succeeded by steep, sterile mountains, from which no springs emerged, and where their feet sank into the sand.

His astonishment was further increased on encountering in this wild terrain the flowers most highly esteemed among us—not only camellias, balsamines[27] and tulips irreproachable

---

[27] "Balsamines" was one of the common names given to flowers of the genus *Impatiens*, also known as jewelweeds and

in color and form, but the most beautiful roses in the world: the tea rose, the king's rose, the rose with 100 leaves.

Why were they not in the Valley of Beautiful Plants, where their place seemed to be established by right? He submitted this question to the master.

"We're in the region of expiation," Fottey replied. "Once, tulips and camellias possessed both beauty and perfume; they became too proud. I took their perfume way to give it to the violet and the reseda, humbler plants whose modesty deserved recompense."

"But what about the rose?" Zoellern interjected. "The rose, regarded by us as the queen of flowers?"

"A title usurped! Her royalty is nothing but a lie; neither her beauty nor her perfumes belong to her; the whole is nothing but a work of art and cunning. Born a simple flower of the fields and woods, her natural grace brightened the bushes in spring that her coralline fruits decorated in autumn; ambition took possession of her; she has had her paradise on Earth, where she was fêted by everyone; now, in this arid and stony grounds, she is expiating her mendacious success; this is her punishment. But misfortune purifies; subjected to this dolorous proof, the rose will recover her primitive state, with her five petals, which make her sparkle in the morning mist, and her original scent, naively sweet, with which she should have been content. Brought back then to the laws of her nature, from which the industry of humans has distanced her so far, along with her pistils and stamens she will recover her soul, for doubled flowers do not have one, and love and maternal cares will easily make her forget her fraudulent triumphs."

Slightly mortified by the regime inflicted on these flowers, which he loved most particularly, Graf von Zoellern continued to follow his guide as far as a chain of black and angular rocks that crowned the peaks of the mountain.

---

touch-me-nots. The one most familiar in Britain is the Busy Lizzie.

Scarcely had they reached them than they were overtaken by a suffocating heat and acrid, caustic and nauseating vapors, by which Fottey seemed not to be affected at all. As for the voyager, he only had time to plunge a rapid glance over the depths of the opposite slope, where sulfurous and bituminous gulfs yawned.

In the profound darkness, he thought he glimpsed a few vegetable forms, spectral in appearance, so shriveled, corroded and withered that no plant buried for ten years in a collector's herbarium could ever have presented a more sickly and wretched appearance.

The uncultivated, sterile place where they had just encountered the roses, balsamines, tulips and others was only a purgatory; this was an inferno. To this had been relegated the venomous plants and the magical plants, those that had aided the operations of witchcraft or the accomplishment of crimes. There too were found plants accused of exciting the human imagination and stirring up deceptive sensualities, at the expense of health, dignity and reason.

Of these latter, Fottey only named three: the opium poppy, which has already killed two million people in China; Indian hemp, with which the Indians manufacture their bhang and the Turks and Arabs their hashish, which lightens their mood, intoxicates and decimates them; and, finally, absinthe, as deadly as the other two, and in the process of cretinizing Europe.

Our friend Zoellern, did not have to beg him to come down again from those heights…

At this point our sleeper brought his narration to a close, and after a few moments of silence, we heard him murmur in a low voice: "Goodbye, good and excellent Fottey… The isle is retreating before me… We're doubling Cape Comorin… Goodbye, Maldive Sea!… Here's Europe!... Here's Paris!... Wake me up, Monsieur Marcillet."

Monsieur Marsillet made the regulation passes.

When Zoellern opened his eyes again, he did not retain any memory of what he had seen and heard in the Paradise of Flowers.

"Well," I said to the doctor, "the séance must have interested you more than any other. It featured a magnetic dream, which I believe you have not yet classified in your scientific theory?"

"Zigzag! Zigzag! Zigzag!" he replied, loudly this time, drumming more forcefully than ever on his snuff-box.

X.B. Saintine: *The Great Discovery of Animules*
(1864)

It is said, and people are generally glad to think, that our souls have already encountered one another in an anterior world, and that some of them have even been paired, giving rise to sympathies that still attract them to one another today and often determine our affections. It is an ancient link that seeks to renew itself across the centuries, a pleasant habituation inclined to continue from heaven to earth. I would willingly endorse the ideas of poets, and lovers themselves, if reflection, and something even better than reflection had not demonstrated to me that they are vain and puerile.

Petty as it is, our terrestrial globe has not neglected to populate itself adequately. How many human beings, and, in consequence, how many souls pullulate between its poles? India and China alone furnish 600 million, before adding Europe, Africa, the Americas, Australia and Oceania to the count. In the midst of such a multitude, dispersed over the surface of the earth, split up and separated to an infinite degree by mountains, deserts and oceans, admit that a meeting of two predestined souls is no more than exceptional. Now, it is the work of a madman to build systems on exceptions.

This cannot happen as imagined. Fortunately, thanks to an unexpected and unlooked-for revelation, I find myself in a position to offer partisans of the ancient dogma something that will take the place of the belief that I have taken away from them, with sufficient compensation, and even some profit.

If our mutual sympathies do not originate so remotely, they are exercised at close range with greater surety, strength and plausibility. Why should souls, like light and perfumes, not have their radiance, or, to put it better, their emanations?

These emanations, these reciprocal attractions, not only attach souls to one another, but also, thanks to another universal law that desires nothing in nature to unite without fecundity, engender by their contact, not a soul—that is the work of God alone—but an *animule*: a more or less viable parcel of soul: *animula vagula, blandula*, as the great Emperor Hadrian once said.[28]

These animules, atoms emanated by our souls, form a sensible atmosphere around us. Our individual soul, or divine guest, partakes more intimately in our joys and pains, our particular inclinations and personal affections; while assisting in that, our animules have another role to play: they compose the great chain, the great network of general affections. Love of family, that other love, broader but sometimes no less passionate, that makes itself felt by an entire people, which, on a given day, lifts them with the same enthusiastic impulse, evidently flows from them. There are ideas in the air, it is often said; in the air there are animules, which imprint thousand of souls with the same impulse simultaneously, exciting them and causing them to palpitate in the magnetic milieu that is their own essence.

"But you have not announced a discovery," it might be objected, "you have given us a hypothesis. Who has demonstrated the existence of these animules? How can you know that they populate the air if, like the air, they are impalpable and invisible?"

As invisible and impalpable as the air: exactly. Listen! Scientists found the means to weigh air a long time ago, to divide it into its elementary components, and yet, in spite of their most complicated optical instruments, they have not been able to obtain any visual perception of it. One day, an intelligent man who was only a scientist in his leisure hours took a

---

[28] The first stanza of the famous Latin poem that begins with this line, from which Saintine presumably derived the inspiration for this story, may be roughly translated as: "Pale, wandering little soul/Guest and companion of my body/Where are you going now/Pallid, rigid and naked/Forsaking the jokes we used to share…?"

piece of card, made a hole in it with the point of a needle, looked through the hole, and saw the air; he saw all the gaseous atoms composing it moving and radiating before him. Well, it was very nearly the same for me with respect to that other supposedly invisible entity, the animule.

Following a long botanical expedition, once evening, having returned home with many plants—aromatic for the most part—and occupying myself with analyzing them by the light of an excellent Carcel lamp,[29] I was astonished to perceive white forms apparently passing under my magnifying glass. I thought it was some reflection of light on the instrument, and set it aside. The forms continued to appear to me, confused at first, then distinct, especially at the borders of my lampshade.

Every great discovery initially causes a distressing hesitation, in which a residue of doubt painfully suppresses the explosion of triumphant joy. Almost frightened by my success, I stood up, went out and headed for the boulevards. Everywhere in the streets, along the house-fronts, around the gas-lamps and in the brightly-lit display windows of shops, I saw before me these floating animules, whose revelation had until then been only a revelation of my thought. This time, I had them, not under the error-prone lens of a microscope, but in my own line of sight, without any intermediary; I had not even needed to pierce a piece of card. To those who are endowed with the gift of prescience, heaven momentarily grants in the same way the faculty of verifying with their own eyes the calculations of their imagination.

Having become calmer, I observed attentively, and made notes.

These animules, almost diaphanous, presented at their central point a sort of dark patch, indicating the presence of some substance, doubtless borrowed from the air in whose environment they live; that is their material aspect.

---

[29] Bernard Carcel patented a new kind of oil lamp in 1800, which used a clockwork-driven pump to bring oil to the wick.

As for their forms, varied according to their different categories, at first sight, they presented the appearance of light shining bubbles of air, with a pearly gleam, surrounding the opaque nucleus I have already mentioned. Not one projected a shadow; on the contrary, the pearly mesh, composed of tiny imperceptible scales, that enveloped their diaphanousness without darkening it, not only amplified luminous radiance but gave off phosphorescent sparks, in all probability electric.

Momentarily, I found in them—regretfully, I confess— the physiognomy of an elongated aerostat floating horizontally. I examined them more attentively. Little silvery oars were beating on their flanks. With their shiny mesh, inflated by air, these oars gave them the appearance of those little feluccas with sails that appear through the morning mists at sunrise in Mediterranean waters.

In the first instance, I had before me the infinitely tiny spectacle of an aerial fleet; in the second, a maritime fleet. But how was it imaginable that these emanations of the soul might be so similar to vulgar machines invented by humans?

Fortunately, at that moment, my eyes, by virtue of an incredible nervous overexcitation, were endowed with the magnifying power of the finest microscopes. My new investigations allowed me to discover semblances of limbs, scarcely protruding from the body, and a conically-shaped and slightly-flattened head sunk between the shoulders—admitting as shoulders the two concave muscular structures between which the head was embedded. An animule of the strongest species, which I was fortunate enough to keep motionless before my gaze or a few seconds, permitted me to rectify my first judgment entirely. The little silvery oars of my feluccas became its slender silky fins, and it breathed air while lifting up, at regular intervals, a membranous partition not unlike the operculum of a fish.

At first I had imagined for my animules a gracious, even mythological form, with wings on their backs, like sylphs or sylphides; I had seen them, in the first place, as balloons, and in the second place, as boats; the turn if the fish had come: I took them for fish, saw their scales, fins and opercula. Was not the air a fluid sufficient for them to be able to live in it and move through it at their ease?

Now that I was no longer thinking of dressing them in a form according to my fancy, in truth, I found them very fine as they were: alert, graceful and charming. I ended up concluding that they were, in every detail, that which they ought to be.

It remained for me to study their habits and inclinations.

The majority swirled in swarms around certain individuals, especially young women and children; they enveloped them like an animate cloud, allowing themselves to be drawn along by the movement that the latter imparted to the ambient air; they crossed the road with them, pausing where they paused.

On occasion, however, some of these little atomistic souls broke ranks and allowed themselves to be drawn into the orbit of another company. Sometimes, encountering one another as if unexpectedly, they made an abrupt movement of separation, which I attributed to an antipathetic influence; but every truth is proved by its antithesis, and if antipathy has its effects among the animules, by the same virtue, sympathy must make itself felt—as I was not long in observing, in the most convincing fashion.

I saw several of them, belonging to different swarms, show themselves two by two, drawing apart and drawing closer by turns, as birds traveling together do, and when they drew closer, their pearly mesh shone more brightly on the two sides that made contact, and they interconnected like a shower of sparks.

Experimenting in the busy street, I could hardly expect to verify the fact, but I do not doubt that, in the right circumstances, two entire groups might be combined by mutual fusion. These groups cannot be content to be thus confused for a few seconds; they accompany, and alternately escort the two individuals from which they have emanated. The latter may not have met yet, but they are already subject to the influence of the magnetic atmosphere that surrounds them; they sense one another and seek one another, without being aware of the invisible magnet that is attracting them to one another. When they finally establish a relationship, the sympathetic effects are immediately manifest, creating, in proportion to their strength and vivacity, those furious spontaneous infatuations that so often have no other rationale, which fade away as quickly as they have come, or the calmer, more rational sentiment of progressive affections, ardent love-affairs and long friendships.

Does this mean that all human beings are equally liable to experience or to communicate these sympathetic impulses? The opposite is easy to demonstrate.

A man walking two paces in front of me was only escorted by a few animules. These, although apparently weak and, I dare say, unhealthy, left his company to mingle with other swarms, but they came back to him hastily, and always alone. I overtook the man in order to inspect his physiognomy; he had a fixed stare, thin lips and a harsh expression—and grey hair to boot. He had to be an old misanthropic bachelor.

I also made many other observations that it would take too long to report; but one that I ought not to pass over in silence is the truly remarkable incident that crowned my experiments.

I was continuing my investigations in the open street, in the corners of squares, in front of cafes and shops— everywhere that a bright enough light permitted my eyes to take advantage of the singular clarity of vision with which I was endowed at that moment—when I suddenly noticed a liveliness, and extraordinary coming-and-going, in my animules. They were no longer arrayed as exactly around certain individuals; all of them, as if obedient to a general commotion, were allowing themselves to be borne along by the same current, into the same whirlwind, like a blizzard of snow blown by a storm-wind—and yet the air was calm, and there as not a cloud moving in the sky.

Without losing its force, this emigration took on a more regular appearance; it was as if invisible leaders had established order and discipline in the ranks, and among these ranks thus aligned I never once perceived the antipathetic somersaults that had previously been possible. Our animules went along the Rue de Richelieu, in such great numbers that the majority were lost in the shade, and even in the darkness, of the upper floors.

Suddenly, as if to give me the power to observe them even at those heights, and in their various directions, all Paris lit up from the bottom to the top of its houses and palaces. Then I was able to see them emerging from every window, descending from every balcony and even from every attic, in order to join the great procession.

On turning into the boulevards, I perceived that the Parisian population, hurled outside by innumerable waves, was filling and cluttering the sidewalks, experiencing that evening an impulse and an agitation entirely similar to that of my animules.

That same Saturday, the 25th of June in the year 1859, when my great discovery should have received its consecration, the news had just arrived by telegraph of the important victory won by the Franco-Sardinian army on the banks of the Mincio.

The victory of Solferino was that of good,[30] which serves to prove the role that the animules play in great popular emotions, whose explosive spontaneity has never before been explained.

---

[30] The crushing defeat of the Austrian army at Solferino, ten days after Prussia had belatedly mobilized against France in support of the Austrians, was the military high point of the Second Empire; Saintine could not know, when he wrote the story, that the vital stimulus it provided to the unification of Germany under Prussian domination would pave the way for the revenge of the Franco-Prussian War of 1870, which smashed and humiliated the Empire in question. Love, of course, often has similar eventual results on an individual level.

Since that day, it has not been given to me to renew my experiments—which, at any rate, have not yet been contested by anyone.

Eugène Mouton: *The End of the World*
(1872)

And the world will end by fire.

Of all the questions that interest humankind, none is more worthy of research than that of the destiny of the planet we inhabit. Geology and history have taught us many things about the Earth's past; we know the age of our world, within a few hundred million years or so; we know the order of development in which life progressively manifest itself and propagated over its surface; we know in which epoch humans finally arrived to sit down at the banquet that life had prepared for them, and for which it had taken several thousand years to set the table.

We know all that, or at least think we know it, which comes down to exactly the same thing—but if we are sure of our past, we are not of our future.

Humankind scarcely knows and more about the probable duration of its existence than each one of us knows about the number of years that he has yet to live:

The table is laid,
The exquisite parade,
That gives us cheer!
A toast, my dear!

All well and good—but are we on the soup, or the dessert? Who can tell us, alas, that the coffee will not be served very soon?

We go on and on, heedless of the future of the world, without ever asking ourselves whether, by chance, this frail boat that is carrying us across the ocean of infinity is not at risk of capsizing suddenly, or whether its old hull, worn away by time and impaired by the agitations of the voyage, does not have some leak though which death is filtering into its carcass—which is, of course, the very carcass of humankind—one drop at a time.

The world—which is to say, our terrestrial globe—has not always existed. It had begun, so it will end. The question is, when?

First of all, let us ask ourselves whether the world might end by virtue of an accident, a perturbation of present laws.

We cannot admit that. Such a hypothesis would, in fact, be in absolute contradiction with the opinion that we intend to sustain in this work. It is obvious, therefore, that we cannot adopt it. Any discussion is impossible if one admits the opinion that one is setting out to combat.

Thus, one point is definitely established: the Earth will not be destroyed by accident; it will end as a consequence of the continued action of the laws of its present existence. It will die, as they say, its appropriate death.

But will it die of old age? Will it die of a disease?

I have no hesitation in replying: no, it will not die of old age; yes, it will die of a disease—in consequence of excess.

I have said that the world will end as a consequence of the continued action of the laws of its present existence. It is now a matter of figuring out which, of all the agents functioning for the maintenance of the life of the terraqueous globe, is the one that will have the responsibility of destroying it someday.

I say this without hesitation: that agent is the same one to which the Earth owed is existence in the first place: heat. Heat will drink the sea; heat will eat the Earth—and this is how it will happen.

One day, with regard to the functioning of locomotives, the illustrious Stephenson asked a great English chemist what the force was that moved such machines. The chemist replied: "It's the Sun."

And, indeed, all the heat that we liberate when we burn combustible vegetable matter-wood or coal—has been stored there by the Sun; a piece of wood or coal is therefore, fundamentally, nothing but a preserve of solar radiation. The more vegetable life develops, the greater the accumulation of these preserves becomes. If a great deal is burned and a great deal created—that is to say, if cultivation and industry evolve, the storage the solar radiation absorbed by the Earth on one the hand and its liberation on the other will increase incessantly, and the Earth will become warmer in a continuous manner.

What would happen if the animal population, and the human population in its turn, followed the same progress? What would happen if considerable transformations, born of the very development of animal life on the surface of the globe, were to modify the structure of terrains, displace the basins of the seas, and reassemble humankind on continents that are both more fertile and more permeable to solar heat?

Now, that is exactly what will happen.

When one compares the world with what it once was, one is immediately struck by one fact that leaps to the eyes: the worldwide evolution of organic life. From the most elevated summits of mountains to the most profound gulfs of the sea, millions of billions of animalcules, animals, cryptogams and superior plants, have been working day and night for centuries, as have the foraminifera on which half our continents are built.

That work was going rapidly enough before the epoch when humans appeared on the Earth, but since the appearance of man it has developed with a rapidity that is accelerating every day. As long as humankind remained restricted to two or three parts of Asia, Europe and Africa, it was not noticeable, because, save for a few focal points of concentration, life in general still found it easy to pour into empty space the surplus accumulated at certain points of the civilized world; it was thus that colonization increasingly populated previously uninhabited countries innocent of all cultivation. Then commenced the first phase of the progress of life by human action: the agricultural phase.

Things moved in this direction for about six centuries, but large deposits of oil were developed, and, almost at the same time, chemistry and steam-power. The Earth then entered its industrial phase—which is only just beginning, since that was not much more than 60 years ago. But where this movement will lead us, and with what velocity we shall arrive, it is easy to presume, given that which has already happened before our eyes.

It is evident, for anyone with eyes to see, that for half a century, animals and people alike have tended to multiply, to proliferate, to pullulate in a truly disquieting proportion. More is eaten, more is drunk, silkworms are cultivated, poultry fed and cattle fattened. At the same time, planning is going on everywhere; ground has been cleared; fecund crop rotations and intensive cultures have been invented, which double the soil's yields; not content with what the earth produces, salmon at five francs a side have been sown in our rivers, and oysters at 24 *sous* a dozen in our gulfs.

In the meantime, enormous quantities of wine, beer and cider have been fermented; veritable rivers of eau-de-vie have been distilled, and millions of tons of oil burned—not to mention that heating equipment is improving incessantly, that more and more houses are being rendered draught-proof, and that the linen and cotton fabrics that humans employ to keep themselves warm are being fabricated more cheaply with every passing day.

To this already-sufficiently-somber picture it is necessary to add the insane developments of public education, which one can consider as a source of light and heat, for, if it does not emit them itself, it multiplies their production by giving humans the means of improving and extending their impact on nature.

This is where we are now; this is where a mere half-century of industrialism has brought us; obviously, there are, in all of this, manifest symptoms of an imminent exuberance, and one can conclude that within 100 years from now, the Earth will have developed a paunch.

Then will commence the redoubtable period in which the excess of production will lead to an excess of consumption, the excess of consumption to an excess of heat, *and the excess*

100

of heat to the spontaneous combustion of the Earth and all its inhabitants.

It is not difficult to anticipate the series of phenomena that will lead the globe, by degrees, to that final catastrophe. Distressing as the depiction of these phenomena might be, I shall not hesitate to map them out, because the prevision of these facts, by enlightening future generations as to the dangers of the excesses of civilization, might perhaps serve to moderate the abuse of life and postpone the fatal final accounting by a few thousand years, or at least a few months.

This, therefore, is what will happen.

For ten centuries, everything will go progressively faster. Industry, above all, will make giant strides. To begin with, all the oil deposits will be exhausted, then all the sources of kerosene; then all the forests will be cut down; then the oxygen in the air and the hydrogen in the water will be burned directly. By that time, there will be something like a million steam-engines on the surface of the globe, averaging 1000 horse-power—the equivalent of a billion horse-power—functioning night and day.

All physical work is done by machines or animals; humans no longer do any, except for skillful gymnastics practiced solely for hygienic reasons. But while their machines incessantly vomit out torrents of manufactured products, an ever-denser host of sheep, chickens, turkeys, pigs, ducks, cows and geese emerges from their agricultural factories, all oozing fat, bleating, lowing, gobbling, quacking, bellowing, whistling and demanding consumers with loud cries!

Now, under the influence of ever more abundant and ever more succulent nutrition, the fecundity of the human and animal species is increasing from day to day. Houses rise up one floor at a time; first gardens are done away with, then courtyards. Cities, then villages, gradually begin to project lines of suburbs in every direction; soon, transversal lines connect these radii.

Movement progresses; neighboring cities begin to connect with one another. Paris annexes Saint-Germain, Ver-

101

sailles and then Bauvais, then Châlons, then Orléans, then Tours; Marseilles annexes Toulon, Draguignan, Nice, Carpentras, Nîmes and Montpellier; Bordeaux, Lyon and Lille share out the rest, and Paris ends up annexing Marseilles, Lyon, Lille and Bordeaux. And the same thing is happening throughout Europe, and the other four continents of the world.

But at the same time, the animal population is increasing. All useless species have disappeared; all that now remain are cattle sheep, horses and poultry. Now, to nourish all that, empty space is required for cultivation, and room is getting short.

A few terrains are then reserved for cultivation, fertilizer is piled herein, and there, lying amid grass six feet high, unprecedented species of sheep and cattle, devoid of hair, tails, feet and bones are seen rolling around, reduced by the art of husbandry to be nothing more than monstrous steaks alimented by four insatiable stomachs.

In the meantime, in the southern hemisphere, a formidable revolution is about to take place. What am I saying? Scarcely 50,000 years have gone by, and here it is, complete!

The polypers have joined all the continents together, and all the islands of the Pacific Ocean and the southern seas. America, Europe and Africa have disappeared beneath the waters of the ocean; nothing remains of them but a few islands formed by the last summits of the Alps, the Pyrenees, the buttes Montmartre, the Carpathians, the Atlas Mountains and the Cordilleras.

The human race, retreating gradually from the sea, has expanded over the incommensurable plains that the sea has abandoned, bringing its overwhelming civilization with it; already space is beginning to run out on the former continents. Here it is the final entrenchments: it is here that it will battle against the invasion of animal life. Here is where it will perish!

It is on a calcareous terrain; an enormous mass of animalized materials is incessantly converted into a chalky state; this mass, exposed to the rays of a torrid Sun, incessantly stores up new concentrations of heat, while the functioning of machines, the combustion of hearths and the development of animal heat cause the ambient temperature to rise incessantly.

And in the meantime, animal production continues to increase; there comes a time when the equilibrium breaks down; it becomes manifest that production will outstrip consumption.

Then, in the Earth's crust, a sort kind of rind begins to form at first, and subsequently, an appreciable layer of irreducible detritus; the Earth is saturated with life.

Fermentation begins.

The thermometer rises, the barometer falls, the hygrometer marches toward zero. Flowers wither, leaves turn yellow, parchments curl up; everything dries out and becomes brittle.

Animals shrink by virtue of the effects of heat and evaporation. Humans, in their turn, grow thin and desiccated; all temperaments melt into one—the bilious—and the last of the lymphatics[31] offers his daughter and 100 millions in dowry to the last of the scrofulous, who has not a *sou* to his name, and who refuses out of pride.

The heat increases and the wells dry up. Water-carriers are elevated to the rank of capitalists, then millionaires, to the extent that the prince's Great Water-Carrier becomes one of the principal dignitaries of state. All the crimes and infamies that one sees committed today for a gold piece are committed for a glass of water, and Cupid himself, abandoning his quiver and arrows, replaces them with a carafe of ice-water.

In this torrid atmosphere, a lump of ice is worth 20 times its weight in diamonds. The Emperor of Australia, in a fit of mental aberration, orders a *tutti frutti* that cost an entire year's civil list. A scientist makes a colossal fortune by obtaining a hectoliter of fresh water at 45 degrees.

Streams dry up; crayfish, jostling one another tumultuously to run after the trickles of warm water that are aban-

---

[31] The lymphatic temperament, associated with one of the four humors of ancient medicine, is better known as the sanguine; it is associated with sociability and compassion, among other traits.

doning them, change color as they go along, turning scarlet. Fish, their hearts weakening and their swim-bladders distended, let themselves drift on the currents, bellies up and fins inert.

And the human species begins to go visibly mad. Strange passions, unexpected angers, overwhelming infatuations and insane pleasures make life into a series of furious detonations—or, rather, one continuous explosion, which begins at birth and concludes with death. In a world cooked by an implacable combustion, everything is scorched, crackled, grilled and roasted, and after the water, which has evaporated, one senses the air diminishing as it becomes more rarefied.

A terrible calamity! The rivers, great and small, have disappeared; the seas re beginning to warm up, then to heat up; now they are already simmering as if over a gentle fire.

First the little fish, asphyxiated, show their bellies at the surface; then come the algae, detached from the sea-bed by the heat; finally, cooked in red wine and rendering up their fat in large stains, the sharks, whales and giant squid rise up, along with the fabulous kraken and the much-contested sea serpent; and with all this fat, vegetation and fish cooked together, the steaming ocean becomes an incommensurable bouillabaisse.

A nauseating odor of cooking expands over the entire inhabited earth; it reigns there for barely a century; the ocean evaporates and leaves no other trace of its existence than fish-bones scattered over desert plains...

It is the beginning of the end.

Under the triple influence of heat, asphyxia and desiccation, the human species is gradually annihilated; humans crumble and peel, falling into pieces at the slightest shock. Nothing any longer remains, to replace vegetables, but a few metallic plants that have been made to grow by irrigating them in vitriol. To slake devouring thirst, to reanimate calcined nervous systems, and to liquefy coagulating albumin, there are no liquids left but sulphuric and nitric acids.

Vain efforts.

With every breath of wind that agitates the anhydrous atmosphere, thousands of human creatures are instantaneously desiccated; the rider of his horse, the advocate at the bar, the judge on his bench, the acrobat on his rope, the seamstress at her window and the king on his throne all come to a stop, mummified.

Then comes the final day.

They are no more than 37, wandering like tinder specters in the midst of a frightful population of mummies, which gaze at them with eyes reminiscent of Corinthian grapes.

And they take one another by the hand, and commence a furious round-dance, and with each rotation one of the dancers stumbles and falls down dead, with a dry sound. And when the 26th cycle is over, the survivor remains alone in front of the miserable heap in which the last debris of the human race is assembled.

He darts one last glance at the Earth; he says goodbye to it on behalf of all of us, and a tear falls from his poor scorched eyes—humankind's last tear. He catches it in his hand, drinks it, and dies, gazing at the Heavens.

Pouff!

A little blue flame rises up tremulously, then two, then three, then 1000. The entire globe catches fire, burns momentarily, and goes out.

It is all over; the Earth is dead.

Bleak and icy. It rolls sadly through the silent deserts of space; and of so much beauty, so much glory, so much joy, so much love, nothing any longer remains but a little charred stone, wandering miserably through the luminous spheres of new worlds.

Goodbye, Earth! Goodbye, touching memories of our history, of our genius, of our pains and our loves! Goodbye, Nature, whose gentle and serene majesty consoled us so effectively in our suffering! Goodbye, cool and somber woods, where, during the beautiful nights of summer, by the silvery light of the Moon, the song of the nightingale was heard. Goodbye, terrible and charming creatures that guided the world with a tear or a smile, whom we called by such sweet names! Ah, since nothing more remains of you, all is truly finished: THE EARTH IS DEAD.

Charles Cros: *An Interastral Drama*
(1872)

La Esperanza, August 24, 2872

Ordinance CXVII of the 32nd Grand-Master of Terrestrial Astronomy has provoked whining from the entire Satirist party. Let us say right away that this party, although it denies it vehemently, is strongly reminiscent of that of the Freethinkers of a few centuries ago. It is so strongly reminiscent that one might fear seeing it go to the same negative extremes, which would consequently necessitate the same repressions.

The Satirists have been talking about a return to the onions of Egypt,[32] to the darkness of the 19th and 20th century; they have proclaimed it a restoration of the clergies of yesteryear, a superstitious measure, a mythological fantasy introduced into that which is most essential to the smooth progress of modern human society.

It will be easy for me to nullify these vain claims. Firstly, it is necessary to observe that the ordinance establishes nothing that has not been actual practice for many years. It does nothing but formalize what already exists in the particular regulations of all terrestrial observatories, and also the results of numerous decisions of the Supreme Court.

---

[32] I have translated "aux oignons d'Égypte" literally, although the phrase in question (from *Exodus* 16:3) only appears in French Bibles, not English ones. The Hebrews, while wandering in the desert with Moses, are said to have regretted leaving Egypt, where they had had enough to eat: the French version of the phrase was adopted metaphorically for reference to nostalgia. The King James version has "flesh pots" instead of onions, reflecting a marked cultural difference in patterns of regret.

Indeed, it requires an ignorance of the most elementary study of administrative law to be unfamiliar with the formalities demanded by all the Observatory councils for admission into the Grand Cupola and the Correspondence Terrace. It is necessary not to have read any of the astronomical publications of this century not to know that the term "Mysteries of the Cupola and the Terrace," so critical in the ordinance at issue, is in common usage, and that certain official documents, already ancient, employ it explicitly. It is part and parcel of the special regime, of the obligatory celibacy of astronomers who desire to surpass the fourth grade, of the oath demanded of them and the particular penalties to which they are subject—penalties that become more severe as the grade of the offender becomes more elevated.

It has been the case for a long time that in requests for admission to superior grades, aspirants mention first and foremost their celibate status and the austerity of their morals, with supporting evidence. Now, these things have been compulsory in reality for a long time, and ordinance CXVII is simply a regularization of a custom recognized as necessary from a moral and political point of view. In this respect, the action of the ordinance, rather than further restricting the custom, has rendered it more equitable and broader in scope, by anticipating the abuse of certain excessively severe restrictions that were beginning to be introduced into several courses in Astronomy.

I know, however, that the Satirists will not be satisfied by these explanations. Custom it may be, they will say, but an unjust and evil custom: an abuse of power, and so on.

With respect to this objection—which, moreover, immediately proves the ignorance and thoughtlessness of those who raise it—I do not want to enter into a debate in the strict sense of the term. I shall limit myself to telling a story that will demonstrate, even to the simplest minds, the necessity of strong regulation of the sort that has naturally prevailed, and which has now been defined by ordinance CXVII.

Perhaps you will recall the sudden and unexplained retirement of a director of the Observatory of the Southern Andes, and the rumors surrounding that retirement. There as mention of culpable negligence and the violation of the Mysteries of the Cupola. The word *mysteries* can even be found in the newspapers of the period. The government wisely hushed up the affair, and the director, although missed by virtue of his remarkable work—especially his work on the equatorial flora of Venus—took early retirement on health grounds. He has now been dead for a long time, as are the majority of those involved. Here, therefore, are the facts as they happened. I shall not give any names.

The director in question—exceptionally, even in that era, as I have said—was married. To be strictly accurate, he was a widower at the time of his appointment—but he had a son of 22 or 23.

The young man, endowed with a vivid, almost undisciplined, imagination, had no taste for astronomical studies, and did not want to do anything but paint and compose verses. He has, in fact, left behind poems highly rated by specialists, although they have a characteristic strangeness scarcely tolerable to those who, like me, only like the normal and uncontestable masterpieces of the 25th century. Let us return to our story.

Studies of the Venusian flora were carried out by exchange, in accordance with normal practice—which is to say that it was necessary to transmit as many specimens of terrestrial flora as were received from Venus. Use was made to this effect of the great battery of 3000 50-centimeter objectives and the adjoining reflectors. It is common knowledge that this battery, which resembles an immense insectile eye, and which cost the constructors 29 years of work and the government 95 millions, is still one of the finest batteries on Earth. Images are reproduced at 1/400th of their diameter by the distance between Earth and Venus, with the consequence that it suffices for Venusian astronomers to magnify the images 400 times on the transmission surface to enable us to receive them at their actual size.

An exchange of Venusian and terrestrial botanical specimens was therefore under way, and the battery was constantly aimed at a Venusian peak, which it is unnecessary to identify. The director, absorbed by the powerful interest of his research, had the idea—more unfortunate than culpable—of making use of his son's help in the fixation and classification of the photographs transmitted to him. Later, he went so far as to confide the direct observation-post at the ocular to the young man. This can only be explained by a sort of senile folly, for, in order to explain such a grave neglect of metaplanetary convention during the inquiry, the unfortunate director simply alleged that he had been suffering *eyestrain* at the time. But let us continue.

The great botanical research project occupied half of the transmission time; the other half was dedicated to current correspondence. The young man was therefore acquainted with the entire procedural operation of that correspondence, without any preparatory studies, regulation, grade or taking any oath!

The subordinate astronomers, perhaps more concerned with protecting their salaries than looking out for the interests of society, or perhaps because of their otherwise-praiseworthy habit of absolute obedience and respect with regard to their director, let things be. At any rate, as they told the enquiry, the correspondence service was conducted, in these irregular conditions, in a very active and fecund manner.

Simply for the sake of the story's convenience, I shall call the young man by the banal and commonplace name of Glaux. Glaux, therefore, seemed suddenly to have taken his ocular functions very much to heart, He asked everyone about possible improvements relating to the transmission process. He even became the first person to put into practice many means previously neglected as purely theoretical and inapplicable. Indeed, it is only since these events that we have been able to transmit and receive sonorous phenomena. The utility of that has been denied; it is argued that we do not have much understanding of Venusian music, and that, with respect to spoken languages, we can only have them pronounced by mechanical articulators. Speaking them ourselves, it is added, would be a waste of time, except in the evidently absurd supposition of an interplanetary voyage. This is, in my opinion, an excessively hasty and ill-tempered conclusion—but I shall move on.

Whence came this sudden astronomical zeal? Its cause would have been easy to anticipate, if the old routine did not bring the majority of men to consider the most natural things in the world as strange or impossible. In truth, science has progressed more rapidly than reason and common sense.

This is what had happened.

Glaux, having concluded the current transmissions one day, was about to quit his post when he saw a creature advancing across the terrace of the Venusian observatory that he did not recognize as belonging to its personnel.

Positing in advance that I am taking account of the distinctions and restrictions of science, I shall say, in order to speak briefly, that it was a *woman*.

Here my task as a narrator becomes difficult. It would be impossible if ordinance CXVII itself had not exactly defined the offences of expression. I shall therefore keep strictly within legal limits and I shall be very sparing with details.

It was, therefore, a woman. Glaux, piqued by curiosity, observed her movements. She went idly back and forth, I cannot say anything about her *extraterrestrial* beauty, or of her attire, of which our most sumptuous flowers give only a dull and monotonous idea. Only sworn astronomers of the 11th grade can be precisely informed in these matters, and that by other means than a description formulated in words.

But here *She* is, arriving at the terrestrial correspondence apparatus, and pausing there. Glaux then makes the greeting customary at the beginning of correspondence. *She* replies very pertinently, repressing what might be called, by virtue of a legitimate analogy, *a burst of laughter*. These details come from a journal in prose and verse that Glaux left behind.

By means of a few exchanged signs, Glaux sees with surprise that *She* is familiar—perhaps more so than him—with the interplanetary language, and the dialogue continues. But Earth and Venus rotate; atmospheric refractions blue the images and soon permit no more than the several-times-repeated signs: Until tomorrow! It is from that day onwards that Glaux is seen to put so much zeal and ingenious activity into his job of correspondent.

Did he imagine for himself those marvelous methods, which one no longer thinks of admiring, now that their usage is continual, or were they communicated to him? Perhaps they were the indiscretions, very advantageous to us, of the young Venusian woman, careless—as women generally are—of keeping the scientific secrets of her planet.

You have guessed, of course, that the two young people were smitten with one another. What folly! What a deplorable consequence of a failure to observe the rules!

They thought they could vanquish the distance that separated them by exchanging the most complete accounts of themselves. They sent one another their photographs in series sufficient for the reproduction of three-dimensionality and movements.[33] In the hours when observation had finished, Glaux shut himself up in a room and reproduced the moving image of his beloved in smoke or dust: an impalpable image made of light alone. He also realized her motionless form in plastic substances.

---

[33] This anticipation of cinema—though not its holographic aspect—might have been inspired by a scientist Cros met at Camille Flammarion's salon, Étienne-Jules Marey, who shared his interest in photographic technology; Marey developed a "chronophotographic gun" in 1882 for analyzing movement by means of multiple exposures, and might have mentioned the possibility to Cros some time before bringing the project to fruition.

It is then that they thought of sending the sound of their voices, their words, their songs. All of that was recorded in curves and reproduced by an electrical tuning-fork apparatus.[34] I cannot say anything about the words and songs (?) that came from so far away.

Everything that I have just stated so briefly—for good reason—lasted three years.

The third year was terrible, a mixture of ecstasy and despair. Would it have been possible to save the two lunatics at that point, by forceful measures? It is doubtful. The harm was done, irreparable. One evening, when our dusk corresponded with dusk in the Venusian country in question, and all the preparations had been made on both sides. Glaux and the young woman exchanged one last kiss across implacable space and killed themselves.

This catastrophe nearly compromised the good relationship between two planets, for the young Venusian woman was the daughter of one of the most powerful astronomers of that world. Everything was settled by precise metaplanetary conventions, which were then put in place. Ordinance CXVII has implemented these conventions of Earth. The unfortunate consequences that were momentarily dreaded will thus be avoided.

All Glaux's papers, photographs, photosculptures and phonographs are filed in the central archives. It is necessary, as I have said, to have reached the 11th grade to have access to them.

Despite what I have just recounted, by superior authorization, I would not be surprised to see the Satirists continue to deny the expediency of ordinance CXVII.

THE END

---

[34] This was written five years before Cros submitted his design for such an apparatus to the Académie des Sciences. It is interesting that Cros subsequently refers to *phonographies* [phonographs] although he called his own apparatus a *paléophone*.

Charles Cros: *The Science of Love*
(1874)

While still very young, I had a fine fortune and a taste for science—but not the airy, pretentious science that believes it can create a world entire and leaps into the blue atmosphere of the imagination. I have always thought, in accord with the tightly-organized cohort of modern scientists, that man is merely a recorder of brute facts, a secretary of palpable nature; that the truth, conceived not in a few vain generalizations, but in an immense and confused volume, is only partially accessible by scrapers, clippers, ferreters, porters and warehousers of actual, observable and undeniable facts—in a word, that it is necessary to be an ant, a mite, a rotifer, a bacterium or anything at all to transport one's atom into the infinity of atoms that comprise the majestic pyramid of scientific truths. To observe and observe, and, above all, never to think, dream or imagine: that is the splendor of present-day method.

It was with these sound doctrines that I entered into life, and as soon as I had taken my first steps, a marvelous project, a genuine scientific windfall, came to mind.

When I learned physics, I said to myself: people have studied gravity, heat, electricity, magnetism and light; the mechanical equivalent of these forces has been or will be determined incontestably in a rigorous fashion—but all those who are working on the expression of these elements of future knowledge are only playing a paltry role in society. There are other forces that sagacious and patient observation ought to submit scientific intelligence. I shall not offer a general classification, because I consider them harmful to study and I have no such intention. In brief, I was led—how or why I do not know—to undertake a scientific study of love.

I do not have an absolutely disagreeable physique—I am neither too tall nor too short, and no one has ever affirmed that I am dark or fair—except that I have eyes that are a little small, but rather shiny, which give me an appearance of stupidity useful in scientific societies but harmful in the world at large. Of that world, moreover, in spite of methodical efforts, I do not have a very clear knowledge, and it is a veritable masterpiece of self-composure that has enabled me to pursue my austere goal there without attracting attention.

I said to myself: I wish to study love, not in the fashion of Don Juans, who amuse themselves without writing, not that of literary men, whose sentimentalize vaguely, but that of serious scientists. To establish the effect of heat on zinc, one takes a bar of zinc, heats it in water to a temperature rigorously determined by means of the best possible thermometer; one measures precisely the bar's length, its tensile strength, its sonority and its calorific capacity, and one does the same at another temperature no less rigorously determined. It was by procedures as exact that I proposed to study love: a remarkable project for one of such a tender age—scarcely 25 years—and a difficult enterprise.

Generally, by virtue of some inconvenient and perhaps culpable repugnance, people in love obstinately refrain from any scientific examination, particularly in those moments when examination would be most fruitful. Given that, my plan quickly ran into trouble. In order to study love, I told myself, it is necessary to take advantage of the best observation-post. The most intimate confidant is sent away during the characteristic interval. Only furniture, and sometimes a dog or a cat, witnesses the mysteries that an inexplicable fatality has so far concealed from analysis. I had, therefore, only one resource, which was to play the role of the amorous individual myself.

Having little in the way of charm, in that the little accorded to me by nature had been etiolated by the shade of libraries and laboratory odors, I had recourse to my profound knowledge to render me worthy of feminine dreams.

Oh, what cosmetic marvels I invented in that era: an insoluble puerile rouge; the blue-black of sleepless eyes; oils to render the skin diaphanous; galvanizations to give my legs a certain dash! But I was not naïve enough to count solely on the appearance of my physiognomy and the allure of my figure. It was necessary to acquire a thorough knowledge of the charming trivia that seduce young women, those ridiculous futilities to which the fair sex submits us.

I went to find Chopin and said to him: "You've played the piano a great deal in society. What is the music that pleases women most?"

He replied, without hesitation: "Rosellen's *Rêverie*."

"40,000 francs, if you will teach me to play that reverie perfectly."

Chopin, ridiculously impractical, excused himself and recommended one of his pupils, Monsieur K***, as better than himself (which was, in fact true). Monsieur K*** accepted the 40,000 francs, and, as an honest man, taught me to play Rosellen's *Rêverie*, and that alone.

I was equipped in that respect.

I went to find Musset and asked him: "What is the poetry that pleases women most?"

Musset placed his index-finger on his eyebrow and said: "Acrostics."

"Here's 50,000 francs; teach me acrostics."

Musset, an incorrigible Bohemian, did not understand that I was his Providence and sent me to Monsieur W***—I don't want to reveal his name—a pupil I found to me much better than his master.[35]

---

[35] What Frédéric Chopin and Alfred de Musset have in common is that they were the most famous lovers of George Sand, whose feverish romantic novels were thought to have had a considerable influence on the attitudes of young women; she wrote at least one acrostic encoding Musset's name. The composer to whom Chopin refers is Louis-Henri Rosellen (1811-1876).

W*** took the 50,000 francs and made me and exquisite collection of acrostics, in all the names of feminine martyrology. Each name had three versions: blonde, brunette and chestnut. There was, in addition, a written promise of delivery for unexpected cases.

Thus equipped, I entered resolutely into society.

After numerous failures—it is so true that only can only learn by experience—which there is no need to relate, I finally found my opportunity. It was in a family living in the Marais, in one of those old parliamentary mansion houses. The whole first floor served as a paper store, and one had to climb the interminable steps of a large, patiently-forged stone staircase to the upper floor, where Monsieur D*** and his family lived. The honest and forgotten appearance of the house pleased me as soon as I set foot in it.

Monsieur D*** had surrendered the paper store downstairs to the husband of his older daughter. Previously, with his pen stuck in his ear and his eyes on the bales, he had acquired a fortune large enough to assure a reasonable dowry to his younger daughter, while retaining enough to excite the "expectations" of his sons-in-law.

They entertained every Saturday—small-scale receptions with tea, little cakes and so on. It was to marry off the daughter that they engaged in these simple joys; in addition, on the other days of the week, they paraded the said daughter around all the houses of the same society. I had passed through an immense number of these interiors, leaping about conscientiously to the sound of polkas and quadrilles that complacent mothers oozed from their soft fingers. As they ran into me everywhere, I was able to get myself invited to M. D***'s home. I had determined, in consequence of comparative examinations, that Mademoiselle D***'s complexion was more suitable than that of any other prospective young woman to my project.

The situation was excellent. I was received in view of a possible marriage; they paid attention to me, they caused me to stand out, cleverly, in a manner calculated not to disgust the

117

perhaps-eccentric character of the young lady. But my plan ran into difficulty. As it has long been notorious that marriage has no connection with love, it was necessary to maneuver to avoid that disastrous conclusion, which had already be offered to me frequently, and which I had fled, not without compromising myself somewhat.

I therefore began by giving some advice to the mother on the subject of her exaggerated plumpness—all, of course, within the limits of the most exquisite politeness and even the most candid benevolence. This advice caused her to adopt a bittersweet tone and to provoke a profession of political faith, about which I had a few reservations. I hung in there, however, not wishing to hasten matters, and started chatting, in a slightly sad and preoccupied manner, with the young lady. I stopped in the middle of sentences that the Devil cold no more have completed than I could: "There are instances when the soul must rise above complexities…" Or: "The heart is a slave whose chains…" Or even: "The heart is a slave that cannot obey…" And so on.

Then, after a sigh, I went to sit down at the piano and the irresistible *Rêverie de Rossellen* earned me delightful glances of submission over the shoulder of the young woman as she drank her tea.

Her name was Virginie and she had chestnut-colored hair. My collection of acrostics included that particular case, in a form which read:

> Vous ne connaissez pas tous nos rêves de fièvre
> Indomptable, où le feu qui brûle notre lèvre
> Rend la vie impossible en ces salons railleurs.
> Grâce pourtant à vos regards (j'en suis comme ivre,
> Ivre d'azur profound), je me reprends à vivre,
> Naïf, aimant les bois. Si nous étions ailleurs,
> Il faudrait oublier famille, honneur, patrie,
> Et pense que je suis tout cela, ma chérie.[36]

---

[36] You do not know all our dreams of fever

These lines, compiled for the occasion by my friend the poet W***, lent themselves marvelously to my project of seduction. As soon as I had slipped them adroitly into Virginie's moist hand, the poor thing was submissive to my power from then on.

One evening, as I took my cup of tea, I squeezed her little fingers beneath the saucer. Due to emotion, or perhaps intention on my part, the cup fell, broke on the corner of the piano, and the hot sugared tea with its cloud of ilk inundated my superb pearl-grey trousers.

"Clumsy fool that I am!" I said, going pale by virtue of the scalding effect, insignificant as it was. "I've ruined your dress, Mademoiselle."

"You never upset anyone else's, Virginie," said her mother.

"Madame, I assure you that it was me, by placing the cup on the edge of the piano...."

"Anyhow, the maid can serve the tea and syrups."

The young woman disappeared. Oh, if I had been able to witness the night she must have had!

In brief, I balanced my actions and gestures so well that the coldness of the parents increased at exactly the same rate as the daughter's love. Subsequently, I exchanged words with her in low voices: she was unhappy, her parents detested me, it was necessary to spare their feelings, etc...

I may appear to be writing fiction, but it would be a mistake to think me capable of such lightness of mind. What I

Indomitable, in which the fie that burns our lip
Renders life impossible in these mocking drawing-rooms.
Thanks to your glances, however (I am drunk on them,
Drunk on profound azure), I am returning to life,
Naïve, loving the woods. If we were elsewhere,
It would be necessary to forget honor, family, fatherland,
And think that I am all of that, my dear.

have said, as briefly as possible, was necessary. Now the science, properly speaking, begins.

We exchanged our portraits. Mine was photographed on enamel, framed in gold, with a minuscule chain, to be carried under clothing. That portrait contained a pair of maximum and minimum thermometers, hidden between and ivory plate and the enamel—two masterpieces of precision in such small dimensions. I was thus able to verify the modifications of the normal temperature of an organism affected by love.

Under pretexts that were often difficult to invent I had the portrait returned to me for a few hours, took note of the numbers and their dates and reset the thermometers.

One evening, on which I had danced twice with a little brunette lady, I recall having observed a reduction of temperature of 40%, followed or preceded—I had no information as to the order of the phenomena—by an elevation of 70%. Those are facts.

At any rate, everything being prepared, I took the following measures. I said to Monsieur D***: "Property is theft" (it's not mine and it's not new, but it always works), and to Madame D***, who had had a miscarriage that she mentioned too frequently: "A woman, from the social economic point of view, can and ought to be considered a fetus-factory—and I hummed, to the tune of *Beside a Cradle*, a few lines of a song by W*** entitled *Beside a Specimen Jar*: "It looked like a white detachable collar/An embryonic substitute for a worthy pose.../If it were not preserved in alcohol/What great things it might have done!"

Then I insinuated this note into Virginie's hand: "I shall explain everything later. Absolute row between your parents and me. The ideal, the dream, the prism of the impossible are what awaits us. To live it is necessary to love... A carriage is waiting downstairs; come, or I shall kill myself and you will be damned."

That was how I eloped with her.

The ease with which this enterprise had succeeded amazed me as, once in the railway carriage, I looked at that young woman, brought up in tranquility, probably destined for some mediocre employee, who had followed me thanks to a series of sentimental formulas—which I had not invented, moreover, and which I could not sufficiently explain.

We were going somewhere, of course. I had, in fact, prepared some time before, with my personal sagacity, a delightful and methodical installation whose purpose will become clear in due course. The train journey took three hours—plenty of time for alarm, sobbing and palpitations. Fortunately, we were not alone in the compartment.

I had made a preliminary study of the situation, so far as I could, in novels: "You... you're sacrificing everything for me... how can I ever thank you..." Then, after a silence: "I love you, I love you... oh, journeys with the beloved! The horizon reddened by the sunset, or the pearly dawn, and we are face to face, after distraction or sleep, in newly-perfumed lands."

The sentence had been written for me by my friend, the poet W***.

We arrived, her like a wet bird, me delighted with the initial success of my research—for during the entire journey, while reassuring the poor frightened girl, without letting myself be carried away by the romantic vanity of the elopement, I had skillfully applied between her 10th and 11th ribs a long-running cardiograph so exact that Dr. Maret,[37] to whom I owe its hypothetical description, had refused to develop it for economic reasons.

Afterwards, a carriage collected us from the station. Terror, embarrassment, anxious intoxication of the demoiselle. My feebly-repulsed embraces permitted the cardiograph to record the visceral expressions of the situation.

---

[37] This appears to be a deliberate misspelling of the name of Étienne-Jules Marey, the pioneering cardiologist whom Cros met at Camille Flammarion's salon, who also shared his interest in photographic technology.

And in the delightful boudoir where, putting her hands over her eyes, she reproached herself for her definitive rupture with the exigencies of morality and public opinion, I was fortunately able to make an exact determination—the moment being of absolute importance—of the weight of her body. This is how:

She had let herself slump on to a sofa, lost in thought. As I paused, contemplating her emotionally and delightedly, I used my heel to press the button of an electric bell lodged under the carpet, and in a secret cabinet, at the end of the balance whose other end was occupied by the sofa, Jean—a devoted and forewarned servant—was able to observe the eight of the fully-dressed demoiselle.

I threw myself down beside her and lavished upon her all possible consolations: caresses, kisses, massage, hypnotism, etc.—consolations that were not, however, conclusive, in view of my research plan.

I shall pass over the transitions that enabled me to remove her clothes, while she was still on the sofa, and carry her to the bed-alcove, where she forgot family, opinion and society. In the meantime, Jean weighed the clothing left behind, underclothes and footwear included, on the aforementioned sofa, in order to obtain by subtraction the net weight of the woman's body.

In the room where, intoxicated by love, she abandoned herself to my fictitious transports—for I had no time to waste—it was as if we were in a retort. The copper-lined walls prevented any connection with the atmosphere and the air was analyzed rigorously, first as it came in and again when it went out. Potash solutions contained in flasks revealed to skilful chemists on an hourly basis the quantitative presence of carbon dioxide. I remember curious figures in this regard, but they lacked the precision justly required by tabulation, since my own non-amorous respiration was mingled with Virginie's genuinely amorous respiration. Let it suffice for me to mention the large excess of carbon dioxide during those tumultuous nights when passion attained its maxima of intensity and numeric expression.

Strips of litmus paper cleverly distributed in the linings of her garments revealed the constantly acidic reaction of sweat. Then, on the following days and nights, there were figures to record relating to the mechanical equivalent of nervous contractions, the quantity of tears secreted, the composition of the saliva, the variable hygroscopy of the hair, the tension of anxious sobs and sensuous sigh!

The results of the *kissometer* were particularly curious. The instrument, which is my own invention, is no larger than the apparatus that Punch-and-Judy men put in their mouths to make their puppets speak, which are known as "whistles." As soon as the dialogue became tender and the situation was established as opportune, I put the primed apparatus—covertly, of course—between my teeth.

Until then, I had been rather disdainful of those expressions of "a thousand kisses" that people put at the end of amorous notes. They are, I said to myself, hyperboles that have passed into vulgar language by courtesy of certain poets of bad taste—like Jean Second,[38] for example. Well, I am happy to bring an experimental verification to these instinctive formulas, which many scientists before me have considered absolutely chimerical. In the space of about an hour and a half, my counter registered *944 kisses*.

The instrument placed in my mouth inconvenienced me; I was preoccupied with my research, besides which, feigned activities never equal real ones. If all that is taken into account, it will be appreciated that the number 944 might often be surpassed by violently amorous individuals.

---

[38] The humanist Churchman Jan Everaerts (1511-1536) wrote in Latin, signing himself Johannes Secundus, which became Jean Second in French. He was famous for the erotic content of his poetry, which was collected in French translation under the title *Le Livre des Baisers*.

That exquisite period of happiness for her and fruitful study for me lasted 87 days. I had established the series of decisive facts on which the science of love must necessarily be founded, save for the ninth and tenth sections within my subdivision. The ninth part was entitled *The Effects of Absence and Regret.*

The study became delicate; fortunately, I was able to count on Jean—the devoted servant—and my faithful laboratory assistants, physicists, chemists and naturalists.

"Virginie," I therefore said, one morning, "heavenly dream of my life, star of my pallid future, while in your arms I have neglected a few invoices that have been contested. I must therefore remove myself temporarily from the gleam of your eyes, the magnetism of your kisses and the dazzle of your embraces and go clear up that aspect of my commercial life."

The scene she made completed what I had determined in a few preceding scenes relative to *The Mechanics of Chagrin.*

Inflexible, I left—not without leaving all my assistants precise instructions to take the final notes necessary to my report, the academic effect of whose publication promises to be explosive.

To tell the truth, though, I had grown weary of that patient research. When a chemist studies a class of reactions or a general theory, with the greatest fervor, he can at least quit his laboratory at mealtimes and at night and abandon his mind to the ordinary facts of life. The problem that I was pursuing did not allow me those leaves of absence. It was necessary always to be ready for experiments; it was necessary, avoiding all distractions, to be constantly on the lookout for the countless and complex phenomena that emerge from what is known as an amorous intrigue.

In consequence, I took advantage from that respite from arduous toil. Sure of my subordinates, I forgot momentarily, in the ballrooms of the barriers and renowned houses of pleasure, the uninterrupted intellectual tension, to which I had subjected myself religiously for the greater glory of science.

As I came back on the train, I congratulated myself privately on the colossal task I had accomplished. I told myself, justly that my report would cause a colossal sensation in the scientific world, like Newton's *Principia* or some other analogous revelation.

Such persistent praiseworthiness, I thought, as I lay back on the cushions of the carriage that conveyed me from the station to the villa, and the disinterestedness of such considerable expenses, would finally have its reward!

"Madame left three days ago," I was told, when I got home.

"Left three days ago! That's not possible…"

"She left a letter for Monsieur."

This is the letter:

You would be despicable, Monsieur, if you were not so stupid.

Oh, how bored I was at home with my parents since finishing my studies at the Conservatoire! You didn't understand that I was very glad to find you in order to get out of that paternal shack. Thanks all the same, dear friend.

Your friend Jules W*** has explained your project to me.

You must be very young, without appearing so, to believe that that's what can be learned with women.

By the way, I've found all your instruments and records. I was nervous—and yet you are a matter of indifference to me!—and I have broken them all and burnt them all.

I've even discovered the mystery of the sash that you left me. Your thermometers and hygrometers (that's the word, I think), so many spies, are in pieces.

Then again, what information would you have obtained from me about love? You have always been extremely boring. Your friend Jules amused me, and perhaps excited me, with his Bohemian audacities. You, never…

It was too depressing in your trick boudoirs.

Goodbye, my little scientist. I'm going to make my own living on the stage, abroad. A Russian nobleman, less serious and more sensible than you, is taking me away in his trunk.

Virginie

All my hopes of glory annihilated, 6000 francs—three-quarters of my fortune—spent for nothing, science held back, in this regard, for several centuries: such is the picture that presented itself to my mind on reading that letter. Not wanting to believe it, I searched the villa from the cellar to the attic.

And as I wandered through those empty rooms, I felt— the final mockery of fate—regret for Virginie's flight! Yes, I regretted the loss of that woman more than that of my finest works! And I went to lose consciousness—O shame!— burying my face in my pillow to recover the scent of the tresses that I would no longer be able to touch.

To cap it all, missing the opportunity to record the analytical elements of such profound heartbreak—such a particular set of violent sensations—I did not think of hitching myself up to the cardiograph!

Charles Cros: *The Newspaper of the Future*
(1880)

I arrived at the offices of *Le Chat Noir*, and was so overwhelmed by the Asiatic luxury of the rooms that I stood for two hours, twirling my hat between my fingers, in a corridor strewn with a thousand busy employees, dressed in the most various and multicolored uniforms.

I was taken into a waiting-room. The curtains, the divans and the incense burning in the corners increased my timidity. Vanquished by fatigue and emotion, however, not daring to let myself collapse on to one of the comfortable ottomans that cluttered the editorial offices, I spotted a little three-legged cane-seated stool and sat down thereon, judging myself scarcely worthy of it.

Immediately, I was gripped by an unfamiliar vertigo: Monsieur Grévy[39] appeared to me with the features of Jupiter, pursuer of nymphs; Salis was holding an Apollonian lyre and, smiling mysteriously, sang to me:

On that tripod, men of the least capacity
Acquire a sibylline perspicacity.

Indeed, the walls seem to be drawing draw away, the ceilings are becoming domes of tropical verdure, and the belated flies of winter multiply in the forms of twittering hummingbirds.

The block-calendar, from which a sheet is torn away every day, was illuminated by an electric light, and a fateful date could be read thereon: March 1, 1986.

"Why that nine instead of the eight?"

---

[39] Jules Grévy was the President of the French Republic in March 1886, having not long begun his ill-fated second term (his resignation was forced in December 1887).

127

"It's quite simple," Rodolphe murmured. "We're older by 100 years."

"We're going to die, then?"

"Don't try to be clever. You know perfectly well that, thanks to the famous American Tadblagson's invention, our brains have been fabricated in platinum by galvanoplasty, and that, when they're worn out, they're replaced by an identical specimen, since the molds are conserved and catalogued at the Town Hall."

"And where are we?"

"In the offices of *Le Chat Noir*."

Indeed, the reporters are seated around an immense emerald table. The reporters are not handsome; they have the faces of furniture-removers; they are all clad in grey linen with an identification-number on the collar. Each of them wears a kind of hat shape like a pumpkin, connected to his forehead by a series of contacts, like those in the measuring-devices used by hat-makers.

5 p.m. chimes.

The ten reporters at the end stick telephones to their left ears and write with their right hands on continuous strips of paper unfurled in front of them by a machine. As the surface is covered in writing, it is drawn through a slit into the basement, where the printing-works are.

Alphonse Allais, in the capacity of an obliging cicerone, explains things to me: "They're the reporters of the Present; the telephones reveal to them what is happening everywhere, and they write with the talent that they extract from those singular hats.

"I should not forget to tell you that the hats contain state-of-the-art metallic brains, with batteries and accessories. The contacts touching the forehead serve to transmit electric currents that can produce talent in the most obtuse of heads.

"This invention, due to the celebrated Tadblagson, has transformed the social order by rendering talent proportional to wealth. That is why the greatest genius of our era is the banker Philipfill, who has been able to afford himself the luxury of collecting the most expensive brains. Among others, he is said to have paid a million and a half for Sarah Bernhardt's brain, guaranteed genuine.

"It follows from this that an end has been put to the socialist demands of the last century. Now the axiom is: no money, no talent. There are very rare exceptions of people without a *sou* who are born with intelligence, but our tribunals apply summary justice to them by expropriating their brains, every model of which reverts to the State.

"*Le Chat Noir* of 1986, which desires to interest its readers at any price, has made the greatest sacrifices to enrich its cerebral collection. Thus, the heads of the ten reporters at the back, two of whom write in verse, are worth more than five million. That one, on the left, has a Victor Hugo brain; just look at it—ten past five, and he has already written 200 verses, 20 a minute."

I leaned forward avidly to read a few verses, but the paper was moving so quickly that I could only read these:

The rough sandstone wheel draws water from the trough
And the steel blade whistles, twists and glints.
The steel must yield to the bite of the flint.
A spark must flash in the supreme collision
Like the spark in the gleam of a lover's vision.[40]

"Oh! That will probably be cut by the sub-editor. The brain of the bearer sometimes has too great an effect on the work. That one is a knife-grinder, and his trade is showing.

"As you can see, we obtain our reporters from the lowest class; they're more reliable, cheaper and less liable to put their own inner being into the work.

"We sometimes link two or three different brains, however, in order to obtain unexpected effects. For instance, look at that reporter bowed down by his two superimposed hats. In

---

[40] I have had to be a trifle inexact in rendering the meaning of these lines, in order to preserve the rhyme-scheme, which seemed necessary in the interest of the parody—all the more so in the next sequence of improvised verse.

addition to his own brain—which has scarcely any effect—
he's carrying that of the poet Theodore de Banville, in combination with that of an advocate known to a few erudite per-
sons. I'll use my scissors to cut out what he's just written—he
won't even notice—and you can assess the effect.

This is what was written on the excised strip.

I had her one fine evening (all things

                                    ......   Considered.)

Her mother was a tailor, vulgar and

                                    Widowed.

I had a mind, despite my colleagues' horror,

                                    To make...

But no one, says Cujas,[41] *alleging her turpitude,*

                                    Could take...

Is that gaze, with its gunpowder flashes,

                                    Profound?

To ask the question, my heart, it to answer it,

                                    Deep down.

I told her: you shan't have a stone from me,

                                    Neither

A diamond, a louis, a franc, a glass of beer,

                                    Nor cider!

Pay? Never! In case her vibrant amorous heart

                                    Faltered...

I'd rather keep my budget wisely

                                    Unaltered!

---

[41] Jacques Cujas (1520-1595) was a famous expert in Roman
law; his most oft-quoted dictum was *Nihil hoc ad edictum
praetoris*, whose approximate significance is "That is irrele-
vant from a legal viewpoint."

"Tonight, it doesn't make sense—but sometimes, it astonishes the reader. Quarter past five...stop! The copy's all in."

All the reporters put down their pens and telephones. They all put their hats in numbered boxes and make their way, as the idiots they were before being coiffed, to collect their 3.50 francs from the cashier.

"The reporting is nothing, as an expense, by comparison with the cost of administrative personnel and furnishings."

The furnishings? It doesn't surprise me that they're costly. Imagine immense hothouses filled with palm-trees and orchids, criss-crossed by bird-flies and hummingbirds! These hummingbirds are something of a nuisance. Fortunately, the American Humbugson has just invented a colibricidal powder.

And the walls that are visible, out there in the distance, and those abrupt crags, are made of reinforced concrete, lit up by night. I won't even mention the basement for the printing-press, where no one is printing, because there are people with exquisite voices dictating copy into phonographs whose tapes, reproduced by the million, will carry the *spoken* newspaper to its subscribers.

No one any longer knows how to read or write—that's progress!—because of the aforementioned phonograph. One only finds a few people, backward in that respect, among the dregs of the population—those are the people employed as reporters...

Crack! My three-legged cane-bottomed stool has broken beneath my contortions—and I fall back into our own sad epoch, into the offices of a periodical in 1886.

What a paltry establishment yours is, my poor *Chat Noir*!

Charles Cros: *The Pebble That Died of Love*

A Story Fallen From the Moon

(1886)

On the 24th of Chum-Chum (Vegan calendar, 7th series) a terrible moonquake devastated the Sea of Tranquility. Horrible or charming fissures opened up in that virgin[42] but infertile ground.

A flint (definitely not from the epoch of chipped stone, more probably that of polished stone[43]) chanced to roll down from a doomed peak and, proud of its roundness, lodged about a *phthwfg*[44] from fissure AB33, commonly known as Moule-à-Singe.[45]

---

[42] Cros inserts a footnote: "We cannot put any credence in the infamous slanders that have been put about regarding this region."

[43] Early French anthropologists subdivided what the English called the Stone Age into three divisions: the era of *pierre éclatée* [chipped stone], the era of *pierre taillée* [carved stone] and the era of *pierre polie* [polished stone], although the first two were never clearly distinct and were eventually merged into the *paléolithique* [Paleolithic] while the third became the *néolithique* [Neolithic]. The chronological order of the two eras is reversed here, in the interests of euphemistic reference.

[44] Cros: "The *phthwfg* is equivalent to a length of 37,000 meters of iridium at seven degrees below zero."

[45] This now-obsolete argot term combines two words, *moule* [mussel] and *singe* [monkey], that are both used abusively to signify something similar to the English "fathead;" it is relevant to note, however, that the fissure presumably resembles the narrow opening of a feeding mollusc, which is cited ana-

The rosy appearance of this region, entirely new to a flint scarcely chipped away from its peak, and the black manganese moss that overhung the new abyss, frightened the audacious pebble, which stopped dead, foolishly.

The fissure burst into silent laughter—the silence peculiar to the Beings of the Planet Without an Atmosphere. Far from losing its grace in the course of that laughter, its physiognomy gained a certain exquisite modernity therefrom. Enlarged, but more elegant, it seemed to say to the pebble: "Come on then, if you dare!"

The latter, whose name was actually *Skkjro*,[46] judged it appropriate to preface its amorous assault with an *aubade*, sung into the void perfumed by magnetic oxide.

It employed the imaginary coefficients of a fourth-degree equation.[47] It is well-known that in ethereal space, one obtains unparalleled fugues in that fashion (Plato vol. XV, ch. 13).

The fissure (whose Selenian name means *Augustine*) seemed at first to be appreciative of this homage. It even softened, welcomingly.

The Pebble, emboldened, was about to take advantage of the situation, rolling further, perhaps penetrating...

At this point, the drama commences—a drama brief, brutal, and true.

The dry surface of the Moon, jealous of this idyll, was subject to a second quake.

The frightened fissure (Augustine) closed again, forever, and the pebble (Alfred) exploded with rage.

That was the beginning of the Age of Chipped Stone.

---

logically in the slang of other languages, notably the Australian euphemism "spearing the bearded clam".

[46] Cros: "This forename, common on the Planet, is an exact translation of 'Alfred'."

[47] Cros: "The original lunar text has 'a fourth-floor landing'— an obvious typographical error."

Charles Epheyre: *The Mirosaurus*
(1885)

What does one need to be happy? A faithful and gentle wife, a modest and honorable social position, good health and reasonable comfort. In my opinion, there's no need for greater wealth.

And that is why Monsieur Perron, the local registrar in Martinville, in Calvados, should have been perfectly happy.

His little house was surrounded by a garden; it shone whitely in the sunlight, when there chanced to be any sunlight, surrounded by greenery. It was the most luxurious house in Martinville, for the presbytery—which could have given it some competition—was old, falling into ruins, whereas the Perron house had been recently repaired. Its youth made a contrast with the decrepit hovels and smoky cottages of the village.

Alas, one always finds, even in the wisest man, something akin to a seed of madness. Monsieur Perron, who had no ambition for himself, became ambitious on seeing his son grow up.

Georges would certainly not grow old in the humble status of his father! He would leave the ignoble province where everyone yawns, and see Paris. He would arrive there triumphantly; he would make a great name for himself, would amass a colossal fortune. He would get his hands on the only two great kinds of wealth that bring happiness: fame and money. He would pierce, by dint of hard work or genius, the immense obscurity in which the petty and the humble vegetate dolorously. That was what Monsieur Perron repeated to himself night and day, while balancing his accounts.

As soon as Georges was ten years old, he was sent to school in Caen. He had a kepi and a tunic; he wore out trousers that were too short, on wooden benches that were too hard.

He tore and covered with ink the masters of ancient and modern literature; he learned to play prisoner's base and tag, to write lines with three pens joined together and to call those who denounced him when he copied his homework lunatics.

Those studies lasted six years. That is how long it takes to form the hearts and minds of children. Monsieur Perron would have been quite satisfied had Georges been able to combine his various talents with the advantage of a baccalaureate, but Greek and Latin had conserved all their mysteries for the poor lad. He failed completely at the first attempt.

During this interval, Monsieur Perron died. His robust confidence in the future was unshaken, and, as he departed for the other world, he had retained all his hopes. Hopes or illusions, it scarcely matters; death is gentle when one still possesses them. May the God of Abraham and Jacob show us such favor at our last sigh. He left three people behind: Mother Perron, a meek and tranquil creature; Nonotte, the busy old maid, simple and loquacious; and finally, Georges, who had no baccalaureate but was no less admired and adored by the two women for that.

It turned out that Monsieur Perron had been very thrifty. He left some capital— government stock, to be exact, with small periodical dividends. It was enough to live quietly, without exaggerated luxury but without anxiety for the future. In Martinville, with an income of 12,000 francs, one can still hold one's head up, and it is permissible to keep a few bottles of burgundy behind the firewood for special occasions.

By dint of perseverance, Georges eventually obtained his baccalaureate. That was a memorable occasion in Martinville. That day, it was almost forgotten that Monsieur Perrron was dead. The poor brave man would, however, have been highly delighted with that fine introduction to glory.

The beginning of a career is fraught with so many rough patches that I am always astonished when anyone dares to commit himself to one. Georges hesitated between the law, medicine, administration, commerce, the army and industry

135

for such a long time that by the age of 23 he still had not made a decision.

Must the truth be told? Our friend was lazy. He did not like activity, effort or strife. Why bestir oneself, exhausting oneself in sterile and tiring attempts, when happiness was at hand, under that humble roof where there was an indulgent mother and a devoted servant? Is there any pleasure greater than taking a nap beside a stove or watching big grey clouds borne along in hurried swirls by the wind from the sea?

Growing pale over boring books, confronting redoubtable examinations, visiting unfamiliar, malevolent, surly and harsh people, depriving oneself of walks, sleep and rest—that was how Georges represented glory to himself, and it scarcely seemed enviable.

He liked the joys of nature. He loved birdsong, which the return of spring recalls to love and joy. Later, in summer, he wandered through the countryside, admiring the large meditative oxen, glad to be alive, grazing meadow-grass. Often, on the cliffs, he listened to the sound of the waves that came to beat the rocks at high tide. For long hours he contemplated the eccentric seagulls, white patches playing with the crests of the waves, or the boats whose sails were filled by the wind, leaning over the abyss. Then a secret contentment took possession of him; he thought vaguely that it must be hard to be an audacious seagull, struggling with squalls, or a valiant boat defying the fury of tempests. He liked it better being Georges Perron, petty bourgeois of Martinville, who, after his excursion to the rocks, was sure of finding the table set and a benevolent maternal smile when he returned home.

Alas, benevolent maternal smiles never last for very long.

Madame Perron's death did not change Georges life of idleness at all. The excellent Nonotte, who had rocked him in his cradle, continued surround him with tender care. After a few months of sadness, the little house recovered its calmness. Everything was orderly and serene again. Georges resumed his solitary walks and continued his dreams.

What was he thinking about as he daydreamed? Where did his chimerical aspirations lead him? Where was that smoke going? Who knows? Perhaps in the direction of great thoughts, perhaps that of great actions.

In his excursions to the shore, Georges had one place that he preferred—a sort of natural grotto that was half-submerged at high tide, but which the low tide uncovered in its entirety. It was, nevertheless, rather difficult to reach and curiosity-seekers never visited it. It was there that Georges spent long hours in meditation.

When he finally went home, he saw from a distance that Nonotte was waiting for him impatiently on the doorstep.

"It's 6 p.m. already," said the worthy woman. "Hurry up, or the joint will be burnt."

She brought warm clothes and slippers. All the wellbeing of the hearth warmed the vagabond's heart again. Then, there was steaming soup, which Nonotte placed on the white tablecloth in a ceremonious manner. And when the dinner was over, Georges, sitting in an armchair, smoked his long pipe, falling half-asleep, lulled by the hum of the stove and Nonotte's chatter.

No neighbor or unwelcome guest ever came to trouble that peace. Their only commensal was Miche, a fat and indolent she-cat who lay at the foot of the armchair.

At 9 p.m. or thereabouts, his eyelids having become heavy, he had to go lie down, languishing on the huge, soft, pleasantly-scented bed with its long white curtains. Georges stretched himself out, snuffed out his candle and, the following morning, feeling much better, felt ready to resume the thread of his destiny.

By virtue of visiting the same grotto every day, he ended up knowing it down to its smallest details. It was adorned with fossil seashells that projected from the clay. Sometimes, Georges detached one of these venerable relics with his knife. He was familiar with their forms and their indentations. Carefully, he studied the structure of each shell, examining the folds, the juncture and the involutions, and often regretted not

137

knowing the names of the various species that he had before his eyes. He knew, however, thanks to a vague memory of his schoolwork, that fossils were ancient creatures that had lived in distant epochs and had been fixed for hundreds of thousands of years within the Earth's crust.

An old book on natural history gave him a few summary indications; he learned that there were Ostreas, Pectens, Rhynchonellas and Ammonites, and became interested in their history. One day, he brought a few of these seashells home, then others, and yet others. He lovingly chose all of those whose stria had been best preserved over time; he put them on a shelf, grouping them according to their forms and analogies, comparing them, turning them round and classifying them as best he could.

An unknown force developed within him, like a secret and mysterious instinct, which pushed him forward. Every day, his little collection became dearer to him; every day it took up more of his time. He was astonished to find himself so ardent about things that he hardly understood. With a certain surprise, he was aware of the birth of a strange vocation and he was a witness rather than a protagonist of the passion that stirred within him.

As for Nonotte, she did not understand the assembly of old shells at all. Georges brought new ones back every day. To the great indignation of the honest servant, an entire room was devoted to this debris. They were on the floor, under the bed, in the wardrobes and the cupboards. It was a museum in miniature; had Nonotte not worshiped her young master, she would have swept away that entire paleontological orgy like unsavory dust.

The solitary walks had an objective now; the daydreams had taken on a precise form. It was a matter of enriching the shell collection, of amassing in the little house in Martinville these witnesses of ancient ages. Georges was no longer living in the present; he was in the past. He was 500,000 years older than his fellow citizens in Martinville. He became a contemporary of the Ammonites, imagining their conflicts, their appetites and their frolics in the seas of the earliest terrestrial ages. He imagined immense beaches animated by the combats of monstrous creatures, and he lost himself in that contemplation of the past, full of disdain for the vulgarities of today.

In his monotonous and comfortable existence, gripped by this strange mania, Georges quickly forgot all the stupid things that one learns at school. He no longer thought about the splendors of Paris and all the pleasures that the capital reserves for young people. All of that phantasmagoria gradually disappeared and faded away in his memory, stifled by the nonchalance of present wellbeing, the force of a nascent passion and the majesty of the solitary and calm nature in the midst of which he lived.

There was an old family friend of the Perrons living in Caen, who was a member of the Paleontological Society of Calvados. Georges wrote to him asking for advice. The worthy man, astonished and delighted, came to Martinville and admired Georges' collection. He weighed the Ammonites, turned over the Terebratulas and read aloud the labels stuck to the oysters.

"You must join our society," he exclaimed, excitedly. "You've become the equal of the best of them at a stroke."

Georges protested at first, judging himself unworthy of such an honor; then, seized for the first time with a confused sentiment of ambition, he accepted.

Twice a month he went to Caen to attend the meetings of the Paleontological Society. There he learned the elements of geology, and was encouraged by honest advice. The Society was composed of worthy men devoid of arrogance and vanity. They led modest little lives, untroubled by any extreme desire. They followed from afar, by means of a few scientific journals, the great movement of progress whose frenzied whirlwind carried away their colleagues in Paris. Alongside those violent conflicts, fecund ideas and desperate efforts, they kept quiet in their petty province, satisfied with their humble station, fanatically amorous of their science and their region. They only spoke about Parisians with irony, perhaps mingled with regret; but they returned to their amours very rapidly. With no other passion than for their fossils, they discussed the stratum of a shell or the classification of a bivalve with more enthusiasm than the taking of Sebastopol or the war in Italy.

At about this time, Georges made a friend.

One of the inhabitants of Martinville having died, his house fell by inheritance to an individual of an animal species totally unknown in Norman villages. This person came unceremoniously to establish himself in the house he had inherited, and for a long time was the object of all the conversations in the main square and everywhere else.

Monsieur Frantz Loch, born in Winterstein in German Switzerland, resembled a spider. He was tall and thin, with arms and hands that seemed to go on forever. Black hair, greying slightly, falling upon his shoulders; blue eyes possessed of a softness and an extreme strength; coarse and angular features, and a deep voice; something wild and benevolent in the ensemble: such was the new inhabitant of Martinville.

He had brought musical instruments with him: a violin, a violoncello and a piano. Every evening, he devoted himself to prolonged musical exercises, and well into the night, sentimental melodies such as Martinville had never heard mingled with the sounds of the wind and the sea.

During the day, Frantz Loch walked on the strand, listening to the whistling of the breeze, the roaring of the waves and the rattle of the shingle. Often, in the midst of the racket, he would take a pencil and paper from his threadbare coat and write feverishly. His long legs strode back and forth on the sand as if running after inspiration.

It was in nearby locations that Georges was searching for shells, sculpting his stone with his hammer, absorbed in the conquest of some Terebratula or an Ostrea. The same disdain for the banalities of life united the two men. They did not take long to get to know one another, to talk to one another, to understand one another. Georges offered to show Frantz his collection; Frantz offered to let Georges hear his music. Frantz admired the collection; Georges waxed ecstatic over the music.

Finally, after a hard life, Frantz was able to find some rest. Until now, the fatalities of life had drawn him through misery and misfortune. That naïve and tender soul had run into human heedlessness, ingratitude and malice. Passionate about his art, Frantz had thought that it was sufficient to eat when hungry, to do no harm to anyone, and to be a great artist. In 40 years, people and events had not entirely succeeded in disillusioning him.

For the good, misfortune is a bountiful school. After having suffered a great deal, Frantz had become better. He, who had been so badly treated by his fellow humans, loved humankind, and if he lived in solitude it was by virtue of timidity, not hatred.

Soon, attracted by a powerful sympathy, by the need for friendship that is as strong as the need for love, old Frantz developed a tender and profound affection for young Georges. He treated him with paternal gentleness, giving him advice.

"My son," he said, "you have adopted a tranquil and happy way of life; you are a true sage. Let my experiences be a lesson to you; don't do as I have done in running after wealth that does not exist. Seek neither glory nor fortune; glory is for the dead, fortune for fools. Life is here, in the midst of this powerful and fecund nature, which never betrays those who love her. Perhaps she will yield one of her secrets to her, and you will have more joy in discovering a new fossil than in climbing into a carriage with eight springs."

Frantz also talked about his art—his divine art, which opened the doors of infinity. He became animated then; his eyes burned with an unfamiliar flame, and his emotional speech penetrated Georges' soul.

In the evenings, until late at night, Frantz and Georges remained together. Frantz played the airs of old masters, so sweet and so pathetic, and Georges never wearied of listening to them. A new world revealed itself within him, full of mysteries. He listened, slightly distractedly at first; then, gradually, he became attentive, gripped by the divinity. The vibrations of the instrument, increasingly sonorous, seemed to make his thoughts vibrate; as the harmonious phases unfolded beneath his friend's agile fingers, an entire world of thoughts traversed his head, and images passed by, tender, sad, ardent, audacious, filling his being with indefinite emotions, full of charm and force.

On those evenings, to Nonotte's great despair, Georges came home late. Frantz's house was some distance away, and, come rain or snow, he had to traverse the entire village of Martinville at 1 a.m. One day, Georges proposed that Frantz should come and live with him, and Frantz agreed. They agreed to share the household expenses.

I know that nothing is more contrary to custom, nothing is less regular. It is quite acceptable to make a friend, but to welcome that friend into one's home! It is necessary to be devoid of any sense of social convention; a self-respecting person would never behave as Georges did. So Georges was much criticized. Unfortunately, he paid little heed to popular opinion. He was simple enough to want to do as he wished, and, not being inclined to interfere with the actions of others, he claimed the liberty of his own.

Soon, the friendship between the two men became profound. Frantz told Georges about his disappointments, his sadnesses, his love-affairs. Yes, the old musician with the long arms had been in love. He had felt his heart swell with joy at a woman's smile—that of a pretty blonde girl from Winterstein, who had toyed with him for two years. When Frantz began that story, he could not finish it. His voice trembled, his eyes became moist, and then, abruptly, he opened his violin-case and, without saying a word, started to play at hazard, feverishly, as if only the divine melodies of Beethoven or Schumann could chase away the bitter memory of the pretty blonde girl from Winterstein.

And Georges too thought about the soft smiles and tender gaze of a woman. A vague desperation gripped him; in the rapid notes emitted by the violin, he saw the forms of women

142

passing by, who extended their arms to him and offered him their kisses. Little by little, the thick envelope of lethargy within which he had blunted himself since infancy was ripped apart. His ideas became more precise, more abundant and vaster. He saw something beyond his seashells. Behind his collection he vaguely perceived the infinity of science: an entire world of powerful facts and vast ideas to which, until now, lost in the observation of meager details, he had remained a stranger.

One day—a memorable day—when Frantz was declaiming on the shore, Georges, who was hollowing out the walls of his cavern, felt his pick arrested by an object of large dimensions. He tried to detach it; the object resisted. Then, with his knife, his hammer and his pick, he set about attacking the friable stone that surrounded the unknown mass. The mass was enormous, half a meter thick, so solidly enclosed in the rock that it could not be budged. After an hour's labor, Georges succeeded in laying part of it bare; then he took a step back in order to assess it more accurately.

Suddenly, an idea illuminated his mind; he felt as if a frisson—the frisson of the sublime—was traversing his body from head to toe.

"Frantz! Frantz!" he cried, breathless with emotion. "Look! A fossil! An immense fossil!"

Frantz came over. "It's only a large stone," he said.

"A stone!" Georges exclaimed, indignantly. "A stone! It's a magnificent fossil, larger than all those in museums."

"Oh!" said Frantz, a trifle skeptically. Seeing that Georges was getting carried away, he added: "I hope that it is a fossil—but it's time to go home for dinner."

Georges did not sleep a wink. The next day, very early, in spite of heavy rain, he resumed his work. After great effort, he was finally able to disengage the so-called fossil. As he had bought the little cavern some months before, no one could interfere with his digging or contest his discovery.

Well, yes, it was a discovery! Fortunes are sometimes reserved for the humble. The enormous object was nothing other than a fossil bone belonging to a great Jurassic reptile, the existence of which no one had previously suspected.

Disinterring the remains was a difficult task. For Georges, it was delightful. He could have brought in workmen, but he preferred to take sole charge of the work. All alone, with an indefatigable ardor, he separated out the bones. As soon as dawn broke he was in the cavern, sculpting the monster's remains, and he stayed there until dusk, insensible to the wind and the rain. Every day brought a new discovery, a new joy. First the limbs appeared, then the colossal vertebrae, and then the enormous head, with orbits as large as immense cauldrons.

The worthy Frantz was amazed and delighted. There was no longer any other topic of conversation between the two men.

Six months of effort, six months of ever-renewed pleasures. The time passed quickly. Finally, the *Mirosaurus maritimus*—that was the name Georges gave it—transported piece by piece, could be reconstituted almost in its entirety. A shed was constructed in which the gigantic skeleton was installed. Standing on its four immense limbs and inclining its colossal head, the Mirosaurus was a truly fine sight. People came from far around to admire it, and Georges composed an explanatory treatise to describe the new species.

This treatise caused a sensation in the scientific world. There was a veritable revolution. For several years, the geologists who were piecing together the history of fossil saurians had always been confronted by a lacuna, an enormous gap, a horrid, gaping, shameful void between the Paleosaurians, whose jaws were straight, and the Archeosaurians, whose jaws were square. Well, the Mirosaurus had oblique jaws. That was the feature connecting the Archeosaurians to the Paleosaurians. The gap was filled in, the void eliminated. Thanks to Georges, the science of fossils no longer had a cruel lacuna. Thanks to Georges, the audacious hypothesis that Monsieur Lissardière had ventured in 1850, regarding the analogy of all the saurians, had been confirmed.

In spite of its triumph, the Mirosaurus remained modest. The poor deformed creature that had paraded its colossal body over Cretaceous beaches 100,000 centuries before, cared little about academic and Sorbonnean disputes. In spite of its success, it was always there, in the shed, silent and motionless, perhaps dreaming of times past and disdaining from the height of its great age the emotions of the young world that had reintroduced it to the benevolent light of the sun.

Neither Frantz nor Georges took much account of the polemics that the recognition of the Mirosaurus had excited in Paris. All that scientific kerfuffle was genuinely of little importance to them. Georges' joy was sufficient for Frantz, and the sight of the old fossil monster was sufficient for Georges. In contemplating his reptile, the honest fellow savored an unalloyed pleasure. At any moment of the day, he could go to the shed, feel the bones of the skeleton, polish them, touch them, run his hands amorously over the old carcass, wax ecstatic over the apophyses and the crests, inventing a new admiration with every passing moment.

Life had never been so sweet for our friend. Never had fortune smiled on him so much. Happy Georges! He did not seek to know whether he was happy. He lived without disputes, without anxieties, without chimerical aspirations. He did not philosophize; he did not reason—which is the best way of avoiding irrationality. He loved Frantz, his house, his cave and his Mirosaurus. No, none of that could betray him, and one could defy malevolent destiny!

The evening musical sessions, interrupted for some time because of the work necessitated by the Mirosaurus, had recommenced. Frantz's violin had never been so eloquent; never had the notes escaping quiveringly from the old instrument vibrated with so much force and gentleness. They were powerful sensations, ineffable tendernesses, enchanting dreams. If the Mirosaurus opened upon the infinite soul of the past, Frantz's violin opened stairways toward the infinity of the future.

As for the present, it still fled by, without disturbance and without sadness. The house in Martinville was upstanding, solid, sane and calm. Old Nonotte made sure that the curtains were very white and that good hot soup was always steaming at the appointed time in the earthenware bowls.

Months passed. Finally, in successive fragments, the Mirosaurus was entirely disengaged from its somber cavern. It could be photographed in its entirety, and Georges sent a print to Monsieur Lissardière, a member of two Académies, Professor of Paleontology at the École des Arts, etc., etc.

Monsieur Lissardière replied that he would come to Martinville himself, to study the remarkable specimen *in situ*. Georges and Frantz went to meet the great man at the railway station. They recognized him easily by the enormous rosette ornamenting his frock-coat. They introduced themselves; they greeted one another and headed, without wasting any time, for the Mirosaurus' domicile.

Monsieur Lissardière was a knowledgeable man, and, moreover, a clever one. He held five important positions, in his own right, with generous salaries. Nothing, however, could satisfy his ambition. Several positions were not enough for him; he needed them all. So, whenever a geologist happened by chance to be offered any official position, however modest, Monsieur Lissardière took it as a personal offense. He pestered successive ministers with acrimonious claims. In the offices of the ministry everyone knew him, from the concierge to the chief of staff. Everyone feared his complaints, but whether by virtue of weakness, dread or indolence, they kept their expressions straight and gave in to him.

He was, however, a fine speaker. He shone in the salons—but in no period of his life had he ever broken stones or scraped fossils. He left such fastidious work to his assistants; he did not like the minutiae of science, he said, and only took pleasure in powerful generalizations. To tell the truth, his assistants were veritable slaves; he gave them neither respite not leisure. It was hard work being an employee of Monsieur Lissardière, and he wearied the most patient—so he was forever

146

complaining bitterly about the disastrous individualist tendencies of the youth of today.

Such was the short, thin, pale and wrinkled man with the pretentious gestures and penetrating eyes who made his entrance at Martinville railway station, and immediately inspired in Georges a superstitious terror.

When he was in the presence of the Mirosaurus, he first inspected the jaw.

"Of course! It's oblique! What have I said? It's an archeopaleosaurian. I foresaw it, your fossil, in 1850. You've doubtless read my paper? It's oblique, perfectly oblique. It had to be, for I'd predicted it. It's a handsome specimen, a very handsome specimen."

He spent about an hour detailing the beauties of the Mirosaurus. Georges gave him two or three explanations which struck Monsieur Lissardière by their novelty.

The savant professor cast a rapid eye over the seashells, admiring them to an appropriate degree. What surprised him, though, was the new classification that Georges had worked out. Our friend was well able to defend it when Monsieur Lissardière attacked it, and the professor was astonished that, far from faculties and academies, in an obscure village, an ignorant petty bourgeois could have had so many ideas.

The morning was well spent. They went to table and had a long and plentiful lunch, as one does in the provinces. Without missing a bite, Monsieur Lissardière, took a greater interest in Georges than the Mirosaurus.

"Would you believe," said Frantz, "that the Museum of St. Petersburg has offered us 200,000 francs for our animal? We didn't want to sell it, though."

Monsieur Lissardière uttered a cry of amazement. "200,000 francs!" he exclaimed. "There's an object that has cost you dear!"

"That's true," said Frantz, "but it's our luxury."

Monsieur Lissardière looked at him sideways. The long-haired musician had displeased him from the start. "You're very rich, then?" he said.

"Enough to refuse ourselves nothing," Georges replied, smiling.

"And to desire nothing," Frantz added.

Monsieur Lissardière opened his eyes wide.

Eventually, he took his leave of the two friends. He gave Georges a vigorous handshake, bowed slightly, almost impertinently, to Frantz, and climbed up into the carriage that would bear him away to Paris, full of hope.

He slept on the way, but it was not of the Mirosaurus that he dreamed. In an enchanting dream, he distinctly saw the ideal son-in-law for whom he had been searching for a long time.

A few days later, Georges received a letter from Monsieur Lissardière.

The illustrious scientist lavished admiring epithets upon the Mirosaurus that he had been able to discover in the depths of a cavern. That discovery was celebrated as the most significant progress made in geology for 20 years. "You have," he said, in conclusion, "discovered that which I thought; who knows what you might be capable of doing henceforth, by following my counsel? Come to my home in Villeneuve-sur-Oise; we shall work together, and it will be easy for us to compose a quite remarkable treatise on the Mirosaurus."

Flattery is the most perfidious of intoxicating liquors; its perfume is so inebriating that it numbs, stuns and generates delirium in the most solid of heads. Georges had no difficulty imagining that he might become a great man. Surges of pride invaded him. No, truly, he did not belong in Martinville. A little beach is a narrow theater for a scientist of the first rank; was it appropriate to let great discoveries rot in a provincial hamlet?

A remote village; a few fishermen's huts; a rustic house; a failed musician! On looking around. Georges found that everything had shrunk. Even the Mirosaurus had lost a little of its prestige, and he could no longer adore it with the same blind affection.

After some hesitation, Georges accepted Monsieur Lissardière's invitation. Frantz accompanied him as far as Rouen. The musician had tears in his eyes.

"What will become of me without you, Georges?" he said. "Don't stay out there, at least. You're fine in Martinville—don't seek your fortune elsewhere. Oh, yes, glory! But there's more glory in the Mirosaurus' cave than Lissardière's villa. Then again, you're not made for people like that, my poor boy. You're a dreamer, a poet, an innocent—what will become of you in their Paris, in the midst of their intrigues and battles…?"

But he interrupted himself abruptly, accusing himself of egotism, and reproaching himself for thinking of himself when a great future was opening up for his friend.

What a surprise was waiting for Georges in Monsieur Lissardière's little house in Villeneuve-sur-Oise! Within a few days of his arrival in Monsieur Lissardière's home, he was far less interested in the Mirosaurus than in young Clotilde, the savant professor's daughter.

Once more, the master's perspicacity had not been found wanting. What he had found in Martinville was not merely a Mirosaurus that gloriously confirmed one of his hypotheses, but, even better, a son-in-law who might serve his glory. Truly, young Perron was the son-in-law he had been waiting for, rich enough for Clotilde to have all the nice things that only wealth can provide, intelligent enough to be a precious collaborator, and sufficiently obscure and docile for that collaboration to be silent and advantageous. With George, one need have no fear of the rebelliousness and ingratitude of the young disciples of the École des Arts, whose foolish vanity made them charge dearly for their petty services.

But Georges could not see so far ahead; he had no suspicion of these tenebrous machinations. He surrendered himself to sensations that were entirely new to him, which penetrated him delightfully. He put on a show of being interested in the diameter of the intermaxillary bones of the Archeosaurians and listened without complaint to Lissardière's dissertations, but in reality, no longer knowing what had brought him to Villeneuve, unresistingly obedient to the caprices of his vagabond imagination, he thought of nothing but escaping to rejoin Clotilde.

Clotilde was pleased by this homage. Strictly brought-up in an austere environment, she had grown up since her earliest childhood in the adoration of the parental individual. She had always heard talk of her father's great intelligence and high status. It was, in the Lissardière household, a fixed and indisputable verity that Monsieur Lissardière was a great man, and that everyone else ought to efface themselves before him. It was almost sacrilege to resist or contradict him. His words were gospel. Madame and Mademoiselle Lissardière accepted them without argument.

Several times already, suitors had offered themselves; they had been rejected. Even young Michenot, Monsieur Lissardière's best pupil and most devoted collaborator, had been sent packing, less for his lack of fortune than his vague inclinations to independence. Michenot evaded the authority of his patron, and Monsieur Lisardière was determined to have his son-in-law under his dominion, like his wife and daughter.

Georges had forgotten Frantz and the Mirosaurus. An unknown life was opening up to him. In the evenings, on the veranda, Clotilde would run her agile fingers over the piano, lit by two candles, while Georges, intoxicated by indescribable sensations, gazed at her and listened to her. Yes, this was true happiness!

And Clotilde, sensing feminine coquetry awakening within her, sometimes affected a joyous familiarity, putting more care into her manner of dress, teasing Georges regarding his savagery and the solitary life he had led on the shore of the Ocean.

After a fortnight, Georges fearfully perceived that the treatise on the Archeosaurians was almost complete, and that he would have to return to Martinville. Then he became desperate. He spent his nights tossing and turning in his bed, repeating all the words and phrases that had been addressed to him by Clotilde, constructing entire worlds on some banal interjection or insignificant remark. Sometimes he was full of hope; at other times, he was profoundly discouraged, sensing the enormous distance that separated the charming Clotilde, the daughter of Monsieur Lissardière, from the humble Georges Perron, amateur geologist, more than half bumpkin.

Meanwhile, Monsieur Lissardière followed Clotilde's maneuvers and Georges' hesitations with a keen eye. He decided to hurry things along. One morning, after a long session on Jurassic herpetology, he asked Georges point-blank whether he wanted to get married.

Georges stammered; it seemed to him that the ground had given way beneath his feet. He hesitated momentarily, not knowing what to say or do. He had to reply, though.

At the decisive moment, he experienced an instant of extraordinary clairvoyance. Like an unfortunate who falls into a precipice while measuring with a glance the depth of the abyss into which he is plunging, he understood that Lissardière had only brought him to Villeneuve to marry him off. He divined that Clotilde did not love him and never would love him. Yes, it would mean losing contentment and gaiety! It would mean leaving Martinville, and Frantz and Nonotte, to embark upon a miserable existence bristling with strife, worries, sleepless nights and joyless days.

He saw all that, and yet he felt himself weakening.

"Well?" demanded Monsieur Lissardière, smiling encouragingly.

And Georges, stammering, admitted that Clotilde was a superior woman, that he was assuredly quite unworthy of her, but that, after all, he must think of the future…

In brief, he asked for Coltilde's hand.

Monsieur Lissardière did what he had to do, coldly and affectionately. He weighed up the services that he, Lissardière, had rendered to science and the fatherland; he spoke about a successor worthy of him, and praised Clotilde's extraordinary intelligence to the skies. For his part, he held Georges in high esteem, but still, he must consult his wife and daughter. In sum, he asked for a week to reflect, and, in order to observe all the conventions, he enjoined Georges to return to Martinville to await Clotilde's response.

When poor Frantz heard the disastrous news, he uttered a dolorous roar. So that was why Monsieir Lissardière had dragged Georges to Villeneuve-sur-Oise! Into what an infernal trap, and with what cunning! In spite of his innate generosity, the worthy musician felt himself animated by a ferocious hatred against all the Lissardières, great and small.

But the roaring and the hatred did no good. Frantz was obliged to listen submissively to the tale of Georges' anguish, when he came back still enfevered by Clotilde's piano-playing and coquetry. Confusedly, in spite of his despair, Frantz understood that Georges was in the right. The bizarre association that had brought an old musician and a young geologist together under the same roof really could not go on indefinitely. It was an abnormal phenomenon, contrary to all custom, which, sooner or later, had to run into the hard reality of things and come to an end. By taking a wife, Georges would be reentering the common run of things, from which he should never have absented himself. His existence could not offend the common sense of his fellow citizens and contemporaries in perpetuity. It is not good to live otherwise than one's peers, and it is only decent, before getting too old, to return to the bosom of bourgeois routine.

The two friends felt, however, as if an invisible barrier had been erected within their communal intimacy.

"Don't worry, my worthy Frantz," Georges said. "I shan't leave you. Could we really draw apart? Is it possible that we could ever be strangers to one another? You will have two friends now, instead of one."

In speaking thus, Georges was lying to himself.

"Let's go see the Mirosaurus," said Frantz, after a pause.

The Mirosaurus was still there, solemn and silent, swaying its denuded head. Before the skeleton that reminded them of so many common joys, so many collective dreams and so many conversations, Georges and Frantz were penetrated by a bitter sadness.

O poverty of human thought! We do not know how to live. What should be our supreme science is the one of which we are most ignorant. When the present smiles upon us, instead of pausing, we think about the future. But the future does not keep its promises, and the present that has been happy is no longer any more than a memory. We can no longer recover the happy days of yesteryear. We shall no longer have those gigantic bones to disinter and classify. Amity, sweet amity, will never smile upon us again. "Madman thrice over," Frantz said to himself, "why did you not pause in the passage of those hours, so gentle, that you regret?"

During the week that followed, Frantz, against all expectation, continued to hope. Monsieur Lissardière did not reply. Who could tell? Perhaps he would refuse.

As for Georges, he no longer knew whether he ought to live in hope or dread. An immense lassitude overcame him. He no longer thought about anything. Every time he tried to pull himself together, the image of Clotilde came to trouble him. He saw her in the little house in Martinville, sometimes sweet and tender, leaning on his arm, sometimes haughty and imperious, imposing her will harshly, cleaning house, chasing away Frantz and Nonotte, sweeping the shells away, selling the Mirosaurus to the highest bidder. He saw all the Lissardières installed at the peaceful old hearth, importing the prejudices, passions, disgusts and idolatries of another caste. Sometimes, he heard a kind of insulting laughter; Clotilde rejected his advances scornfully. Then, seized by self-pity, he closed his eyes, as patient animals do which no longer resist the insults heaped upon them, tolerating blows in silence and awaiting a better destiny.

You have doubtless seen, from a river-bank, an unfortunate cork agitated by various currents. One wave carries it away, another brings it back, and the feeble object bumps into obstacles to the right and the left, ahead and behind, shaken in every direction, dragged along by the changing caprices of the flow, alternately sinking and surfacing, colliding with every projection, swayed by contrary eddies, eternally recommencing the same blind curse without reacting to those superior forces.

It was thus that Georges, thrown into the midst of the events, passions and conflicts of real life, allowed himself to be guided by things and people. Over the cork tossed by the waves he had the sad superiority of being able to reflect and meditate upon the agitations that drew him along.

It was not a letter that arrived; it was Monsieur Lissardière himself. He had come to Martinville to bring his provisional consent to the marriage.

"It's true that Clotilde is very young," he added, "but it's unnecessary to conclude the matter right away. While waiting, I've decided that it's necessary to come to Paris. If you follow my advice and direction, a fine future is in prospect for you. You will show me your drawings, your collections." He added, modestly: "I have some experience—at least, people are kind enough to think so—and I can be very useful to you. We shall work together, and, with me, you might do anything."

He said very little about Clotilde, though, and seemed scarcely to be concerned with anything but the immense labors that awaited Georges as soon as he had arrived in Paris—so our friend was more alarmed than satisfied. Frantz tried to put on a brave face, but, in spite of his efforts, he was unable to appear cheerful.

Before leaving, Monsieur Lissardière wanted to see the Mirosaurus again. "Let's take a look at my Mirosaurus," he said. "Yes, that's what it is. Admit that it's a fine discovery." And he admired the magnificent fossil with a paternal affection.

A few days later, Georges was in Paris.

He rented a small furnished apartment near the Sorbonne. The accommodation was ugly, dirty and cold, quite miserable by comparison with the little house in Martinville, but what did it matter? Was not Clotilde here, and would her sweet smile not chase away all the clouds?

In truth, he found Paris less frightening than he had had first thought. He discovered unfamiliar satisfactions there.

Monsieur Lissardière introduced him to a few eminent masters: Professor Valuzot, the director of the fossil museum; Monsieur Le Croquet, the engineer of several railways; Monsieur Durant, a superior employee at the ministry—that was his only superiority; Monsieur Riffard, a senator, considered by his family to be a genius of the first order. All these illustrious men heaped eulogies upon Georges; they took an interested in the Mirosaurus, affirming that it was a fundamental discovery and that after such a glorious conquest it was not permissible to bury oneself in a provincial hole.

All these eulogies resounded in Georges' ears and troubled him. It was an agreeable noise, a soft and sonorous harmony by which he allowed himself to be lulled. Truly, he was soon convinced. He deigned to believe what was said about is importance. He took himself seriously, observed himself, contemplated himself. In the street, he walked with a certain dignity, saying to himself: "The son-in-law of Monsieur Lissardière and the inventor of the Mirosaurus is certainly not just anybody."

He soon became acquainted with the great men of the capital. He was shown the exceedingly formal manner in which men are judged by success, in the opinion of society—Parisian society, of course. That was the real and enviable thing here, and one could not be happy if one was not well-placed in the opinion of society.

Georges was rapidly initiated into the mysteries of Parisian high society. He even received an invitation from Madame de Crussac, whose salon is the antechamber of al the Academies. Madame de Crussac congratulated Georges, and congratulated Monsieur Lissardière.

There was an enormous crowd at the salon, everyone greeting one another, detesting one another, bowing to one another, shaking hands and, once backs were turned, tearing one another apart. One would be too bored otherwise. Occasionally, the buzz of slander suddenly paused. There was a

155

celebrated virtuoso, the illustrious Raggiletti, who was playing a symphony; then everyone listened. The symphony was one that Frantz loved. How many times Georges had heard it back home! As the celebrated Raggiletti developed the melody, with strange contortions, Georges felt himself gripped, as he had been in Martinville, by a sort of exaltation. All the flatteries, the engaging words, went to his head life a deadly blast. Their bitter perfume had intoxicated him. He told himself that he was able to do better than all the marionettes surrounding him; that one day, he too would have positions, salaries, medals, that people would come from one end of the salon to the other to greet him, to admire him, to congratulate him. This was no longer, as it had been by the Ocean, a vague aspiration toward a mysterious future, toward an ideal and ungraspable science; it was a sort of ambitious rage, a determination to succeed, to crush rivals, to dominate an elite assembly—to be, in a word, like the great Lissardière family, into which he was entering triumphantly.

He felt pity for the humble condition of the people of Martinville. Was it possible to live like that, semi-fossilized, in an obscure village? Martinville was nothing but a hamlet, a tongue of land lost in the waves. Glory would not seek out anyone there. Glory was in Paris, in Madame de Crussac's salon. What good did it do Frantz to play his divine melodies? There was only Nonotte, the Mirosaurus and the seagulls to hear them. But Raggiletti, what a marvel! He was surrounded, congratulated; ladies of the first rank were giving him an enthusiastic ovation; journalists were there, who would make the name of Raggilletti famous tomorrow, and spread its echoes throughout the civilized universe.

To begin with, Georges had been full of ardor; he visited museums, followed courses, listened, while taking notes, to Monsieur Lissardière's savant lessons. Now, however, his zeal has relented; the hope of a vacancy at the École des Arts finds him less enthusiastic.

That vacancy is an invention of Clotilde's. For the first time, Clotilde has not shared the opinion of her father, and, although Monsieur Lissardière does not approve, she has convinced Georges to apply for one. In the meantime, in order to be nominated, it is necessary to take an examination for which the preparation is long, difficult and fastidious. Sulkily, Monsieur Lissardière has promised to put in a good word for his future son-in-law with the assessors, but it is still necessary not to appear too ignorant.

So Georges has shut himself up in his study. He re-reads chapter LXVII of the *Traité des coquilles*. He gets up and walks around the room, numbed and sickened by the monotonous reading. He has forgotten Madame de Crussac's salon, and tells himself that the *Traité des coquilles* is a high price to pay for the honor of being seated to the right of that illustrious lady on gala days. The weather is superb; it is one of the first fine days of the summer. From his window, Georges can see students walking gaily in twos and threes, chatting. The trees have that spring greenery that is so charming after winter stripped bare. The orchestra in the Luxembourg sends forth gusts of joyful sonority.

Chapter LXVIII: Distinctive characteristics of the Brachiopods of the lias.[48]

"What are you doing at this moment, my poor Frantz? Perhaps it's low tide, and you're doubtless walking in the rocks, amid the seaweed that the tide has just abandoned. You're watching the flow of the limpid streams heading out to sea; the pools are slowly emptying; the little crabs are hiding under stones. Don't forget our old cavern, with its seashells, though. One never knows whether someone else…"

Chapter LXIX. Distinctive characteristics…

The door opens suddenly. It is Monsieur Lissardière.

"Look," he said to Georges, showing him a newspaper, "this will make you rejoice! You've been given a dispensation from the examination; in a fortnight, you'll make your debut at the École des Arts."

---

[48] The lias is a group of strata identified in Britain, extending from the late Triassic to the early Jurassic.

An immense sigh of relief filled Georges' breast; with an indescribable satisfaction, he closed the *Traité des coquilles* noisily and shoved it away. He was no longer listening to Monsieur Lissardière, who was talking about his influence, the benevolence of the minister, and the considerable importance of a debut at the École des Arts.

"Oh yes," he said to Georges, "it's necessary to do me honor, my friend. You know that I always have 400 people at each of my lectures; you need no fewer. I'm counting on you. You'll draw your own glory from it, of course, but you'll have to work. Hold on, here's the exact *Traité des coquilles* you need, on your table—you'll find all the necessary information in that excellent work."

Alas, Georges understood only too well. It was the end of contentment, of repose, of patient and obscure research. And for what? Must he grow pale spending long hours over that odious book?

"You haven't thought of thanking me," said Monsieur Lissardière, with a hint of discontent. "It's a very good appointment, though, my dear Georges, and everyone will envy you. Think about it: that's worth some gratitude, damn it! You don't have a degree from the École des Arts, and it's an exceptional favor to be given a dispensation from diplomas. Here you are, introduced to a position without having passed through the twists and turns of the hierarchy."

And Georges was obliged to thank Monsieur Lissardière.

The decisive moment—the opening lecture at the École des Arts, that is—approached with fearful rapidity. Georges had never spoken in public, and he trembled at the idea of confronting the 400 auditors of Lissardière's course in the great amphitheater of the École des Arts. How should he make his entrance? How should he explain the principles of Jurassic paleontology? How should he begin? Georges was paralyzed by terror in advance; a cold sweat and little shivers overcame him when he thought about the solemn moment of his arrival in the lecture-hall. 400 listeners—perhaps 400 enemies?

Sometimes, though, he became more hopeful. He looked at himself in the mirror, studied the rhythm of his first sentence, and draped himself in his dressing-gown to judge the effect produced. Then he cast his eyes over the list of the professors who had taught at the École des Arts in the last two centuries, and found the most illustrious names in France there. He swelled up with a vast pride then, when he thought of the immense honor of succeeding all those glorious masters.

He passed from triumph to despair and from despair to triumph.

He was no longer living any but a feverish, insupportable life. In front of Monsieur Lissardière he put on a brave face, and feigned all the confidence that he did not have, but when he found himself alone, he was unable to hide his anxiety, his discouragement or his anguish. Sometimes, he shared his dread with his fiancée. With some hauteur, Clotilde reassured him, but only half-heartedly. Involuntarily, she felt herself gripped by a sort of disdainful sympathy for the poor young man—the pity that kills affection more effectively than the bloodiest offenses.

To lift Georges' spirits, a spectacular success was needed. There was, instead, a spectacular failure.

When he appeared in the amphitheater he was welcomed very coldly; the young students of the École, well known for mockery, had already made a joke of the Mirosaurus. Like a stone falling into a pond, the sudden arrival of this provincial had raised up a concert of indignation and jealousy. Monsieur Lissardière's assistant, Monsieur Michenot, who had passed all his examinations with flying colors and had his eye on the chair of the École des Arts, had fomented a kind of cabal. All his friends were there; a dull hostility was circulating through the assembly. A caricature was passed from hand to hand in which the Mirosaurus, decked in a miter, was solemnly blessing Georges and Lissardière.

Perhaps, by force of eloquence and knowledge, Georges might have been able to avert the storm, but from the very start he was nervous; he stammered, said silly things, and talked about Monsieur Lissardière, his illustrious master. When he pronounced the word *Mirosaurus*, he was interrupted by a gale of laughter. Then there was a profound silence, during which Georges thought that such a torture was worse than death. He tried to summon up his courage and stammered a few inconsequential words; the audience laughed and shouted. Then our unfortunate friend, suddenly sensing the enormity of the disaster, left the room in the midst of booing.

Thus began and ended Georges' first and last lecture at the École des Arts.

On this occasion, Monsieur Lissardière's conduct was truly inexplicable. He did not seem saddened by his pupil's failure. When Clotilde came to inform him of the deplorable outcome of Georges' lesson, he could hardly conceal his satisfaction.

Poor Clotilde! In spite of the sage advice of her father, she had wanted to see Georges triumph; on arriving early in the great hall, however, she had sensed such a current of enmity passing through the crowd that she had not dared to stay. She had retreated into a small adjacent room, where the usher had offered her a chair. From there he could follow nearly all of what was happening in the amphitheater; she therefore heard the initial silence, then the laughter, then the booing. Powerless and shivering, she witnessed the miserable abortion. Then she saw Georges, defeated, haggard and bewildered, crying like an infant.

"Poor boy!" she murmured.

A few days later, there was a long discussion between Monsieur Lissardière and his daughter. Clotilde wept, declaring that she would not consent to be Madame Georges Perron for anything in the world. Monsieur Lissardière, by contrast, defended Georges.

"He won't be a professor right away, but don't worry; his time will come. You really aren't being very kind to the excellent fellow, who would throw himself in the fire for you."

Clotilde gave in, but her respect was lost, and her confidence was dead.

Georges too felt that something within him had broken. He knew that Clotilde had witnessed his distress, had seen his humiliation. That was unforgivable. From that ill-fated day onwards, he could not face Clotilde without a certain dread. *She despises me*, he thought. His manly vanity and his scientific pride both suffered.

As for Monsieur Lissardière, he was entirely consoled. A few days later, he offered to take Georges to Villeneuve. There was a new geological horizon at Villeneuve itself, difficult to grasp in its details. It was necessary to set Georges to work. They would see there of what the inventor of the Mirosaurus was capable; and, since he was not cut out to be a great professor, it was necessary to find out whether he had the rare qualities of a scrupulous and sagacious observer.

The two geologists left for Villeneuve, therefore. Initially, Monsieur Lissardière took part in the excursions; then, as he was not interested in details, he stayed home reading his journals while Georges roamed the countryside. Our friend left at dawn and walked all day. He did not return until the evening, at nightfall. Then he listened in silence to the fastidious dissertations of his savant collaborator, refraining from opposing them by a single syllable. Then, when dinner was over, fatigued by his labors, he went to sleep in his chair.

Those long marches through the fields were Georges' consolation. The École des Arts and the *Traité des coquilles* had not entirely filled the geologist with disgust. He found some pleasure in exploring the rich fossil strata in the environs of Villeneuve. He resumed breaking rocks, shifting stones and examining shells. He carried a bag and a hammer with him, and as time passed, took pleasure in comparing the specimens that hazard offered to him. In this way, he made a local collection that grew quite rapidly. He devoted himself to it ardently, disdaining the useless lumber of books, and recovered in vigorous and omnipotent nature his self-respect and love of great things.

Every time he interrogated Monsieur Lissardière he was surprised by the insufficiency and the sufficiency with which his master judged everything. He preferred chatting to the peasants and field-workers, simple rustic folk, perhaps coarse and intellectually uncultivated, but who, at least, did not crush him with the weight of their incontestable superiority. He let them speak, taking an interesting their lives, their mores, their tastes and their observations; he laughed wholeheartedly at their jokes. Let Professor Lissardière and his colleagues to mock such deplorable simplicity.

Most often, Georges set out on his own, but sometimes he took with him a worthy man to whom he had taken a shine. He was a Breton, a former mariner, whom the hazard of various circumstances had washed up as a domestic servant in Paris. Pierre knew nothing about geology, but he loved to accompany Georges. He listened with religious admiration to the minute details that his master gave him regarding fossil seashells. Together, they searched in clay or chalk for Terebratulas, Cerithiums and Pectens, excited by their discoveries. Then Georges talked about the ancient terrestrial ages. He explained the sequence of living things; he explained how they developed according to deterministic laws, improving as they became more distant from their initial origins. And he abandoned himself to inspiration. He no longer dreaded seeming vague or dull, and he would have swapped all the crafty and skeptical students at the École des Arts for that naïve and docile listener.

When they returned, bending their backs beneath the weight of their specimens, they strode along the long white highway. Then Pierre, to alleviate the tedium of the road, would relate his travels—his voyages to Senegal, in Oceania, to Chile—his ocean crossings, punctuated by petty events: catching a shark, salvaging a ship, passing through a cyclone. He recounted these slender facts with infinite detail. Georges listened attentively, and the two men—simple souls, evidently—forgot the social barrier erected between them.

After a month or so, the work was nearly complete. Georges drafted a substantial account of what he had observed. He added a few sketches to it, and gave the whole to Monsieur Lissardière. The professor seemed quite satisfied.

"Very good, my dear Georges," he finally said. "We've done some truly fine work, and it will create a stir in Paris."

Instead of returning to Paris, Georges would rather have gone to Martinville, if only for a few days, in order to see Frantz and Nonotte again, but Monsieur Lissardière opposed it.

"What are you thinking, my dear chap? What about your marriage? This isn't the moment to go out there. We have other things to do than make music with your old German!"

Georges' marriage had now been announced publicly. Monsieur Lissardière treated him almost as a son-in-law, telling him what he wanted and tracing out a whole plan of conduct for him—including, among other things, the necessity of disposing of the Mirosaurus.

Poor Mirosaurus! It was the source of all Georges' glory, and the young man's heart sank at the thought of abandoning his old friend. Yes, it was almost a dirty deed to get rid of that faithful companion, that modest and indispensable auxiliary. Has one the right to be ungrateful to things, any more than to people?

It was Clotilde who was most insistent, criticizing the poor skeleton relentlessly. One evening, there was a sort of family meeting at which the fate of the Mirosaurus was debated. Weakly, Georges defended his fossil against Clotilde, who attacked it bitterly, mingling her mockery with practical considerations and the full force of a bourgeois reasoning that evaluates things at their exact material worth.

"A skeleton worth 200,000 francs is a luxury befitting a millionaire, but you're not a millionaire. An extra 10,000 francs of income is comfort, while the Mirosaurus is almost poverty. Then again, is it really so beautiful? At the Museum, you can find many more remarkable, which cost nothing, and you can look at them at your leisure."

163

And all these dry words, with an irrefutable logic, chilled Georges' heart, all the more so because he had no reasonable response. He felt vanquished, not convinced, and there is nothing more painful than being put in the wrong when one feels, deep down, that one is right.

Georges had to do it. Although the rebellion of his wrath was growling dully in his heat, he obeyed. He wrote to Frantz—it was, moreover, the only letter he had written to his friend—and Frantz, without any vain recrimination, meekly sent the Mirosaurus away. Need it be said that he shed a few tears as he packed the fossil's bones into a dozen large crates? The Mirosaurus was now, alas, the pride of the Museum of St. Petersburg and the joy of Kramalasov.[49]

This time, Georges' love was entirely interred. The departure of his beloved Mirosaurus completed the destruction of what remained in his heart for Clotilde. And yet, he dared not admit to himself that it was all over. Perhaps did not even know what he thought. He scarcely had time to think. Monsieur Lissardière had reduced him to the status of a slave or a liegeman; he granted him neither distraction nor pleasure. Writing to his dictation, drawing diagrams, doing research in libraries, visiting some scientific conference or other, attending great ceremonial dinners—such where the only occupations permitted to our unfortunate geologist.

It was the gala dinners, most of all, that were unbearable. He imprisoned himself in an imperturbable silence, noting in passing all the stupidity and nonsense that were spoken in front of him, sensing that he was regarded as a kind of curious animal, called an imbecile and a poor wretch as soon as the dinner was over. But that scarcely bothered him, and he rendered all those poseurs scorn for scorn.

---

[49] This reference is enigmatic, although it might be a mangled version of the Krasnoselsky district of St. Petersburg. The museum in which the Mirosaurus would have been installed is presumably the Kuntzkamera.

Monsieur Lissardière, however, affected a great admiration for his pupil and future son in law in public. He freely admitted that Monsieur Perron was an exceptional individual—a slightly primitive scientific mind, to be sure, but one whose genius was ahead of its time.

"He's a man who makes discoveries," he added, "and I wouldn't be surprised if he finds us something someday that will turn science upside down!"

Science! Well, no. Georges has renounced science. He has understood, perhaps a trifle belatedly, that she is a person of easy virtue, easily seduced by a promise or a caress. She is cold, bad-tempered, pitiless, and one must sacrifice everything one loves to her, for a long time, in order to obtain a few insignificant favors in return. No, science is not for Georges. He likes quietness, tranquility of mind; he detests effort, and he detests boredom even more. He would rather read La Fontaine's fables than the *Traité des coquilles*. He prefers an excursion to the beach at Martinville to the most savant deductions of Monsieur Lissardière and his friends.

The aberration that took hold of him in Madame de Crussac's salon has quit him now, and forever. Monsieur Lissardière's laurels no longer prevent him from sleeping. He thinks mad ambition pitiful; he tells himself that he is, in sum, a peasant, and a peasant he will remain.

When Monsieur Lissardiére's affairs were concluded, he wandered around Paris. There, instead of collecting seashells, as in Martinville, he collected ideas—sad ideas, moreover, although they sometimes made him smile bitterly. He went through the streets, lingering in front of shop windows, causing passers-by to elbow him out of the way, contemplating all that feverish activity—the impassioned movement carrying all those frenzied individuals to their work or pleasure—with disdain.

Alas, nothing is forgotten in the human soul; and everything that has existed in our consciousness, as at the surface of the sea, if only for a second, leaves an indelible trace. The fit of ambition, temporary as it had been, had cast a kind of foul leaven into Georges's soul. He was no longer the same man as before. The cheerfulness and insouciance of times past had not returned. All his thoughts were now mingled with a bitter sentiment. In the vastness of Paris he felt his inferiority, his humility, his weakness. He saw himself small and unknown, lost in that human ocean. The name of Perron had slipped back into obscurity. A chocolate-maker with his posters is better-known—which is to say, more famous—than a scientist who has discovered a Mirosaurus.

Oh, how he regretted the happy time when he had nothing beside him but the blind tenderness of old Nonotte, the passionate friendship of Frantz and the compassionate deference of the fishermen of Martinville. How sweet is the odor of seaweed compared with the stink of the faubourgs! And he had left it, that seaweed! He had left his fishermen and his old Nonotte and his worthy Frantz—to run after a chimera, he had abandoned his life, his good life full of serenity, sweet dreams and tender affection!

What strange inertia holds him thus, chained to this detestable existence, far from his beloved Martinville? Georges curses himself 20 times a day, indignant at his cowardice, the manner of his weakness, which insults and rebukes him without being able to give him any energy. Why does he remain, since neither glory, nor science retained him? Now, when Georges sees Clotilde, he no longer blushes and trembles, as before, with delightful and invincible fright. The banal handshake on arrival and departure is as cold as an obligatory politeness.

The wedding date has not yet been fixed. Georges is in no hurry. He no longer resists Monsieur Lissardière; he has abdicated. He does what his master commands; his will-power has been annihilated by a will more powerful than his own.

One day, satisfied with the docility and intelligence of his pupil, Monsieur Lissardière finally told Georges that the moment had arrived, that it was necessary to prepare for the great event, and that the invitations could be sent out.

Georges attempted a few words of gratitude, and as he had not yet penetrated his own sentiments, was astonished not to find more delight in his heart. That evening, he went to pay his first official visit to his fiancée.

When he entered the drawing room, there was no one there yet. While awaiting Clotilde's arrival, he began riffling through the newspapers strewn on the table and the scientific journals that Professor Lissardière received. Suddenly, he made an angry gesture, and abruptly threw away the *Revue* that he was holding, crumpling it slightly.

At that moment, Monsieur Lissardière came in. He seemed even more self-satisfied than usual, and he extended his hand to his future son-in-law with an authentic bonhomie full of condescension.

Georges was pale, and his lips were trembling. His attitude was so confused that Monsieur Lissardière was taken by surprise.

"Don't worry—Clotilde is coming."

Instead of replying, however, Georges picked up the inopportune *Revue* he had just thrown down and turned it this way and that.

"Have you read my article?" asked Monsieur Lissardière.

"I've read it," Georges replied.

"Well, do you like it?"

Georges did not reply. The professor scowled.

"If you have any criticisms to offer, don't hold back, my dear chap! You should know, however, that the entire scientific press has adopted the conclusions of my research at Villeneuve."

"You mean our research," said Georges, boldly.

The breath of revolt was blowing through him; an immense indignation was swelling within him. All the servitude and humiliation of recent months was returning to his heart. He felt as if he were transformed. It was no longer his master and father-in-law, the illustrious professor, who was before him, but a rival, a plagiarist who had taken from him the most cherished thing in the world dear, which is thrice sacred: the supreme consolation of the scientist and the artist—which is to say, the honor of a labor accomplished. Such authorial pride is unfathomable. Georges, humble and hesitant a short while before, was now an intrepid aggressor. The weak sometimes have these audacious impulses.

"Our research, then," said Monsieur Lissardière, pinching his lips. "But we do not share in it equally; since I'm the one who provided all the ideas, it's only just that my name alone should be attached to it."

"How can you say that?" Georges replied, exasperated. "Don't you know that they were my ideas as much as yours? Even…"

He stopped.

"Well, speak," Monsieur Lissardière replied, having become pale in his turn, trembling with anger. "Say it…"

But Georges did not say anything. He tried to control himself, without succeeding in stemming the seething flood of indignation that was rising up in his breast.

"Is the Mirosaurus yours or mine? Your friends and your journals talk about it every day. But to hear them, it seems like your discovery; everyone affects to forget who made it. I'm not very important, to be sure, but at the end of the day…"

"You're an ingrate," Monsieur Lissardière interjected, in a resounding tone—for he also felt stifled by indignation. "Who were you when I took you from your village, to bring you here, to give you lessons—which I've never done for anyone else—plucking you from the obscurity in which you were buried, introducing you to the foremost scientists in France, giving you my daughter, my beloved Clotilde? Who were you, Monsieur Perron? And this is how you repay me! No, truly, such conduct…apologize to me, or I shall never see you again as long as I live."

"Apologize?" Georges exclaimed. The audacity of the man disconcerted him. Him, the spoiled, the enslaved, the crushed, apologize to his tyrant! Such courage was beyond his strength. He remained silent.

Monsieur Lissardière strode back and forth around the drawing-room. "My poor daughter," he murmured. "My poor daughter!" Georges' ingratitude appalled him—but, remembering the magnanimity of which he had given evidence with respect to that wretch, he admired himself. "Look," he said to Georges, after a long silence. "You've had a moment of aberration. For my daughter's sake, I'll take pity on you and forgive you."

"Monsieur Lissardière, Monsieur Lissardière," Georges relied, with restrained rage. But he could not find anything to say; his anger was choking him. "Goodbye," he said. And he left.

What should he do now? Against Monsieur Lissardière, against Clotilde herself, against Paris and all the scientists in Paris he felt animated by a ferocious, inexhaustible hatred. He had acted without calculating the consequences of his action. Yes, it was a rupture! Yes, it was the end of all his dreams of glory and love! Well, no matter. He had but one idea: to leave behind—far behind—the diseased atmosphere that had weighed upon his life like an odious nightmare for a year.

Then, as if impelled by a superior force, half-awake and half-asleep, disdaining the opinion of the world, he walked to the station and boarded a train that was about to depart.

A whirl of trees, houses and bridges pass before his eyes, flying past at top speed. Finally, the train stops. Here is Martinville. He recognizes all of the places where he spent his life, his lovely life of yesteryear: the station, the presbytery, the bell-tower, the main street—and, at the far end of the main street, in the distance, he perceives a little white house. One last effort, and he has arrived. He knocks; no one answers. He knocks more loudly; a light appears and footsteps are heard on the sand.

"Who's there?" says an uncertain voice.

Thank God, it's Frantz! "Frantz, Frantz—it's me!"

And Frantz and Georges are in one another's arms.

A few days later, Monsieur Lissardière hosted a great dinner-party. He had never been as triumphant. He had just been named president of an important official committee charged with organizing the fossil Archives of France. It was that appointment that was being celebrated. Over dessert, the name of Georges Perron was mentioned.

"Don't speak to me about that man!" said Monsieur Lissardière, with virtuous indignation. "He's an ingrate!"

Everyone smiled; then they talked about something else.

Meanwhile, out in Martinville, the Sun was setting—a beautiful October sun fading away into the ruddy mist extended over the Ocean. Frantz and Georges were rummaging into the grotto of the Mirosaurus again. They had picks in their hands, and numerous pieces of debris were cluttering the ground.

It was Georges who paused first. "It's over, my poor Frantz. There's no more Mirosaurus."

"Patience," said the worthy Frantz. "We'll find something, we'll find something."

"Alas, it wouldn't be the same."

They sat down and contemplated the sea. The sublime spectacle delighted them; they had no need to speak to understand one another, and, remembering past misfortunes, they shook hands.

Thus their life passed; no troubles saddened them; no dissent drove them apart.

Georges did not spare a thought for Clotilde or marriage. He devoted his attention to his collection of fossils, which grew by the day. He discovered two Ostreas whose structure was extremely curious, and he sent a paper to the Paleontological Society of Calvados. The Parisian Societies were too scientific for him, and he dreaded prompting some other Lissardière to come to Martinville.

In the evening, in the old dining-room with the wooden dressers, gently rocking back and forth in his armchair, he listened to Frantz's violin singing the harmonies of the old masters. Then Georges dreamed while awake.

He has made a great discovery that has turned science upside-down and opened up a new world; all the scientists in

170

Europe come to admire his work and listen to his lectures. Hundreds of listeners hang on his every word, following the progress of his thoughts.

Then the scene changes. Another dream, just as beautiful, inflates his heart with pride. He is in Africa, in regions burned by an implacable Sun; he is the leader of a little band of valiant men; he has conquered immense lands unknown to other men and planted the tricolor flag in those barbaric regions.

Sometimes, again, he sees himself as an omnipotent minister, reforming the laws and institutions of France, reversing abuses, unmaking hypocrites, confounding the envious, followed by a shivering Assembly.

Often, too, there is a theater auditorium, shining with light. The prettiest women in Paris, the most seductive actresses, cluster around him; the curtain goes up; people listen, stupefied with admiration; frantic applause bursts out from all sides, and the name of Georges Perron is greeted with shouts of enthusiasm.

Frantz has stopped; the music falls silent, and all those chimeras fly away. Georges finds himself back in Martinville, a bumpkin as before.

"What a pity!" he murmurs.

But Frantz does not reply. He knows that one does not forgets glory, once one has imagined that one might possess it one day. He knows that illusion is sweet, but that reality is bitter.

Charles Epheyre: *Professor Bakermann's Microbe*

A Tale of the Future
(1890)

In the latter days of the months of December 1935 Professor Hermann Bakermann returned joyfully to his lodgings, striding through the streets of the little town of Brunnwald as rapidly as his generous girth would permit.

He was rubbing his hands as he walked, a sign of profound satisfaction—a legitimate satisfaction, for, after long labor, Professor Hermann Bakermann had finally found the means of creating a new microbe, more redoubtable than all the known microbes.

It will doubtless be remembered that in the last half-century, microbial science had made extraordinary progress. In the mid-19th century, a celebrated Frenchman, Louis Pasteur, had proved that certain minuscule creatures exist, which penetrate surreptitiously into the bodies of humans and animals. He had called these perfidious parasites "microbes." He had even indicated ingenious methods of recognizing them, collecting them and cultivating them. Now, in 1935, the works of Pasteur had been long surpassed. Obedient to the impulse provided by the master, all the scientists of Europe, America, Australia, and even Africa, had set to work. Thanks to them, the most difficult problems had been clarified, the most obscure problems resolved; there was no longer any disease that did not have its microbe, labeled, classified and stored. The forms, the behavior, the habits and the tastes of all terrestrial, marine and airborne microbes were known, and microbial science had become the basis of medicine in all the universities.

In Germany, as elsewhere, mores had changed considerably in the last 30 years. The reign of the spiked helmet had finally come to an end. The professors and the scientists had resumed their place in the sun; they no longer trembled before a beardless corporal, and the ancient German customs, honest and peaceful, had succeeded the regime of the saber.

That was why the noble town of Brunnwald possessed a brilliant university, sumptuous laboratories and excellent professors. Now, none of these masters had more zeal or talent that the celebrated Hermann Bakermann. At an early age he had flung himself impetuously into microbial science; later, having become a professor, he had been able to construct the laboratory of his dreams. It was there that he spent his life. Disdainful of his patrons, he lived amidst his flasks and his culture media, surrounded by the most powerful and most deleterious viruses.[50] In order not to be infected by his poisons, however, he had taken all the necessary precautions. By means of a skillfully graduated series of vaccinations, he had eventually rendered himself almost invulnerable, with the result that his health did not suffer at all for that existence passed entirely amid the germs that afflicted poor humankind.

However, as not everyone in the world was as well-protected as he was, Professor Bakermann had taken care to construct, at the extremity of his laboratory, a special room, to which he jokingly referred as the "infernal chamber", which he did not permit any other human being to enter at first. This little room, heated and lit by electricity, was equipped with powerful disinfection apparatus, and the prudent Bakermann never came out of it without first purifying himself with the most active antiseptic fumigations.

As he went home that day, then, Professor Hermann Bakermann was content. The problem that he had sought in vain for such a long time to solve had finally received a simple solution. The means of rendering harmful microbes inoffensive were known, but that was only one aspect of the problem.

---

[50] When this story was written, the terms "virus" and "bacillus" were considered interchangeable, no fundamental distinction yet being possible between different types of "microbe."

Bakermann had found a means to render inoffensive microbes harmful.

When we say "harmful" we do not mean to imply mildly harmful, but terrible, overwhelming and irresistible. The microbes presently known only kill in a day, half a day at the worst, and are also possessed of a fragile vitality. It does not take much to attenuate them or render them harmless. The problem, therefore, was to have a virus powerful enough to kill in an hour, at a dose of a hundredth or a thousandth of a drop, in such a manner that no living creature could survive it. Above all—and this was the most delicate part—the terrible microbe must be very resistant, incapable of allowing itself to be weakening by intemperances of climate or the medications that artful humans were inventing incessantly.

Gradually, Bakermann had succeeded in making his great discovery. "A microbe," he said in his course, "is like a human being. We humans need a varied diet. We need soup, sauerkraut, beer, caviar, butter, cakes, mutton, fish, lobster, pâtés, honey, almonds, fruits, sardines, Rhenish wine, champagne, potatoes and kummel. Our health improves as our alimentation becomes more sophisticated and more complicated. Well, microbes have the same needs as we do. Let us give them a very varied and rich nourishment, and we shall make them increasingly vigorous—which is to say, energetically malign, for the vigor of a microbe is proportional to its destructive power."

So, all Professor Bakermann's concern was lavished on the confection of his culture media. In this respect, he could have given tips to the best French chefs. In his latest medium, he had found the means of introducing 87 different alimentary substances, and the microbes within it were developing with a truly prodigious vital intensity.

We cannot enter into detail here regarding the famous scientist's scientific techniques. At any rate, thanks to improved culture media and certain electrical procedures that he was still keeping secret, Bakermann had profoundly transformed a vulgar microbe, the microbe that turns butter rancid—very widespread, alas!—by submitting it to a whole series of complicated cultures, and he had made it into an extremely nasty microbe.

A hundredth of a drop killed a large dog in two and a half hours, and a single drop could kill 3000 rabbits in two hours. It goes without saying that Bakermann had not been able to try it out on such a large quantity of rodents, but he had caused a considerable number to perish, to the great indignation of Frau Bakermann.

Frau Bakermann? Well yes, there is no life that does not have some secret distress, no fruit that does not conceal a poisonous worm, no rose that does not have an unfortunate thorn. For the illustrious Bakermann, the poisonous worm, the treacherous thorn, was Frau Josepha Bakermann.

Frau Bakermann had never understood microbial science. Every time the unfortunate scientist tried to talk to her about it, she looked at him suspiciously.

"What good is all this fuss about futilities that make everyone laugh? Instead of going to the theater or for a walk, you shut yourself up in an unhealthy room with rabbits, toads and pigeons! Is that a job for a man who respects himself and his wife? If only you imitated Dr. Rothbein, who, while being just as much of a scientist as you, makes ten visits a day and is paid 20 marks for every one—but you're incapable of making a simple pfennig. You're nothing but a poor man, Bakermann, and it's me who tells you so; I'm astonished that there's a single student on your course, for you only know how to tell them the same story over and over again."

In brief, Frau Bakermann detested microbes.

She hated something else too: that was the tavern.

All the greatest men have their faults, and, on searching hard, one will always find a defect, a stain or a weakness in the best of them. Professor Bakermann had his weakness too; it was the tavern.

All things considered, Bakermann's conduct was excusable.

Drinking tankards of good beer one after another, in a joyful row, with cheerful comrades, while playing a hand of piquet or discussing the condition of Europe and the progress of microbial science, is certainly more agreeable than listening all evening long to bitter recriminations regarding the exorbitant price of rabbits, the high cost of the exquisite foodstuffs that it was necessary to buy to nourish the microbes, the uselessness of delicate thermometers that cost 100 marks, and the necessity of having a fur cape like Frau Rothbein, or Oriental door-curtains in one's drawing-room like Frau Scheinbrunn, the president's wife.

When Bakermann had succeeded in getting to the door without being seen, he was saved. He only came back very late, with his head a trifle heavy and his face crimson, but quite satisfied, and submitted, without saying a word to an avalanche of bitter words. He even—which is a terrible thing to say—got used to it, ending up only being able to go to sleep to the sound of lamentations and invective.

This evening, however, as he went home, Bakermann gave no thought to his wife. He was thinking about his terrible microbe.

"I've found it…I've found it!" he repeated to himself. "Yes, I have it. Oh, the brigand! It's given me enough trouble! But what shall I call it? It's necessary to give it a name, for every new microbe must be given a name, and this one is definitely a new microbe. It can almost kill at a distance. Ah! Yes, that's it! That's it! *Mortifulgurans. Bacillus mortifulgurans.* That has a really fine ring to it!"

"Ah, there you are!" cried Frau Bakermann. "Not bad. 8 p.m.! Did you even look at the time? I thought you weren't coming back—and that wouldn't have been any great pity."

"Calm down, Frau Bakermann," said the worthy man, "And get ready to rejoice, for I'm bringing you good news."

"Really?"

"My word, yes—very good news, and very important. You know, my dear, what I've been seeking for such a long

176

time, the microbe that kills rabbits in two hours, at a dose of a thousandth of a drop…"

Poor Bakermann, with a perseverance worthy of a better fate, stubbornly told his wife about all his scientific experiments, and the snubs that he met with every time had not yet discouraged him.

"If you think I'm going to listen to your nonsense! Yet another stupidity! Isn't it pitiful! At your age!"

"But, Frau Bakermannn…"

"Come on, it's dinner time—and no tavern today, you know. I know all about your accursed microbes. Every time you claim to have made a discovery—a discovery!—you take advantage of it to spend the night drinking with good-for-nothings like Rodolphe Müller and Cesar Pück. I warn you, thought, that I'm not in a patient mood tonight."

I can see that, Bakermann thought, sighing.

Nevertheless, he did not lose all hope, for Frau Bakermann often fell asleep after supper, and Bakermann took cowardly advantage of that respite to get away.

Bakermann ate with a good appetite, therefore, and paid no heed to Josepha's threats. She, becoming increasingly irritated, to a great extent than ever before, told her husband quite bluntly that if he went out, she would cause a scandal; that she would go to his sanctuary—which is to say, his laboratory—and even to the infernal chamber itself, in order to carry out a search.

"It's there, I'm sure, that you're hiding Eliza's letters."

Bakermann contented himself with sighing and raising his eyes to Heaven.

Eliza was a servant girl that Frau Bakermann had once been obliged to sack, for she suspected her husband of kissing the little rogue on the sly. We do not know to what extent the accusation was justified, but it was still the case that, as soon as Eliza's name was pronounced, Bakermann lowered his head and was unable to make any reply.

"Yes, Eliza's letters! That's certain. What's become of her now? She hasn't left the town, and you're still seeing her.

Frau Scheinbrunn told me that she's been seen in a silk dress and pearl earrings."

Bakermann did not breathe a word, and tried to distract himself by repeating: *Bacillus mortifulgurans!*

"Guess, Josepha, what name I have given it!" he suddenly exclaimed. *"Bacillus mortifulgurans.* Eh? It's a good choice, isn't it? My colleague Krakwein is capable of making a disease of it!"

"I'm sure," Frau Bakermann continued, "that you still write to her. A girl who is always badly coiffed, a liar, a glutton, a debauchee…"

"Wife!" Bakermann groaned.

"I'll go to your accursed laboratory—yes! I'll go and I'll search everywhere, and I'll find the proof of your wretched conduct.

"Wife, my dear wife," Bakermann murmured, "you mustn't do that. Remember that my *mortifulgurans* is there, and that I alone can enter the infernal chamber without danger. If you knew all the precautions I take. Think of your health, your precious health, my darling."

Deep down however, he scarcely took any notice of Frau Bakermann's threats. Almost every evening, there was the same anthem, and thus far, Frau Bakermann had never dared cross the redoubtable threshold of the infernal chamber.

Later, Frau Bakermann, wearied by quarrelling, dozed off in her armchair.

My word, Bakermann thought, *it's not far from here to the tavern. I'll go along to say good evening to Cesar Pück and tell him the great news. I'm anxious to have his advice about the* mortifulgurans. *Josepha's well away for an hour, and she'll still be asleep in the same place when I get back.*

With that, walking on tiptoe and making himself very small, Professor Bakermann went into the hallway, put on his coat and hat, and went out.

Once he was outside, he uttered a deep sigh of relief, and smiled involuntarily at the thought of the tavern when Cesar Pück awaited him.

Cesar Pück, Valerian Grossgeld and Rodolphe Müller were, indeed, there, faithful to their posts. They uttered a joyful hurrah on seeing their illustrious friend arrive.

"I can see that there's news!" exclaimed Pück. "You're wearing your finest smile!"

"Yes, indeed!" cried Bakermann. "Boys, I have my microbe, and I call it *mortifulgurans*."

"Bravo!" said Müller. "I knew that you'd get there in the end. But you mustn't rest on your victory. Do you know what you ought to look for now?"

"My word, no!"

"The bacillus of good humor—and you can try out its effects immediately on Frau Bakermann."

"That would, indeed, be a glorious success," Bakermann murmured. "But we're here to talk about cheerful things. Come on—a tankard! And let's get the party started!"

Beer had never been so exquisite, nor a game of piquet so interesting. With insolent good luck, Bakermann won as often as he could have wished. Aces and kings flooded his hands. In the meantime, tankards were emptied effortlessly, while pipes and laughter kept pace.

Time passed, though. There was always one last tankard, one last hand, one last pipe, to the extent that Bakermann finally drank to the health of *mortifulgurans*.

In the end, he had to leave his friends—but his head was heavy and his gait unsteady…

Frau Bakermann was in bed, asleep or apparently asleep. He wasted no time in contemplating her, and, without even bothering to get undressed, lay down to sleep the profound sleep of the triumphant.

About 6 a.m., however, he was forced to pry an eye open. Frau Bakermann was shaking him violently.

"Hermann!" she was saying, "Hermann!"

He pretended not to hear—and, in fact, hardly could hear, for the fumes of the beer were still numbing him with their thick shadow.

"Hermann! Hermann!"

"Can't you let me sleep?"

Frau Bakermann was gripped by atrocious pains. She was sitting up in bed, very pale, with haggard eyes.

"Ring for Theresa, my darling," he sighed. He pulled the bell-cord, and then went back to sleep.

But Frau Bakermann's suffering was getting worse. Theresa, the chambermaid, was scared when she saw her distraught face. A livid December dawn appeared in the windows.

"Sir, sir!" Theresa cried. "Madame is very ill! Very ill!"

This time, Bakermann woke up completely. Yes, truly, Frau Bakermann was very ill.

"Go fetch Dr. Rothbein immediately," he said to Theresa, "and go to the pharmacist's to get morphine and quinine."

Frau Bakermann now had very cold hands, a purple face and terribly dilated pupils.

"Josepha! Josepha!"

"My love, my love," she said, in a soft and feeble voice, "forgive me...for I sense that I'm going to die, and that I've brought it on myself. I've been...I've dared..."

"What have you done?" demanded the professor, gripped by anguish.

"You know...the infernal chamber! The infernal chamber! Well..."

"Well? Speak! Speak!"

She could not say any more. A frightful spasm sealed her lips.

"The infernal chamber," murmured Bakermann. "Speak, Josepha, speak, I implore you."

But Josepha was no longer able to reply. She had lost consciousness. Spasms of agony were agitating her icy limbs. Then she fell into a profound torpor.

At that moment, the doorbell rang. It was Professor Rothbein, Bakermann's friend, famous for his irreproachable diagnoses. He examined the sick woman for a few moments, and shook his head despairingly.

"Well?"

"Be brave, my friend, be brave."

"But what is this rightful malady?" Bakermann ventured to say.

Rothbein reflected momentarily; then, after a further scrupulous examination, he said: "This is an extremely rare malady, which is almost never seen in Europe. It's the koussmi-koussmi of Dahomey."

"Really!" said Bakermann. In spite of everything, he felt relieved of a great weight, for he felt overwhelmed by a secret terror that he dared not admit to himself.

"It's koussmi-koussmi," Rothbein repeated, firmly. "My dear Hermann, there's no mistake about it. Everything is there, and the symptoms are obvious: the suddenness of the onset, the pallor of the face, the dilation of the pupils, the spasms, the chill, the torpor…"

He would have continued in that vein for some time, if Frau Bakermann had not rendered up her soul at that moment.

It was 8 a.m. Everyone in the house already knew the disastrous news. Little Theresa, as she went to the pharmacist's, had not been able to prevent herself from telling the story to two or three of her peers. A crowd had begun to gather, and the cause of the illness as already being discussed.

As for Bakermann, he was plunged into a profound distress—but his distress was nothing compared to his anxiety. Rothbein's coolness and self-confidence had diminished a few vague dreads…but Josepha had mentioned the infernal chamber. Why?

Suppose, in a fit of absurd jealousy, in order to search for Eliza's letters…

Unable to bear the terrible uncertainty, he ran to the laboratory…

The door of the infernal chamber was open, and Bakermann perceived, to his horror, that someone had opened the microbe cupboard and rummaged through the flasks! An imprudent hand had even knocked over one of the phials in which the terrible *mortifulgurans* was growing.

This time, no further doubt was permissible. Yes, in spite of her husband's solemn instructions, Frau Bakermann had dared to penetrate this redoubtable refuge, and had knocked over a bottle of *mortifulgurans*!

At all costs, it was necessary to avert greater misfortunes. A terrible microbe had taken possession of Frau Bakermann's body, and now, by a rapid contagion, it was going to reach the entire town. He had nothing to fear himself—he was too thoroughly vaccinated to be affected—but the others…the others!

Bakermann shuddered at the thought that Rothbein, Theresa, the neighbors and their wives were going to fall victim to *mortifulgurans*. And who could tell how far it might go? Herman Bakermann's thoughts dared not take that frightful supposition to its conclusion.

Bakermann raced home and began a thorough disinfection of the house. Alas, what good would it to?

Indeed, at 10 a.m., Theresa began to suffer from an intense headache. Then there was a great shiver, followed by spasms. After two hours, the malady had made terrible progress, and the unfortunate Theresa expired at midday.

With a dry eye, Bakermann witnessed her terrible death-throes. Yes, it was definitely *mortifulgurans*. There was no possible doubt; all the anticipated symptoms were there, and none was lacking. What vitality there was in the microbe, though! In spite of his anguish, Bakermann could not help admiring, with all the pride of an artist, the conquering march of his microbe. As soon as it had penetrated, it triumphed. In three hours, it was all over. First the nervous system, then the respiration, then the temperature, then the heart; it was methodical, punctual, inexorable; neither quinine nor morphine could do anything. Yes, certainly, *mortifulgurans* was tenacious and irresistible, and all the physicians' drugs could not defeat it.

What could be done now? Halt the propagation of the disease? That was impossible. Let it continue its victorious march, then? This was insane—a monstrosity surpassing everything imaginable! Bakermann knew his *mortifulgurans*. He knew that nothing could make it retreat. It was a true microbe, that one, as superior to others as electric light was to a miserable candle. So be it! The die was cast! *Mortifulgurans* would spread throughout the world!

That evening, there had already been 17 deaths in the town: the pharmacist's apprentice at 3 p.m., then Rothbein at 4 p.m., two of the pharmacist's customers at 5 p.m., four of Rothbein's clients and five of the pharmacist's at 6 p.m., plus four neighbors—the same ones that Bakermann had seen chatting to Theresa that morning.

The local newspaper announced the outbreak of the fatal epidemic in these terms:

We regret to inform our readers that a disease, originating in the Orient, has fallen upon our industrious city. At the time of going to press, 17 deaths have already been recorded, and our specific information allows us to affirm that there are a great many sick people in various parts of the town. The illness comes on suddenly, and kills in a few hours, defying all therapeutic resources. It is probable that it is caused by a microbe that none has yet been able to study; but according to competent authorities, the malady is none other than koussmi-koussmi, a kind of infectious disease rife in Dahomey. One can only speculate as to the manner in which koussmi-koussmi was able to reach Brunnwald. The facility of communications between Africa and Germany offers some slight explanation of that propagation, but why have the intermediate countries not been affected? These are questions that our hygienists will soon be able to resolve...

Whatever the case may be, it is a matter of a redoubtable evil. We are counting on the science of our physicians to avert it, and in the good sense of our people not to abandon themselves to vain panic.

Meanwhile, Professor Bakermann had plunged into a profound despair. The death of a wife is certainly cause for grief, but Frau Bakermann was mortal, after all, and in the end, one ends up being consoled. What was horrible, defying all expressions of horror, was the extension of the epidemic.

183

He tried to reflect, but his head was whirling. What could be done, since *mortifulgurans* was invincible? Ordinarily, in an epidemic, not all those affected die; there are individuals who escape. Perhaps physicians are able to cure some of them; some people contrive to avoid the contagion. Above all, the malady comes to an end; the microbe ends up becoming less redoubtable, becoming attenuated, and thus less and less dangerous. Here, though, there was no hope of anything similar. *Mortifulgurans* would not be attenuated. On the contrary, it would gather new strength as it was disseminated throughout the world. It was too vigorous, too robust, too well-constructed to weaken. The human species, retreating before it, would be driven to extinction!

A terrible unprecedented battle was joined in Bakermann's soul. No mortal, in all probability, had ever felt such a heavy, crushing responsibility weighing upon him. If only a solemn confession could avert the disaster! But no, a confession would be futile. Whether he spoke or remained silent, the epidemic would run its course, so why speak? Yes, why? If a loud public confession would save a single victim, certainly! But it would only serve to render the name of Bakermann permanently shameful to future generations—provided that any human beings were able to survive *mortifulgurans*. Future generations? Bakermann smiled bitterly, as he thought that, thanks to him, there would be no future generations.

Besides, he thought, *is it really* mortifulgurans? *Rothbein had no hesitation. He immediately affirmed that it was koussmi-koussmi. Why should Rothbein not be right? Why contradict him, and become one's own executioner? It is a culpable presumption for a lone man to claim to know more than the masters of a science. They have pronounced sentence—well then, their verdict is irrevocable: it is koussmi-koussmi. And after all, if I speak, I won't save anyone. I shan't say anything! I shan't say anything!*

In spite of all this reasoning, the voice of conscience was stronger. "Bakermann," the voice said to him, "you are lying to yourself. You know perfectly well that your wife died of *mortifulgurans*, that there is no koussmi-koussmi, that you are the sole cause of the terrible epidemic that is going to cause the disappearance of all humankind. If you want to diminish the atrocity of your crime, it is necessary to confess it freely. Be an honest man, Bakermann, for, if you keep silent, you are the most frightful villain to whom the earth ever gave birth."

He went out. He felt the soul of a great martyr within him, and he had made a heroic resolution.

Yes, he wanted to drink the chalice to the dregs. He had an enemy, a mortal enemy: Professor Hugo Krankwein, his rival in microbial science; a short, bald man with a grimacing, ferrety face, very knowledgeable and very envious. It was to Krankwein that Bakerman would confess his crime.

Krankwein lived alone in an isolated suburb. He opened his own door—but he recoiled in fright when he was confronted by the distraught face of his colleague.

"In Heaven's name, is it really you?"

"It's me," sighed Bakermann. "My wife died this morning."

"Yes, I know," said Krankwein, raising his eyes to heaven. "The poor woman was one of the first victims of the koussmi-koussmi."

"Don't talk about koussmi-koussmi!" cried Bakermann. "There is no koussmi-koussmi! There's only *Bacillus mortifulgurans*!"

Well, well! thought Krankwein, not without some satisfaction. *The poor fellow's gone mad.* "Come on, my dear colleague," he said, gently, addressing Bakermann with the kind of slightly-scornful patience that one has for children and invalids, "I know the horrible story. Dear Frau Bakermann had bought an Oriental carpet that came straight from Dahomey; no more was required, alas!"

"There is no koussmi-koussmi, I tell you!" Bakermann cried. "Can your koussmi-koussmi kill a vigorous and healthy man in three hours? Can it strike without remission? Can it resist quinine and cold baths? No, a thousand times no, it's my microbe, I tell you, my *mortifulgurans*, that killed Josepha."

185

Krankwein smiled. "My dear Bakermann, pain is leading you astray; *mortifulgurans* is a dream of your sick imagination, and the situation is too grave for us to linger over implausible hypotheses."

"Hypotheses!" roared Bakermann. "Hypotheses! Do you know what you're saying? *Mortifulgurans* exists. I created it, brought it out of nothing. I constructed it in its entirety, unassailable, irresistible, defiant of medicine and doctors. I've kept it in my phials; by means of it, I've poisoned Frau Bakermann, Rothbein, Theresa, and 500 others! And you talk to me about hypotheses!"

"Calm down, I beg you, my dear colleague," sighed Krankwein. "Look, tomorrow morning, if we're still alive, I'll come to visit you, and you'll realize that you aren't being entirely reasonable."

"Don't you understand, then, that *mortifulgurans* has no effect on me…!"

He had hardly finished the sentence when he had a sudden flash of inspiration. It was a dazzling lightning-bolt—one of those sublime and grandiose conceptions that cast their blinding light over the entire soul.

"I've got it! I've got it!" he cried. And, without bidding farewell to the stupefied Krankwein, he precipitated himself into the street, bare-headed.

Thank God! thought Krankwein. *Bakermann has gone mad. He certainly wasn't strong before, but now he's veritably insane.*

With that, Krankwein went to bed. He too was vaccinated against all epidemics, and had no fear of koussmi-koussmi. The fate of his fellow citizens was of very little interest to him. As for *mortifulgurans*, he had the misfortune of not believing in it.

In the middle of the night, in the desolate streets of Brunnwald, one might have seen a man walking with great strides, his hair in the wind, gesticulating and talking aloud, without paying any heed to the snow that was falling thickly or the thick, cold slush that was covering the pavement.

"I've got it! I've got it!" Bakermann was repeating to himself. "Of course! My *mortifulgurans* has been cultivated on negative electricity; positive electricity ought to kill it instantly. It's fatal, absolutely fatal, as certain as two and two make four. With positive electricity, it will be destroyed, annihilated, pulverized instantly. It will become as harmless as it was in the beginning, when I extracted it from rancid butter. What am I saying? It will be even more harmless. And people will live; they'll have nothing more to fear. With positive electricity, the world will be saved, and humankind won't end, and he name of Bakermann will be gratefully celebrated by innumerable future generations—for there will be future generations! Let's go, Bakermann—to work! You've done harm, but you alone can repair it. To defeat *mortifulgurans*, it requires no less than the man who gave birth to it."

Meanwhile, the epidemic was making giant strides. To begin with, in the town of Brunnwald, it had broken out everywhere. In almost every house there was at least one victim, and the victims immediately fund themselves in desperate straits. No remedy interrupted the march of the scourge. The consternation was universal. No one dared leave home any longer. The administration, with its invariable foresight, poured torrents of phenol all over the town, which steam pumps distributed in the streets.

The news brought by the telegraph was very grave. On the morning of December 23, in Berlin, ten cases of death were reported, disseminated in various quarters. A traveler who had left Brunnwald in a third-class carriage had contaminated the seven travelers in the carriage with him, and all of them had succumbed, leaving behind them the contagion of the terrible scourge.

The rapidity with which the accursed microbe developed prevented all preventive measures; there was no possibility of quarantine, or closing borders. In 12 hours, with superheated steam trains, one could go all the way from Cadiz to St. Petersburg; it was no longer the 19th century, when it was difficult to travel more than 60 kilometers an hour. In one night, therefore, the entirety of Europe was poisoned.

The town of Brunnwald was half-annihilated. Vienna and Munich already counted a few fatalities, and were probably infected at all points. Paris, London, Rome and St. Petersburg were invaded, without anyone being able to prevent the invasion, and the current evaluation was that the entire human race would be doomed within 48 hours. It was enough to make the greatest heroes shiver.

Bakermann, however, was not afraid. He no longer dreaded *mortifulgurans*. He worked unrelentingly for the greater part of the night, and in the morning, at dawn, the astonished inhabitants of Brunnwald were able to see an immense poster what had been set up in the market-place, which read:

PROFESSOR BAKERMANN CURES KOUSSMI-KOUSSMI BY MEANS OF ELECTRICITY!

If Bakermann had made use of the term koussmi-koussmi, it was by virtue of a craven condescension to the general opinion. In fact, the public, the newspapers and the scientists were talking about nothing but koussmi-koussmi; any other name would have been incomprehensible. Not without bitterness, Bakerman had resolved to employ the vulgar expression, which had become unanimous.

He regretted the term *mortifulgurans*, which he had chosen himself, lovingly—and, after all, he had a right to give his microbe the name he preferred—but he had given way, for it was a matter of making known without delay the victorious treatment that would stop the scourge in its tracks.

A large platform was established on which were set chairs, sofas and even beds. An electrical conductor led from this platform to an immense battery. The negative electricity, which invigorated *mortifulgurans*, went from there to ground, but the positive electricity, which was fatal to the microbe, went entirely into the platform. People climbed up to the platform—its dimensions were sufficient to allow 15 of them to take up positions there at their ease—and after a few seconds, they were charged with positive electricity. They could then repel the infection.

The first sick man to take his place on the platform was Cesar Pück. He was suffering atrociously, and his livid limbs were prey to atrocious convulsions. He was hoisted up on to the platform, in the presence of Krankwein, who was smiling sarcastically, and all his afflictions immediately ceased. The cramps, the spasms and the chill disappeared in a matter of minutes as if by a miracle. The moribund face of worthy Cesar Pück became joyful and smiling, as of old.

On seeing this result, which he had anticipated, but about which he had still had doubts until a demonstration had been given, Bakermann was overwhelmed by joy. There had been too much emotion in such a short time, and he lost consciousness.

He was brought round eventually. Soon, the whole world knew about the miraculous cure of Cesar Pück. The news spread in the blink of an eye. In less than half an hour, all the Brunnwaldians knew that Bakermann had cured koussmi-koussmi with electricity. Electrical batteries and platforms modeled on Bakermann's were set up everywhere. By noon, there were no less than 50 large positive electricity platforms actively functioning.

The death-rate diminished very rapidly. Between 9 and 10 a.m., there were 435 deaths; that was the maximum. By 11 a.m., the figure had declined to 126; at noon it was no more than 32, at 1 p.m., eight, and finally, at 2 p.m., there was only one—that of a stubborn old physician who would not hear mention of the electrical treatment, saying that it was stupid, that in Dahomey koussmi-koussmi as cured without electricity, and that he, Meinfeld, was too old to swallow the so-called discoveries of modern science.

There was now tranquility in Brunnwald—but what a disaster further away! The telegraph brought frightful news with every passing minute. At the very moment when, thanks to the positive electricity platform, the population of Bunnwald was entirely reassured, there had been 45,329 deaths in

189

Berlin, 7542 in Vienna, 4673 in Munich, 54,376 deaths already in Paris, and 58,352 in London.

In brief, there had already been a total of 684,539 deaths in Europe.

The Americans, on hearing news of the frightful scourge, had implemented precise measures to prevent its propagation to the new world. The fleet had been placed on a war footing, and they had taken the heroic resolution to get any ship trying to force entry with cannon-fire and torpedoes loaded with tetranitrodynamite.

Desolation reigned. Everyone was repeating that the end of the world had arrived. A large number of individuals, preferring a rapid death to the anguish of the painful and invincible malady, killed themselves in order to escape death. All business was suspended. There were no more railway trains, no more boats, no more police and no more administration. Few crimes were recorded. Some ordinarily-peaceful people went crazy, greeting tradesmen who tried to get into their homes with revolver shots. Human savagery, latent in us all, had regained the upper hand. The civilized world, so proud of its civilization, had become barbaric again, as in the early days of humankind. It was a reversion to the paleolithic era, perhaps earlier.

The telegraph, however, was still functioning, well enough that by noon, the whole world could be acquainted with the fact that a cure for koussmi-koussmi had been found—that a celebrated professor at the university of Brunnwald had, by a stroke of genius, discovered a means of opposing the terrible disease. Bakermann! Bakermann had invented a treatment for koussmi-koussmi! It was sufficient to place oneself for a few minutes on a platform charged with positive electricity.

The news spread with prodigious rapidity. That same evening, in all localities throughout Europe, great and small, immense electrical platforms were at work. Floods of positive electricity spread over the terrestrial globe. Everywhere, colossal machines, gigantic electrical piles, were installed in public squares; everywhere, the marvelous effects of positive electricity were manifest.

Thus, mortality decreased as rapidly as it had increased.

Koussmi-koussmi had met its master. The epidemic, which might have caused humankind to disappear, had proved once more that human genius finds no obstacles, and that rebellious nature is always tamed by the superior forces of human science and intelligence.

There were a few victims, to be sure, but all administrations had been subject to such overcrowding—3000 applications for a single job—that the petty bloodshed, though certainly dolorous for a few families, was, on the whole, rather beneficent. Once the alert was over, koussmi-koussmi could hardly be considered a veritable calamity.

In Brunnwald, Professor Hermann Bakermann bathed in full glory. Telegrams flooded his home. A few sovereigns deigned to thank him personally, for sovereigns value their health as much as, if not more than, other men, and with good reason. Bakermann therefore received great honors: the Orders of the Garter, the Bath, the Golden Fleece, the Black Eagle, the Red Eagle, the White Elephant, the Green Dragon and the Thistle. The name of Bakermann, which had not emerged until then from a small circle of initiates, became the greatest name in science in the space of half a day.

Modestly, he savored his triumph. He welcomed with frank cordiality a deputation of notables and students who wished to congratulate hm.

"My God, my friends, I had a good idea, that as all. Your gratitude is sweeter than any reward."

Even Krankwein came to pay him a visit. "Well, my dear colleague," he said, sourly, "you're a great man now! Admit, though, that you were lucky. If Frau Bakermann hadn't received her Dahomey carpet, there wouldn't have been any koussmi-koussmi in Brunnwald, and you wouldn't be so proud."

In all the countries of Europe, a subscription was organized to erect a statue to Bakermann. Several millions were

191

amassed in less than a day, and the committee decided that the statue in question, ten meters tall, should overlook the public square in Brunnwald.

In spite of his glory, however, Bakermann has no vanity or mad pride. He has resumed his cherished research in his beloved laboratory, and he is working away there, doggedly. He no longer has any fear of the infernal chamber. It is open day and night, and any curiosity-seekers can go in.

In the evenings, he returns to the tavern. Thanks to *mortifulgurans*, no one now prevents him from drinking tankards to his heart's content, so he prolongs his partying with Cesar Pück and Rodolphe Müller until dawn. He certainly has the right to give himself a good time now and again, after such terrible anguish and such a service rendered to humankind.

But there is no perfect, irreproachable happiness in this world. Professor Hermann Bakermann still has one great annoyance: he regrets the term *mortifulgurans*, and every time the name koussmi-koussmi is pronounced in front of him, he pulls a face—for he knows full well that koussmi-koussmi does not exist, and that a wrong has been done to the microbe made and reinforced by him. Nevertheless, he finds some consolation in trying to make a better *mortifulgurans*, more vigorous, more invincible than the first, whose irresistible effects no electricity, nor any medication, known or unknown, will be able to combat.

Paul Adam: *A Tale of the Future*
(1893)

I

Philippe sensed in his uncle's letters a plan to marry Philomène to Commandant de Laclos. The extreme anguish that
gripped his heart in consequence astonished him at first. His
cousin was five years old her than he was. Besides, she had a
serious turn of mind, and she was certainly unlikely to approve
of the turbulent ways of a cornet in the Guides, which is what
he was.

By virtue of this reasoning, however, and as the Colonel,
in his correspondence, dissipated any hope of a refusal, Philippe became accustomed to dolor. The image of the young
woman watched over the torture of his amorous spirit pitiless-
ly.

Now, here he is, devoid of strength, sprawled on the cushions of the railway carriage. Dully, he follows the meager
gestures of the Colonel, attentive to the 100 little boxes
brought to the capital, which contain the wedding presents.
How is it that neither the Commandant nor the Colonel perceives his despair? How did they not see him turn pale when he
entered the Guides' mess brandishing the permission obtained
from the general "to attend a family wedding"?

They do not notice anything: neither the atrocious taut-
ness of the smile with which he replies to their joyful remarks,
nor the sweat that chills his temples and the leather of his police helmet.

The Colonel is even going peacefully to sleep.

Through the windows, the passing countryside makes the
memory of the hours of that same voyage, previously undertaken with her, more precise. His uncle had come to collect him
from the École Militaire after the final examinations, and dur-

ing that journey, she had appeared to him to be an extraordinary individual, knowledgeable in all the sciences and making unexpected judgments on the world.

"Yes," replies the Commandant, "unexpected judgments. She has studied everything, has she not, while isolated in that fort to which her father's position attached him? There's no longer a wall in her home that isn't covered in books..."

"This is the heart of our fatherland, Commandant, she'll tell you...this very spot, where the ferruginous soil reveals itself by that slope suddenly surging forth in front of the flat factory buildings...."

"The heart of our northern republic? Look how it rises up, that ground, toward the pale firmament of mists. On the horizon, it gradually covers up the smoking chimneys of distilleries and forges."

"Has she told you about her love for the poor?"

"She has an extraordinary love for the poor."

"Here, she said, at this height, the pasturage is better because the mass of the land muffles the sound of industrial bells, the appeal to the quotidian suffering of the herds of workmen..."

"She's one of the elect, Philippe, one of the elect. Shall I be able to make her happy enough?"

They examine one another; they listen to their silence.

"The plateau!" says the Commandant.

There, the ground seems to have leapt up all of a sudden from the plain browned by labor, and in its leap to have drawn up chalk cliffs, inaccessible crags, clumps of pines and birches, patches of meadow, and entire beech-wood, and even a few villages huddled in cavities full of ferns and holm-oaks.

"Did you know her mother?"

"No, Commandant, I didn't know her mother. She died so young!"

"Philomène resembles her, spiritually. Her mother was always contemplating her idea of God; she contemplates the world's pain as well..."

"Christ—the same Christ in two forms..."

"Mystics! Look, here's the plateau displayed above the land…the earth is red with iron ores…"

"Oh! Doesn't iron flow like blood, all red…"

"You don't say! The earth is so red that the people, by dint of working it, have taken on the same color…"

"Oh, I get it…she told you that too—that the little children hereabouts already bear on their red bodies the blazon of the metal that provides their livelihood."

"Why that bitterness in your voice, Philippe?"

"No reason, Commandant…no reason. We've reached the region of Blast Furnaces, with its pit-villages full of people and flamboyant keeps."

"Look—it forms a great circle extended within a fixed perimeter."

"Beneath the cannons of the octagonal city, whose ramparts are there, at ground level."

"Prudence is necessary, Philippe, with these poor people, for they sometimes get exasperated."

"Are we getting out? We're going past the claustrophobic little houses where the families of magistrates, tax-collectors civil servants, and whatever live."

"Wake up, Colonel! A 40-minute stop, for the customs. We're going to stretch our legs…"

"Eh? What?" says the Colonel. "Are we at the frontier?"

"Very nearly. You know the place well—it's the last station before the Fort."

"Damn! Look—to the left, the red brick house…where you can see the primroses in the little flower-bed, eh? That's the executioner's house."

"Ah! The executioner's house. There are many murderers, because there's no enough food."

"Then again, the people lack distractions…"

In fact, Philippe thinks, *if the features of my face do not change at all, nor reveal my pain to their eyes, it's because I'm exaggerating my suffering. It's necessary to believe that misfortune won't crush me. Even so, it's as if there were stones in my breast when it rises to take in air…*

195

They go for a walk.

At the pinnacle of the rococo cathedral, the divine symbol of torture, the iron cross, imposes its significance upon the narrow, hard streets through which the life of the city is circulating. They lead from the belfry, rigid within its stony lace, to the barracks and the brothels, to a theater modeled on Greek architecture, to a Louis XV courthouse, to a hospital in the Empire style, a vast and simple prison solely ornamented with a few nasturtiums kept in a window-box by the wife of the concierge. Closer to the citadel, they encounter military depots and storehouses, and young beardless soldiers who, in their long tightly-belted greatcoats, resemble servant-women in skirts, and officers with spurs and moustaches, as round as eggs or as slender as ears of corn, with short riding-crops under their arms.

Broad, well-swept and lit by electric bulbs, the boulevard cuts through the city between sumptuous department-stores, which alternate with the headquarters of insurance companies, metallurgical companies and banks. Gentlemen are strolling there, evidently proud of their cares, and women eager to love, for the benefit of their purses or their hearts. Workmen laden with bales, and slightly drunk, are running back and forth. The fabric of dresses is neatly arranged in the carriages.

The boulevard leads out of the city to the railway station. After that, it becomes a highway following a route almost parallel to the railway. Trains go through the Blast Furnace region quite rapidly, passing between human beehives made of burnt bricks, red tiles and cement....

The Colonel resumes his nap in the right-hand corner.

"There, Commandant, look at that," says Philippe. "The children swarming over the earth—one might think they were a swarm of flies crawling over dung."

"Oh, Philippe, why talk about children like that?"

"The linen that hideous old women is washing in the tub...oh!...it's tearing. What a heart-broken expression! In truth, that linen has torn all the way to my heart."

"Why are you talking like this?"

"You have to laugh, though, at that exceedingly busy mother...all at the same time she's breast-feeding, wiping a nose with one hand, delivering a slap with the other, scolding with her mouth and rocking a cradle with her foot, making eyes at the porter who's passing by. Those little girls whimpering as they pick vegetables, or fetch water from the well—laugh at their ugliness! And the adolescent girl knotting dirty ribbons in their thin hair..."

"Philippe, why are you looking at the world through black glass?"

"There are no old people to be seen, Commandant, in this city of the poor..."

"No, that's true...there are none to be seen..."

"But there are little square cemeteries everywhere...one, two, three..."

"The adults are not to be seen, either, Philippe."

"Apparently, they all live within the enchanted flame that roars among the screams of the metal, beneath the domes of the factories..."

"The bars also seem to be full of pipe-smoke..."

"Pain is numbed by brutalization..."

"She told you that too, Philippe—Philomène told you that...and now you're reflecting her soul almost as much as her little sister Francine..."

The cornet turns round. He looks out of the carriage window. The plateau becomes a hump-backed strip of rocks. Giant ferns are growing there. Gradually, the terrain becomes greener. Trees cluster. Iron trellises keep pheasants in the hunting-grounds. Along their length, in order to prevent the birds from getting out, little boys are whistling. The chilly air turns their hollow cheeks purple. A guard is keeping an eye on them.

The forest is about to begin. It is already overflowing the hills on the horizon. Meanwhile, the screams of the metal pursue the train's flight. When they die away, the train is already going through a region bordered with birches and ash-trees, punctuated by clearings in which herds of deer are lingering.

Abruptly, the train emerges from the branches. The forest stops dead. The express glides over the crest of a rock that plunges steeply into a profound valley full of villages whitening the edges of woodlands. From nearby into the far distance, a river curves, its waters cramped by the frequent arches of bridges.

The rock forms the spur of a long narrow plateau, which has become the defensive point of the fatherland overlooking the frontier river. In addition, rounded mounds cover the strategic earthworks of the Fort. Steel cupolas are mounted on the rock. Brickwork blocks the caverns. Electric wires run from tree to tree. Soldiers emerge from subterranean tunnels through posterns. Ravines are the location of barracks in which artillerymen are quarrelling, their gibes raising echoes upon echoes.

At the tip of the rock there is a garden in front of a white house, and an iridescent jet of water above a shallow bowl, where the Colonel-Governor's daughters, clad in polka-dot dresses, are counting the primroses newly emerged on the lawn that morning.

"Hello, Philippe," she says, and adds in a whisper: "We sensed your sadness as it approached…"

II

The soldiers are attaching lamps to masts along the patrol-routes. Flags replete with the names of victories are hoisted. Veterans are teasing the monkeys brought from Asia by Commandant de Chaclos' troops, who are celebrating their success in the Oriental lands this evening. The fort is host to 1000 singular animals: hairless dogs, domesticated ibexes, loquacious parrots skilled in the recitation of barbaric poems. Trophies have been constructed out of strange weaponry, reminiscent of jagged scythes, curved sabers covered with damascene-work, breastplates of iron and lacquer-work. Captured standards bearing crescent moons and magical dragons float over triumphant arches made of fir-branches. Patriotic songs ring out in canteens full of people, and painted paper lanterns dance in the wind.

In the Colonel's house, they are finishing dessert. As the night is preparing to display the light of all its stars, the windows are open. The two sisters go out on the balcony to look at the heavens. Down below, the windows have also been opened in the guest-room where the adjutants are dining. Aided by the wine, they are telling tales of their exploits. An emphatic rumor of gaiety bursts out there, to be propagated throughout the fort, between the fiery yews, the tricolor light of lanterns and the lamps in the canteens.

Further down, the band tunes up, and then the brass section gives wings to the sound. It expands toward the course of the river, which sparkles in the shadows.

Francine and Philomène are leaning on the balcony. The younger sister is chattering away to the Commandant.

Philomène murmurs to Philippe: "Since I shall be unable to have love, since no one will ever possess my soul entire, what does it matter to you? Alone here, isolated from society and human contact, amid this wretched population in the livery of war, I have created for myself a second life, full of crazy and magnificent ideas. I have retreated to it permanently. Human affairs will no longer affect me, except superficially and according to the décor of existence."

"The Commandant's glory has affected you."

"I certainly love him less than I love you—yes, less—but he won't try to penetrate my inner being, to possess any more of me than I give him."

"Your body..."

"That's how your youth reveals itself, which frightens me. What is it, the body? Less than nothing. I don't refuse to recognize my beauty—but even so, I don't intend to become no more than an instrument of joy for the ardor of your youth. That would be an insult..."

"Leave that. Tell me, Philomène, do you think you'll be forever incapable, be it out of compassion or admiration, of

199

consenting to sacrifice your intellectual pride and absorbing yourself in anyone…?"

"Out of compassion, who knows? Out of admiration, yes. But for me to admire someone to the point of adoration…what an unexpected hero he would have to reveal to me!"

"Merely the man whose actions realize the dream of your soul."

"I shall only cherish a dead man, then. For anyone who preaches a new faith to human beings and attempts to convert them; anyone who, like Christ, wants to offer them a living example of his doctrine, will incur the hatred of men, to the point of death. And he must sacrifice himself for the sake of sacrifice, ignorant even of the consolation of knowing that he has been useful in the redemption of the world. He must love sacrifice for its own sake, without the lure of glory, simply for the beauty of dying needlessly…but you don't understand…"

"I would understand if you initiate me."

The silence of the band, which had stopped playing, interrupted their conversation then. In the sudden atmospheric calm, the boasts of the adjutants could be heard.

"Oh, during the Indus campaign, we fed our Asiatics to the fire, feet first, and shoved them into the fire as they were consumed. What brave fellows—they pulled horrible faces, but they didn't scream…"

"In the Legion, we cut the tendons in their feet with a pen-knife first…"

"In Ethiopia, we gathered our prisoners 20 at a time in the depths of caves, in front of which we set fire to green wood, and they sneezed their lives away in the smoke. Do you remember, Firmin?"

"When the general forbade us to waste powder shooting the Chinese, we piled them up in ditches in the paddy-fields and smashed their heads with rifle-butts for fear of spoiling the bayonets. Their skulls stuck out like rows of onions. The first pained me—so young, wasn't he? With lovely oriental eyes, imploring…well, war's war. One can't take them forward, nor leave them behind the column…"

"Then again, when one goes into their villages, doesn't one find the heads of comrades taken by surprise in forward positions stuck on bamboo poles? They sometimes look like two rows of lamp-posts on the city boulevards—except that he poor devils' eyes no longer light up."

"All that, my old mates, still isn't worth as much as Commandant de Chaclos' coup."

"My God, lads, I was there! What a mess! I put the charge under the pile of the bridge myself…we let them get on to it, and when they were plenty of them there, the commandant pressed the switch on the electric battery. Bang! The whole lot went up!"

"We found fingers and noses, taking a stroll all alone more than 200 meters away, and eyes stuck to trees, between bits of brain and nerve-ends…and the eyes were looking at you. It was frightful, my dear chaps, frightful! The survivors beat the retreat straight away. We took their positions without any trouble…and here we are, victorious, glasses in hand. Triumphant arches have been erected; the commandant has his medal…so three cheers for war! When one comes back from it…"

Francine, who had a bunch of primroses in her hand, suddenly dropped them—and she passed the palms of her hands over her temples, as if to dissipate a nightmare. Presumably, she did not see Monsieur de Chaclos bend down to pick up the scattered corollas in order to give them back to her, for she immediately ran away. Before she had reached the door, she collapsed on the ground with frightful cries, shaken by nervous convulsions.

During the illness that followed this fit, the young girl was subject to sinister hallucinations. In the fever she saw the memories of war recounted by the adjutants traced out in tangible images. All military apparatus had to be taken away from her: uniforms, weapons and engravings advertising historic bravery. The distant sound of a drum sufficed for the bloody evocation, and it was a horrible thing. She sat up, slender and haggard, her hands open and extended to shove away the hideousness of the dream...

"Oh!" she said. "Those poor lives cut short... The river of blood leaking out of the ditches... The heads rolling like balls... The fingers clenching on the saber that severs them... Oh, the eyes of the dying...! The eyes! The eyes! The eyes! The blood rises, rises...it's in my mouth...ugh! It's choking me...I don't want..."

And she fell back into another fit...

Philomène's marriage was delayed by the grave condition of her little sister. She never left her side. Her affection for the creature that everyone was cursing only became more fervent. The Colonel had fits of fury in which he wished the unhappy child dead. Even though they affected indulgence and pity, the officers of his entourage spoke uneasily about the delirium that withered their glory.

Besides which, the legend of the little prophetess soon visited the imagination of the soldiers, and they talked about it in whispers in the barracks before lights out. Their courage threatened to weaken. In the ranks, twice over, recruits rebelled against orders, and it was murmured that the hour would soon come when men would cease to learn the art of killing. Cannon would be melted down to make ploughshares. Universal fraternity would not be long in blossoming.

III

This was very serious, because it was feared that the immense conflict of the Northern nations anticipated for 30 years, for which preparations had been patiently made, was now imminent. Certain omens of battle were beginning to appear in the heavens and in the speeches of diplomats. The first days of spring had arrived, and spring seemed, in the opinion of all men of war, to be the best time to undertake the mutual massacre of nations. Activity was redoubled in the arsenals and the drill-squares. The Colonel dreaded that the poor morale of his troops would be blamed on him by the marshal-inspectors, and to distract the minds of his soldiers from reasoning he drove them relentlessly on marches and maneuvers calculated to weary their moral strength with physical fatigue and render them docile to his hand.

Running around the villages and miner's hovels, however, they became even more troubled. They lamented: "What a barbaric epoch we're still living in, for so much poverty to remain in the world. Our mothers give birth to us with the sole objective of hard labor, and we slave more than animals, without having the leisure to think, as animals do. Oh, cursed be the moments of brief joy in which our sad fathers hurled their semen into the loins of their skinny spouses. What right had they to create us, since they were unable to leave us any other legacy than desires that can never be satisfied?

"And the scientists say that generations succeed one another on a path of progress, and that humankind is marching to the conquest of God. Can we believe them, since we learn nothing but the art of cutting our throats, when all our strength is employed with the sole purpose of ameliorating our fate, no longer succeeding but very meagerly? In truth, the young prophetess is right, who cries by night that we remain as barbaric as wolves, and that we shall never be happy, because we love blood too much…

"See how the drums and flags are being prepared now…we shall have to hurl ourselves upon the poor devils of other nations, without even being able to understand the reasons for our rage. Our feet have already been hardened on the roads, and our shoulders no longer feel the weight of our haversacks….

"Let's see—will there rise up among us a strong man, who will finally proclaim the revolution of universal Love?"

And the petty soldiers shoved one another, saying: "You, you…" But none of them dared to say anything.

Finally, Francine's delirium was attenuated. She recovered her health and her reason. But when Monsieur de Chaclos wanted to raise the matter of the wedding again, Philomène told him that she would remain single. He understood then that she shared her sister's sentiments, and that he horrified her by virtue of the blood in which he was covered.

A little later, he learned that Philomène was engaged to Philippe. That did not surprise him, because he had overheard some of their conversation on the evening of the primroses.

The cornet changed garrisons, and came to the fort with a detachment of Guides.

After that, Monsieur de Chaclos was sad, for he cherished Philomène with all the tenacity of late passions. The near-certainty that he had had of marrying her had rendered the love of the 40-year-old even more unbreakable. Nevertheless, he had a noble soul; he persuaded the colonel to let Philomène marry Philippe. And when the young woman remarked on his intervention with astonishment, he told her that he loved her for herself, not for his own sake, and preferred to see her happy in another's arms rather than unhappy in his. That would be infinitely less painful.

When they came out of the church, the cornet said to his wife: "Now that you've sacrificed yourself to me out of compassion, I shall try to merit your admiration…"

The war began…

The Fort was guarding the frontier; the first cannon-shots were fired from its emplacements.

The troops from the city arrived, and then the troops of workers and peasants who got off trains. They were put into uniform and weapons were distributed to them.

Outside, the highways are filling up with mothers and children, who were begging. Young women are prostituting themselves for next to nothing. On the horizon, the keeps of the factories cease to glow for the first time in 30 years. The boulevard in the city is full of activity because public funds have been gambled away in the headquarters of the insurance companies, metallurgical companies and banks. The money men are already surreptitiously buying back bonds in order to resell them at a profit as an initial advantage is announced.

In order to gain that initial advantage, which dispatches usually exaggerate, the Marshals hasten to gather men at that part of that frontier. They are snatched away from mines and furrows. Fanfares sound. Flags flap. Actresses in white dresses, draped in the national colors, sing in the open air on hastily-constructed stages about the sacred love of the fatherland. And the red men of the ferruginous soil file past in enormous masses, filling the overly narrow space of the streets with their bodies. Company administrators order casks of bad wine to be unearthed to warm their enthusiasm. It is a matter of gaining that precious advantage, of making a profit on the markets…

Gendarmes are herding the wretched hordes, a sea of red heads whose waves are beating the stages where the actresses in white dresses, draped in the national colors, and tousled hair besides, are singing untiringly about the day of glory…

A few more hours to pass, a few jolts of the railway-wagons, and the herd, furnished with uniforms and insignia of rank, coiffed in kolbacks,[51] mounted on requisitioned horses, is ready to seize the advantage—two-and-a-half per cent on the Bourse tomorrow.

The gun-carriages roll over the pebbles of the roads. The squadrons gallop amid the screech of metal. The regiments trample down the soil beneath 6000 regimental boots. The officers prance amid the gleam of their new leather-work—and now, on the crests of hills where low-lying clouds unfurl, here come the brief flashes of the enemy guns.

In the ranks there are men who suddenly turn somersaults, with clown-like grimaces, or fall to their knees, like visionary fanatics, bewildered by the sight of the world beyond. Others are lying down, as if to go to sleep. And when the columns have passed, when the lines have stretched themselves out, there are good red heads that remain in the risen dust, coughing over redder pools…

The countryside remains green and bright to either side of the fast-flowing river. Wheat covers the plain with its ten-

---

[51] Kolbacks were the spiked helmets popularized by Prussian uhlans.

der shots, and there is, in the hollow of the great valley, a fine nest of abundance, with its little white houses and its luminous waters, and its propitious hem of gently-sloping hills.

Philippe, at the head of 60 cavalrymen, is in command of an observation-post. He sees the roads blacken with human swarms, the grass flourishing with bright patches donated by uniforms, rigs galloping frantically over ringing pathways. Here at there, at a stroke, flame drapes itself over the roofs of small farmhouses. Lines of infantry broaden out over the plain. They advance, running, lying down, crackling and spitting, getting up, running again, gaining shelter, abandoning it, leaving corpses huddled in the grass at every stopping-point. Around him, the fusillades are making so much nose that the air seems to be frying.

And close at hand, the large red heads of his men are turning blue beneath the polished chains of kolbacks and the violent pomp of tassels. Boots are trembling in clicking stirrups. Hands thickened by labor in forges are sponging sweat from foreheads. Sad bargains are struck in huddled groups. Bachelors take the first rank in order to conserve he more useful lives of fathers.

"Go…hang back, you have children…I don't have any…if I die, you'll look after my old mother…"

"Understood…forward march!"

The adjutant tries to re-establish the ranks, and growls frightful curses…

"Let it go," says Philippe. "Let them prepare themselves for death as they see fit, in order that they will not execrate us…their executioners!"

A murmur of astonishment causes the shoulders of the Guides to shudder, and they look at the young cornet, whose dolorous face lights up…

He thinks about that human desperation, and suffers. His wife's compassion grieves him, because she cannot offer him any other kind of love. Oh, to conquer her admiration by a great sacrifice, by the beauty of a death without glory…!

A cavalryman races toward his troop. The Captain orders the cornet to lead his men at the gallop in a charge, concealing themselves in a sunken road. He will surely reach, by that means, the enemy battery that is trotting unsuspectingly to take up a position... The regiment will launch itself forward to support him.

"Do you see them, my boy? There are scarcely 1000 of them. That larch-wood is hiding us from their scouts. We have them. Charge! At the gallop! Forward!"

Philippe feels his horse leap forward at the command. The animal carries him away against his hesitant will. He wants to shout: "Back! Stop the murder! My comrades..." The animal carries him away in the forced gallop of the platoon. It carries him away like the force of events, the fatality of life, the superior rhythm that leads men to pain, to death, and to God.

The hedges pass by, with their topped willows, their branches spreading out like drunken arms. The ground flies past beneath the iron horseshoes. The men are breathless with fear. They will never arrive...they will arrive too soon...

The hedge has come to an end, and before them, there are 20 poor louts covered in mud, hanging from the harness of a cannon, which a team of horses is dragging awkwardly and laboriously. Frightened and livid faces are turning toward the Guides. Incomprehensible howls are exchanged. A man on horseback fires a shot; the flame seems to spring from his fist. The platoon rouses itself for one last surge, and is about to fall upon the wretches, whose trembling hands can no longer find the triggers of their rifles...

"Halt!"

Philippe has shouted; the horses are yielding to the pressure to the bridle...and now he finds himself stupid in the relative silence, no longer knowing why he has ordered that halt...since the riflemen are taking aim...

"Peace!" he shouts, again...and he continues in their language: "We could slaughter you...but the time has come for love...we must stop killing one another...we must stop killing

207

one another…we don't want to kill one another…we're brothers…poor human brothers… Peace! Don't you want that? Let's make peace! Love us!"

Undoubtedly, the enemies thought that he was announcing the good news of a real peace, suddenly concluded, for they threw down their arms and there was an immense outburst of joy. They ran to one another and embraced. The Guides started to laugh too, without knowing. The Adjutant turned his horse round and departed toward the regiment.

Philippe was no longer speaking. Between his fingers, he clutched the spring of lilac given to him, on his departure, by Francine and Philomène…and he rejoiced, thinking that he had just acted in accordance with their generous prayers.

He was about to resume his exhortations to love when he perceived that the enemy troop had grown. Soon, the Guides were surrounded by the green and white uniforms of the artillery. He wanted to explain, but an old officer arrived, who snatched away his saber…

He was taken prisoner.

On Sunday, the following Sunday, in the morning, he passed in front of the Colonel-Governor's house. The blooming lilacs looked like snow hanging from the walls. The sisters were there, waiting for him at the gate. Francine melted in tears, but Philomène seemed radiant. Her increased beauty exalted her. She threw him a sprig of lilac that she had pressed against her lips. A soldier in the escort picked it up and gave it to him. He raised it to his mouth.

They went down by the patrol circuit. Philomène shouted down to him from the terrace…

As he went along the wall she said to him: "I admire you and I adore you, because you have opened the new era of love, and because your blood will sanctify it…"

Philippe felt dazzled internally by an indescribably light. He took up a position in front of the stake and stripped the lilac of its leaves while the sentence of death was being read out. Recovered from enemy hands, the court martial had found him guilty of treason.

"Have you anything to add?"

"No. I preferred dying to killing. I'm ready to submit…to that fate…"

He was taken away. For a moment, his gaze embraced the esplanade, the square formation of troops gleaming in the young sun, and the dozen executioners who were stepping forward. Above them, on the terrace, Philomène was standing upright against the sky, kissing her hands. And she was, to him, the black angel who opens the doors of the new life to souls.

Without quitting her with his gaze, his heart singing, he gave the order to fire.

Louis Mullem: *The End of a Monopoly*
(c. late 1889s-early 1890s)

One can be certain that the numerous recent excursions of the Parisian executioner in lofty endeavors have provoked a rather sharp discontentment among certain people in the provinces. This kind of "representational artist," who has returned to the ascendant in the capital, seems, in fact, likely to discourage departmental natives who are thinking of becoming actors in the same, assuredly dramatic, career. It will therefore not be surprising that requests of this sort are being addressed to the parliamentary commission responsible for the consideration of petitions.

Lacking in numbers as the signatories doubtless are, their arguments nevertheless merit examination. In the first place, they attempt to emphasize the insufficiency of the monopoly—or, rather, the mononecropoly—that the State has assumed in this business. Critics also highlight the difficulties that the transfer of judiciary woodwork has occasioned, and the relative lack of employment that results for local constructors.

It also requires to be noted that the present manner of procedure is in complete contradiction with the egalitarian principles of free concurrence.

The guillotine, as has been so often and so rightly said, maintains a stubborn presence in our judiciary mores. Every French citizen, therefore, ought to have the right to maintain one, if he so desires, as one may install a newsstand or a refreshment-booth.

The expense would now be much less and a permanently-established apparatus would lead to salutary reflections on the part of those tempted to commit crimes—who, in spite of the pretext of the example invoked in favor of capital punishment, rarely have the opportunity to witness it as simple spectators.

In the good old days, gibbets and pillories were erected on a long-term basis in places of execution. There are, therefore, sound precedents with regard to this fashion of usefully ornamenting public highways.

Ever-practical, the Americans do not represent instruments of official murder in mysterious terms. They have recourse to "electrocution," a barbarous but scientific term, as befits an ultra-civilized device, and they can aliment the battery that must receive the condemned individual from any street-light.

Then again, the project in question offers unprecedented advantages. It is not only more-or-less attested malefactors who are mortally judged. One may add, on the evidence of the quotidian social thermometer, the quantity of sad individuals whom the lack of any resources leads fatally to the same extremity. The free and "automatic" guillotine would become an indispensable suicide machine for heir use, with an annexe containing everything necessary for writing, according to custom, their last and impotent testaments.

The mechanism would, in any case, be very simply conceived in a familiar manner. A slot would open beside the aperture, captioned "Insert 10 Centimes."

Louis Mullem: *The New Year*

(c. late 1889s-early 1890s)

As radiant as a deity made of dreams, as beautiful as a form detached from the Ideal, she is about to quit the spaces of infinite duration.

Daughter of time, her turn has come to preside over the flight of hours on Earth.

She will be the awaited year. She will experience, as a force outside herself, the distancing of the fabulous spheres of extent, and she understands that she is ready to descent along the highway of the heavens.

She remains motionless for one more instant, letting her eyes wander over the magnificence and the mystery of the naïve regions with which her memory will delight itself during her absence.

It is a strange land, extending boundlessly into an indescribable depth of light, where there are beings and crowds of uncreated unhumanities, whose supernatural existence expresses nothing but confidence and joy. The gaze cannot grasp the vast plenitude of that enchantment, of which the thought of the exiled infant has a vision that trembles at times, being interrupted, like a reflection of foliage in water, and sometimes fading away, as if in a dream, straying too far into the future.

"It is the life that might be," the contemplator says to herself, "and also the life that will become, according to its purpose, so gentle, no noble and so pure...."

And the sentiments of tenderness, enthusiasm and pity are exalted in the heart of the new year that is going toward human beings. She rises up in the majesty of her mission. She would like to convey to the Earth all that she has just foreseen of possible felicity, all the harmony that a decree of supreme will might render certain.

But where will the energy and power for such an effort come from? Perhaps from "The One Who Will Be," the rebel Spirit of invincible and supreme Revolt, whose palace, tracing an edifice of gold and light in the dark blue atmosphere has just surged forth before the Exile on the slope of the sky.

A multitude flooded the steps and portal of that edifice. The garments of these visitors were made of art, their hands bore works of as-yet-unknown science, their faces revealed beings of bold and serious thought.

The voyager crossed the threshold and penetrated into the high-ceilinged room with hangings of flame in which Satan was resting on his elbows, absorbed in a mass of books and manuscripts.

"I know," he said, raising his severe forehead and letting his genius flow back into his audacious eyes, "yes, I know…you're going to Earth, like your sisters, the years of the past; you're ambitious for the glory and the power to ensure humans of the entirety of wisdom. Alas, what can I do for you are present? My return to divinity is still far off. I still have a great many things to do. Until they're accomplished, I shall remain unruly. I shall create prodigies that will vanquish the last resistances of matter. I shall impose laws in opposition to all deceptive veneration of the past. I shall dissipate forever the shadows of ignorance, suffering and oppression. Perhaps, eventually, I shall establish liberty, fraternity and justice. Who knows?—perhaps I shall even obtain the defeat of oblivion, the eternity of life for the intelligences that know and the souls that love. Then the mirages that I evoked in your path just now will be realized—and that will be good, and I will become once again the true God, for I was and I am Science. But how many more centuries will vanish before I reach my goal? Maintain courage, though. Dispense as best you can your love and your virtue during your few hasty days down there…"

Slowly and sadly, the departing individual set off again. A cruel premonition troubled her with fear. She felt herself diminished of all that she left behind her of hope and beauty. She ceased to be the august virgin of imperishable essence and

213

was transformed into a frail adolescent whose heart was tremulous and required support.

As she directed her course, moreover, the ambient images became more rigid, symbolizing the horror of imminent realities. Faces were drifting, telling fortunes in indolence and pride. Other apparitions displayed poverty, hunger, debauchery and opprobrium. In the distance, peoples were rushing around, disheveled and bloody, in the fury of war. Death floated, its mask turning green with hatred and annihilation.

Once again, who would dry the tears of that future of folly and anguish?

A temple loomed up on the horizon. The vaults resounded with the hymns of the organ; the nave extended, thousands of believers kneeling in the candlelight.

The desperate individual advanced, in supplication, to the sanctuary ruled by "The One Who Is."

"I can do nothing," he said, lost in clouds of incense. "I leave Creation to draw from itself the consequences that it embodies. I remain outside the ideal that is dreamed or pursued. I start nothing, I help nothing and I retreat into myself. On the day when my work was concluded, I proclaimed that 'it was good'. I was called God—but I am only the Fatality against which you struggle beneath the sky. Go, then, and expect nothing but the triumph of Chance, the impassive sovereign of good and evil."

The departing individual set off again, in a terror of fear and prayer. The dolorous miracle of her destiny was complete. She no longer had even the sickly grace of young womanhood. She became a naked child, puny and irresolute, who knew nothing but obedience…

But she as she reached the extreme limits of the eternal land of chimeras, a cloud enveloped her, in order to guide her to the entrance of the world of verities, in which everything happens.

Her sisters, the years gone by, were weeping as they departed. They too, when they flew toward somber humanities in their turn, had brought the great hope of deliverance and joy.

All of them came back having scarcely begun their task of salvation.

The night became profound, and the cloud fell into the abyss from on high. The voice of the twelfth hour struck space; an immense rumor rose up of terrestrial life. People cheered, celebrated, sang…and also mourned the advent of the new year.

Louis Mullem: *The Invisibility of Monsieur Gridaine*
(c. late 1889s-early 1890s)

It is necessary to believe that the inhabitants of
Loudéac—particularly the bourgeois and commercial elite of
that charming little town—had given evidence of a certain
systematically malevolent prejudice with respect to the person
of their honorable fellow citizen Monsieur Paulin Gridaine.

There was nothing very serious, all things considered, in
ridiculing Monsieur Gridaine slightly regarding his public
actions and gestures, but the gossips made the error of going
beyond that, to devote themselves to malicious inductions
concerning the private life of the honest taxpayer in question,
and even to the propagation of unworthy suspicions regarding
the most secret tendencies of his character.

The evil tongues of the elite in question were thus, in
truth, going too far.

It is true, nevertheless—let it be said unambiguously—
that the appearances of M. Paulin Gridaine during his rare
peregrinations in Loudéac lent themselves to ironic commentary. For example, he deliberately chose the most deserted
streets, and hugged the walls as if he were afraid of being seen
by anyone. He rebuffed with a coldly distant reverence any
attempted approaches by people he knew, and his eyes turned
away with an expression of dolorous ennui whenever he happened to make visual contact with any stroller whatsoever—
even those of the sex for the sake of which members of the
other go strolling.

There are, in any case, innocent manias about which
there is no need to get unduly excited, the more-or-less valid
causes of which it is wiser to investigate—for, with the exception of a few rare notabilities, the commercial and bourgeois
society of Loudéac does not present, at first glance, any very
striking esthetic interest, and, even without being entirely mi-

santhropic, an independent stroller could, in all justice, refuse them a reciprocity of attention.

Perhaps our man made the great mistake of ostensibly manifesting that indifference or general antipathy toward others which well-brought-up people hide beneath the veil of politeness—but would such a minute fault suffice to place Paulin Gridaine at the head of the list of the eccentrics of this native town, to lead people to nudges one another on catching sight of him and profess amazement or stifle laughter? Would it suffice, finally, to explain the detrimental propagation of the local, even regional, legend of *the man who did not want people to look at him*? That surpasses the limits of indiscretion.

When the authorities, having been alerted by nasty rumors, appeared to want to intervene, Monsieur Grisdaine, who wanted to go unnoticed, became all the more convinced that, on the pubic highway, anonymous policemen "had their eye on him". Was his case really to be exaggerated to the point of suspecting insanity, and would he then be put under surveillance as danger to the public?

Such a persecution, both popular and administrative, definitely ceased to be supportable. That was the point at which Paulin Gridaine started to write, from time to time, to the public prosecutor, to warn him about obscure tittle-tattle. He sent that magistrate a series of notes written in the most moderate terms, utterly devoid of acrimony, of which it will be sufficient to reproduce a few extracts here, to give evidence of their author's state of mind, in contrast to the superficial appreciations of current opinion.

In the course of these confidences, spaced at wide intervals, Monsieur Gridaine did not, at first, explain the fundamental idea behind his mysterious contemporary actions. He went over his past history, the events of which had produced the genesis, and finally the predominance, of his present opinions.

The first fragments of autobiography, thus confided to the officer of the court, summarized Paulin Gridaine's educa-

217

tion in Paris and his fruitless efforts, once his studies were concluded, to embark with any chance of success upon any of the careers open in the capital to intellectual energy. He was a born dreamer. The law, medicine, history, theology and other hard-labor traps of that sort became, by turns, the theater of his inaptitude for any methodical discipline.

Every year, his holidays took him to Loudéac, where the knowledge of his obstinate fiascos inclined him to depressions in which he became very acutely aware that his family "had its eye on him".

At this point, one might object that the impressionable Gridaine was perhaps giving way to an excess of imagination. With a little more experience of the human heart, he would doubtless only have perceived a little vague sympathy, if not a complete indifference with respect to him, in the ocular investigations to which he seemed to be obsessively subject.

The annoyance that Monsieur Gridaine experienced could, nevertheless, be imputed to the fact that, for centuries, the dynasty whose name he bore had been exclusively devoted to the sale of vegetable preserves; he was the only side-branch that had emerged, by some mysterious spontaneity, from that genealogical tree of invariable tradesmen.

Then again, in the bitterness of his failures, Monsieur Gridaine doubtless estimated that the anomaly of such a random graft on the trunk of his family ought to have been legitimated by a magnificent flowering, by something evidently superior to the vegetables comprising the abovementioned traffic. There was, however, nothing like that; no superiority burst forth in Monsieur Gridaine, and, whether it was unconscious or deliberate, the "family eye" appeared to be scornful of the absence in the young scion—at least for the present—of any fecund seed whose produce might one day surpass, or even attain, the value of the most ordinary dried fruit

At any rate, whatever the reason was, the gazes aimed at him by his relatives made Monsieur Gridaine's hair stand on end—his notes to the prosecutor explained—by reason of the striking resemblance that existed between Monsieur Gridaine's own eyes and those of his kinfolk. Products of the same atavistic mold, these organs functioned in a similar manner. They all possessed the same coldness, with the same alternations of rapid sarcasm that Monsieur Gridaine launched into space unawares whenever his reflections returned to the theme of his individual mediocrity—and when his ancestry scrutinized him, Monsieur Gridaine sank into the frightful sensation of seeing his own eyes observing him against his will.

According to the confessions transmitted by Monsieur Gridaine, these scruples had nothing at all to do with exaggerated modesty or overweening vanity. They derived entirely from a pessimistic system of philosophy, from which Monsieur Gridaine concluded that the fabrication of human beings had been a practical joke played by the force or farce of things.

As a specimen of that sad species, it seemed no less humiliating to him to be examined in his external appearance than in any activity of his mental being. The former case, he said, concerns a vain configuration that only separates itself from inert matter for a fleeting instant, while in the latter, one only encounters incoherent impulses of a thought that cannot claim the immortality that it imagines and which, by virtue of that very fact, remains incapable of demonstrating any reason for being, private or social, of any kind whatsoever. It became exasperating for Monsieur Gridaine to live as a member of such a pitiful creation, and, in consequence, he hated the idea of anyone analyzing the superfluity of his efforts to live as much as he dreaded considering them himself.

In brief, Monsieur Gridaine confessed a keen repugnance for the spectacle of his identity in the present conditions of anthropomorphy, and wrote to the prosecutor that if someone could only put him on the track of a method of liberating his "self" in an incorporeal state—which implied the possibility of his infinite fusion with the breath of intelligence spread throughout the universe—he would at least attempt to free his "external self" from confrontation with crowds: in a word, to irrealize his terrestrial effigy by relentlessly perfecting the artifices by means of which he had so far only obtained "a modest commencement of invisibility." It was, however, necessary for him to abandon this obscure and difficult enterprise, for new arrangements of his intimate existence claimed all his attention for the time being.

At the age of 30, he had cut short his Parisian disappointments and settled down in Loudéac within the bonds of matrimony. His fortune, filled out by the contribution of the charming Mademoiselle Claire Blondot, left him abundant leisure to pursue his work in the vein that has just been indicated. Unfortunately, Monsieur Gridaine reported to the magistrate, as soon as he had entered into marriage, he had been forced to defend his freedom to study against obstinate intrusions. Visitors laid siege to his home and passed him through the sieve of an extreme microscopism, which heightened to extremes the anger aroused by the optical exercise accomplished by the "Gridaine gaze" with its aforementioned particular acuity of bourgeois sarcasm. Imagine, in fact, a right eye opening its blue bleakness very wide, while the left eye, clenching its eyelid over the rictus of the cheek, only lets through a vivid spark of irony. By what right did that latter eye carry its insidious question mark everywhere it went? What undercurrents of ennui or disillusionment were being launched via the ingenuous features, very soft and still virginally exotic, of his young wife?

The expulsion of that clan of nuisances could only be obtained after several years of the prudent maneuvers demanded by provincial propriety and concerns regarding prospective heritages—after which Monsieur Gridaine only accorded access to his home to his young cousin César Blondot, an artist with a sensitive soul who, although he surreptitiously surrounded the exquisite Madame Gridaine with a continuous ecstasy, gave great pleasure to the master of the house in compensation, and only affected a very vague awareness of his actual presence.

A favorable era began. They lived, ignored and calm, in a pretty hereditary cottage situated on the very edge of Loudéac, whose grounds, shaded by old trees, bordered open country. The moment seemed to Paulin Gridaine to be appropriate for the resumption of his speculations.

One day, he was leaning on his elbows at the table in the garden in front of a few immaculate sheets of paper, with his forehead in his right hand, armed with a pencil. They had just finished lunch. The ravishing Madame Gridaine, whose features no longer displayed all the enigmatic candor of earlier days, abandoned her nonchalance to the accustomed contemplation of cousin César. The indolence of the hour produced an atmosphere evocative of inspiration. It was charming, and Monsieur Gridaine did not hesitate to inscribe in large capital letters the title of a projected thesis on "The Research of Invisibility".

Unfortunately, Madame Gridaine, perhaps seeking a diversion from the assiduities of her young cousin, took it into her head to lean on her husband's shoulder and manifest a semblance of curiosity in the subject of his work. Monsieur Gridaine experienced the natural repulsion of any writer when someone spies in this fashion on the idea at the end of his pen, especially when the idea in question is in no hurry to manifest itself. Abruptly, he scattered torn pieces of paper like snow and swore to avoid in future any attempt to write at home. Fury had brought all his cerebral faculties into play, however, and, as if guided by a sharp need to take his revenge as a thinker, he seized an axiom on the wing, which he judge marvelously valuable for the clarification of his theory and its practical realization.

He had, in fact, concluded that "invisibility can only be determined by means independent of the real."

This luminous principle stemmed, to tell the truth, from the incident itself. Monsieur Gridaine noted that his recent abstraction had been much better represented by the page that remained blank than by its titular trace, unfortunately glimpsed by Madame Gridaine. A vast perspective of ameli-

221

oration was opened up by that reasoning with respect to invisibilist methodology. What followed logically, for Monsieur Gridaine, was the task of "immaterializing his actions and gestures" within the scope of human accessibility, and acquiring the gift of "mental non-appearance" within himself as well as externally.

It is easy to imagine the obstinacy of his repeated reflections and experiments, and it was precisely in the course of that laborious period that the idlers of Loudéac exasperated Monsieur Gridaine with a multitude of taunts that were as absurd as they were devoid of respect for the liberty of others. Monsieur Gridaine's complaints to the prosecutor only became more energetic.

Even if, he insinuated, the legend of "the man who does not want to be seen" were founded on an exact basis, would that give the stupid indigenes the right to treat him as a maniac dangerous to the security of the citizens? He stuck close to walls? My God! That was because he hated to be surprised while transporting himself from one place to another, when, for a sensible man, there is nothing in the world worth the trouble of going anywhere whatsoever, nor in coming back. Furthermore, he only went out to get a little air, something "invisible in essence" and yet without which no vitality could be maintained. If he did not like being "stared at" that was, again, out of reciprocal commiseration for the pitiful ensemble of psychological incoherence and unstable carnal aggregates that constituted the human race. Thus understood, "invisibility" would simply be comparable to that politeness, said to be typical of drawing-rooms, which only admitted people "impersonally" and which, without any allusion to their intrinsic infirmities, excluded from the problem as equal quantities, confounds them all in the false ideal of a single "superhumanity."

The aim of these mundane strategies, he continued, is to shield "imperfectible" beings temporarily from ephemeral criticism, but only "invisibility" could render such a desideratum effective and durable—and that would be the conquest of true liberty for particular individuals whose mental life could exercise itself without any exterior collaboration. The need "to be seen" is comprehensible among actors, priests, military men, orators, workmen etc., for they are the inseparable instruments of their professions. Save for the categories of workers or apparitors, however, the individual presence is merely a foolish adequation of arbitrary and superfluous superficialities.

Such being the opinion of Monsieur Gridaine regarding our planetary role, one wonders whether he might have acted wisely in having recourse to suicide—a rather simple objection against which his arguments did not lack finesse. His voluntary "non-existence", he wrote, could only be proven in confrontation with the ambient actuality, in the same way that the intimate conviction of not being ostensible could only be confirmed by receiving from others evidence of "imperception."

Monsieur Gridaine had no difficulty in recognizing that these truisms were fringed by the naivety of a science in its infancy and that "the plausible hypothesis of a mental evolution outside substance remains one of the most formidable problems of transformism that the future will decide."

In the meantime, he begged the officer of the court to recall his myrmidons and warn the jokers of Loudéac that the suspicions of buffoonery with which they were harassing Monsieur Gridaine were only founded on the chimeras of their dull stupidity. He proudly claimed the right to maintain his inoffensive appearance as a petty rentier and to continue his studies of "invisibility"—in which, he said, his progress was becoming, at least mentally, increasingly significant.

Among other proofs in this regard, Monsieur Gridaine indicated the sudden progress that he had achieved in the fundamental thesis of his ideas, thanks to a recent circumstance. The incident in question was the performance given by the great actress Anna Bérard while passing through Loudéac.

Expressed entirely, he wrote, by the clamor of her tirades and the fury of her gestures, transubstantiating body and soul in her role, it was the totality of what her body and soul could exteriorize of beauty that the actress delivered to the enthusiasm of the auditorium. And the most ordinary motor of social action—which is to say, the instinct of life reciprocally seen and shown, rose that evening to the level of the supreme syntheses of art.

The excitement of his spectacle modified, from top to bottom, Monsieur Gridaine's former reasoning. He recognized at a stroke the error that had made him attribute his hopes of isolation to some unknown quintessence of timidity and pride. No! Those two sentiments were not involved in any causal manner. "Invisibility" and "inaudibility"—of which he would make a special study in due course—now appeared to him as natural attributes of inner being, constituting the indispensable counterpart of the "qualities of expansion and resonance" for which the actress was glorified. In this combination, the philosophical superiority evidently turned in favor of Monsieur Gridaine, for Anna Bérard, "only excited the noise and glare of a human hour that had the appearance of being forgotten" while, by means of "the unexpressed," our great thinker represented "the eternal secret of the origins and conclusions of our being."

At the fall of the curtain, he thought that the actress was struck by the mutism and rigid immobility that he opposed to the general effervescence. She seemed wounded by that unusual attitude, and it was as if her acquired power to speak and depict "the ephemeral instantaneity" broke before the brilliant determination assured by Monsieur Gridaine of "retrenching himself in the durable depths of the unknown."

Indifferent, from that evening on, to the pitiful jests of the Loudéacians, Monsieur Gridaine remained inflexibly of the opinion that "invisibilism is well and truly a positive and progressive science, of which it only remains to determine the usual procedures."

His gracious spouse supported him at first in this meticulous occupation with a great deal of devotion and subtlety. Yes, at first!—for there soon occurred a number of conjugal incidents correlative of a complexity that Monsieur Gridaine's subsequent letters to the magistrate only elucidated imperfectly.

By means of the single word "invisibility," once snatched from the manuscript, Madame Gridaine had penetrated the motive for the exceptional distraction of her husband and had adopted the duty of disciplining his autonomous familiarities. Cousin César still indulged overtly in ecstatic impertinences. The agreeable female, opening hostilities, pretended to lend herself to these exuberant Platonisms and even set out to encourage them, to the extreme limit at which Monsieur Gridaine would depart from the impassivity that he manifested as a spectator.

This tactic, perhaps designed by eternal femininity to provoke a useful and belated explosion of marital jealousy, only produced diametrically opposite consequences. During these gallant interludes, the fortunate Monsieur Gridaine clouded himself in an absorption that won him a notable sum of relative invisibility. But they waited in vain—Monsieur Gridaine's correspondence with the prosecutor here exhibits the difficulty of explaining such a delicate situation clearly— for the experiment to reach its final conclusion. Cousin César's ardors were, it is true bordering on paroxysm. Madame Gridaine finally responded to them, it is certain, with an attitude of undeniable tenderness. It cannot be denied that both of them brought the most praiseworthy zeal to repressing their effusions as minimally as possible, leaving the husband to his flattering illusions of "unreal presence." But with what result? The two young hearts only allowed themselves to hesitate at decisive moments, and Monsieur Gridaine's ambitions were never crowned by a flagrant vicissitude of nature that signified *visible* evidence of his impersonality…

War-weary, the two lovers plotted to complete the imbroglio in a distant escapade in private, the unscheduled return from which would depend on the duration of their happiness. Still put at ease by Monsieur Gridaine's detached manner, the two Cytherean tourists experienced no great anxiety on seeing him, faithful to his method, escort them distractedly to the railway station.

The adventure only procured Monsieur Gridaine the meager satisfaction of an intrinsic invisibilism. Henceforth, he was alone in his deserted home, and the absence of intimate witnesses prevented him from measuring externally his progress in the solution of his great problem. Far from being discouraged, however, he soon impressed on his imagination a prodigious flight of genius—or obsession—following a singular event that his letters to the magistrate recorded succinctly.

For a month, Monsieur Gridane recounted, the Parisian newspapers had been commenting excitedly on the sudden, complete and exceedingly strange disappearance of Mademoiselle Anna Bérard, the incomparable actress. A love story, a womanly caprice, or the weariness of fame, the reporters and diarists speculated, in their banal fashion. Monsieur Gridaine gave no credit to these excessively vulgar interpretations. He knew better, for he recalled the expression of avid curiosity that the actress had turned toward him during her triumph in Loudéac, and did not take long to conclude that he had made her, by virtue of the inherent magnetism of a strong will, into an "invisibilimaniac adept."

Having embarked on that path, his idealism surpassed the final limits. He waited with total confidence for the "disincarnated spirituality" of Anna Bérard to occupy the space vacated by the prosaic Madame Gridaine; he even succeeded in the inevitable persuasion that the phenomenon was accomplished in the form of "psychic perspiration." Monsieur Gridaine was exultant. He cohabited in spirit with the superb daughter of the theater and—a notable thing—for the first time in his life, he was in love: the noble love of thinkers, which manifests itself so well outside or beyond its object. The extrasubstantial object of his worship, he wrote, was possibilized between the void and himself, as the conceptual image sensed in advance by a painter must float between the canvas and the model that he is about to reproduce.

Invisibilism was finally affirmed in his pure immateriality, corroborated by the absence of any sensible proof to the contrary. The eminent researcher was already thinking of popularizing his discovery by the acquisition of a patent, when the whimsical Anna Bérard returned to the boards and gathered, thanks to her calculated flight, a fine second crop of popular acclaim.

Hard as the blow was, Monsieur Gridaine did not lay down his arms. On the contrary, he launched himself with even greater intrepidity into his attempts, and cloistered himself in strict isolation, where no one could interfere with his experiments in "invisibilization in itself," which he claimed, finally, only to be manifest when he was alone, and only to himself. Could he, in any case, avenge himself more worthily on the base perfidy of Madame Gridaine and the intellectual treason of Anna Bérard? Was not the silence in which his laments were stifled the surest power of invisibility for the secret of his soul?

In one last plea to the prosecutor, he insisted, nevertheless, that his freedom of concentration remained permissible, and should be legally defended against the ignorant attacks of the idiots of Loudéac.

The magistrate did not remain insensitive to these entreaties. He went so far as to propose to Monsieur Gridaine that he convert his petty fortune into an annuity, in order to establish his residence in a national and "philosophically sanitary" institution where his remarkable work as an "invisibilator" could continue in total security, under the protection of the State.

Monsieur Gridaine greeted these overtures calmly, but without pleasure. According to him, he only required an act of simple justice in the solicitude accorded by central authority to "the inventor of a new order of scientific ideas." Governments sometimes thus correct the indifference of crowds to the scientists on whose obscure efforts the future is founded, and governments are doing no more, in such occasional instances, than their duty.

Accepted nevertheless, with a good grace, the transfer was carried out without delay.

Monsieur Paulin Gridaine presently lives beneath the roof of a former monastery, in a pleasant little room that rejoices in the dances of sunlight and shadow activated by the tops of old trees. The simple furniture of that retreat involves no superfluity that might distract Monsieur Gridaine's meditations from their goal; he does not even run the risk, as he once did, of seeing his calculations of invisibilism given the lie by the inopportune appearance of his image in a mirror.

Walks in the garden also offer him charming hours, although limited according to the hygienic rules imposed by the house. All in all, Monsieur Gridaine's heart overflows with a grateful satisfaction that he did not hesitate to make manifest in a *postscriptum* to the prosecutor.

It seems evident to him that official assent has definitively classified "Gridaine Invisibilism" in the certifications of a number of French institutions. The conclusive demonstration of that fact emerges from the conduct observed in his respect by the other people who, by virtue of their genius or their extraordinary talents, have doubtless succeeded in becoming inmates of the same abode by virtue of national gratitude.

My new colleagues, he wrote, these illustrious men with various titles, who would undoubtedly be ridiculed by the wretched people of Loudéac—among whom, I am not unaware, my present refuge passes for a madhouse—do not manifest any symptom of attention at my approach in the garden. Nothing distracts them from the mystery of their thought or extracts them from the preoccupations with philosophy or science that are the essence of their being. They only look at me, as I pass by, with mute, aberrative eyes, devoid of any indication of refraction and animated by a simple muscular mechanism of unconscious vision. In their vicinity, I am quite imperceptible. Nothing! They no longer see me, any more than they see the void, and they continue their progress toward their dreams of infinity without suspecting that "the Invisible" has just passed before them.

Louis Mullem: *Club Conversation*
(c. late 1889s-early 1890s)

The shadows were already gathering in the main hall of
the Art and Industry Club. Two of the gas-lamps distributed
around that pleasant location had, in fact, just been extinguished, in view of the fact 10 p.m. was about to strike, and
that was the time when night is thought to begin in our placid
and orderly little town of Béthune.

The club in question participates in the delicate virtues of
the modest locality. Industry and the arts are only debated very
superficially by the members, who are voluntarily ignorant of
the former and even more voluntarily weary of the latter. They
have merely been led to adopt that respectable appellation in
order to justify the express prohibition on talking politics or
religion prudently imposed on the society members by article
375 of the statues. Honest people of all parties can thus meet
one another on what is termed, in similar cases, "neutral
ground," around the green baize of a billiard table, without
diplomacy, and play cards that were not at all electoral.

The meeting-hall is very simple too, situated on the first
and only upper floor of a house on the main square, offering
little more luxury than an ordinary restaurant in the good old-
fashioned North. The walls, lined to half way up with stucco
painted the color of old oak, conclude in white plaster, on
which are mounted, in frames, the usual brightly-colored ad-
vertisements by inventors of inventors of aperitifs, symbolizing the Bacchic ecstasy of their clients. The frantic recom-
mendations of the texts conjoined with these images suppress
any flicker of uncertainty regarding the choice of the most
poisonous absinthe or the most corrosive "bitter."

At the back of the room is the aforementioned quadruped
billiard-table, now immersed in shadow, but installed beneath
a lantern-hood that pours a uniform light down upon the over-

ly-frequent frustration of cannons. To the right, toward the foreground, stands the venerable counter, laden with scintillating glassware and equipped with a large beer-pump, like an altar consecrated to the so regrettably national cult of the god Gambrinus.[52] Above this, its open battens pushed back against the side wall, is a sort of tabernacle in black wood filigreed with gold, where sparkling pewter beer-mugs hang, and a rack of seasoned clay pipes.

The furniture is completed by square tables, wicker chairs, and a huge ceramic stove extending its sheet-metal flue toward the ceiling. The latter must be very cold, for we are in the shivery month of October and the furnace is not to be lit, according to article 411 of the statutes, until All Hallows.

No poetic superfluity, therefore, bursts forth in the environment of this bourgeois rendezvous, except that, as the lights go out, certain livid gleams are projected from the billiard table and the shining mugs and crystal bottles, which allow the triangular neo-Greek summit of the Town Hall on the other side of the main square to be glimpsed through the windows, silhouetted in black against the blue moonlight: a fantastic transfiguration of that aediliatory edifice, the diurnal aspect of which is the acme of banality.

In addition to these melancholy motifs, the room was chilled, as we have said, with the bitterness of the first shivers of autumn. The manager, costumed as a waiter, was drowsing behind the counter, protecting his head from the cold beneath an exceedingly unceremonious cloth cap. Sometimes, as he nodded off after serving a glass or a pint pot, he restored the circulation to his fingers with the aid of copper spirit-lamp whose flame was maintained for relighting pipes.

In spite of the slow torpor of appearances, the Cub comprises the only decent place in Béthune where, at such an hour,

---

[52] Gambrinus was a legendary king of Medieval Flanders credited with the invention of brewing beer. His name is still preserved in the names of various brewing companies, but its origins and etymology remain murky.

a few recalcitrant citizens, differentiating themselves from the majority of indigenes who have already gone to bed, might persist in seeking some distraction. The laggards in question are widowers, bachelors and even a variety of husbands, all middle-aged, whom no prospect of amusement hastens back to their lodgings, or to whom the encroaching night truly seems to offer the piquancy of a slight disorder, or at least a little Platonic protest against the local customs of the excessively home-loving. There remain, in consequence, at a few tables around the big stove, four pairs playing piquet, impériale or bezique and a trio playing whist, with a group of spectators.

Few words are spoken in the miserly light, but rather murmurs: the occasional exclamation, a few whistles of admiration at the play of a trump or the exhibition of an "86" or some other stroke of good or bad luck in the eternal farce of chance; then silence falls again and it would be difficult to describe the amplitude of the calm that extended thereafter.

Thus had resumed, every evening at that hour for about half a century, the intimate pleasures of the club, which the subscribers, in their declining days, reproduced exactly, according to the habits of their deceased predecessors. Only at very rare intervals was some exceptional incident observed—for example, the unexpected visit of some unassiduous member, such as the two whose sudden entrance occurred that evening, exactly at the somnolent hour at which this story began.

Monsieur Brunel Isidore made his entrance in the company of Doctor Fauber Théodule. Both took off their stiff black hats, low in form with very large brims—a style gladly adopted by the old people of the province, whose desire to seem important, stable principles and suspicion of changing fashions obtained obligatory external representation in that invariable severity of coiffure. Both removed their ample brown cloaks with velvet collars, according to the fashion of the legitimist opposition under Louis-Philippe. Then, when both had deposited these objects on chairs, they installed

231

themselves next to the left-hand wall, at one of the tables least exposed to the glare of the last gas-lamps.

They each used the spirit-lamp to light a long pipe brought by the manager, along with a pitcher of beer; having clinked their glasses, the emptied them by half—after which, sounding the gloom with his hard black gaze, beneath graying bushing eyebrows, M. Brunel said: "How is it that the Bonsor brothers hasn't yet arrived?"

"He probably won't be long," was Dr. Fauber's reply.

The irruption seemed at first to provoke a certain ill ease among the card-players; a tremor agitated the cards, from which eyes were turned away in order to examine the newcomers surreptitiously. It was as if the two old men had introduced an element of night-terror that they had brought from outside, or as if they emitted some mysterious effluvium of an inexplicable Satanism.

They did, in fact, trace rather strange outlines in the semi-darkness: the long, thin face with a very prominent brow that Isidore Brunel framed with a tangle of white hair gathered into a forelock; and the strong head with the cunning features that Dr. Fauber rounded out beneath a cap of close-cropped grey hair. And did not both of them, with the carefully-shaven faces of scrupulous old egotists, seem to light up as the gleams of their narrow eyes scanned the audience with a premeditation of rascally joviality?

In addition, it was soon observable that, without invoking too many considerations of superstitious diabolism, the club members were examining the newcomers with a rather aggressive interest, mingled with a strong dose of anticipatory irritation against the tendentious speeches with which Fauber Théodule and Brunel Isidore would doubtless excite their dialogue, according to their well-known custom.

After all, it must be confessed that the Béthune Club only possessed legendary information regarding the title of doctor brought back by Fauber Théodule from a journey to America undertaken in his distant youth, by virtue of the marvelous surgical innovations that he had learned during that studious period from the principal Yankee pathologists. Nothing conclusive had ever been indubitably established regarding the origin and outcomes of M. Fauber's superiorities. A similar veil of indecision clouded the functions of correspondent for numerous foreign periodicals of which M. Brunel Isidore boasted, and the profound philosophical articles that he supposedly addressed to those important publications. Sometimes, people even dared to call into question the authenticity of the multiple decorative diplomas to which the two gentlemen insinuated their entitlement, the respectable signatures of which—with a disdain more colored with ostentation than shaded with modesty—they always neglected to display, partially or totally, in public.

It is to be supposed that the possession of a tidy fortune, inflated by individual supplements of annual income from unsecured loans, permitted the two old boys to wander over the summits of conveniently abstruse sciences without their being obliged to compromise their daily needs by any contact with any institution or profession. Furthermore, the two friends closely guarded the secret of the essential nature of the absorbing project on which they were working—of which, during their rare chats in the Club, they only allowed glimpses of the most deceptive conclusions: generalities that were always excessively sardonic and funereal, which our bitter tricksters, giving the appearance of assuming *a priori* the credulous stupidity of the *profanum vulgus*, reeled off with the all-too-evident intention of troubling the serenity of listeners and sowing, in their candid optimism, derision, disenchantment and fear.

Such was the inveterate grievance against these captious doctrinarians, which the present company attested by the severe absorption that they soon feigned to devote to the continuation of their card games, as if they were armored with intolerance against all nuisance.

The hostility softened slightly, however, thanks to the fact announced by the two old quibblers regarding the probability of a visit from "the Bonsor brothers"—an individual

233

whose bizarreries, however pronounced they might be, at least did not result in any acrimony with regard to the susceptibilities of the members of the Cub.

Besides, "the Bonsor brothers" retained the sympathy of the honorable society, even though he had thus far foiled the ever-despotic exigencies of regional curiosity. He had been able to keep the secret of his biographical particularities under the eventually-sidetracked investigations of the little town, and no one, without being overly bothered about it, knew what kind of scientific or whimsical pastime the ex-banker had adopted since his retirement from business. The hints that he dropped regarding various machinations of occultism had not yet been accredited with anything outrageous of the indigenous prudishness. He seemed, on the contrary, only to seek out his friends Brunel and Fauber at the Club in order to make polite fun of their unbridled speculations, thus making himself the instrument of the prevailing rancor.

Then again, there was a preliminary and almost mythical interest in the region In the very existence of the individual summarily indicated by the cooperative name of "the Bonsor brothers," derived from an old social cause. Was it Évariste or Sébastien Bonsor who had formerly led their prosperous finance house? No one knew, and no one, in any circumstances whatsoever, had even clapped eyes on the "two brothers" simultaneously. A near-identity in age—for they had definitely taken care not to represent themselves as twins—a striking resemblance and a methodical mutual exchange of journeys and returns executed by night, favored a system of mystifying substitutions, which the alternating Bonsor brothers amused themselves by continuing, having made a fortune, in the isolated house that had been built for him on the outskirts of Béthune.

The joke remained constant. Évariste finally became a chimera in the eyes of those did not believe in the implausibility of Sébastien, and—by a strange complication of the headache—Sébastien was only incarnate as the sum of an illusion that ceased to exist in the possibility of Évariste. Thanks to this skillful alter-egoism, the Bonsor duality avoided, at least by half, the annoyance of being "too frequently seen" that sojourns in narrow localities inflicts. They were only ever encountered "alone," and the person who then passed for one of them was then hurriedly greeted by the celebrated name of "the Bonsort brothers," which resolved synthetically, and politely, the suspicion that one might be talking to the other one.

"He claimed, though, to have something curious to tell us," said Dr. Fauber, observing in his turn the regrettable lateness of the authentic or supposed Bonsor. "Exactly what time is it, then?"

M. Brunel took his large gold watch from his waistcoat and turned the face to the doctor. "Exactly what time?" he said. "Why, just the nothing at all of the present moment between the nevermore and the not yet."

The sentence, delivered in a slow and profound voice, burrowed into the silence of the club—whereupon the insistent chime of half past ten emerged from the melancholy belly of the big clock, marking like a knell the continual decease of duration between never and always.

"Bravo!" applauded Dr. Fauber, putting on an apologist zeal somewhat in opposition to the audience's opinion. "It neglects the trivial in favor of laughter, your philosophy!"

"Yes, I confess, my philosophy will be joyful from now on," M. Brunel let slip, in the wake of a long puff of smoke. He continued: "It has become cheerful, my philosophy, because I have finally been able, through the inextricable confusion of opposed facts and theories, to summarize it in a precise formula: in the accurate—or perhaps false, but at least explicit—expression of my own personal point of view."

"Formularization is everything!" Fauber stated, doctrinally.

"But it also requires much obstinate research for its extraction," Brunel complained.

"Oh, we know what a hard worker you are," Fauber joked.

"And how much anguish that effort causes us," Brunel sighed, again. "What disenchantments. On seeing one or other of the most celebrated theories falsified, what despairs arise in confrontation with the vain pursuit of the conclusive idea!"

"Those are the true torments, utterly unknown to the vulgar," M. Fauber emphasized, with a glance of utter scorn for the assembly deemed incompetent in such deductions.

"Materialism, for example, seduced me for many years," M. Brunel began to recount. "It satisfied me completely in everything concerning the observation of accessible nature—but how could I not accuse it, finally, of an absurd contradiction with its own principles when it strays beyond the firm ground of certainties and claims to determine analytically the unexperimentable unknown that predominates around us, and even within ourselves?"

"It is certain," M. Fauber agreed, "that the most ingenious assertions of that school leave us unable to explain anything of the speculative operations of the mind, to take account of even the simplest phenomena of intellectual initiative."

"No, Messieurs the Materialists," said M. Brunel, rudely, "there is manifest within us a faculty creative of ideas, a conceptive life independent of sensory mechanism. Some of the abstractions of that reasoning power—that soul, if you wish—are not, whatever you might say, reflections or images, or repercussions of sensible facts. You will never—no, a thousand time no!—justify all that with your bundles of motor and sensory nerves and their attachment to the cerebral pulp, a simple inert mass to which, out of the pure expediency of affirmers short of proofs, you attribute some unknown intellectual energy, or some unknown interpretative automatism of sensation.

"Your corporeal being, which you make into the perfect circulus of the psycho-physical assembly, only shows us an arbitrary aggregate of tissues, humors and saps, each able to vegetate independently, into which nature infiltrates nothing more that its properties of cohesion, reproduction and imperishability; and you advance nothing but a petition in principle—which is to say, a stupidity—when you declare the soul absent at the birth of an individual because the imperfection of the embryonic organs has not yet permitted that soul to become manifest. To say that that intellectual virtuality appears subsequently *ex abrupto*, among elements that only contain it in essence, is equivalent to the ultra-metaphysical absurdity of having it emerge from nothing.

"You thus dispossess human beings of the original gift of continual and perfectible thought, which they believe their race to have and to transmit. It is in that hypothesis of an attachment to the human weave that people find a reason to exist, and you will never make them accept by preaching that problematic notion, in the ultimate depths of their consciousness, other than as a bitter and foolish derision for the suffering of living only to die, that they are not linked to anything anterior to them or succeeded by anything that surrounds them. Why, then, O too-exclusive materialists, do you refuse our organism accessory mentalities, which, in spite of their imperceptibility, are, after all, only material facts?"

M. Brunel continued to reason in a rude and resounding voice, with that invective manner—perhaps a trifle provincial—which consists of impersonally but furiously ticking off imaginary individuals with opposed opinions.

"Assuredly, assuredly!" exclaimed Dr. Fauber. "The senses and their annexes are only ever determined as the points of support of the vibrations or transmissions of the soul that haunts us and which conceives or expresses, through us, its ideative particularities. Of what importance to us, against that, are the rigorous denials of anatomists? Their microscopes have not encountered the soul. So what? Have the most exact descriptions of musical instruments, the most meticulous calculations of their sonority, the most limpid demonstrations of the rules of harmony and the most searching analyses of symphonic structure revealed any other origin for the lyrical emotions than the brain of the composer? There you are, then!"

"Very good! Very good!" M. Brunel confirmed, "although it's not the best argument to oppose to the detractors of animistic interference. I was forced, as you will easily under-

237

stand, to fall back into the ancient groove of the spiritualists.[53] But therein, instead of the blind fatality of things, there was the metaphysical illusion of words—nothing but the endless string of words proceeding to the obligatory consequences of their etymology: words that are both causes and effects and, by virtue of the artifice, drifting on a current of logic that has no source but the dictionary.

"Materialism adapts us without restriction to organic agencies instituted by mere chance, by virtue of which everything that exists might be otherwise or might as well not exist at all. With spiritualism we are the tributaries of a heap of Absolutes that flow according to the signification imposed upon syllables, becoming the prisoners of a sequence of syllogisms and conclusions of which the brain is no more than the verbal keyboard. We find ourselves conduits—damn it!—with a mystical drive toward belief in eternity, divinity, finality, etc., which it is necessary to accept in themselves, for they have no other proofs and, more especially, no other relationships between them than the definitions of the names that are given to them.

"Materialism arrests the independent flight of the Idea by restricting itself to the evident realities of substance. Spiritualism only builds its faith on the unstable imagery of phrases. The negations of the former rest on the facts; the latter bases its affirmations in the void. The principal objective of the two methods seems, therefore, to be to demonstrate their reciprocal insufficiency and, leaving us to our intimate manner of appreciating our present existence, they plunge us to a similar extent

---

[53] M. Brunel is not referring to practitioners of the occult art or religion known in English as spiritualism, who were more usually known in France as "spiritistes," but to the philosophical opponents of materialism who had been designated by that term long before the Fox sisters and a host of other imitative "mediums" got up to their shenanigans in the mid-19th century.

into the most frightful uncertainty regarding the necessity of living or having lived!"

"Certainly. The stupid affirmation of one or other of these theories does not stand up to examination," Dr. Fauber agreed, cynically, "and it's doubtless the humiliation of having cultivated the ineptitude of one of them for too long that creates a vindictive pleasure in preaching the other."

"Quint and quatorze!" the piquet table cut in, the players feigning total monopolization by the fascination of the game, but perhaps using that cry of victory as a kind of anathema against these fallacious dialectical absurdities.

It is true that one could not more deeply offend the sentiments of the honorable assembly, composed, as it usually was, of facile freethinkers in the anticlerical mode, partisans of returning "politely" to the oblivion from which one has come, or sectarians of a good God without hindrance who is supposed to protect for as long as possible the existence of his worshipers in modest little towns, demanding nothing more, via the voices of parish priests, than a formal adhesion, and promising them in exchange a happy perpetuity in future worlds full of honest bourgeois folk.

"Yes, such was the horror of my doubts!" Brunel went on, his acrimony increasing and his melancholy becoming more contagious as the extinction of another gas-lamp by the manager propagated the gloom within the room more harshly. "Such as my intolerable oscillation between those systems, which bring us no assurance with respect to what will become of us and do not present us with any plausible explanation of our present necessity. It was necessary, in consequence, for me to try to extract a truth from these various contradictions in correcting each of them by means of the other—and, after a thousand efforts to avoid a superficial eclecticism, I then arrived at what I call my own formula, my fixed principle, the definitive compass of my judgment."

"Let's have it," cried Dr. Fauber, widening his enthusiastic eyes in the thickening obscurity. "Let's have it!"

"And since then," Brunel went on, "I permit myself to say to Messieurs the materialists: we have a soul and it exists in parallel, if you please, with our substantial and vital mechanism. At the same time, however, I proclaim in the face of spiritualism that that soul, being wedded to matter, must necessarily be subject to material modifications. It's as simple as saying hello. It is necessary, come what may, that the soul in question is extinguished, disaggregated and volatilized in order to be resuscitated, with us and like us, in the various chemical, vegetable or gaseous particles into which we are destined to be redistributed. Consequently, and contrary to the obsolete claims of the Schools, we should—listen carefully; this is my formula—we should finally announce, affirm, extol and impose *the mortality of the soul*!" Brunel, finally sublime in his cold mockery, was resounding: "Yes! A thousand times yes! We need the mortality of the soul. We need it. It is high time!"

"Superb!" proclaimed Fauber, excitedly. "Superb!"

"Having understood this," Brunel continued, "and being fortified by the fact that nothing in nature can disappear, death becomes, logically, the phenomenon of transformation which melts a corporeal human being, soul included, back into a spiritualized matter in which his sensations—and, perhaps, his individual consciousness of a continuation of his being in eternity—reside. It is thus perfectly foolish to repeat that 'philosophizing is learning to die.'[54] Such a study is merely one way among so many others of killing time, and we would establish a more useful precept in declaring that it is necessary to

---

[54] In the French version quoted by Mullem ("*philosopher, c'est apprendre à mourir*") this dictum is associated with Michel de Montaigne, whose *Essais* include an elaborate meditation on its implications. Montaigne credits it to the Roman orator Cicero, who did indeed formulate it as an axiom, but Cicero was himself reflecting on an argument allegedly put forward by Socrates, as quoted by Plato, regarding his puzzling insistence on meekly accepting the death sentence passed on him by the Athenian state.

learn to die in order to enter into philosophy. A similar rule, in practice, would teach us the art of dying progressively and continuously, and about a radically intrinsic death—which is to say, one delimited by its exclusive and evident properties, beyond imaginative appreciations of belief or doubt.

"To that effect, we would analyze precisely the daily sum of proportional decline that every one of our plastic actions and intellectual efforts determines within us. We would keep an orderly account of our expenditure of life in the petty coin of muscular and cerebral activity, or even mere idling. 'Time is life,'[55] the English would as well be able to say. Each blow struck upon the anvil of time detaches a spark from the vital block.

"The scientific world will, I hope, admit as new and useful my idea of little quotidian death-throes, measured in proportion to the probability of our existence. But what am I saying? Quotidian? It is from hour to hour and minute to minute that we collect these delicate indications of continual death; we shall employ in grasping them all the known resources of histology and physiology, scrutinizing its progress with the most inflexible rigor, in order to advance gradually and in full knowledge of causality toward the form of material and mental immortality that we retain in infinity…"

"An odd play!" observed the bézique table, without being precise as to whether the allusion referred to the curiosity of a "500" or old Brunel's deplorable necrological buffooneries.

"It's magnificent!" insisted Dr. Fauber, in a voice tremulous with funereal admiration. "It's magnificent! One may affirm, in consequence, that 'the art of dying,' so neglected and so stupidly feared until now, will henceforth be informed in a clear and practical manner, which will bring it within everyone's range."

---

[55] Mullem renders this phrase in English, playing on the well-known Anglo-American dictum that "Time is money."

"Let us assume so!" M. Brunel conceded. "But have you not, my dear doctor, introduced a few good ideas yourself into the same category of ideas?—which, moreover, are admirably concordant with my theories. Eh, my lad? Rumors to that effect are running around the medical world! There's talk of a new 'Method of Pathology', by means of which you will demonstrate the incessant and congenital presence of morbid alterations latent and in development in all organized beings—something that might be called, democratically, 'the universal disease'."

"I cannot deny that my studies have, in recent times, headed in that direction," Fauber confessed. "According to my calculations, based on practice and in accordance with the evidence, there is reason to assign to each of our vital actions a proportional fraction of the quantity of successive alterations of which our death indicates the total. We therefore decline constantly, and by virtue of that fact are destined to perish. Now, each of these minuscule alterations—activated by its particular microbes—is necessarily accompanied by a relative measure of pain and, for their part, these sequences of pains realize the particular and regularly lethiferous[56] unhealthiness that each particular temperament possesses at birth.

"The most undisputable of philosophical observations is the one that sees our progress toward the grave commencing in the cradle—but why do the vulgar so willingly lose sight of the necessary consequence of that axiom, the knowledge that, between the point of departure and the terminus, the morbid principle *innate within us* follows is natural progression with no possible pause? Strong in their vigor and insouciant as to the question, human beings admit as healthy and intrinsically vivified the period of growth up to and including adulthood. Error, my friends! The vital fluid of an organized being, like the sap of plants, embodies the necessary against of degrada-

---

[56] This neologism, which I have transcribed directly into English, is derived from the same Latin root as "lethal" and means "death-producing."

tion in its original essence. That is a simple truism. There is, therefore, strictly speaking, no fixed and integral health. It is pure infatuation that makes people believe that they possess it. There is always something in one fraction or other of our existence that is, insensibly but irremediably 'getting worse.'

"Note that, in response to the ordinary question 'How are you?' people instinctively offer replies that are exceedingly banal but nevertheless lugubrious: 'not bad;' 'so-so,' etc.— which is to say: 'I'm pursuing, without any deleterious breakdown or murderous accident, my punctual process of decomposition.' That is how one considers one's health, for want of knowing one's personal constitutional disposition. And one flatters oneself on being the target of, or succumbing to, some indisposition or other exploited by the cunning of some modern Aesculapius, or even believing oneself to be a victim of some epidemic that has become fashionable on the word of journalists. Well, those are only superficial effects, pathological exteriorizations that merely translate the imperfection of certain fundamental—by which I mean constitutional—infirmities."

"So fevers," Brunel helped him, slyly, "consumptions, ataxias, apoplexies…"

"Are nothing but masks," attested Dr. Fauber. "Nothing more I tell you, than the various peripheral expressions of mortal elements that every one of us is fomenting internally. Ah! Nature, providence or fatality, is an absolute joke!"

It seemed that the doctor's laughter had passed like a gust of wind over the last gas-lamp, which the manager had just extinguished. Nothing remained lit but the fantail burner of the central reflector, whose exceedingly pale radiance was dancing over the irritated stupefaction of the card-players."

"It is only fair to recognize, however," M. Fauber continued, "that Science had singularly neglected this field of investigation until now. The docile credulity of patients is, therefore, to a great extent excusable. They have hardly any means of control in such matters, and are constrained to allow their diagnoses to be orientated toward a small number of maladies that are, so to speak, officially imposed upon them. I conclude, in consequence, that a pathologist has a rigorous duty to extend his discoveries as far as he can into that inexhaustible repertoire of infirmities of every sort.

"Agronomists, carefully increasing our means of leguminary nutrition, searched among as-yet-uncultivated vegetables for new comestible resources. In the same way, within his entirely contrary art, the medical investigator, disdaining the all-too-easy observations of collective affectations—which is to say, adventitious maladies not inherent to his client—will try to extract from the human plant the radical secret of its auto-destructive virtualities, and will only try to lead his invalid toward a decease that will allow him personally and—if you will allow me to us the word—legitimately to pass over.

"I am devoting myself to this task, in my modest fashion, and what an inexhaustible mine I have immediately glimpsed of as-yet-unanalyzed deteriorations and breakdowns. Nothing is stable, in sanitary terms; nothing, I tell you, is unscathed by the exacerbation and usury of the mechanism of death that operated within the physiological individual unremittingly. There is not a single one of the 1000 fibers of the living body that is not making a contribution to the work of final degradation. The most infinitesimal nerve embodies its special disorder, which it communicates to the entire system and impacts upon the brain. The muscular tissue weaves a perpetual alternation of atrophy and hypertrophy. The skin, in its entirety, is nothing but a porous filter for the absorption of subtle rheumatizing and microbial agents from the atmosphere. The bones, in their apparent opacity, are perforated by myriads of microscopic channels infiltrated by the intoxications that our humors pour out. Embryonic sensitivities—which is to say, vital sacrifices—operate at the root of every fingernail and hair of any sort.

"It is admirable, given all this, to think that the most minimal irritation of the surface provokes, by a mysterious process of transmission, shooing pains in the profound layers. What prodigious artistry! What humorless fatality! What mistaken damage inflicted by nature of things on the extollers of final causes! And I need not mention, after you, my dear M. Brunel, the continual current of deleterious impressions that flow from thought to the cerebral substance, and from there to the rest of the economy. I shall limit myself to recalling incidentally the impotence of the imagination to concentrate its own unease without projecting anxiety to other sensitive regions. But let us not omit to specify that the brain itself is modified according to the character of the emotion appropriate to every thought, and that it localizes in the organs the subsequent anomalies of perturbations.

"Who can say, for example, whether a cardiac affection[57] determined by political deceptions is entirely similar to a similar infirmity produced by the frustration of literary ambition or disappointment in love? It is no longer a matter, you see, in all of this, of that meager half-dozen classic maladies by which the coterie of orthodox physicians claims that everything is circumscribed. In my opinion, I have begun to establish, at least in its general outlines, the nomenclature of these innumerable causes of irrepressible alternations, which it is necessary to specify nerve by nerve, globule by globule and atom by atom—each one of which, according to its virulence, is susceptible of supplementation by the diseases that surround it. Members of the public, thus informed, nothing less than liberated from their hygienic illusions, will then only have to observe themselves in order to determine exactly what sort of life will lead to their death."

---

[57] As with much of the wordplay in this speech, this item does not quite translate into English; the phrase that I have transcribed directly carries two distinct meanings, dependent on whether one construes "cardiac affection" as "fondness" or "heart disease." I have refrained from footnoting several similar instances, because it would become tedious; all I can do is inform the reader, regretfully, that the original version of this entire passage is a trifle wittier than its English equivalent.

"*Avons le mort,*"[58] said the three-handed whist table, whose tenants abruptly changed seats.

"That's exquisite!" Brunel supplied, compliantly. "You will leave behind a renown exceptional in science: that of an inventor of diseases."

"One invents nothing; one merely discovers," Dr. Fauber temporized, "but I shall, at least, have revealed the art of being ill in order better to die, as you are revealing the art of dying in order better to philosophize…"

"And I have found something better!" interjected a new-comer whose entrance had passed unnoticed, and in whose configuration the club believed that it recognized one or other fraternal exemplar of the rare Monsieur Bonsor.

The last gas-jet still alight did not illuminate the corner in which the conversationalists were sitting. Monsieur Bonsor could be seen sitting down in the moonlight filtering in from outside—which, enveloping him with vague light, projected an exact shadow of his person on to a neighboring seat, almost a disquieting silhouette of a second "Bonsor brothers."

"Is that the important communication for which you summoned us?" asked Brunel.

"We've been waiting for you impatiently," Fauber assured him.

"Yes, Messieurs," said one or the other Bonsor. "I willingly render homage to the progress resulting from your work, but I repeat that I have found something better than cultivating the philosophy of dying or detailing the disease of living; I have acquired the means of living without existing, or, if you prefer, bearing witness as a mere spectator to my entire and positive non-existence."

---

[58] There is, alas, no English equivalent (so far as I know) of this arcane technical term, let alone one that preserves its essential pun. Its literal meaning is, of course, "let's die." In three-handed whist, one player has to be partnered by a "dummy" hand, so what the players are doing is switching round so that someone else has that dubious privilege.

A study in length and weakness of profile, tightly costumed in the anglomaniac style, Monsieur Bonsor brothers punctuated his words sarcastically with a tremulous elevation of the index finger, which caused the shadow sitting beside him to tremble in parallel.

"Non-existence! Damn it, that's saying a lot," M. Brunel remarked.

"That would require very assiduous study," opined M. Fauber.

"I shall not deny," said M. Bonsor, "that before attaining my goal, I was obliged to dedicate myself for a very long time to the most subtle experiments of 'automentalhypnosis'— which is to say, the art of hypnotizing oneself mentally." The wagging of the index finger separated every syllable of these great words to signify their importance. "My God!" he added. "One can say that in all modesty. The science is nothing very new. The Buddhists of India procure a state of abstraction of that sort called *nirvana*, thanks to practices of autosuggestion whose traditional formulae go back to the remotest antiquity. The profundity of the catalepsies obtained by that method is such—as travelers believed to be reliable report—that the ecstasized can be subjected to an astonishingly prolonged temporary burial. During their reclusion in the grave, these Buddhists, by the application of powers of astrality—forces still obscure for us—disengage some sort of vaporous tissue imitative of their corporeal structure, and achieve in that way the visible and tangible flight of a part of their soul.

"At this point, I ought to remark that during their burial, it is the essential part of their soul to which these strange individuals release, while they simultaneously immobilize the part of their soul that remains terrestrial. I mean by 'terrestrial' the amalgam of education and instruction that familial and social authority instills in us; it is the fraction of the adventitious soul by means of which we cease to be ourselves to become 'others,' by means of which, in the enigmatic drama of consciousness, a person incessantly remains the disconcerted interrogator of his own role In other words. It is the 'acquired' soul or, if you wish, the supplement of experimental intellectuality that we receive from objective—which is to say, material and external—interventions. It is therefore natural that it shares in the somnolence of the purely physical faculties that bring it into play.

"As for the part of the soul freed from its carnal prison during these brahmanic lethargies, that is our original soul, liminally innate within us—what philosophers have called 'the soul of our soul.' It is the 'native' soul that ordinarily complicates the 'acquired' soul, without ever reaching the point of knowing it well or being in complete accord with it. It is the arcane element of the soul, in which our primal aspiration, our suddenly emergent passions and our exclusive and irreducible entity are fomented. It is, in fact, the only aspect of our formation in which we are autonomously free, where our thought finds the security of its own reason for being, but which mercilessly steers the other half of the indoctrinated soul to obedience and imitation.

"This primordial fraction of the soul—or, if you wish, this autopsychy—is the one that the Hindus disengage from its corporeal anesthesia in order to free it, without substantial shackles, from contact with the ambient world. In contrast to these Indian mores, however it is the "self" of our soul, the "elementary self" that is amenable, among we Europeans, to occlusion in the impassive meditation of nirvana. On the contrary, it is the other half of us, the mechanical, educable, intractable, active and reproductive individual that it is necessary to expel from thought and deliberately abandon to its animal task of pure imitation.

"This is obtained, I repeat, by a mental concentration of the will toward the conquest of a doubling—which, although it is regarded as chimerical by the profane, is no les confirmed, for certain adepts, with the full degree of certainty that their conviction can embody. With respect to myself, I believe that I have succeeded completely. I no longer confront with myself anything but a separate, nirvanic impersonality, in which my intellect is adapted to the ideal. Once again, I do not exist, relative to my mundane exteriority, and I have taken the necessary steps to send that exteriority to circulate by itself, but selflessly, in the tedium of society. Pardon me, though—in this respect, I forgot to…permit me…"

M. Bonsor brothers stood up very straight, copied instantaneously by the adjacent shadow, and with a formal gesture, said: "Messieurs Brunel and Fauber, I have the honor of introducing you to my Survivor."

There was an exchange of bows in the lunar obscurity, whose cold gravity augmented the suspicions of the Club that this apparition of the Bonsor brothers, finally simultaneous, might be more or less supernatural.

"All our condolences," said M. Brunel, necrologically, bowing to the second Bonsor, whom he considered as having fallen from elevated speculations to life itself, condemned henceforth to wander in the flat reality of communal existence.

"And we shall pray for you until the hour of your free resurrection," added Fauber, in the same funereal tone of commiseration.

The doubled Bonsor then, finally, resumed speaking.

"Suicidophilic in appearance," he said, "my brother has organized this means of making known the authenticity of his claimed decease. This is the whole of the mystery. He will henceforth retrench himself in the bliss of his dreams and leave me in charge of his daily routines. I shall be subject without release to the brewing of business affairs, visits, soirées, weddings, etc. I shall have to take part in carious administrative councils and parliamentary assemblies. It will be necessary for me to play the wallflower at receptions, affect amusement in false pleasure parties, sketch consternated expressions in the presence of other people's misfortunes, and, finally, to fulfill the obligations of the human number, with contrived sentences, rigorous politeness, requisite hypocrisies, dinners, indigestions, draughts, rheumatisms and all the rest. It's infinitely tedious!"

Your annoyance is certainly understandable," confessed M. Brunel, "and your generously abdicated thought certainly merits a less ambulatory corporeal internment.

"So I thought of devoting myself, for a few days, on my own account, to a mortuary comedy played out in the desired conditions of plausibility—but imagine the difficulties of every sort to which I would be exposing myself. The Church demands confessional and oleaginous demonstrations. The town hall insists on the emission of a last sigh attested by a municipal physician. Add to the exorbitant cost of funeral ce-remonies the price of their ill-assorted processions and their dispensation of land, especially when one adds in the illusory clause of concessions in perpetuity. It's intolerable. There's no principle of *laissez faire et laissez trespasser*[59] such as the modern mind desires. So here I am, relieved, for the time be-ing, of any obituary whims, and resigned to my tribulations as a social mannequin. Besides, the fault of being able to appear deceased has as its rigorous corollary the semblance of being able to be alive...."

The last gas-lamp expired. The Club members poured out on to the staircase and made their farewells in the main square, while Brunel, Fauber and the double Bonsor disap-peared into the shadow spread by the tall façade of the town hall—from which, at that moment, the chimes of midnight emerged.

There were a few moments of further chitchat among the groups.

"What bores and braggarts!" said the card-players, brisk-ly and vengefully.

---

[59] Given that English has found it necessary to import the phrase *laissez faire* [let be, or let alone] in the sphere of eco-nomics, for lack of an adequate expression of its own, it seemed appropriate to leave this entire phrase in the original; the nearest English equivalent, which does not have the same elegant dash, would be "let live and let die."

"What a miscreant that Brunel is!" said a contentedly theistic piquet-player.

"What a clergyman that Fauber is!" declared a Voltairean impériale-player, at hazard.

"Curious, all the same, about that other one who availed himself of death!" mused a whist-player, anxiously.

"That's all right," said a resigned bezique-player, "it's a long time since we've had such an amusing evening in Béthune!"

Louis Mullem: *The Shadow and His Man*
(c. late 1889s-early 1890s)

"Free! Free at last!"

Yes, that really was, it seemed to me, the refrain mumbled by the singular individual next to whom I chanced to find myself on the bench.

We had met a short while before at a funeral, and nothing about either of us had particularly interested the other, each of us being the kind of unostentatious stranger that makes up the numbers of such processions. Now, I could not help sparing him a sideways glance. He was tall and thin, poorly dressed in a black frock-coat—as I was myself—with a tall, unfashionably ceremonious hat like mine. A few linden leaves extended between the morning sun and the two of us poured a trembling green pallor over the fellow—and doubtless over me too.

"Finally free!" he continued to mutter, with slow sighs of relief, like grief extending its wings toward forgetfulness. Was he really speaking? Was it not merely my imagination that pretended to detect meaning in the indistinct breath of his lips?

I analyzed the man in greater detail. He represented a complete insignificance, apparently devoid of any sentiment worth the trouble of mentioning. His fragile and timorous silhouette described a very humble uselessness—and yet, one divined in him a strange mystical satisfaction, conceived of that very excess of non-value: a sort of internal semi-gaiety; perhaps a discreet reaction of irony against the need to fulfill his bleak destiny of being an absolutely nonentity in any social role whatsoever.

Then again, he was scrutinizing with a rather sardonic eye the medley of grass and flowers surmounted by a crucifix—the common grave—before which, bringing a halt to our funerary excursion, we were taking a moment of leisure in the middle of the necropolis.

Was he evoking some deceased person buried in that nameless mud after a purposeless existence? What it that person whom he deemed justly delivered from terrestrial disappointments? Or was he remembering a bad parent, a perfidious mistress, or some false friend or other, of whom death had conveniently rid him?

My curiosity was awakened on that subject. Our recent inhumatory collaboration furnished sufficient pretext for a conversation between people who had nothing to say. I extended a forefinger toward the banal popular tumulus. "Loved or hated, we find them there, don't we, Monsieur?" I said, with a brusque cordiality, as if to jump smoothly into the supposed depths of his reflections.

He turned his pale face toward me. The features, already clawed by old age, revealed a certain joy, rather disconcerting for me, in embarking upon an ordinary conversation. It appeared to be the satisfaction of a maniac seizing a fortunate opportunity to expound his obsessions. I already feared being drawn into the tedium of an endless discussion in the philosophico-soporific mode customary in the presence of tombs, but his response filled me with surprise.

"Is the person I neither hated nor loved lying there?" he said. "Is he alive or dead? Was, he in fact, ever alive? I don't know. The materiality of his being imposed upon me an illusion that has effaced the years. That's all! And I feel that I am free of him...for I was his shadow."

"His shadow!" I exclaimed, bewildered by the agreement of the word with my interlocutor's costume and physiognomy. "His shadow?" I repeated. "Oh, that must be a curious story."

"More harrowing than strange," he remarked, his voice meditative and his eyelids half-closed on a gaze reaching into the distance of memory. He went on: "I had been going about for 20 years when I first observed the existence of the chimerical creature that resembled me, feature for feature, and which moved in front of me as if my own body were preceding me.

253

"I was waiting, in that era, for the radiant romance of life, as promised in stories, and I was intoxicated by ideal transports toward any beauty floating on my horizon. It was especially at those moments of foolish exaltation, during time spent in the wind and the sunlight of the streets, that the phantom rose up whose double I was.

"I thought at first of simple mirages, for the apparition was limited within the range of my vision. In the distance, it became iridescent and dispersed into fluid; too close, it was suddenly absorbed into me; then, in the fading of dusk and darkness, I no longer saw it. Soon, though, I discerned the true character of the prodigy. It was full of terror. The composite of human light clad in my form acted in my stead and in my place, drawing me inertly in his wake. He went forward in the desire whose dream I caressed, in the resolution of which I formed the will. He gave gestures to my most secret thoughts; boldly or cynically, he incorporated my soul and compelled me, as I have told you, to be no more than the shadow of my own individuality.

"Consider, for example, how things transpired when, in the course of my 20th year, the beauty of a woman advanced toward me, a temptress of infinite hope. Immediately, my damned specter filched a seductive effigy of himself from the reflection of a shop-window, and then confronted the lady's young splendor with an attitude of infallible conquering audacity; he displayed his foppish fatuity in a greeting; He affected to put one hand on his heart—on mine, alas, which beat as if to burst!—while the other, undulating and romantic, abandoned itself to the blowing of a kiss. Strange success! The beauty, as if dualized by a similar phenomenon, appeared delighted; the brush of the imaginary kiss set a tremor on her lips; a glint of pleasure gleamed between her eyelashes. For a few moments, entirely beside myself, I imagined myself becoming the real hero of the exquisite adventure! But almost as quickly, the fantastic couple dissipated in the evasive play of light, while my own distressed being—oh, how unnoticed!—was subjected to the lady's haughty indifference!

"Such, my dear Monsieur, was my vain amorous youth; he, my passionate projection, lending himself incessantly to the exuberant pantomime of sensations that I put forth; me, never being anything but his shadow and his silence..."

My comrade paused. He had expressed himself constantly in his dull murmur, which also seemed the echo of a silence and the shadow of voice. Again I was in doubt as to whether he really was speaking, or whether I was merely hearing in my own skull the nebulous story to which the mortuary appearance of my companion gave rise.

"My days, however," he continued, "had charm then. The unreal actor who was the image of me exerted himself in the impetuosity of the noblest enthusiasms. The disappointment that rebounded therefrom upon the timidity of my soul left me, at least, a certain sweet reverie compounded out of sadness. Ten years later, those gentle impressions were no more.

"That decade had produced no more result than the augmentation of the two or three derisory *louis* of my monthly wage, in the somber indigence of a lowly judiciary clerk. The poor fellow's cares, humiliations and rage stirred up a crescendo in my mind—but if I resigned myself, apparently being too much of a coward, if faint attempts at revolt only groaned confusedly in the depths of my consciousness, that was not the case with my prestigious alter ego, who now permitted himself an unleashing of wild insurgency. His face grew green with hate and fury on encountering so many upstarts who paraded in the insolence of fortune and pride. I imagined hearing the bitter cry of the insults he hurled against the costumes of strollers in luxury. He almost contrived to provoke some of the wealthy individuals by virtue of whom his poverty—which is to say, alas, mine, so black it was—seemed muddied with scorn. These affectations procured me the delicious anticipation of a vengeance that would obtain him room for maneuver.

"I confess that I wished that he might commit the spiteful absurdities that he sketched out on my behalf. In the depths of consciousness, I premeditated trepidations on tiptoe, punches breaking noses, the vertiginous trampling of thorns under-foot—but externally, I observed the most prudent impassivity, in order to avoid any reprisals. How superfluous that precaution was, though. By the time the insults reached me, my demon had fled; I was his shadow, in which everything faded away; I became once again the said ruined wretch that no one noticed, and of whose boasts no one deigned to take any notice. Truly, those whimsical effervescences of the street were breaking me, and the following evenings were worse. As I have told you, in the darkness of the garret, the sprite, the gnome, the sylph or the djinn—call him what you like—infused himself within me. We were nothing but an exaltation of rancor, and we were subject to cruel insomnias full of howls against the torments of existence, of which he was only the vain play of light, and which amassed in me an obscure and inexpressible dolor…"

The narrator stopped for a second time, his face grimacing in remembrance of the furies of the past.

"Fits of despair, frightful although futile," I said, compassionately.

"Certainly!" he continued, having pulled himself together. "There were ten more years of torture, but finally, appeasement had it hour. My goblin was captured by age. He manifested himself outwardly in the most anodyne fashion, and we gradually came into harmony, in the eternal frippery of my black frock-coat, the entirely inoffensive type-specimen of the good little clerk in his den. A conclusive reform! He exhibited from then on a timorous and prudent appearance. He greeted our fellow citizens decorously in their Sunday walks, and even condescended to take off his ceremonious top hat—the one that, unfortunately, I am presently wearing—to salute any ladies and gentlemen that he judged to be important.

"Privately, I protested a little against these platitudinous courtesies. The old revolutionary leaven still fermented from time to time under the whiplash of egalitarian convictions—but I was fated to be the shadow slave; against my wishes, I imitated the polite gestures; I too took off the top hat and dedicated bows to notable individuals at a respectful distance; and by virtue of pure automatism, my coarse impulses were finally transmuted into amiable imitations of urbanity.

"Time completed the dispersal of the vexations themselves. It brought old age with it, and that methodical egotism which dispels emotions for hygienic reasons, if not for philosophical ones. In probably-rational consequence, the dolled-up Lucifer of my own stamp—was that not my own vanity too long contemplative of itself in the reflections of shopwindows?—my Lucifer, I repeat, now ceased to open my wake along the streets. He no longer animated, in the guise of my features, the being devoid of radiation whom he allowed to reach a terminus. Is that enough to make me boast of being free? A fine affair! But I sometimes, all the same, how I miss that aerial twin, by means of whom all that surged within me of bold aspiration, noble desire and judiciary audacity simulated the power of life. I am still a shadow, but the shadow of something that has vanished forever, a patch of shadow on the effaced trace of my soul, dead before me..."

We had risen to our feet toward the end of this prattle, and were going out into the remote quarter overlooked by the hill of the cemetery.

"Your case is very simple," I told him, by way of conclusion. "In Germany, the tale was once told of the misadventures of a man who had lost his shadow.[60] You my fear Monsieur, are a shadow who has lost his man."

I expected a reply to this subtle explanation, but the person I had been talking to had, I think—I don't know how—slipped away.

I found myself alone, sharply cutting out on the sunstruck walls the tall, thin outline of an old bailiff's man in a worn black frock-coat, in a tall ceremonial funeral-hat, and I lost myself among the crowd of passers-by: shadows, like me, of the supreme heroes they once believed they had within

---

[60] Adalbert von Chamisso's *Peter Schlemihl* (1814).

257

them; shadows still of what they wanted to be and could not become.

Louis Mullem: *Chemical Eternity*
(c. late 1889s-early 1890s)

Doctor Gipson is only known to the public at present by virtue of the launch of a "manifesto" that he has communicated to the newspapers, and which is to serve as a sort of preface or explanatory program to a full-length book that he intends to publish imminently.

In that preliminary document, however, he posed as the absolute reformer of the medical art and he anticipated the amazing results that the art in question would obtain in future, by virtue of the application of his method. He was, moreover, confident of demonstrating and proving these prodigies in his future volume.

The noise generated in the scientific world by this was immense. Some opined, quite unceremoniously, that our man was a charlatan; other affected a boundless admiration in his regard and confidently fabricated biographies decorated with the most extraordinary therapeutic successes.

By virtue of this concert of anthems and exaltations, in which irony doubtless played an even greater role than certainty, Dr. Gipson emerged, some 15 months ago, as the hero of the day—which ensures, I think, that our readers (it is a reporter from the *Go-Ahead*[61] who is speaking) will obtain some amusement from an intimate sketch of the man. To obtain this pleasure, I made some preliminary inquiries, the result of which was that a one-to-one meeting over a fine dinner was the best means of encouraging the doctor to confidences, and

---

[61] Mullem gives the name of this periodical in English, to confirm the various other clues he offers to the effect that the story is set in England. I have, however, refrained from altering the name of the doctor to the infinitely more plausible "Gibson."

after a rapid exchange of correspondence, I obtained permission to collect him from his domicile one afternoon and take him to my club as a guest.

I carried out this enterprise yesterday, and was received in Dr. Gipson's vestibule by a lady whose dark costumed augmented the melancholy expression of a face whose handsome features were accentuated by thinness.

"My husband is waiting for you in his laboratory," she said, having seen my visiting card. "Would you care to follow me?" There was no need for her to reveal her conjugal status; one recognized at first glance one of those spouses with a bruised soul who submit resignedly, in the shadows, to the extravagances and effervescences of a man of genius—or one who believes himself to be a genius.

No technical equipment was visible in the apartment to which that attractive wife introduced me; nothing was to be seen there but a divan and a few chairs, and also an occasional table supporting the apparatus necessary for mixing hot toddies.

The place was quite cheerful. The windows framed a section of garden where a few snowdrops were fluttering slowly in sparse winter sunlight. A blazing fire in the hearth doubled with a dance of light shadow of Dr. Gipson's long black garment on the pale green of the opposite wall. The light emphasized the tallness and thinness of his upper body and colored the disorderly mass of grey hair on his head. It faded away in the distracted expression the depths of his black eyes, but by way of compensation, it sparkled in the facets of an enormous diamond—perhaps too fabulously enormous—which stood out against a white cravat in a fashion that one could only compare to fragments of a blaze.

I noted these details while the doctor, after a few words of welcome, constrained me, in view of the cold outside, to take my share of a toddy that, even though divided between us, appeared no less vigorous. During this interval, Mrs. Gipson handed her husband his carefully-brushed hat, and then we left the house.

Rapid as this departure was, however, I had time to note the pensive glance that Mrs. Gibson directed at the immense diamond that the doctor was wearing. Was I mistaken? One might have thought that she was attributing a fateful significance to that circumstance—or did she simply regret seeing her spouse take that prodigious item of jewelry out of the house?

In spite of the aforementioned cocktail, the cold of the street froze the words on our lips. We hastened to my club, where a well-laid table awaited us. Our wellbeing was quickly restored by the preliminaries of the meal, and I finally embarked upon the scientific conversation into which I needed to draw my gust.

I began by announcing to the eminent practitioner my desire to obtain a few autobiographical details, while depreciating my ability, as a simple reporter, to follow him into more abstract discourse. As proof of my layman's sincerity, as much as to ask him to correct my errors, I then set out to summarize what I had read about him in various specialist periodicals, without neglecting certain items of information that, doubtless due to my ignorance, seemed to me to be buffooneries of the most extravagant sort.

"Your admirers and your adversaries," I said, "agree, each from his own viewpoint, in calling attention to your extraordinary manner of practicing autoplasty.[62] At a young age, it is said, you invented a host of 'transmutative' instruments adapted to the sad necessities of war, and that, also being endowed with an incomparable promptitude of execution, you accomplished the boldest operations imperturbably under a hail of bullets. You were seen, on one of the last battlefields of the old world, to relieve combatants of their shattered limbs

---

[62] Strictly speaking, autoplasty is the repair of lesions by means of tissue-grafts taken from elsewhere on the same body (the only sort of grafting that had been successfully exemplified in Mullem's day); as will quickly be seen, however, Gipson's supposed expertise lies in transplant surgery of far more extravagant kinds.

and to replace them, *hic et nunc*,[63] with similar appendices taken from freshly-killed soldiers.

"Bellicose rage and nervous surges of heroism or terror favored these surgical improvisations on living flesh. Arms switched shoulders without letting go of their rifles, firing continually all the while. Cadavers were seen lying on the ground by their own eyes, introduced into the blind orbits of brothers-in-arms. The heads of private soldiers suddenly found themselves on the bodies of officers—a prodigious promotion imposed by the pressure of the circumstances of battle.

"Taking advantage of the recent carnage executed by Europeans in Asia and Africa, you transported in your wake caravans of exceedingly rich clients, who had been treated with extreme disfavor by nature, on whom you effected transplantations and connections that were all the more fruitful for benefiting from a mixture of races. And it is certainly consoling to think that these frightful butcheries, in which conquerors persist under the pretext of being civilizers, will no longer serve in future for the exclusive satisfaction of inhumanity, but that, thanks to you and the popularization of your method, will work to the advantage of scientific progress."

I thought I had surpassed the most extreme limits of exaggeration, but the doctor listened to me with a sly benevolence, and fixed upon me the gaze of a superior individual who is delighted to learn what the ignorant irony of the public is saying about him.

Thus encouraged, I continued—while we were emptying our first two or three glasses—to tell him in a eulogistic manner about certain other extreme farces that were being laid at his door.

"These marvels were nothing, however," I said to him, "by comparison with the mighty feats that you accomplished later, after long studies whose mystery no one has penetrated. Not satisfied with your superficial applications, you pushed the audacity of the vivisector so far as to inaugurate modifica-

---

[63] There and then.

tion in the internal organs of the human species. It is asserted that, during a sojourn in Paris, you opened a 'cooperative ovariotomy dispensary' that was a great success.

"That sort of feminine ablation gave rise to ardent controversy at the time. The ruling classes, which demanded plebeian abundance for the needs of war and industry, feared the propagation of that mode of sterilization among the populace. The clan of sociologists, persuaded that a wealthy minority is better than a limitless proliferation of poor people, praised the timely utility of the artifice in question, and embraced polemic as firebrands of its paradoxes. Then, terrorized by the speeches of conservatives, and, most of all, by clerical objurgations, the majority of your desexualized individuals fell into the most bitter remorse—but your art brought them salvation. You were not the routine kind of surgeon who limits himself, once and for all, to cutting out the organ that displeases him. You hold that organ in reserve, in conditions that permit it, if necessary, to resume its original place, and you were counting on a quantity of fashionable women who would eventually undertake alternately to abandon and recover the means of fecundation according to their interests or whims.

"Your skill, in what I dare to call subjective surgery, then seemed to have attained the final limits of the possible, and yet you were to cause the scientific world even more astounding surprises. You eventually shed complete light on the fact, scarcely glimpsed at the time, that sexual specialization remains indecisive during uterine life. The distinctive marks of each genre, although they seem very clear after emergence into the world, sometimes retain a few more of less profound indications of that original hesitation. For example, some men, integral in other respects, look at life with eyes that seem to have a feminine constitution, and their visual sensations have the advantages and inconveniences of that anomaly. Some women provided with the most specific external attributes of their sex nevertheless embody, without emphasizing vague corporeal deformations, some fragment of masculinity, and a

263

brain imprinted with a persistence of virility that inspires them with all its actions and, sometimes all its extravagances.

"I shall not expand further on the innumerable natural imbroglios of this sort, for they often give rise to more-than-scabrous eccentricities of which contemporary literature has too often provided an ignorant echo, solely in the desire to hook the curiosity of numerous readers. What I can venture to say is that, in more than one household in which some such disparity afflicts both spouses instead of than amusing them, you have brought about a concordance or exchange of organs by a prodigious series of interpolations that would have made you the most admired man of our century if the honorability of your fortunate clients had not rigorously constrained you to professional secrecy..."

My statements were beginning to take on the appearance of an impertinent "leg-pull," and, no longer knowing exactly what I was doing, I had refilled a certain number of glasses to the brim when doctor made a gesture indicating that he was about to speak in his turn.

"Let us leave there, I beg you," he said, "these trifling operations, of which those that are not yet authentic will necessarily come about in the course of time. Surgery, that purely manual art, benefits from equipment whose sequential improvement will proceed indefinitely and will vanquish all mechanical obstacles.

"Besides, a living being is not, as the vulgar suppose, a pure unity. It is, on the contrary, composed of a multitude of substances that retain, within the agglomerate, their own function, their particular progress and, ordinarily, their independent activity. It is therefore, in the destiny of the profession that I have long practiced eventually to attain, gradually but surely, absolute mastery in the faculty of making all desirable modifications in animal bodies by the separate treatment of their parts. These results, already foreseeable, should not astonish us, even in advance.

"The surgeon, however, limits himself to the relatively simple task of carnal mechanization. It is not within his competence to go back to the sources of life, to extract that phenomenon from the mystery that envelops it, to direct its course and, at will, to extend it. Such is the problem on which I am now mounting a frontal attack, with the hope—almost with the certainty—of a solution. It is in that respect only that I propose to affirm my personal and creative role in the history of science."

On the last words of that exordium, the doctor made me a sign to refill the glasses, as if as an oratory precaution, in view of a long speech, and I summoned up all my attention.

"Yes," Dr. Gipson continued, "to extend the gift of human life for as long as possible, and to devote all medical resources to that end—that it is the task for which I wish, at least, to construct the theory, while simultaneously furnishing the first elements of the procedures to be put to work on the service of that *desideratum*.

"In truth, existence has thus far only appeared in each of us as a temporary configuration of matter in motion, like a bubble dissolving after a brief moment into the liquid that the air has buoyed up. We can therefore assume that there can be no permanence in our present form. However, that permanence manifests itself as a possibility to some observers.

"On this matter, before any other explanation and for the purposes of greater clarity, permit me to affirm with Virchow[64] that 'the continuity of life must be, for us, a dogma'. Whether it is a matter of the birth of an organism or of a disease, the great scientist declares, it is a living cell that we find at the point of origin. Darwinism emerges in its entirety from that idea—as Virchow alleges—and the continuity of cellular life suffices to explain the hereditary transformations of the most complex organisms.

---

[64] Rudolph Virchhow (1821-1902) popularized the dictum *Omnis cellula e cellula* [every cell originates from another], which was actually coined by François Raspail, after adopting the dogma in 1858.

"To this I will add that, 40 years ago, Monsieur G. Ville[65] showed that certain vegetable enjoy the singular property of transforming the mineral nitrogen in the air into organic nitrogen—which is to say, into living cells. We are therefore entitled to suppose, with some plausibility, that the vital continuity or permanence of which I speak resides at least in the admixture of our posthumous decompositions—that is to say, of the aforementioned still-living cells—with the analogous and imperishable particles of the environmental substance, to which we thus restore that which we have borrowed from passive and sensitive elements.

"Until now, physicians have made scarcely any progress in this direction, because they have not understood the intimate mixture of vegetation and sensation that constitutes animality, even though the ancient philosophers and even the Church Fathers glimpsed this state of affairs a long time ago. One of the most assiduous reasoners among the latter, Tertullian, whom I have studied extensively, made a considerable contribution to the emphasization of this truth: 'The soul,' he wrote, 'is made of matter. It is composed of a special substance that differs from that of the body. It has all the qualities of matter, but it is immortal.'

"The ingenious theologian did not imagine that matter is equally indestructible. He thus affirmed, without knowing it, the simultaneous perpetuity of the soul and the body. In another work—concerning, I believe, the resurrection of the flesh— this same theologian tells us: 'The soul is the director and, in a sense, the coachman of the body. It has the exclusive power of forming thoughts, willing, desiring and disposing what it proposes, and, when it acts to that effect, it expects the flesh to do

---

[65] Georges Ville claimed to have demonstrated this hypothesis experimentally in 1853; it had first been proposed much earlier, by Joseph Priestley among others. This sentence implies that the story was written in 1893 or thereabouts, which is consistent with the earlier implication that Virchow was still alive at the time of writing.

the work. The flesh is the carriage of the soul, its adornment and its wealth. The soul does not withdraw alone, like the flesh, it has its retreats, which are waters, fires, birds and beasts of every sort, as well as plants of all kinds. Our double personality does not dissolve in these substances, it merely flows within them, and also in mires—and if those mires dissipate, it still flows within them, and, as if it emerged in alternate turns and returns, is thrown back thrown back into the earth, its ultimate origin.'"

Toward the end of this tirade I had filled a few glasses, half of which the doctor absorbed very calmly, and I the other half, a trifle bewildered by this unexpected Tertullian cited by Dr. Gipson in tone of freshly-revived memory, like an introduction to a set of axioms that he was about to extract.

"Yes, Tertullian was very largely correct," he went on. "Yes, the mind, the thinking faculty encounters appropriate receptacles in scattered matter—and it is marvelous to think that if the body proceeds germinatively, and if the soul, by the same token, proceeds intellectually in communion with imperishable matter, we finally hold the complete solution to the entire metaphysical problem. You see, in addition, how the chances of demonstration abound in favor of those penetrations that operate between us and surrounding organisms—for the naïve Tertullian only forgot one thing, which is the law of reciprocity that must necessarily preside over these transfusions.

"Can we, for example, deny a transitive exchange of vitality between ourselves and animals, the masks of which are imprinted on our faces, and whose spontaneous penetrations also act in the secrecy of our instincts? May it not be, on the other hand, from our animistic atoms that coffee, tea, tobacco, hashish, opium, ether and so on borrow the effects of stimulation, excitation and hallucination that their usage restores to us? There is evidently a human humor latent in these substances, the mental action of which one cannot logically attribute to simple inert contact. By the same token, the cellular emanations of our thought must be present in enormous quantities in various alcoholic beverages, since their absorption generally causes within us a prodigious outflow of gaiety and imagination, and sometimes tenderness, bitterness, sarcasm, anger or fury, and that their abuse turns our intellect upside down, in an irrepressible and tumultuous chaos of faculties."

At this point, I could not help noticing on the table the already-considerable number of bottles, the aroma of which, equally savored by each of us, seemed, in spite of the doctor's sustained impassivity, to be volatilizing in an increasing eloquence on his par. Meanwhile, the gigantic diamond in his cravat sparkled with an ever-more-vivid joyful fire.

"So what if people raise an objection to the purely rational principle of molecular affinities?" Dr. Gipson continued, in a tone of lofty pity for those supposed contradictors. "What does it matter to me if the present lack of proofs attracts vulgar suspicions of illumination or ineptitude? The lack of evidence of a fact—which is to say, the mystery of things—is merely an appeal to scientific effort in the search for the truth. We march all the more surely on the track of the truth because it elevates its beacon light in the darkness. I shall always steer toward that distant light, which marks the relay where plausible hypotheses are elucidated to which I shall hold firm so long as their lack of exactitude has not been demonstrated to me. Experiment, in fact—that guide-donkey of graduate scientists—only enquires into things that are. Independent minds want to exercise their foresight on the subject of what is to come—which is to say that, if pure science desires to exceed its limits, as is its incessant duty, it must accumulate its experiments to discover rather than to explain.

"Such is my own method, and I have already extracted therefrom the conclusion that the true role of the physician is to prepare, support and facilitate our posthumous dispersal. The Bible calls that returning to the dust from which we have emerged. The metaphor is even more exact than it is eloquent, for that dust contains an ensemble of molecules, living or otherwise, reduced to impalpability; it contains, integrally, the

268

supply of organic substances that the phenomenon of life temporarily coordinates within us. Taken and rendered to the cosmic universality, a human being is only matter, and matter, as we have just seen—and mark this well!—is merely chemistry.

"It is, therefore, now up to chemist-physicians to appropriate human beings, by an adequate hygiene, to their destiny and to their material evolution—for those two terms, one naïve and the other pretentious, have exactly the same fundamental meaning—and to render humans equally apt to their various modes of life, concentric or diffuse."

The doctor allowed these final words to be followed by a brief silence—time for us each to empty a glass of champagne—and I took advantage of it to examine the orator, while making every effort to remain serious. He was speaking with his eyes staring into nowhere, as if he were making a public speech—but the wonderful diamond in his cravat was directing frolicsome rays of light at me, which seemed to be mocking my internal alarm.

"My theory," Dr. Gipson went on, "thus consists of proposing to our descendants a chemical regime in harmony with both their zoomorphic state and their final dispersion in nature. Oh, I'm not the first person to have made this discovery"—and the doctor, with my collaboration, drank a glassful less measured than his modesty—"the idea was in the air. Some time ago, a celebrated foreign scientist[66] made a speech at a banquet given in his honor, and prophesied a future hu-

---

[66] This notion was popularized in France by Marcellin Berthelot (1827-1907), who synthesized numerous hydrocarbons and anticipated a glorious future for such techniques in *Chimie organique fondée sur la synthèse* (1860). The idea crops up routinely in French scientific romance, having been anticipated prior to Berthelot's popularization by Charles Nodier in a Utopian satire published in 1833 and translated as "perfectibility" in the Black Coat Press anthology *The Germans on Venus*.

mankind exclusively nourished on chemical substances—which, by virtue of the abundance and condensed volume of mixtures would reduce the problem of daily bread to a minimum. Let us not hesitate to say that it was only an intellectual joke, which the illustrious guest was only inspired to make by the excess of the feast in which he had shared—but it was a flash of light for my intuition. Without delay, I formed the thesis and offered a preview of the consequences of chemical alimentation in the *Manifesto* with whose renown you're familiar, although it barely touches on the subject.

"The trajectory of matter through our period of individuality cannot be accurately measured within the limitations of our present methods of analysis, and I am only assuming the simple role of initiator for the benefit of future researchers. The results of their labor will be to incorporate in human beings all the particles of ambient energy of which they might be the recipients or centers of attraction, and, by means of that intussusception, to enrich the anthropomorphy of the sum total of 'humanizable' thought that the chemical elements imprison. We shall then have authentically scientific funerals, in which our remains will immediately be redistributed by special incinerators between the various conglomerates that they synthesized during life, and these posthumous substances, residues of our generations, will be further improved repeatedly by their return to human form. As for our deceased, they will experience the delight of finding themselves scattered in the disseminated atoms of the personality that they had initially embodied in concrete form."

At these words I felt that, in spite of my best efforts, my face was bound to betray an urgent need for explanation, and having disposed of another mouthful of sparkling wine, I stammered, somewhat at hazard: "That's magnificent, to be sure, but how will this marvelous project commence?"

"In the imminent volume announced in my *Manifesto*," the doctor replied, "I explain that the alimentations of the future will not be for the sole purpose of satisfying the vulgar and bestial instinct of appetite, and I indicate the composition of a certain number of concentrated elixirs, the list of which my disciples will only have to increase, by following the fundamental principle. When the catalogue is complete, human beings will be constituted physically, psychologically and even psychically by integral and exclusive chemical action. The first experimental applications that I have already made of a few electuaries have been such as to give me a hopeful confidence in the eventual triumph."

The doctor had let slip the word *applications* with serenity. It caused me to shudder. I remembered the pale and thin appearance of Mrs. Gipson. The thought naturally occurred to me that her husband might have carried out a few trials of progressive nourishment on her, from which he had sagely abstained himself—but that was a matter of an intimate nature, which I was prohibited from raising directly, and I got around the difficulty by remarking to Dr. Gipson that in his admirable deductions, he had not yet told me about the scientific treatment specially reserved for the delightful sex of which Mrs. Gipson was a part.

"It is indeed," I added, to justify my observation, "a sex which, by its temperament, its needs and even its originalities, seems to me to require a physico-chemistry quite different from ours…"

The doctor's face took on an appearance of perplexity in confrontation with the task of elucidating such a delicate problem. He put his chin in his hand, and for a few moments, that hand seemed to occasion a sort of eclipse between myself and the incisive fires of the knot in his cravat.

"I haven't yet made any serious experiment in that regard," he said, after a brief meditative silence, "but I think it necessary, on this point, henceforth to make a *tabula rasa* of the mass of stupidities that have been voiced at all times on the subject of love, from which our interest in sexual variation predominantly arises. That passion that must, in itself, legitimate conjugal union, will only cease to be an imaginative lure when the couple has been scientifically and respectively chemicized. The experiment would be indecent. It would require

271

not merely the perfect accord of the purely physical particles but also the production, as you have just insinuated, the harmony of animating functions with the aid of substances collaborating in the alimentation of thought. There would only be happy marriages by virtue of the equipment of similar chemical souls in identically composed bodies. The illusions of future spouses regarding their reciprocal charms, the irreflective impulses of desire and the cruel disappointments of characters in conflict, which cause so many hidden miseries and belated regrets today, would be avoided—or at least corrected—thanks to the new method, by studying the degree of sincerity of amorous and sentimental declarations, hostile and hateful ones, and so on, by the manner in which the exhalations, the effluvia and vital emissions of the interested parties influence, for example, litmus paper, or some other reagent whose increased sensitivity will respond in a peremptory manner to those investigative necessities."

The doctor was becoming unspeakably obscure, and in order to get him out of that thorny phase, I decided to ask him a question about the final passage of the Manifesto—a passage that was quite clear, for once, but whose preposterousness had raised a particular clamor.

"My dear Gipson," I said to him—for the infectious benevolence of the feast had already occasioned a commencement of familiarity between jus—"does not your program, as you have publicized it, make allusion to something much more extreme than all the marvels we have just passed in review? Have you not confided to the physicians of the future the sublime and definitive mission of vanquishing death and assuring all human beings of the enjoyment of a sort of eternity? That, I believe, is what has unleashed the most ardent protests and anger directed against you."

Dear Gipson replied in the detached tone of an inventor who willingly, but without obstinacy, admits the corollary consequences of his discoveries. "I only permit myself one hypothesis in that direction, and I limit myself to furnishing, in that respect, a few preliminary indications for the use of those who will come after me. From now on, however, it seems to me permissible to suppose that after numerous successions of heredity, thanks to the regime that I propose, and thanks also to the increasingly purified quality of the compositions that will be employed therein, that future races, materially refined from top to bottom will be provided with unalterable chemical organs. From that will result the terminal conquest of rational anthropomorphy, the ultimate logical coronation of life—by which I mean living immortality!"

While the doctor's reasoning dived into the worst accumulations of shadow, the diamond in the cravat tormented me with a fulguration of almost impertinent gleams. I don't know why that had finally started to irritate me, but it was very irritating. I knew that I had to control myself, however, and I attempted to make a show of an excess of enthusiasm for the dazzling postulate that had just been formulated.

"Bravo, my dear Gipson—that's sublime!" I exclaimed. "That will conclusively relegate the old philosophies that are still divided, without proofs, between dubious ultraterrestrial revenges and imbecilic returns to nothingness. Enough of these threads of consolation or despair, and let us have immortality in life itself!" Timidly, I risked: "But it is necessary to assume that our successors, in spite of the perfection of their mental and physical chemistry, will eternalize themselves on Earth without experiencing the need to reproduce themselves, thus avoiding its eventual overcrowding?"

In order to reply, the doctor adopted a rather solemn expression, by way of paying homage to the importance of the objection.

"If I now proceed to affirm my initiatives as the laws of the future," he said, "that is because I sense in myself a participation of the divinity. Now, as you know, God in humankind is merely successive and, due to the fatality of progress, must always leave himself, humanly, something to do. In the matter of prolific immortality, it is absurd to anticipate that our composite matter will still have a tendency to disaggregate into fragments when it wishes to amalgamate in new cellular syntheses that it will find more sympathetic. We have all the more right to form that conjecture because the immortal Terrans, being of an identical and transmissible facture, will be led to fuse with one another, by means of penetrations, with the worthy aim of representing themselves and containing themselves in the most perfect unity—but this will be in incalculable remote eras, for that will be the authentic God-Human, and the definitive culmination of progress."

The doctor's intellect was going adrift in the densest abstractions, and his face, doubtless like mine, seemed to be enveloped by a certain dreamy fog—but his inflexible diamond began to scatter powdered sunlight and sting me with flashes that definitely seemed to me to be outbursts of laughter.

I could not help bursting out myself in the face of such provocation. "I say, Gipson, my dear friend" I exclaimed—we were drinking liqueurs after the coffee, and I was beginning to address my guest in an intimate manner—"what is that satanic diamond planted in your cravat like a searchlight? Has it a soul? Does it understand what you're saying, or is it mocking me because it thinks that I don't understand you?"

"You're not so very far from the truth," he told me, without turning a hair. "This diamond is a cadaver, neither more nor less, and its history is quite simple. I was once wandering in the wildernesses of the Far West when the idea occurred to me of studying the *incineration* that was then in vogue. Guided as ever by plausible hypothesis, I presumed that the ignition of an animal, dead or alive, might develop certain shiny silicates, and gave myself the task of verifying the susceptibilities of their condensation.

"Sowing dollars in abundance, I had an immense furnace installed, provided with a ventilation system capable of producing a maximum heat and directing it toward an octagonal receptacle in which the crystal would be produced. My wife, whose devotion is unbreakable, accompanied me, as did a young student whose love of science—or so he claimed—attached him to my footsteps. The truth is that, while spying on my discoveries, he was paying court to my wife—but that detail is unimportant, for my faithful other half had immediately warned me, and I was able to devote myself entirely to my research.

"I believe that you will have no trouble, now, in guessing the outcome of the anecdote. Know, however, that the absence of inhumatory organization in the country did not permit me to experiment legally on any human cadaver, even for money. I was reduced to building my furnace, which was not very elevated, in the form of a humpback bridge that a buffalo lured by cereal tidbits had to scale to the culminating point. Then, I only had to activate a spring suddenly to lower the descending slope, with the result that the quadruped was immediately engulfed in the crematory machine.

"One morning, everything was ready. I had displayed my vegetable bait while a buffalo was wandering about the prairie. The animal, however, scarcely moved forward; it seemed suspicious, and was in no hurry to make its contribution to an illustrious invention. I was breathless with impatience, when I suddenly felt as if I were being watched. The student was, in fact, on the lookout to see and comprehend. *Oh, that boy!* I said to myself. *He not only wants my conjugal prerogatives, he also requires half my glory!* Abruptly, I turned round, and with a prodigious leap I thrust the spy into the orifice. A marvelous confirmation of my hypothesis! I took him out again, after a month's cooling, in the form of the splendid specimen of carbon to which you are devoting your curious attention. Believe me, the beauty of that find freed me from any idea of remorse, but Mrs. Gipson, whom I informed about the adventure, always manifests a little ill humor when I wear the jewel…"

The meal had terminated in the apotheosis of a *flambée* of punch, and we said our farewells at the door of the restaurant.

The propagator of nourishment by science and the bold precursor of chemical Eternity had not forsaken his apparent tranquility throughout the conversation. He seemed to me to be a man capable of accommodating himself for a long time yet to the kinds of food, and especially the kinds of liquids, that will constitute the pleasures of our present feasts until the new order begins. For proof of that, I had the tall, flexibly perpendicular figure that swayed lightly from one sidewalk to the other, while his magnificent diamond detached from the street-lights a coming-and-going of stars—and until the vanished from sight at the far end of the avenue, I wondered whether he was dragging through the night the darkness of insanity or the blinding visions of a brain troubled by too audacious a comprehension of the future.

He left me, moreover, with a fantastic impression. His theories took possession of my being and put it in astounded communication with universal nature. An ethereal atmosphere flooded my brain, seemingly wanting to bear me up toward the clouds. Involuntarily, and my body abandoned itself to the attraction of the multiple consubstantial atoms that linked it to the Earth...and I went home to transcribe the interview, God knows how!

Louis Mullem: *The Supreme Progress*
(c. late 1889s-early 1890s)

The morning sunlight was dancing gaily in the trembling foliage of tall trees, and the walls of the attic perched beneath the roof of the vast edifice received pretty pale green reflections embroidered with threads of silver.

Save for this natural ornamentation, the furniture of the cabin-like space was of the simplest sort. It comprised two iron bunks enveloped in white curtains, several chairs and a little imitation-mahogany table. It was all scrupulously neat. In a corner, a nightstand supported a few toilet items.

Such an environment, reminiscent of a furnished hotel, contrasted strongly with the venerable aspect of the room's two occupants—a married couple, according to all appearances—who were at that very moment welcoming, with abundant ceremony, a young gentleman dressed in black, with a white cravat.

Few preliminary words were exchanged, the principal motive for the conversation having doubtless been determined in advance. After a few words of apology regarding the lack of luxury of the abode, which gave evidence of an improvised and probably temporary residence, the Thinker—such was the pseudonym evoked at first glance by the aged husband—took his place, with the other individuals, at the little table, which was cluttered with papers.

Very tall and very thin in his monastically-tailored dressing-gown, his eyes pale blue and full of dreams beneath the large forehead fringed by a cloud of grey hair, the Thinker prepared to read aloud from an unpublished manuscript, the pages of which he rearranged.

The wife of the Thinker—one must regret here that neither custom nor necessity yet imposes the urgency of a term applying that epithet to the fair sex[67]—seemed to be a respectable lady whose more-than-modest costume nevertheless indicated slowly-ruined former wealth. She gave the impression of a wife resigned to an ideology in which her voyages in higher intellectual realms had long distracted her from the cares of her fortune. She manifested toward her husband an attitude of obstinate admiration, ostentatiously matrimonial to an even greater extent than rational.

As for the gentleman dressed scrupulously in black, with the scrupulously white cravat, he demonstrated by his attitude that the purpose of the interview was to make known to him as quickly as possible the tenor of the manuscript, the threat of which had just been indicated as imminent.

Then the Thinker, raising his severe and meditative face to the light, read out the following fragment of a thick work that he entitled *The Supreme Progress*, while the gentleman, now even more rigidly clad in black and even more intensely cravated in white than ever, never ceased to listen with scrupulous and mute attention.

Introduction to the Work

The parties engaging in dialogue in the present work, *the Thinker read*, assume for a setting the idea that everyone's imagination is able to form, approximately, of the Unreal.

It is in that vaguely ethereal and indescribable milieu that "the Gentleman and the Lady," the two characters endowed

---

[67] This interpolation makes little sense in English, where women can be describes as "thinkers" as easily as men— although custom does militate against it somewhat—but in French a female *"penseur"* would be a *"penseuse;"* Mullem is rightly pointing out that the language had never found much use for the latter term. That situation is, of course, no less regrettable nowadays than it was when Mullem made his observation, and Mullem—as readers of this story will soon observe—did absolutely nothing to oppose or alter it, despite his sarcasm.

with eternity that we set on the stage, are pursuing an endless conversation, of which we can only reproduce a brief extract here. On this particular day, an indescribable well-being was spread around—something, if one might put it thus, like a more-than-usually lucid diaphaneity in the hectic undulation of space. For this reason, He and She felt even more pleasure than usual in abandoning themselves to the current of their reflections.

Possessed of the patience that coincides with absolute wisdom, the Gentleman immobilized himself in his aerial contexture, spherically and diametrically equal to the ancient terrestrial globe. The Lady, although confounded with the subtle effluvium of her spouse, gave evidence of her joyful humor by means of a few undulatory quivers that slightly irregularized the contours of their extremely light communal volatilization. The oceans of yesteryear had once agitated their moving lace around the around the rigid form of the planet in a similar manner.

This episode is occurring, as you have doubtless guessed, at a time in the most incalculably distant future, when the terrestrial organism, finally emancipated from any substantial matrix, occupies an extent of some sort in an exclusively fluid state. The Gentleman and the Lady are, in fact, the couple in whom the collective soul of extinct humankinds are summarized, and know no other employment of time than to devote themselves to the purely disinterested elucidation of eternal abstractions.

Obviously, these two essentially atmospheric individuals are not employing an articulate language. Their reciprocal ideas are only exchanged by means of a differentiation of internal currents. Let us also note that the slowness of their speech is proportionate to the incessant series of centuries that succeed one another during their conversation. One of the consequences of that fact is the phenomenon that each of their remarks—as will be more comprehensible shortly—is equivalent in duration to that of the epochs described by the historical and other events to which those remarks apply. Our present faculty of calculation, and even the present state of our sentiment of infinity, cannot, therefore, conceive of the incommensurable sum of centuries-long periods embraced by the rapid chat that follows.

It is understood, moreover, that the two interlocutors are disembarrassed of the sensualism of ancient anthropomorphism to the point that the delimitation of their respective sexes is henceforth manifest—as we shall see in due course—only in the insouciant playfulness enjoyed by the caprice of the Lady and the inflexible love of truth cultivated by the Gentleman. A fortunate harmony is maintained nevertheless in their debate, for they have no other desire than to fall into agreement. Even in the most advanced of our future descendant, however, as among us nowadays, philosophical discussion rarely produces a result, and the entente that can ensue therefrom remains a matter of politeness rather than persuasion.

The conversationalist duo is, in fact, incessantly divided between the various appreciations that continue to haunt the subject of first causes: Providence or Fatality; Hazard or Predestination; Incoherence or the Necessity of Causation, etc., etc. The Lady leans towards whichever theory flatters her imagination most agreeably. For his part, the Gentleman, guided solely by reason, nevertheless refrains from imposing it under the pretext of marital authority—but he becomes slightly confused when, in order to humor his spouse, he tries to establish an intermediate term between the aforementioned "contradictory" ideas, which is apparently difficult to specify exactly.

He soon became almost irritated by an inconvenience of that sort, because the conversation, emerging from the abstract, had started to rotate around out defunct planet, the Earth, of whose history the Gentleman claimed to have a complete command, in spite of the infinity of centuries of forgetfulness that had accumulated since its complete vaporization.

Without displaying an overt opposition to the renovatory arguments of her husband, the Lady could not hide a brief vibratory flutter, which would be roughly equivalent in the present feminine form to the gesture of stifling an involuntary laugh.

HE: "You're always laughing! That displeases me somewhat, for I never know whether your irony is directed at the things I say or at myself."

SHE: "It's one or the other. It's another one of those terms intermediate between two extremes, of which you continually make use. You're retracing events that strike me as surprising, and I find your certainty as to their authenticity a trifle comical…"

HE: "Will you never admit the surety of my investigative procedures, then? Of course not! That's the problem! Do we not possess, to the last detail, an account of the modifications and alterations to which our previous humankind was subject? Are you not able, as I am, to perceive the images echoed by the planets and corroborate the details in question by exact synthetic calculation. Now, my dear, you are no longer unaware that at more-or-less lengthy intervals, from one incidence to another, the various worlds are reflected through luminous space.[68]

"What does it matter, if you please, that some of these worlds are now molecularly dispersed, since the ancient reflections departed from their surfaces are still pursuing their eternal course, and since all matter subsists in its present attributes as long as contingences do not impose transformation upon it, and since, finally, these same superficial reflec-

---

[68] Camille Flammarion's *Lumen*, initially published in the late 1860s and continually reprinted and augmented until the end of the century, had familiarized writers and readers of French scientific romance with the idea that the finite velocity of light in an infinite universe implied that the history of the Earth could be viewed in its entirety from sufficiently distant points in space, by souls possessed of a prodigious acuity of vision and immune from any limitation of velocity—and would still be subject to such inspection long after the Earth had ceased to exist.

tions are at the disposal of worlds that still gravitate, or which will be born in future into the parabola of clarity.[69]

"Thus, our native globe once received, as scientists observed, the intense light of certain stars that were extinct or swallowed up long before our Earth made its appearance in the cosmogonic ensemble. Active planets also sent us their reverberations, but our ancestors—ignorant then, it is true, of the importance of those astral reactions—neglected their analysis and were unable to distinguish their particularities. Of course, they also lacked the privilege of being, like us, an integral part of the luminous principle and being in direct inherence with every one of its vibrations.

"Let us, I beg you, leave your malicious skepticism there, and, in preference, turn our attention to the relatively recent satellite that is displayed down there, relatively close to us in the plains of infinity. It was only a few centuries ago that it began to refract the radiations of several qualities of the universe. I assume, my dear Madame, that you will not maintain that these radiations, in perfect accordance with those that previously passed over the surrounding stars, are mere chimeras? Examine, for example, that little transparent bubble rotating amid multitudes of other planetary effigies. That modest spheroid—don't take offence—is our humble Terran abode of yore, and none other."

The Gentleman had expressed himself with a certain warmth, and even thought he knew perfectly well, as a rule, how to contain himself, his aerogenic density manifested a notable dilatation.

It would have been dangerous to overexcite him further in that explosive state. The Lady reassembled her atmospherism in an exceedingly slender ellipse, perhaps sketching a pout in a hydrocarburated fashion, and then affected to support her-

---

[69] There is an untranslatable double meaning here, the French word *parabole* signifying "parable" as well as "parabola" thus conferring an extra metaphorical dimension on the florid phrase.

self in a gracious semicircle upon her husband's poles, in one of those very feminine attitudes in which the fear of fainting simulates a surfeit of attention

The Gentleman had the good sense to note this last appearance and resumed his speech...

Brief Interruption

At this paragraph, the Thinker paused, doubtless in the hope of accentuating the impression of what he had just read. His physiognomy displayed, to some small degree, the solemnity attributed in the above pages to the male spirit.

The Thinker's wife, probably by a similar effort of mechanical imitation, struggled as the empyrean lady had against the encroachment of drowsiness.

The gentleman clad in a fresh outbreak of black suit, and cravated like an ignition of white, advertised with a feverish gesture his keen desire to hear the continuation of the marvelous story—upon which the Thinker hastened to continue his reading in these terms:

Continuation of the Story

"I therefore permit myself," said the Gentleman to the Lady, "to draw your entire attention to the phantasmagoria of terrestrial incidents that is unfolding in the mirror of the satellite in question. Thanks to their renewal, these reappearances have a particularly vivid clarity. Look at that! Let us not hurry. Let us run over this short period of a few tens of millions of centuries during which our little planet is, before our very eyes, solidifying out of its original chaos. For us, who no longer possess the sentiment of a delimitation of duration, is not the imaginative passage of accumulations of time in the continual recommencement of eternity—so to speak—a continually renewed pleasure?

"You will pardon me that vain digression, will you not? Let us watch the indicative heavenly body.

"At present, we are viewing the scene of terrestrial matter unfolding in the era when it is finally emerging from its

283

atomic disorder, in order to set forth again according to the various affinities implicit within it, and to distribute its unique force in a multiplicity of effects that has been called Nature. It seems certain, therefore, that each of these originatory atoms—or, if you prefer, each of these molecules constitutive of substances—contains a germ of intelligence, since it is following a necessary and purposive direction. Ulterior facts have, moreover, proven that the most intelligent of the aforesaid atoms will forsake inert bodies to localize themselves in animate bodies, notably in humans, which lend them, until a new order arises, the best available instrument of expression and comprehension.

"Now, it is precisely this dispersal of integral reason, this fragmentation of the intellectual principle, of which one is able to say: *Tot capita, tot sensus*;[70] the interminable sequence of misfortunes suffered by our ancestors must result therefrom.

"If I insist on this circumstance somewhat in anticipation"—he had, in fact, been insisting upon it for the better part of 2000 years—"it is to allow time for a few more thousands of centuries to unfold on our objective whose silhouettes offer nothing much of interest. That is merely the period when prehistoric humanity succeeds in extracting itself from its initial stagnation. But now, in the following epochs, man acquires the notion of his individual value and requires a social condition. It is worth the trouble, at present, of following the phases of that new mode of existence with the aid of the representations of our celestial reflector.

"Among these reverberations, a few fixed, or scarcely-changing points stand out. They are the regions of plains and mountains, as well as the towns that our forefathers inhabited. The rest of the little luminous trace, by contrast, sparkles and palpitates with a continual iridescence. We thus observe the

---

[70] Roughly, "so many heads, so many ideas"—meaning that there are as many different ways of looking at things as there are people looking.

turbulence of an incalculable multitude of molecular extracts, in each one of which moves the ephemeral activity of a human specimen, or some individual of the animal order. Whence comes this perpetual wriggling? Why did our ancestors, as I think I have already said to you, indulge in this ceaseless confused and seemingly purposeless agitation?

"Let us pause momentarily, my dear friend, on that incidental question, which is more serious than it seems. Its perfect solution gives rise, in fact, to important consequences, which might perhaps allow us, in due course, to determine the causalities of the entire system of the universe, almost in their entirety.

"If it will not annoy you to submit to a brief demonstration in this regard"—it would, in fact, only last for six thousand years at the most—"do not forget the primordial fact that the organized beings on our planet, especially humans, only participated in the gift of intelligence to the extent of an infinitesimal mini-portion per individual. Remember too—this is a very important point—that this fractionation of intellectual resources was not merely the terrestrial rule. The same order was strictly observed in all cosmogonic regions, for all the active beings of the present and future plurality of worlds—the "world to come", as it was so elegantly put at the time whose image is gliding over our satellite at this moment. Such an arrangement, however, as you will easily understand, could only be transitory. Otherwise, that bizarre disposition would be comparable to a vast and multiple analysis that could never become a synthesis.

"Whatever the objectivities or appearances were that occasioned its thoughts, in fact, terrestrial reason could not remain satisfied indefinitely with its lot of partial truths; it tended incessantly toward absolute logic; it was subject to the secret aspiration of its faculties, provisionally divisionary, toward an integral intellectuality that would eventually embrace the spiritual contribution of other planets. And from that concentration of the universal idea would stem the entire, unique and divine science, the Word that revealed the true nature of things.

"Now, this need for a synthetic ideality was the driving-mechanism of life in all its known milieux, and those yet to be known. If we restrict ourselves in this respect solely to the history of our ancestors, we shall see that every human being then traversing the fatality of existence felt incessantly over-excited by a desire for progress, the results of which remained enigmatic and unforeseeable, for lack of the superior compre-hension by which those results could be calculated in advance.

"Thus, dear friend, you may take it for granted that the preventive solutions admitted by those unfortunates were sin-gularly inefficient, when they were not simply inept. Some attempted to satisfy their tendency to the exclusive well-being of their sensual structure. Others subordinated the repose of their consciousness to the observation and increasingly expe-rimental manipulation of the matter of which they recognized themselves as an intrinsic part. Yet others, more inclined to hypothetical inventions, glimpsed the appeasement of their souls in the belief in a force exterior to directive impulsion or conclusive wisdom, which they named God, but to which he gave an anthropomorphic interpretation—by which I mean that they measured that pretended intelligence in proportion to the exceedingly minimal parcel of judgment that they persona-lized themselves, etc., etc. I am leaving aside here many in-termediary nuances among these antique fashions of con-struing life, none of which carried the full conviction of those who professed them

"It is sufficient, for the moment, to observe that each of these unfortunate petty nothings of temporary beings at-tempted, more out of pride than certainty, to make his own theories prevail to the detriment of adverse opinions. And of all those who dreamed of the ideal, the greatest and the least alike could imagine nothing better than putting himself in what he was able to conceive as the most flattering light, as if to make his own individuality stand out. From that followed obstinate rivalries between individuals, constant revolt of crowds, and endless duels between nations. Let us analyze once again the recent successions of epochal reflections on the gleam of our star; we find nothing therein but traces of war and vestigial ruins."

At this passage of the marital history, the Lady could not repress certain indescribable fidgetings of meteoric femininity, which could not be interpreted other than as a sign of slight impatience. "In truth," she exclaimed, "speaking for myself, I cannot make out anything very precise in these stellar projections on which you are basing such strong arguments. All that we perceive therein seems singularly vague and vaporous to me."

"I must confess," the Gentleman replied, without any external emotion, "that they are mere patches scarcely distinct within their tissues of light. The mirages in question need to be understood as a sort of hieroglyphic writing, each sign of which symbolizes a series of identical incidents that are produced in similar milieux, the luminous transmission of which confuses the details.

"Look, among others, at this figure, or rather, this schema—I am still only talking about a minimal segment of the reflection occupied by the terrestrial phantom—which is irregularly inscribed down there, becoming the emblem of war, which, save for a few unimportant variations in armaments and strategy, constantly recommences in a similar fashion. We thus possess sufficient means of deduction. The taut filaments that twist and become entangled over the major part of our instrument of observation summarize, as I have already said, the frightful multiplicity of labors that humans inflict upon one another in what they call 'the struggle for existence.' Here and there within that swarm, one encounters a few streaks standing out against the background. They are the juxtaposed photoscopies[71] of a sequence of individuals who, during these falla-

---

[71] Unlike many of Mullem's linguistic improvisations, this is not a neologism; the term "photoscope" was applied to at least three different 19th century optical devices, more than one of

287

cious periods of societarism, strive for success in some art, science, criticism or prophecy, or succeeded one another in illusory vocations of perfectionist propaganda. Their efforts must have been curiously indefatigable and tenacious persevering for an approximative wake of their undivided spectrality still to be manifest in this astronomical fog..."

Here, the Lady deigned to give evidence of a brief revival of interest. "And what, I pray," she enquired, "were the names that these brave men bore, or by which they were designated?"

"That's marvelous, dear friend," the Gentleman replied. "Your question demonstrates a notable aptitude for reconstituting long-gone things. Can one imagine, in fact, such pride in such ephemeral inanity? Did not each of these imperceptible globules of thinking matter assume a special appellation, each going so far as to advertise his or her respective sex, and take pride in being a distinct 'someone'? I do not even exaggerate in suggesting that every one of them, doubtless believing himself to represent the genius of the species, dared to cultivate the illusion of transmitting his personal memory to us!"

SHE (complacently): "That seems perfectly risible."

HE (but with a hint of melancholy): "Led astray by the frenzy of individualism, our ancestors radically misunderstood the necessity of centralizing the intellectual force of which each one of them only possessed the most infinitesimal quota. Thus, they continually delayed the instauration of God in humankind—which is to say, the cohesion of the unlimited totality of comprehension that was assigned, within the hierarchy of the universes, to terrestrial intelligence. For it would be absurd and contradictory to recognize in God any other attribute than being the most philosophical expression of the ensemble of causes and effects.

---

which produced an image that could be, and sometimes was, called a "photoscopie" in French and a "photoscopy" in English.

"At any rate, humans maintained themselves in the emulation of a continual advancement toward the amelioration of their condition—but each one, as I have said, limited those ameliorations to the scale of his irreducible molecule, in proportion to the insufficiency of reason. The antagonism of vanities thus continued, and civilization, in the final analysis, was no more than an *impasse*. While incoherence reigned, the human elite divided itself into two opposed categories, one of which, as you already know, flattered itself by trying cheapen physiological laws by means of some dream or other of the free materialization of mind, while the other was ambitious to attach itself to the incessant evolution of substance. Between these two extremes the bewildered masses became irresolute, not knowing what to think about the faith of overly subtle dialecticians, nor how or why they should support the excess of industrialization and exploitations with which the positivism of scientists oppressed them.

"It was, nevertheless, the latter mode of, so to speak, economico-passive socialization that seemed to be bound eventually to get the upper hand. As regards metaphysics, it was judged sufficient to establish the relationship of the mental power of humans with their mode of activity. Ultraterrestrial explanations of any sort whatsoever fell into the deepest discredit. The entire domain of the possibilities of the unknown was limited in advance to the knowable. The complete utilization of matter was decreed by rigorously determining that goal. The human organism was now reduced to the role of a simple cog in a dynamic and mechanical arrangement of natural forces. The problem of discovering whether or not the aforesaid arrangement proceeded in accordance with some preliminary law was abandoned as forever insoluble. Soon, in fact—and I invite you, my dear, to admit that the phases of existence that the star continues to rememorize graphically are interesting—soon…"

A Parenthesis

Here, replacing the volume on the table, the Thinker interrupted his reading momentarily and made the observation that the author of these pages was about to devote himself to the exposure of a series of facts that were to unfold in times inexpressibly ulterior to ours, and which, although reported in the verbal past tense, had to be considered as absolutely defunct in relation to a futurity so distant that it defies any equation with the sum of the future susceptible to calculation in our own day.

The events to which the remainder of the story refer, therefore, occur at times so advanced that one cannot even attempt to anticipate them today. By the same token, the contemporary imagination, in its most extreme audacities, is even more incapable of supporting the posteriority of the epoch in which these events, having disappeared in their turn, will have become mere memories.

The very nature of his narrative, however, constrained the author of *The Supreme Progress* to draw his pictures merely as retrospective sketches. He thus requested his listeners, insistently, to make the effort of increased attention.

The Thinker's Other Half welcomed this advertisement with condescension. She thus continued to borrow the various more-or-less sincere attitudes of the cloudy Lady characterized in the dialogue.

The gentleman visitor extracted an affirmative gesture from the blackness of his frock-coat, and contrived an occipital oscillation over his white cravat, making it known that, for his part, not one word of the subsequent part of the incomparable work would be lost.

Continuation of the Manuscript

"Soon, in fact," *the reader continued*, "mechanism had become preponderant. By virtue of ever-improving inventions, steam contrived to equal, if not to replace, the vital principle. Industrial machines were complicated by generative or constructive organs thanks to which the excess of their manufac-

290

turing power was employed in reproducing and coordinating the equivalent of their instrumental details. The consequence of these self-propagatory augmentations—their steel joints, metal intestines, fiery breath, and, finally their souls, proceeding from mysterious effluvia of electricity—and the transmission of their actions was an effective redoubling of automation. For example, while a locomotive as devouring distance, it engendered by its side an identical specimen of its tractional apparatus.

"In sum, a regime of mechanical vitality was established in which humans no longer filled any role but that of a mere vocal and visual adjunct. Led by nature, however, to impart as much of their strength as possible to the objects that they employ as auxiliaries, humans adapted themselves to these instrumentations in a fashion so intimate that they infused them into own external appearance, including their various sexes, with the benefits of the impulses and passions that followed therefrom. From then on, the machines were disencumbered of their surplus of extrinsic production. Eventually, clothed with animalism, they were able to devote themselves to the usual affectations of genital specialism, with the advantages of an immediate heredity."

THE LADY: "What a terrible joke!"

THE GENTLEMAN: "Disabuse yourself, dear friend, I am speaking with all the seriousness of which I am capable— but don't be too surprised by a phenomenon that is not without precedent. By going back to the remotest of the annals buried in my memory, I can, in fact, inform you of infinitely primitive epochs in which certain very powerful Terrans who claimed to be owners of the land undertook to furnish the motive energy of agricultural labor by means of individuals of a more-or-less dark hue known as 'serfs'. It is probable that, by virtue of a disinhibition analogous to the one sketched above, these black-skinned individuals, these agitators of energy, were nothing but a concentration of coal in human form."

SHE: "Once again, you're taking facetiousness to burlesque lengths!"

HE: "Be persuaded, on the contrary, that I am doing my best to avoid badinage. We have just seen a striking example of professional appropriation. One cannot, after that, be astonished by what our species, so long supplemented by machinery as an agent of impulsion and transference, would finally become: purely and simply, machine-humans. Thus they attempted to justify, during that transitory era, the theory of a reciprocal penetration between creatures and their environments.

"This very considerable evolution, however, did not bring about any very extraordinary change in the mores of that society. As I have frequently said, by virtue of lack of suspicion of their true predestination, our forefathers remained convinced of their present worth, and paralyzed the progress that they still had to make—for one characteristic of powerlessness is constantly to admit the provisional as definitive. From the viewpoint of the intellect, there was still concurrence, instead of any haste toward fusion, and disputes persisted as ardently as ever between the ideophiles and the utilitarians.

"A few sects, without actually participating in them, praised the maintenance of old beliefs as a discipline salutary to economic innovation. For example, the question of whether or not young anthropolocomotives should receive religious instruction provoked several thousand centuries of civil war. As usual, however, the last word went to the defenders of common sense; and, not content with propagating and multiplying themselves to provide for the exigencies of relentless labor, the machine-humans—or, if you wish, the transport-humans, the ship-humans, the aerostat-humans, the bulldozer-humans, the mining-humans, the agriculture-humans and the factory-humans—persisted doggedly in improving one another indefinitely.

"It would be impossible to express in sufficiently descriptive terms how much anguish, subjugation and overwork our ancestors were subjected to in that period, being constrained to render themselves amenable to such excesses of utilization.

292

"We can see that, as this episode ran its course, the Earth began to cool, by virtue of the extinction of a certain number of suns. Note, in fact, how the reflection of these things on our indicator star has paled during the last few millions of centuries. Matter was disaggregating, and visibly returning to its former state of atomic turbulence. The machine-humans struggled desperately against the rarity and increasing inertia of supplies of indispensable energy.

"A few obstinate progressivists proposed as-yet-untried expedients to avert the crisis, and declared that the maintenance of obligatory labor was justified by the very quest to find new ways of working—but humankind, overstretched and stupefied, began to ask questions. Why the Devil had people always wanted to do something, and why stubbornly persist in doing things, no matter what? History—more than empty of details regarding guilds and trades unions—scarcely traced a confused and hypothetical account of their enormous centuries-long efforts in the past. Would it be for the same negative result that they would accumulate their achievements during the terminal phase of an exhausted Earth? Were they not still living in an erroneous and deluded insouciance, like the existence that must doubtless have been led in the remotest eras of the past?

"Reasoning in this manner, they recognized that feeling and relaxing—or, quite simply, living—was the happiness that it was necessary to protect in advance, or recover after, any attempt at social planning. They fell into agreement on the point that, after having exploited to exhaustion all the resources of substance, there remained no further progress to industrialize. That irremediable lack of any reason to remain material finally brought us to the principal of the intelligence that was still subdivided between us, which it was necessary to constitute as a unique force in order to furnish, at least, a plausible pretext for continuing to live…

"Alas, the Earth crumbled away before the reign of comprehension in simplicity was ever able to establish itself. No other recourse remained but to erase the presence of humankind from the fragment of the universe that was ready to give way beneath it. The facile employment of certain electrochemical elements, which had fortunately remained destructive, assisted the cataclysm; the smoky fog and the red glow of flame that has just slid over our star, down there, is indicative of that explosion. Its inhabitants—its creatures and its peoples—were dissipated in single breath in a scattering that skillful preparations made a century in advance had rendered instantaneous.

"In consequence, the spiritual particles, simultaneously disencumbered of corporeal enslavement, combined with the thinking molecules that had previously only attained their liberty in a posthumous capacity, and their assembly ensured the coherent unity of intelligence in the fluid state…"

An Observation

The Thinker—who, during these final words, had taken on the enthusiastic tone befitting the revelation of important truths—detached his gaze momentarily from the unpublished composition.

"By virtue of what excess of stupidity," he said, "are we obstinate in holding back the advent of that hyperphysical fusion, when we could so easily obtain it by any means of combustion that comes to hand?" The generous prophet's voice grew louder. "And we—yes, the people of today—lack all prescience of the true duty, when we avoid sublimating ourselves into an essence, or any sort of volatilization whatsoever, and remain so childishly attached to the flesh! And if it would be useful to offer an example to the future, what prevents me, then, from furnishing it by my own combustion?"

At this cry of ardent marital conviction, the Thinker's wife seemed to be half-gripped by a sudden zeal also to dissolve herself in the ether.

The gentleman visitor struck the black of his frock-coat abruptly with his hand and rose to his feet, putting the forefinger of his other hand to his cravat to signify that, of the number of reflections evoked by the author of *The Supreme*

Progress, the one that had just been proffered appeared to be the most important to take under advisement.

These audience reactions, however, passed unperceived. The Thinker was in a hurry to finish reading the pages that he had never ceased to hold in his hands.

Conclusion of the Manuscript

"Our former world," *he read*, "had been annihilated, with the result that no reflection of it any longer appears on the star that we have been consulting. And that is why we find ourselves today in a virtuality of abstractive irrealism in which we summarize anthropomorphic thinking: I, the man, the rigid and indefatigable searcher for causes; you, the woman, more excited by the versatility of effects…"

Perhaps ruffled by this allusion to the special genius of her sex, the Lady raised a slight objection. "And what becomes, in the midst of all that, of animal instinct?" she asked, not without a certain hint of persiflage. "What do you make of the parcel of intellect that you say is included equally in every cell of inert matter, or hard bodies, or whatever you care to call them?"

The Gentleman marked by a furtive tremor the extent to which this slowness to comprehend the most obvious things on the part of his companion hurt and humiliated him, but his reply was no less imprinted with powerful forbearance.

"The brute elements of which you speak," he professed, "implicate their dose of intellectualism in their latent or adventitious qualities. Their manner of having consciousness as an objective is dull and passive. It consists of manifestations such as acquiring or receiving a configuration, being modeled according to the exigencies of the surroundings, containing weight, yielding to the impulsion of a movement, submitting to and reflecting the shock of ambient vibrations. Their relative spirituality is translated into the actions of penetration, modification and disaggregation that they exercise upon one another.

"These faculties survive them today in the centralization of their atoms, and concur with us in giving our former planet its present physiognomy. Bodies now retain the impalpable equivalence of all former forms, in the same way that our souls enclose the totality of all former thought. The product of a universal order in which everything is transformed but nothing disappears, the material amalgam adds to our intangible ideality the circumference, the plenitude and the gasified dimensions of our former terrestrial globe—which, commuted as it is into an entity of pure thought, thus maintains its aeriform presence within the system of gravitation. These are the quintessential properties of substance, which assure us today—which is to say, for a vast number of billions of centuries—of the indispensable collaboration of a kind of physiological function, permitting us to remain in rapport with vibratory sensations by means of light, to note the limitations of our present duality, to interpret the diversity of our sentiments by means of interior language, etc, etc, etc.

"Don't you find, dear friend, that our purely moral synthesization is a delectable state of affairs by comparison with the incoherent multitude of individuals and objects that we once were?"

Whether out of malice or a residual sulkiness, the Lady could not help disputing this last opinion. "You have rightly said, if I've understood you correctly," she observed, "that these ancient varieties had the virtue of setting in contrast a host of characters and temperaments. In going through life like that, one experiences an incessant curiosity, the interest of an unending struggle, of an eternally incomprehensible dream, a total ignorance of the universal goal that everyone circumscribes in his own way, according to his own tastes. You have rightly said, I repeat, that all that can be whimsical, comical, enigmatic and painful—so be it!—but it is charming even so, by virtue of the secret pleasure of felling fear. And what of us? What diversion can we obtain in our sempiternal stagnation in this void wallpapered with reflections? How do we kill pitiless time, without the hope, which we had before, that time is killing us?"

With the most perfect calm, the Gentleman replied: "Don't be guilty of infantile impatience, and let us savor, as is fitting, our immense joy in the interminable possession of the future. As for the retinue of our distractions, think of the multitude of other planets, still living, that will unfold during new periods of relative eternity before our eyes. Those myriads of constellations, so different from ours in their conditions of vitality, are no less in possession of a packaged deposit of the wisdom that, when those same constellations volatilize, will condense integrally and fuse with ours. Can one imagine a pleasure more grandiose than being both actors in and witnesses of such a marvel?"

"And after that ultimate phenomenon, what will remain to us?" said the Lady, anxious and unconvinced.

"After?" proclaimed the Gentleman, in a tumult of internal verbalization that unleashed his divinatory exaltation. "After! Our two spiritual sexes will receive their complements of intelligence originating from the dematerialization of the other cosmoses. O sublime prevision of an era in which all that is extent and form, movement and force, action and idea will fuse in the homogeneity of a thinking aspiration! Having thus attained the most absolute result of universal experimentation, our duality itself will disappear in the entente and harmony of a single consciousness.

"Then I shall be, or, rather—permit me this residue of old-fashioned gallantry—*you* shall be the final possessor, to the highest possible degree, of everything that was comprehension—which is to say Wisdom, which is to say God— during the entire duration of the Past. You will then know why that Wisdom or God—who implies boundless perfection, and could in consequence dispense with action—thought it necessary, on the contrary, to incarnate himself and plasticize himself in ideas and allow himself to produce, for such a long time, the illusion of an existence of objects. You will have the key to the frightful enigma of causes, which has thus far remained inaccessible to us.

"Above all, though, you will be the thought that exists beyond all objectivity, since it possesses the power of its own rationality, the thought that will understand why destinies have ceased to be, the thought that will know the effective and directive value embodied in the nature of things—and you will be informed of everything that could, should or must be created again it there is to be a renewal of the future..."

Postscript

The dialogue had ended. With a reassuring gesture, the Thinker displayed the last page that remained to be read, and which contained the conclusions:

"One may wonder, *that addendum said*, whether the imponderable couple, during that conversation, was really occupied with our Earth, or whether they might have confused it with some other planet long since rendered fluid. It is, besides, rather surprising to hear the Man-Woman, that double spirit of all defunct humankind, conversing with itself about these circumstances of eternity, which can only appear elementary and banal to its eyes, something akin to the ABC of the system of worlds. But why must we, whose fate it at least foresees by cosmic analogy—we, its sad predecessors—stagnate in the ignorance of this indispensable truth? By virtue of what bitter stupidity must we oppose, during so many centuries of doubt, error, sophism, revolt, anguish and vain endeavor, our predestination of immaterial intellectualism? Why do we put so much persistence and pride in engraving the imprint of our labor and our desire on the ephemeral surface of a perishable substance? Why, I repeat, do we misunderstand the rigorous duty to liberate ourselves from the concrete, and direct our free souls toward that ungraspable effluvium where free ideas reign?"

Denouement

On this final line, the Thinker rose to his feet and displayed by his attitude an intrepidity of conviction entirely ready to put theory into practice. His broad pale forehead, his long grey hair—shaken by the horror of the gift of prophecy—and his eyes, staring into the distance, left no room for doubt in that regard.

And while he stood tall in that lofty attitude of a seer, the gaze of his spouse enveloped him in one of those conjugal adulations that are all the more passionate as their object veils himself in obscurities more sublime.

As for the gentleman visitor, he hurriedly took his leave, then ran down the stairs from the attic to the ground floor with such aerocole[72] agility that the white of his cravat seemed to be lending wings to the black of his frock-coat, and dived like a premature gust of wind into the room where the Grand Council was sitting, under the presidency of the Director.

This gathering, whose curative purpose may be guessed, was deliberating as to the more or less vigorous treatment that it was appropriate to oppose to the opinions and behavior of the various inmates most recently confided to the care of the Institution by their families. The Thinker was one of these, and the gentleman inspector, unbuttoning the black of his frock-coat and loosening the white of his cravat slightly, immediately delivered his report on the manuscript and the principal aphorisms of which he had just received communication.

The scientific conference discovered nothing therein, in sum, that surpassed in an abnormal and disquieting manner the habitual hypothetical divagations of the philosophers of the day. They even judged that the author of *The Supreme Progress* gave evidence of a noble solicitude with regard to

---

[72] I have transcribed this improvisation directly from the French; its second part is derived from the same Latin root as "colony" and means "inhabitant," so the whole signifies a native of the air, embracing birds, flying insects and other airborne life-forms.

his contemporaries in advising them as soon as possible of the purely ethereal situation that the extreme future had in store for them.

The gentleman reporter emphasized, nevertheless, the gravity of a certain observation of which he had made a particular note. It was the matter of the example that the Thinker was considering offering to his contemporaries by effectuating as soon as possible his assumption to the enviable fluidity.

The learned assembly judged this pretension to be too subversive, at least in the present state of our mores, which only tolerate assumptionist operations in religious intimacy, and it was deemed that the tonic quality of a few hydrotherapeutic refreshments would combat these tendencies to evaporation in an opportune manner—on which note the Director rang his bell to summon the attendants and ordered the inflexible distribution of a number of irremissibly icy showers. Unfortunately, however, it was too late to take measures of urgent prophylaxis.

The Institution suddenly resounded with tragic murmurs. Employees surged forth, pale and trembling. The Thinker, they said, had taken advantage of a momentary negligence on the part of the watchers. Taking his wife with him, he had just precipitated their physical and moral duality into the Sanitary Establishment's enormous gas-generator. After a few seconds, the cremation had been, according to all appearances, complete. The unfortunate household had been transformed, several hundred billion centuries too soon, into the indescribable essential breath that, once the time in question has elapsed, will become the ultimate contexture of anthropomorphism.

As soon as he heard this, one of the most distinguished members of the Council—the gentleman visitor himself, moving so rapidly as to fuse the black of his frock-coat and the white of his cravat into a single shade—lit the nearest candelabrum, in order to assess the value of the human gas, in terms of its output of light.

SF & FANTASY

Guy d'Armen. *Doc Ardan: The City of Gold and Lepers*
G.-J. Arnaud. *The Ice Company*
Aloysius Bertrand. *Gaspard de la Nuit*
Richard Bessière. *The Gardens of the Apocalypse*
Félix Bodin. *The Novel of the Future*
André Caroff. *The Terror of Madame Atomos*
Didier de Chousy. *Ignis*
Captain Danrit. *Undersea Odyssey*
C. I. Defontenay. *Star (Psi Cassiopeia)*
Charles Derennes. *The People of the Pole*
Georges Dodds/Paul Wessels (anthologists). *The Missing Link*
Harry Dickson. *The Heir of Dracula*
Jules Dornay. *Lord Ruthven Begins*
Sâr Dubnotal *vs. Jack the Ripper*
Alexandre Dumas. *The Return of Lord Ruthven*
J.-C. Dunyach. *The Night Orchid; The Thieves of Silence*
Henri Duvernois. *The Man Who Found Himself*
Henri Falk. *The Age of Lead*
Paul Féval. *Anne of the Isles; Knightshade; Revenants; Vampire City; The Vampire Countess; The Wandering Jew's Daughter*
Paul Féval, *fils. Felifax, the Tiger-Man*
Arnould Galopin. *Doctor Omega*
G.L. Gick. *Harry Dickson: The Werewolf of Rutherford Grange*
Nathalie Henneberg. *The Green Gods*
V. Hugo, P. Foucher & P. Meurice. *The Hunchback of Notre-Dame*
Michel Jeury. *Chronolysis*
Octave Joncquel & Theo Varlet. *The Martian Epic*
Gérard Klein. *The Mote in Time's Eye*
Jean de La Hire. *Enter the Nyctalope; The Nyctalope on Mars; The Nyctalope vs. Lucifer*
André Laurie. *Spiridon*
Georges Le Faure & Henri de Graffigny. *The Extraordinary Adventures of a Russian Scientist Across the Solar System* (2 vols.)
Gustave Le Rouge. *The Vampires of Mars*
Jules Lermina. *Mysteryville; Panic in Paris; To-Ho and the Gold Destroyers*
Jean-Marc & Randy Lofficier. *Edgar Allan Poe on Mars; The Katrina Protocol; Pacifica; Robonocchio; Tales of the Shadowmen* (anthologists; 7 vols.)
Xavier Mauméjean. *The League of Heroes*

John-Antoine Nau. *Enemy Force*
Marie Nizet. *Captain Vampire*
C. Nodier, A. Beraud & Toussaint-Merle. *Frankenstein*
Henri de Parville. *An Inhabitant of the Planet Mars*
J. Polidori, C. Nodier, E. Scribe. *Lord Ruthven the Vampire*
P.-A. Ponson du Terrail. *The Vampire and the Devil's Son*
Maurice Renard. *The Blue Peril; Doctor Lerne; The Doctored Man;.
A Man Among the Microbes; The Master of Light*
Albert Robida. *The Adventures of Saturnin Farandoul; The Clock of
the Centuries.*
J.-H. Rosny Aîné. *Helgvor of the Blue River; The Givreuse Enigma;
The Mysterious Force; The Navigators of Space; Vamireh; The
World of the Variants; The Young Vampire*
Han Ryner. *The Superhumans*
Brian Stableford. *The New Faust at the Tragicomique;The Empire of
the Necromancers (The Shadow of Frankenstein; Frankenstein and
the Vampire Countess; Frankenstein in London); Sherlock Holmes &
The Vampires of Eternity; The Stones of Camelot; The Wayward
Muse.* (anthologist) *The Germans on Venus; News from the Moon;
The Supreme Progress*
Jacques Spitz. *The Eye of Purgatory*
Kurt Steiner. *Ortog*
Villiers de l'Isle-Adam. *The Scaffold; The Vampire Soul*
Philippe Ward. *Artahe*
Philippe Ward & Sylvie Miller. *The Song of Montségur*

MYSTERIES & THRILLERS
M. Allain & P. Souvestre. *The Daughter of Fantômas*
A. Anicet-Bourgeois, Lucien Dabril. *Rocambole*
A. Bisson & G. Livet. *Nick Carter vs. Fantômas*
V. Darlay & H. de Gorsse. *Lupin vs. Holmes: The Stage Play*
Paul Féval. *Gentlemen of the Night; John Devil; The Black Coats
('Salem Street; The Invisible Weapon; The Parisian Jungle; The
Companions of the Treasure; Heart of Steel; The Cadet Gang)*
Emile Gaboriau. *Monsieur Lecoq*
Steve Leadley. *Sherlock Holmes: The Circle of Blood*
Maurice Leblanc. *Arsène Lupin vs. Countess Cagliostro; Lupin vs.
Holmes (The Blonde Phantom; The Hollow Needle)*
Gaston Leroux. *Chéri-Bibi; The Phantom of the Opera; Rouletabille
& the Mystery of the Yellow Room*
William Patrick Maynard. *The Terror of Fu Manchu*

Frank J. Morlock. *Sherlock Holmes: The Grand Horizontals*
P. de Wattyne & Y. Walter. *Sherlock Holmes vs. Fantômas*
David White. *Fantômas in America*

SCREENPLAYS

Mike Baron. *The Iron Triangle*
Emma Bull & Will Shetterly. *Nightspeeder; War for the Oaks*
Gerry Conway & Roy Thomas. *Doc Dynamo*
Steve Englehart. *Majorca*
James Hudnall. *The Devastator*
Jean-Marc & Randy Lofficier. *Royal Flush*
J.-M. & R. Lofficier & Marc Agapit. *Despair*
Andrew Paquette. *Peripheral Vision*
R. Thomas, J. Hendler & L. Sprague de Camp. *Rivers of Time*

NON-FICTION

Stephen R. Bissette. *Blur 1-5. Green Mountain Cinema 1*
Win Scott Eckert. *Crossovers* (2 vols.)
Jean-Marc & Randy Lofficier. *Shadowmen* (2 vols.)
Randy Lofficier. *Over Here*

HEXAGON COMICS

Franco Frescura & Luciano Bernasconi. *Wampus*
Franco Frescura & Giorgio Trevisan. *CLASH*
L. Bernasconi, J.-M. Lofficier & Juan Roncagliolo Berger. *Phenix*
Claude Legrand, J.-M. Lofficier & L. Bernasconi. *Kabur*
Franco Oneta. *Zembla*
L. Buffolente, Lofficier & J.-J. Dzialowski. *Strangers: Homicron*
Danilo Grossi. *Strangers: Jaydee*
Claude Legrand & Luciano Bernasconi. *Strangers: Starlock*

ART BOOKS

Jean-Pierre Normand. *Science Fiction Illustrations*
Raven Okeefe. *Raven's L'il Critters*
Randy Lofficier & Raven OKeefe. *If Your Possum Go Daylight...*
Daniele Serra. *Illusions*